THE

Restless

SEA

W9-AMM-566

THE
Restless
SEA

VANESSA DE HAAN

HarperCollins*Publishers*

HarperCollins*Publishers* Ltd
1 London Bridge Street,
London SE1 9GF

www.harpercollins.co.uk

First published by HarperCollins*Publishers* 2018
1

Copyright © Vanessa de Haan 2018

Vanessa de Haan asserts the moral right to
be identified as the author of this work

A catalogue record for this book is available from the British Library

ISBN: 978-0-00-824576-4 (HB)
ISBN: 978-0-00-824044-8 (TPB)

This novel is entirely a work of fiction.
The names, characters and incidents portrayed in it are
the work of the author's imagination. Any resemblance to
actual persons, living or dead, events or localities is
entirely coincidental.

Typeset in Meridien by Palimpsest Book Production Ltd, Falkirk, Stirlingshire

Printed and bound by CPI Group (UK) Ltd, Croydon CR0 4YY

All rights reserved. No part of this publication may be
reproduced, stored in a retrieval system, or transmitted,
in any form or by any means, electronic, mechanical,
photocopying, recording or otherwise, without the prior
permission of the publishers.

MIX
Paper from
responsible sources
FSC™ C007454

This book is produced from independently certified FSC™ paper
to ensure responsible forest management.

For more information visit: www.harpercollins.co.uk/green

To my weird, wonderful and extensive family
– you know who you are –
and to Amelia Grace Jessel, in memory.

Eternal Father, strong to save
Whose arm does bound the restless wave
Who bidst the mighty ocean deep
Its own appointed limits keep
O hear us when we cry to thee
For those in peril on the sea

O ruler of the earth and sky
Be with our airmen as they fly
And keep them in thy loving care
From all the perils of the air
O let our cry come up to thee
For those who fly o'er land and sea

O Trinity of love and might
Be with our airmen day and night
In peace or war
Midst friend or foe
Be with them wheresoe'er they go
Thus shall our prayers ascend to thee
For those who fly o'er land and sea

This famous hymn, written by William Whiting in 1860, is also known as the Navy Hymn and sung at naval occasions around the world. This is a version frequently used by the Fleet Air Arm.

Prologue

The roof stretches across the railway station like the skin of a drum, magnifying the sounds: the tapping and pounding of feet, the trains clanking, the rumble of wheels, the shout of a guard, the whistle of a porter. At the ticket office, there is no sense of where the queue ends or where it begins. A man bashes on the glass, his voice raised in anger, frustration. Tickets are scarce. Everybody here wants to get away, to follow the children who have been evacuated to safer parts of this now unsafe country. The air is sticky and humid. In the haze, little things stand out: two sailors balancing on a stack of cases, one singing as the other accompanies him on a squeezebox. The drifting smoke from the newspaper seller's pipe; the neat rows of black-and-white print on his stand. A cluster of soldiers, their uniforms smart, the leather of their boots supple and clean, their dark, heavy rifles pulling at their shoulders.

A policeman tails a group of suspicious-looking lads that trickle away from him like mercury, slipping through gaps that close as quickly as they open. He loses them again as they circle a girl dressed in a pale-green coat, a cerise ribbon tied around her matching hat, a bright splash of colour among the drab browns and greys of suits and caps. The policeman glimpses the lads once more as they sidestep the expensive leather cases at the girl's feet. Then they are gone again, like the brief flash of the bracelet she is fiddling nervously with beneath the cuff of her jacket: now you see it, now you don't.

The sounds swirl into one cacophony – the sobs of children,

the wails of babies, the tinny squeezebox and the guard shouting into the loudspeaker, the scream of another train pulling free from the throng and towards the light. And then suddenly all noise is drowned out by a new sound, one that Londoners will soon grow accustomed to, but this is the first time they have heard its ear-splitting warning. For a moment, the station freezes, caught in a sliver of time. The babies stop wailing. The man stops banging the window. The squeezebox exhales with a breathless sigh. A thousand pairs of eyes widen, a thousand hearts stop beating.

And then there is chaos. Hands fly up to ears. People scream and clutch at each other. Others gape, bewildered. 'It's the gas!' 'A bomb!' 'They're coming!' Some people throw themselves to the floor while others blindly follow each other, staggering from one foot to the other, unsure which way to run. People fumble for their gas masks, trying to remember the drill. The straps pinch and catch at their hair; the rubber digs into their faces; the horrible smell fills their nostrils.

The crowd takes on a life of its own and surges towards the Underground, sweeping everything before it, pushing aside anything that will not join the plunging wave. The girl in the pale-green coat is caught up in the rush. She stretches out for her luggage, but it has scattered and she is knocked one way and shoved another and then swept along for a little while, all the time trying to reach back with a pale hand for her bags. The policeman is too busy trying to calm the uncalmable to notice that the girl has been swept up by the hoodlums he had his eye on. Now her bags are lost, but at least she has been carried on the tide to the safety of the Underground.

The siren wails through the empty station. The concourse is a mess of scattered things. Luggage is strewn across the floor like flotsam, bags split open, a favourite teddy has been trampled, the newspapers have toppled to the ground, the thick headlines declaring war smudged and smeared by a myriad of shoes. The ticket seller cowers beneath his desk. The guards and porters have disappeared. The only sign of

2

life is a group of naval ratings who have remained on their platform and are being lined up by a young officer. The officer issues his instructions and smooths his impeccable uniform. The boys do not take their eyes off him, drawing confidence from his easy manner, the authority borne of fine breeding and education. They form neat rows of bell bottoms and white-topped caps. The officer calls out another command, and this time the words echo clearly across the silent emptiness. The wailing has stopped.

The alarm is a mistake, a faulty air-raid siren. The station begins to fill up as people return to search for their lost companions, their abandoned luggage. Soon it is as if the concourse never emptied. The ticket seller clambers up from the floor, dusting the dirt from his trousers and resetting his cap upon his head. A new customer bangs at the window while the people behind him jostle for their original positions in the reformed queue. The policeman has long lost his intended targets. No doubt more will be along any moment. Pickpocketing is as much a problem today as it has always been in these crowded places, and the chaos of a war is not going to help matters. He spies the girl in the pale-green dress grappling for her bags and goes to help, his hand resting on his truncheon, his chin sweaty beneath its strap. Together they count the bags. None is missing. Now another figure emerges from the crowds, small and bird-like beneath a thick fur stole – the only one to be seen in such weather. The girl reaches out to her mother, and the policeman summons a porter to place the bags on a trolley, then touches his helmet in farewell as the porter relays the lady, the girl, and their luggage towards the sleeper for Inverness, skirting around a jumble of bicycles, freight, prams and trunks.

The sleeper is already at the platform. Men are rubbing cloths over its black and maroon paint. The girl and the lady search for the correct carriage. Further along the same platform, the young naval officer is ushering the ratings into the dining car, the only carriage with any space left. The boys

3

chatter and laugh as they jostle for a seat until the officer reminds them that they are representing His Majesty's Naval Service, and they stifle their smiles behind their hands. Three pregnant women heave themselves into another carriage. A child cries, snotty hiccups that she tries to blow into a handkerchief. A toddler holds her other hand, sucking bleakly at his free thumb. Passengers already on the train lean out of the windows, hands grasping like sea anemones for a last touch of friends and family. One of them is the girl in the pale-green dress, but the woman she has left on the platform has already issued a brief goodbye and turned on her heel, and there is nothing to do but retreat reluctantly into the safety of her compartment.

There are fewer people on the platform now, more guards and porters in their dark-blue uniforms, polished buttons and cap badges glinting. The doors slam and slide. The guard blows his whistle, and there is the whoosh of steam, and slowly, slowly the train starts to move. A woman with puffy red eyes runs alongside, trying to catch a glimpse of a friend or child slipping away. A guard manages to grasp her by the shoulders and hold her back. Someone screams, but the sound is drowned out by the train's whistle. The carriages jerk forward, away from the confines of the hot and crowded station and out into the warm light. In the dining car, some of the boy seamen are already resting their heads against the windows, eyelids drooping, while others play cards or elbow each other and giggle when they think no one is looking. Their officer adjusts his tie and then runs a finger over the golden wings stitched on to his sleeve and smiles to himself. In the sleeper berth, the girl in the pale-green dress runs her hand over the starched white sheets and sighs. Outside, London begins to slip by faster and faster as the train gathers speed, past narrow gardens and rows of houses, the sun reflected in their windows, making it seem as if the city is on fire.

CHAPTER 1

Jack

The boys tumble out of the station and on to the streets, laughing as they go. It is warm out here, but the air is fresh, and they enjoy the feel of the sun on their skin and the space to move away from the crowds. They follow the tallest of the boys, Stoog, a skinny, athletic-looking lad with hooded eyes and a pent-up energy like a coiled spring. He hustles along a line of people waiting to go in to the cinema, knocking a man's hat to the ground. 'Hey! What do you think you're doing?' shouts the man, shaking a fist, but the boys don't care. They laugh and run faster until they finally reach the river and stop to catch their breath.

It is high tide. In the afternoon sun the Thames gleams amber. The boys lean over the railings and watch the ships as the water slaps at the wall below. The shimmering expanse is as busy as the crowded streets behind them. Along the opposite bank a row of Thames barges, their sails neatly furled, swing and turn together on the tide. Sturdy tugs shoulder through the flow, hiccuping black smoke as they go, while another barge tacks across the running river, her dusky red-brown sails flapping and cracking in the wind. Motorboats carve their way past dredgers. The smell of river mud mingled with coal smoke, sewage, oil and tar is as familiar to the boys as the smell of their own mothers.

Stoog is the only one who doesn't lounge lazily against the rails. Instead, he prowls up and down the pavement. 'Come on, then,' he says. 'Show us what you've got.'

The boys turn, leaning back against the metal and digging into their pockets. They casually pull out a variety of watches and wallets, a lady's purse, a gold watch chain. Stoog nods down the line, until he reaches Jack.

Jack keeps his hands plugged deep in his trousers. He can feel the bracelet, the smoothness of the pearls under his fingers, the cooler sharpness of the sapphire surrounded by winking diamonds. It is the most expensive thing he has ever held, more valuable than a year's worth of wallets and watches.

'Go on, then,' says Stoog.

Jack shakes his head, gripping the bracelet more firmly in his fist.

Stoog steps closer. 'Go on.'

'Not this time,' says Jack.

'It's off my patch.'

'It's not your patch. We all work it.'

'You work it because I let you.'

'I can work anywhere I want.'

'And who's going to sell it on for you?'

'You don't own this city, Stoog.'

Stoog takes a step towards him, his eyes narrowed. 'Is that a challenge?' he says.

'What if it is?' says Jack, and he takes a step sideways, dodging the hand as it darts towards him. He legs it without looking back, Stoog's curses ringing in his ears, leaving the rest of the boys standing there, open-mouthed. Jack is the only one who would dare question Stoog, but they all know that they never get a fair price. Well, if Jack's going to take one last risk like this, he wants it to be worth it.

Jack has already reached the other side of the bridge, but Stoog is not far behind and Jack knows that he won't give up easily. He forces himself on, down towards Tooley Street. This is his territory, where he was born and brought up. But it's Stoog's too, and sure enough, Jack can hear the ragged breath of the older boy closing in. His only chance is to get to somewhere Stoog can't follow. But he is still a long way from the docks.

He hears the familiar swish of trolleybuses swinging along on their cables. Even better, there is the tail end of a queue, and a vehicle is beginning to pull away from the stop. He lunges and swings up on to the platform, bending double to catch his breath and grinning at the sight of Stoog receding into the distance.

The conductor's legs come into view, and Jack takes his time to right himself. He is panting and his legs are shaking. He pretends to fumble for loose change, but the conductor knows his type and is shaking his head and getting ready to see Jack off at the next stop. And now Jack can see another trolleybus close behind, and he knows that Stoog will be on it.

Jack is already down and running again. The docks are within reach. But Stoog is after him, reinvigorated too. Passers-by jump out of the way. Jack is fast, but Stoog is gaining. Now Jack can see the entrance to the docks, and he is almost there, and he finds the strength from somewhere, urging his legs to move, and his chest is about to burst and the breath is burning in his lungs.

He dodges the new sentry, posted fresh this week in case of Nazi invasions. Stupid guard isn't even looking in his direction, but the man does catch sight of Stoog, which makes Jack smile again. But the sentry can't stop Stoog: the older boy shakes him off and is now yelling Jack's name, and pushing past bemused gangs of dock workers. Jack begins to wonder whether he's made the right choice. Carl isn't going to be happy. Carl's dad even less so.

Although it is evening, the docks are still in full swing: there is always cargo for the lightermen to deliver ashore or for the stevedores to load carefully into holds. There is such a tangle of masts and funnels, cranes and ropes that it is hard to determine what is river and what is dry land. Dockers and sailors whistle and shout to each other, struggling to be heard above the whir and grind of machinery, the bump and clatter of barges, and the splash of the water. Jack has the advantage of surprise, being the first runner, but the gathering crowd soon closes up on Stoog. Dockers don't take kindly to outsiders. Stoog is swearing and wriggling, but he is no match for men who spend their days hauling and heaving freight.

'Stop that bloody thief!' Stoog is shouting. And now hands are reaching for Jack too, grasping fingers with torn, black nails, knuckles stained by tobacco. He tries to dodge, but he is tiring. He manages to pull away once more, jinking down behind the metal feet and runners of one of the large cranes and then between a stack of crates. He is alone, but it won't be for long. His brain is working at high speed, his eyes processing in double-time. There is a wooden shack. He twists into it before his followers around the corner. It is a risk he has to take; he cannot push himself any further.

He is in a putrid darkness. The air is close, the stench makes him gag. He hears the crowd approaching, Stoog still shouting his name. His heart hammers in his chest. The footsteps draw nearer. He presses himself into the inkiest of shadows, the bile filling his mouth as the smell infests his nostrils. The door swings open and a ray of light picks out the pole suspended above the trough of muck. Jack holds his breath and shrinks into a ball. He hears the scuff of boots on the ground, senses the energy of the crowd.

Then his heart lurches. Something shifts in the gloom. He is not alone.

His companion moves to block the door, a large, impassable, barrel-chested shape.

'There's a lad on the run,' says one of the pursuers. 'You seen anyone?'

A low voice growls back: 'Can't a man take a shit in peace?'

Jack's knees are seizing up, but he does not dare move. The man stands at the door, and the crowd mutters and moves away, the shadows through the slats of the shack darkening and lightening as they go. They drag Stoog with them, still kicking and biting.

Jack collapses to the filthy floor and retches.

The crowd has gone, and now the creak and crunch of the cranes fills the air once more, the sound of foremen shouting their orders and the trolleys and trucks rumbling past. The man at the door steps out into the light. 'Come on,' he says. 'Let's be seeing you.'

Jack has no choice but to follow. Even though the air outside is still fetid with the stink of the river, it is nothing compared to the latrines. And now there is also the faint, sweet scent of cut wood, for Surrey Docks is a timber dock and there are planks piled in every corner, huge logs bumping and rolling against each other in the water, packed on to the narrowboats that wait on the canal, even swinging above their heads.

Jack eyes the man warily. 'Why didn't you turn me in?' he says.

The man shrugs. 'You want to watch yourself with those dockers,' he says. There is a tear in the arm of his shirt that reveals the striking colours of blue and green tattoo ink on his skin. Great patches of sweat have stained his armpits, and even the creases of his face are ingrained with grime.

'I can handle it,' says Jack. 'My dad and my brother both worked the docks.' His legs have stopped trembling and he pulls himself up straighter, squares his chin.

'And where are they now?'

'Fighting the Jerries.'

'Sorry to hear that.'

'I'd be doing the same if I was old enough.'

The sailor shakes his head. 'What are you? Fifteen? Sixteen? Give it a couple of years and you'll be squeezed into a uniform too; sent off to the knacker's like those carcasses we bring in to the Royal Docks.'

'I'm no coward.'

'What are you running from, then?'

Jack looks at his feet. 'Nothing. A misunderstanding.' He feels the weight of the bracelet in his pocket and colours.

The sailor sighs, his cap lifting as he scratches the back of his head. 'You want to steer clear of a lad like that,' he says. 'He's got a badness about him that ain't going to lead nowhere good.'

'Does it look like we're friends?'

'It looks to me like you is on the edge. One push and you'll end up just the same.'

'I'm different. He doesn't want me working here, but that's what I'm doing from now on.'

'I ain't talking about working here, boy. Just as I ain't talking about signing up to another man's war. I'm talking about freedom. Changing your destiny. Choosing your own path. I'm talking about the ships.'

'Ain't that just swapping one uniform for another?'

The man roars with laughter, youthful eyes bright beneath his tattered sailor's cap. 'I don't mean the Navy, boy. You want to be a merchant seaman. No one telling you what to do except for your own kind.'

'But I ain't never even been on a boat.'

'Ent nothin' to it. Listen.' The man leans closer. 'I was like you once, except I had no ma or pa, not a penny to my name. I slept in ditches and drains until I was eight, and then I found myself a berth. Now I've sailed to every country you can think of and plenty you can't. I've seen wonders you'd never imagine: beasts of the ocean, castles in the sky, men that breathe fire, women what change shape. I'm free to work when and where I want. Hell, I've even got me own stash of gold.'

And he laughs and his great jaw opens, and Jack can indeed see the yellow metal glittering in the back of his dark mouth.

Jack shakes his head. 'There's my mum, my sister . . .'

The man is suddenly serious again, urgent. He thrusts his face right up against Jack's, and Jack can smell the tobacco on his breath. 'I can see you're a brave lad,' he says, 'but it takes a proper kind of bravery to turn your life around.'

Then he puts his head back and laughs again, moving away as he does.

Jack catches sight of something in the sailor's hand, winking and blinking in the sunlight. 'Oy!' he says, snatching at the bracelet. 'That's mine.'

The sailor holds the jewel out of reach. 'No wonder you was running,' he says. 'It's a fine piece . . .'

Jack blushes, ashamed, but the anger is a stronger emotion, and he lunges again, grabbing the bracelet from the man's hand and backing away.

The man grunts, as if satisfying some inner itch. 'Perhaps it's too late already,' he says. 'You's in too deep.'

Jack doesn't want to listen any more. He has inched far enough, and now he turns and stumbles away from the latrines, slipping back among the dock workers, those men with the same worn and weary expressions as his father. He keeps his head down, cap pulled low, occasionally throwing a glance back over his shoulder, but the gold-toothed sailor has vanished into the maelstrom of the docks.

A little further on, he finally reaches his destination. Carl nods a curt hello. He is shorter and stockier than Jack, and he keeps his hair shaved close, which makes his neck look thicker and his shoulders broader. 'What're you doing here?' he says.

'Thought I'd come and check we were all right for tomorrow.'

''Course,' says Carl. He peers at Jack more closely. 'But what're you really doing here?'

Jack shrugs and tries to look nonchalant. 'Fancy going to the pictures?'

But Carl knows him better than that. 'Whatever you've done,' he says, 'you better have left it at the gates. My dad's not going to let us work together if—'

Jack cuts him off. 'It was nothing,' he says. 'Just Stoog kicking off . . .'

'I thought you were putting all that behind you?'

Jack cannot meet his eye. 'I am. I have . . .'

'A new start, you said . . .'

'Just drop it, will you?'

Carl doesn't push it. He and Jack have been best friends for as long as they can remember – brought together on the docks, and in the same class since they were sent to primary. The boys watch Mr Mills work for a while. He is a deal porter: unloading and stacking the long planks that arrive on the steamers from overseas and the narrowboats from upcountry. It's a skill that's up there with the best on the docks, and means regular employment, a far cry from the casual labour that Jack's dad had to rely on. But it's still hard work. Jack can barely lift one plank; Mr Mills carries three or four at a time. He wears a leather cap with a long bit dangling down to protect his shoulders. It is like watching an acrobat, the balancing and judging where best to lay the next plank on the towering pile, the skipping from mound to mound, and all the time the planks on his shoulder tipping up and down while his legs and feet work to keep his body stable.

When he spots Jack, Mr Mills jumps down from the top of the mountain as sure-footed as a goat, his muscles bulging and flexing with effort. He is breathing heavily, his broad chest expanding and contracting against his braces. His calloused hands are full of splinters. 'Jack,' he says, his low voice betraying his dislike. The scar on his cheek is a pale, raised streak down his red face; Carl's family have Jewish blood, and the mark is a souvenir from the fight against the fascists in Cable Street.

'Mr Mills,' says Jack, nodding back.

'I thought you two was going to work tomorrow?'

'We are. But since he's here now, can we go to the pictures?' says Carl.

Mr Mills rubs his scar and eyes Jack. 'You'll have to be up early . . .'

'We know . . .'

'I want you back by dark.'

'Sure.'

'Or I'll have your mother on my case . . .'

'I'll be back.'

Mr Mills gives Jack another narrow look and then rubs Carl's head, and Carl pushes him away, laughing, then the boys disappear once more into their city.

Jack settles the cap firmly on his head, pulling it down tight. He creeps out without waking his sister. It is easier now that she sleeps in their mother's bed. He will pick her up later in the morning, once his mother has been at work for an hour or so. The guilt that plucks at his insides is tinged with worry: Betsy still can't read properly, and now that the school has relocated to the countryside it looks as if she never will. He knows she will be cross when she wakes – she likes to stick as close to him as his own shadow these days – but the docks are no place for a child.

Dawn is breaking. The sky is leaden, pressing down on him with a suffocating heaviness. It is cold, and he half jogs down the high street to try to keep warm. Past the air-raid siren. Past the navy blue police box, and the sandbagged shop fronts – the fishmonger, the greengrocer, the hosiery shop, the tobacconist, the pawnbroker. The stillness is broken by an ancient fire engine and a taxi pulling a water pump that trundle past in the opposite direction. Probably a drill. Everything's a drill these days. Sometimes he wishes the Nazis would come and drop a bloody bomb. That at least might be exciting.

Jack has been good as his word, working the docks with Carl for the last two weeks, avoiding Stoog and the others. Today the boys are heading to the East and West India docks, Jack's favourites, where the air smells of spices and oils, of spilt rum and sacks full of tobacco left to mature in the warehouses. Much of the work is still beyond even Carl's ability – rolling or repairing the heavy barrels, or portering coal and grain – and they stay out of the way of the seasoned gangs with their vicious case hooks, but there is still plenty of work to be found. The boys take what they can get: an hour here or there loading and unloading the smaller carts and trolleys, separating cargo on the floors of the warehouses, jemmying open chests for the customs officials.

They cross from dock to dock, hitching a lift in a cart or a truck or a barge, or they take the train from the Royal Docks, with its vast refrigeration sheds packed with ghostly pale slabs of meat. There is cheese arriving from Europe, and fabric from India, apples and grapefruit from Australia, Palestine. Persian carpets, and silks from India pass beneath cars and buses dangling from great chains. Passenger liners deposit travellers from New Zealand, the Canaries, South Africa, Brazil. Everything is in multiples: lines of people, crates of food, stacks of timber, barrels of wine – once, even, four elephants for the circus.

Carl catches up with Jack on the bridge. The sky has lightened to a pale grey, and there is an eerie mist like a sheen on the river. They are dockside before first call-on, down where the cavernous warehouses and towering chimneys loom reddy-orange in the watery light. The familiar thud and crash of boat and barge mingles with the shouts and curses of men. Jack hears the warning to look out as an unsecured load crashes to the ground, sees the glint of metal as another worker digs his sharp case hook into a sack, savours the smell of coffee and cocoa beans on his tongue.

Today there is a shipment of bananas. Jack watches the green bunches trundle down from the ship's holds on creaky conveyor belts. A man with a horse and cart waits patiently while the first lot of fruit is loaded on to trolleys for the waiting trains and lorries. Carl and Jack have worked with this man before. Once the bulk of the bananas have gone, they help him place the fruit into wooden crates and pack them around with straw. The conveyor belt creaks and squeaks and groans. Jack glances up to the gunwale of the ship, but the gold-toothed sailor is not there. The sailors looking back at him have skin the colour of the roasted chestnuts that he sometimes buys as a treat for Betsy in the winter, their white teeth flashing like chalk on slate.

The driver jumps on to the back of the cart and Carl and Jack hand the crates up to him. Jack's arms ache: bananas are heavier than they look. There are other crates of fruit here already, apples and grapefruit that make the back of the cart smell like sunshine and sugar. Jack's mouth waters.

When they have finished, the man hops down and chats to the dockers, while the boys rest their weary arms. The horse seems unfazed by the constant commotion. It stands with its head low, eyes half-closed, ears flicking one way or the other, resting each hind leg in turn. Jack runs his hand along the animal's flank. It is soft and warm. He leans against it, sucking up the heat through his sleeves. After the hard work, his sweat is starting to cool.

'Make the most of these,' says one of the dockers to the cart driver, removing his flat cap and scratching his head. 'Reckon you'll be lucky to see any more for a while.'

'Problems with supply?' asks the cart driver.

The docker shakes his head. 'Not at the other end. But these poor bastards are having a job getting through.' He indicates another man, a sailor.

The sailor nods his head. 'Sea's swarming with Nazis,' he says.

'Going to starve us out?'

'Don't seem to make a difference what the cargo is. They'll take a pop at anything. Even passenger ships.'

The men shake their heads and suck their teeth.

'What if the country runs out of food?'

'That's never going to happen.'

'Government's talking about rationing butter and bacon in case we get short.'

'Let's hope it don't come to that.' The sailor shares cigarettes out around the group. They light them, the smoke curling in thin blue lines into the air. The smell reminds Jack of his dad.

'You heading back out there?'

'Got to.'

'Got anything to protect you?'

15

"Course not. But I heard we might get a Navy escort.'

'I'll believe that when I see it.'

They stand in silence for a bit, pulling on their cigarettes. The tobacco burns and crumbles and turns to ash that flies away, dissolving into nothing.

Above them, someone starts to rattle the conveyor belt. The sailors are leaning over the edge. One of them whistles, a shrill note that makes the men on the ground look up. 'That's us, then.' The men start to disperse. 'See you next time.'

'Let's hope.'

'Good luck.'

'See you.'

The men tip their hats at each other. The cart driver drops his butt on the ground, grinds it out with his boot. At last he is ready to go. He jumps up on to the driver's bench and the boys clamber up on the back of the cart. They lurch off, past queues of lorries, their goods covered in canvas, waiting to be sent to all the corners of the world. Past a warehouse full of vast tusks sorted into piles of various sizes. Past men in top hats, stroking their glossy moustaches.

Jack leans against a bouncing crate. Carl tips his cap to the back of his head and rubs at his short hair. It looks soft, like the fur of the rabbits that hang in rows outside the butchers' shops.

Jack swings his legs, enjoying the ride. 'You ever thought about getting work on a ship?' he asks.

'Funny you should say that,' says Carl. 'My dad's been on at me to give it a go. Says the docks are a mug's game. He's not fifty yet, but his back's done in and his shoulder's all but seized up. Sometimes my mum has to help him get out of bed in the morning . . .'

'What about them Nazis?'

'If the war lasts, then we'll all have to face them somewhere, I guess.'

The cart bounces and bumps as the city unfolds behind them: streets clogged with men and women and horses and

16

carts and bicycles and buses and trucks. The shops are busy now, chalkboards propped up outside, doors swinging open and shut beneath bright hoardings advertising brown ale and Rowntree's pastilles.

At Covent Garden, the boys help place the boxes of fruit on to wooden barrows. A man walks past with a dozen wicker baskets stacked on his head, the tower swaying like a huge snake. Broad-bosomed women sit on the kerb, flowers in their hats, deep in conversation. Men pull barrows and crates this way and that. Horses chomp at bags of hay. Vehicles come and go. You'd never believe there was a war on.

The cart driver presses a ha'penny into Jack's hand. 'Thanks, lads. See you again,' he says.

Jack pockets the shiny coin, swallowing his disappointment. Three hours of honest work earns less than the brief second it takes to snatch a wallet.

They drift towards the arched entrance to the market. The air is a pandemonium of people bartering over fruit and vege-tables and flowers. Beyond a clump of ragged children, Jack spots a familiar face. Vince.

Carl puts a restraining hand on his shoulder. 'Leave it,' he says. 'You're doing good without them.'

Jack shakes him off, pulling the ha'penny from his pocket and shoving it into Carl's hand. 'We can't split this,' he says, 'it's not enough.'

'You got to stick at it.'

'I've just got one more thing to offload.'

'There's always just one more thing . . .' says Carl, but Jack is already making after Vince, who is sliding down a back alley, hugging the wall as if he wants to sink into the brick-work.

Jack blocks his path. 'I've been looking for you,' he says.

'Well now you found me,' says Vince, his eyes glittering like the sewer rat that he is.

'I've got a bracelet,' says Jack.

'I heard you had something.'

'It's a proper fine one.'

Vince narrows his eyes. 'Thing is, jewels is tricky things to get rid of,' he says.

'Oh, come on. It's never stopped you in the past . . .'

'Give me something to go on, then.'

Jack describes every pearl and stone in detail. He has taken the bracelet out from beneath his mattress nightly to admire its workmanship.

Vince is quiet for a moment, as if mulling over the sum in his head. 'I'll give you ten pound,' he says eventually.

'Ten pound?' says Jack. 'It's worth ten times that.'

Vince shrugs. 'Maybe through the proper channels . . .'

'You mean through Stoog?'

'That's the way it works, my friend.'

'I'm not your friend,' says Jack, grabbing him by the collar.

Vince throws his hands out to the sides, twisting on the end of Jack's fist. 'It ain't my fault,' he says. Jack yanks the neck of the shirt hard before releasing his grip so that Vince yelps, then backs away, rubbing the pinched pale flesh of his neck. 'What you do that for? You know I got to keep Stoog sweet . . .'

'I'll find someone else to take it,' says Jack.

'You can try. No one else is going to touch it. Stoog's put the word out.'

'Who does he think he is? Al fucking Capone?'

Vince shrugs. 'Someone's got to be in charge,' he says, 'or else the whole system falls apart.'

Jack feels the anger bubble up inside him. 'I don't need the money, anyway,' he says. 'I'm doing fine going straight.'

'Looks like it,' says Vince.

Jack glares at him for a moment and then spits his contempt on to the ground at Vince's feet. But Vince is already sidling on down the alley, as slippery as a jellied eel.

It takes Jack some time to find a pawnbroker who will accept the bracelet and its tenuous provenance. The shops with their three gold baubles hanging above the door are easy to find, and he makes sure it is far enough north not to impact on his patch. The price is pitiful – worse, even, than what Vince offered – but Jack cannot take the risk of the bracelet hanging around the house any longer – and he does not want to have to crawl back to Stoog, cap in hand.

Carl and Jack take the day off on Sundays, even though Jack could do with the extra work. Betsy and Jack like to meet Carl down by the river at Cherry Garden Pier. It's become a tradition. The siblings don't even bother to say goodbye to their mother. She likes to lie in on Sundays. Dead to the world now that she's toiling all hours. It seems wrong to Jack that his mother is working on site, building a new bridge across the river, of all things. He can't get used to her leaving in her overalls, walking like a man in those clumpy boots, with that scarf around her head. In the evening her face is smudged with dirt, and she stinks of grease and oil. He wonders what his dad will think when he comes back. He wonders where his dad is. On the Belgium–France border, they've been told. But Jack's not sure exactly where Belgium is.

Carl is waiting for them in the usual spot. The tide is out, and they roam the muddy beach, searching for treasure among the slimy pebbles and bits of smooth, gnarled wood. Sometimes there are old coins, medieval pins, Roman pottery to be found. Stoog says he once saw a severed hand, but no one believes him.

They find a place to sit on the driest bit of the shoreline furthest from the water. In the distance Tower Bridge sticks two fingers up at the sky. The river oozes towards the sea. Ships of all shapes and sizes run with it and against it. The dredgers are at work scraping their clawfuls of silt away from the banks and dumping them into the middle of the river. Jack breathes the smell of the dank shore deep into his nostrils.

Carl throws a stone as far as he can. It plops into the water. 'My dad's inquiring about that place at sea school,' he says. There is an apologetic tone to his voice.

Jack's heart sinks, but he can't blame his friend for wanting to do something about his life.

'You could come?' says Carl.

'I can't,' Jack says, tilting his head in Betsy's direction. 'You know my dad wanted me to keep an eye on the girls.' He tries to raise a smile, but it's impossible. He is destined to be stuck here, scraping a living while other people travel the world, or fight the Jerries. It isn't fair.

'Any trouble from Stoog?' Carl asks.

'I'm steering clear.' Carl still does not know about the bracelet business, and Jack has managed to avoid Stoog for now. There is an uneasy truce on the streets as the city waits to see what the war has in store for it.

Carl is silent for a moment, watching Betsy sift through the rubbish on the shore. Her shoes and socks are wet, and her hands are filthy. Her long dark hair is matted like a bird's nest. 'Don't give up now, Jack,' he says. 'You've worked hard at staying out of trouble.' Jack does not tell him that he has already started to thieve again. Three wallets in almost as many days. He had forgotten what easy money it was compared to the lugging and scrimping down at the docks. Blackout has its advantages, after all.

Betsy tugs at Jack's sleeve.

'Look,' she says. She holds a piece of coloured glass up to the light. Although it has been polished smooth to a hazy green on the outside, inside it there is an imperfection – a crack – that looks just like a star. 'It's for you.'

'Don't you want to keep it?'

'Promise you won't send me away like the other kids?'

'I'm not planning on it.'

'Promise.'

'Fine! I promise.'

'Then I want you to have this to remember your promise.' It's the most she's said in weeks. Her solemn brown eyes peer out at him from under the tangle of her hair.

'I don't need it to remember,' he says, grabbing hold of her and rumpling the top of her head.

'Take it.' She presses the glass into his hand until it hurts.

'All right!' he says. 'I won't forget. You're not going anywhere.' He pulls her down next to him and gives her a squeeze. They watch the sky darken and lighten as clouds shift across it, chasing each other away from the city. They are each lost in their thoughts.

It starts to drizzle, blobs of cold on their skin. Jack stands, yanking Betsy up too. 'Come on,' he says. The three of them make their way towards the embankment. The rain trickles down their backs and over their gas mask boxes, softening the cardboard and making the doodles on Betsy's blur at the edges.

The boys start to run, but Betsy can't keep up. Carl grabs her and hoists her over his shoulder as if she weighs nothing more than a coat. She hangs there giggling as he trots up the beach and the uneven stone steps towards the road. Jack laughs too: he had forgotten what Betsy's happiness sounded like. It rolls and falls from her mouth like a song in time with Carl's strides, and her long hair flies out behind them like seaweed.

CHAPTER 2

Sunday, a year later, and they no longer meet at Cherry Garden Pier. In fact, Jack has not seen Carl for weeks. The Nazis have started to fly their bombs across the Channel, and Mr Mills keeps an even tighter rein on his son.

With fewer and fewer ships making it through, there is hardly any work at the docks. The men clamour for jobs; the gangers struggle to keep them under control. There is nothing for Jack. He is bottom of the heap. It is no longer a question of whether he stays straight. He does what he can to survive.

Betsy and Jack wander the streets and parks, making the most of what little daylight there is and enjoying the break from the daily drudgery of their lives. It has been raining heavily, and there are dirty puddles on the road. The pavement is dark and shiny. The wheels of the traffic splosh through the water and spray them with mud. They wander past their old school. It has been taken over by the air-raid wardens, and doubles as a first-aid post. The playground where they used to play hopscotch and marbles and kick-the-can is empty now, apart from sandbags and a big board with a clock face on it, telling them what time blackout is tonight. An ARP warden has just finished moving the hands. It's the same warden who patrols their street, shouting through the letterbox if he thinks there's any light showing at night.

They are at the edge of the park when Betsy tugs on Jack's sleeve. 'Look!' she says. It is the first time he has seen her smile for weeks. The cumulative effect of fear, poverty and boredom has ground them both into near silence; his face is as pinched and drawn as hers.

Carl is waving at them across the grass. The boys greet each other warmly, and Betsy lets Carl hug her. He lifts her clean off her feet. She looks pitifully scrawny dangling there against his stocky frame. The three of them linger in the park, relaxing in each other's company, catching up on all those weeks missed.

'I'm going at the end of the month,' says Carl.

'Going?'

'Don't you remember? Sea school.'

'So it's actually happening? You're leaving me for dust.'

'It's not too late, Jack. You could still come. There's space . . .'

'You know I can't . . .'

Carl shrugs. There is no point pressing on. 'How you been keeping anyway?'

'I get by.'

Carl frowns, but there is no time to expand, because at that moment they see more familiar figures approaching: Tommy and Vince are swaggering along the path. Beside them is Stoog, carrying a football and walking with jerky movements, as if at every step he expects trouble.

Jack can sense Carl's irritation. 'Come on,' he says, 'they're not that bad. Have a game? It'll be like the old days.'

'I thought you two had fallen out?'

'We fell back in again.' It is true that they have buried the hatchet for now, but there is always a simmering tension where Stoog is involved, and Jack knows that he has not forgiven him. But Jack needs Stoog again, as he needed Carl before. Stoog can get him work. On the street they're brothers of a kind.

'You know you can't trust him . . .'

'I have to trust him. I've got no choice.'

'There's always a choice.'

'Please?' Jack puts a brotherly arm around Carl, and Carl rolls his eyes, but nods.

The incomers are upon them. 'Up for a game?' says Jack.

Stoog shoots Carl one of his looks. They have never got on. The other boys watch in silence. Stoog puffs out his chest, enjoying being the one on whom the decision rests. He nods slowly. The boys grin.

They call to a couple of the other boys who are scattered across the park. Jack recognises Eddy, who used to be in Betsy's class, one of the many kids who trickled back to the city after the first round of evacuations to the country. 'Why don't you two go and look for conkers?' says Jack.

Betsy nods at Eddy shyly and they wander off towards the large horse chestnut tree on the edge of the path. Eddy swings his gas mask up into the tree. Betsy giggles and does the same. They run to where the green balls are knocked down on to the wet grass, cracking them open to see if any are worth keeping.

The older boys set up a football pitch, using their gas masks to mark the goal posts. 'Only thing they're bloody good for,' says Jack.

'And this,' says Stoog. He takes his mask out and holds it over his face, making a loud farting noise. The boys laugh. Stoog is in charge again, and everyone is in their rightful place.

It has turned into a breezy day, and the ground has dried a little but it is still slippery. Jack soon warms up. It is good to be doing something physical, to be chasing his friends and to feel his heart pumping and to be thinking of nothing else but the ball. Soon they are caked in mud. Stoog forgets his attitude, and Carl belongs for a moment. They point and laugh at each other, and their cheeks glow as steam rises from their skin and dissipates into the cool afternoon air.

But their fun is short-lived. A man in a tin hat is making his way across the grass towards them. 'Come on, lads,' he shouts. 'Time to get home now.'

It's the ARP warden. The boys roll their eyes at each other.

'Just a bit longer . . .' says Tommy.

'No,' says the warden. 'The dark's coming in fast tonight and we're expecting trouble.'

The other boys moan too, and then Stoog picks up the ball and flings it at Jack, who flings it at Tommy, who pretends to fling it at the man. The man reacts instinctively to catch it, but there's nothing to catch. The boys laugh, and Tommy drops the ball on to the ground as if to start the game again.

'Come along, now.' The man's cheeks have turned scarlet. 'It's time to be going home.'

'All right, all right. Keep your hair on, old man,' says Stoog.

'Watch your mouth, sonny.'

'Who're you telling to watch their mouth?'

'Who do you think?' says the man, squaring up to the boy. The rest of the boys form a ring around them. Betsy and Eddy stop looking at conkers. The tension vibrates in the cool air.

Carl steps in. 'Let's leave it there. He's only trying to help.'

'Never thought a Jew boy would be on the same side as a fascist,' says Stoog, spitting the words as he cranes his neck around Carl, trying to push him out of the way. The ground is soggy beneath their feet. The sky is darkening.

'Don't you call me a fascist,' says the warden.

'Why? What you going to do about it?'

'Yeah. What you going to do?' Vince says, the excitement high in his voice.

Stoog and the man circle each other like tomcats.

'Jack?' says Carl. 'Don't let this happen . . .'

Jack is torn between backing both boys. 'Maybe we should go,' he says. 'It's almost too dark to play anyway . . .'

Stoog snaps around, shoving his face close to Jack's and saying, 'That'd be just like you. Running away . . .'

And the warden says, 'Now, now. I don't want any trouble . . .' But Stoog is already turning on him and he pulls his arm back and thumps the man in the side of the head with his bony fist, knocking his helmet on to the ground. There is a cracking sound and blood but Jack isn't sure whether it's from the warden's ear or Stoog's knuckle.

25

And Carl is yelling, 'Stop it,' but Stoog is already swinging again, and this time he is aiming at Jack and hissing under his breath, 'This one's for the docks,' and he lands a punch right in Jack's eye, and there's a stinging pain and a mist descends and all Jack can think of is whacking him back.

Carl is still shouting at them to stop, but Jack doesn't care. Stoog may be skinny, but he's fast and he's accurate. Tommy steps in to help Jack, and then Vince thwacks him in the mouth, and all of a sudden the game has turned into a brawl of fists and teeth and pulled hair and ripped clothes and no one is really sure who is hitting who but all Jack knows is he's furious – furious at Stoog for hitting him, furious with curfew and blackout, furious with feeling hungry all the time, furious with his dad and his brother for going away, with Carl for getting out and doing something with his life, furious with the whole bloody lot of it. And he's thumping and smashing and he can taste the blood in his mouth and hear the crunch of bone and the thud of flesh and it feels good to be in the moment, not to worry about where it's all heading.

It is Carl who manages to stop him. He grabs Jack with the grip of a deal porter's son, pulling him out of the fray.

'Let me go,' says Jack, twisting away from Carl, trying to scratch at his face, kick his shins, anything to release the hold. But it takes more than that to bring Carl down. 'Let me go,' says Jack again.

But Carl is furious. There is a vein throbbing in his neck and he is panting. 'What's bloody wrong with you all?' he says as the other boys draw back sheepishly, spitting the blood from their mouths. No one has seen Carl lose his temper before. 'Take a look at yourselves!' He points at the warden. 'He could be your father. Your granddad.' And now he turns on Jack. 'And you,' he says, 'you're the worst of all. You had a chance to do something different, but you're going to end up just like them. Well, I wash my hands of it. You go ahead and kill yourself. I'm out of here.'

He has finally released Jack. They stand chest to chest, eye to eye. Jack clenches his fists, the rage still pumping around his system. He hears a whimper, and a small, cold hand closes around his wrist. He glances down. Betsy. He looks at the warden, a grey-haired old man who is picking his helmet up with trembling hands. He takes a step backwards. The boys and the warden wait for the explosion. He takes another step backwards, and grabs hold of Betsy's hand. 'Fuck you, Carl,' he says. 'And fuck you, Stoog. Fuck the lot of you.' And he turns and staggers away, dragging his sister with him across the muddy grass.

The other boys begin to disperse, and the warden doesn't leave until the last boy fades into the twilight.

A month later, and the raids have grown steadily worse. London has now had nineteen consecutive days and nights of relentless bombardment, of noise and smoke, flame and dust. The docks have been obliterated, the mighty cranes are twisted and contorted into strange shapes, the warehouses flattened, the barges charred embers. Barrels of alcohol explode like gunpowder; paint melts and pours into the Thames, turning it into a river of fire. The deal porters' timber went up on the first night of the raids. The firemen couldn't get close enough to quench the inferno. It still burns, lighting the way for the next bombs.

The money from the bracelet is long gone. The only good that came of it was the sewing machine that Jack's mother uses to make new clothes out of the old. But clothes don't put food in their stomachs, so Jack has found new ways of getting by that inevitably involve Stoog.

He pulls a package wrapped in paper from his bag and offers it to his mother. Six fat sausages peep out. 'Mostly gristle,' he says. His mother takes the parcel. She's given up asking where he gets these things. She places it on the side in the kitchen. She cannot bring herself to look at him.

Later, Jack lies on his back and stares up into the darkness, listening to his mother's dry cough, the wail of next-door's baby, the hollow thud of an air raid in the distance. They have moved their mattresses into the small front room. They sleep in their clothes. The shelter Jack so proudly built with his brother and father is useless. It is cramped and smelly, and most of the time inches deep in fetid water.

In the distance the sky is bright with flames. There is the whine of sirens. Probably another attack on the docks. He is so used to it, he feels himself begin to drift off. A floorboard creaks and a ghostly shadow moves from his mother's mattress towards him. A small voice says, 'Jack? You awake, Jack?' Betsy climbs in next to him. She is so slight that she easily fits on to the single mattress.

'Come here,' he says, hugging her trembling body tightly. As he smooths her dark curls, Betsy's breaths begin to lengthen. She scratches at her head. Lice. They've all got them.

Jack cannot remember what it was like not to feel hungry. Food is rationed, there are queues at the shops, and their mother doesn't have time to wait in them because of her job. Jack has plenty more profitable things to do than wait for a slab of butter, and Betsy refuses to be separated from him. There are rats everywhere. Tommy says they're as big as terriers down his street. Stoog has been catching them and selling them for meat.

There is a whistle outside the window. Speak of the devil. Jack and Betsy are immediately wide awake and scrambling out into the cool air of the streets. Stoog leers at them in the moonlight. 'Got a good feeling about tonight,' he says.

Tommy and Vince are here too, and other faces that Jack and Betsy recognise. They make their way through the park where they used to play cricket and football, now home to the anti-aircraft brigade. They hug the shadow of the tree line. Jack can just make out the pale wall of sandbags and the dark shape of the three-inch gun behind it, the movement of the men of the Royal Artillery, too tense and expectant to notice the youngsters who should be safely tucked up in a shelter.

They move in silence. There is no point in trying to talk above the squealing sirens that send everyone else scurrying under tables and staircases, deep down into the underbelly of the Tube stations. But not them. They know there will be rich pickings about.

They pause at Tower Bridge, lining up one by one to gaze at the river. The moon glitters in oily patches on the surface of the water. There are shapes down there: boats battered and sunk by the previous nights' raids. Fuel and timber still burn, pale lights flickering among the ripples. Above them, searchlights criss-cross the sky, illuminating the trailing tendrils of the monstrous barrage balloons that float fatly there. Further away, black smoke curls up from the docks, blotting out the moon like a cloud.

They hear the German planes before they see them. They can identify each type as well as any anti-aircraft regiment. No British up there yet. They can just make out the bombers, flying wing tip to wing tip above the river, following the trails of moonlight flashing on the surface, searching for the small fires lit by the incendiary devices that exploded earlier, mythical birds seeking their prey. Betsy's eyes grow wider. Time stands still. The sound of the engines roars in their ears, rumbles in their chests. *Thud thud thud*. Like a heartbeat.

The planes are almost on top of them. The *rat-a-tat-tat* of the anti-aircraft guns starts up. Suddenly the planes swing to the left, to their side of the river, the south side, over the docks again. They catch a glimpse of light in a cockpit. And then . . . *Boom!*

The noise slams through them. They are running again, this time in the wake of the planes. The searchlights try to pick out the bombers in their pale beams, but they fail. The drone of more bombers joins the battery from the ground. Shrapnel tinkles like metal rain on the roofs. The fire engines come clanging along the road.

And now the Allied planes come swooping in to try to fight them off. But the boys aren't interested in dogfights these

29

days. They are running over rubble, and the air is full of dust and bangs and wails – human and inhuman. Fires rage across the city. Boy Scouts run from warden to warden, shouting above the din. But relaying messages won't fill empty bellies.

Jack and Betsy stay together, but the others fan out, looking for the butchers and the grocers, anywhere for a bargain. 'You all right, Bets?' says Jack. She nods. Her teeth shine white among the smudges of dirt on her face.

There is a flash of light to their right. Jack is sure they haven't been hit, but a split second later they are lifted clean off their feet. They slam back into the wall of a house, whose windows are blown in at the same time. The air is knocked right out of Jack's chest and it takes a good few seconds for him to realise what has happened. All he can hear is a high-pitched ringing. Betsy is lying next to him. She has hit her head, and for a moment he isn't sure whether she's alive or dead. There is a trickle of red on her forehead, but then her eyes flicker open, and relief rushes through him and he leans over to grab her bony body in a hug, her wiry little arms gripping him back.

Around him, the world seems different, as if he is looking through a prism: the objects are crystal clear yet haloed with coloured light. He blinks and shakes his head, trying to clear the outlines that are seeping into a haze. The piercing echo of the blast is beginning to subside in his ears, but the sounds are still distorted. There are groans coming through the blown-out window next to him. He struggles to his feet and squints into the yawning hole. There is glass and splintered furniture and smashed crockery everywhere, dust settling over it like snow. He cannot locate the source of the moaning.

Jack tells Betsy to wait where she is. He takes off his coat and lays it over the windowsill where jagged glass still sticks up from the wooden frame. He climbs carefully into the house. The pictures have been blown clean off the walls, and a large dining table has been thrown on its side, and now he sees there is a man sitting on the floor next to it. Jack stops, unsure whether to climb straight back out. The man is ghostly pale, covered in dust. He appears unharmed, but confused: 'Have you seen her?' he keeps saying. 'Have you seen her?'

There is no sign of anyone else.

Jack stands there for a moment. Behind him the torn curtains flutter and flap in the breeze. It is the perfect opportunity to grab something, before the man comes to his senses. Jack's eyes flicker across the room. He is quick to recognise the objects of value. He snatches up a bent photograph frame and a twisted silver candlestick.

On the floor, the man is still moaning as he starts to dig into the pile of plaster and brick with his bare hands. Jack knows he could recover at any moment. He starts to back away, towards the window, clutching his loot in one hand. At the sound of glass crunching beneath Jack's feet, the man suddenly stops digging and stares up at Jack with eyes large as saucers. Jack is ready to run, every muscle tense. But the man doesn't seem to be able to see anything through the tears that are making dark tracks down his pale cheeks. 'I know she's here,' he says. 'Have you seen her?' And he turns back to his scrabbling in the debris.

Jack is almost out of there. He allows himself one last glance around the place, in case he's missed anything. It is then that he spots the headscarf. It is hidden from the man on the floor by the great broken back of the dining table. The horror hits him like a blow to the chest. The scarf has the same pattern as his mother's favourite one. He cannot help taking a step forward. His eye picks out the arm, the legs, the body of a woman who, apart from a light dusting of ash, seems untouched, as if sleeping peacefully among the ruins. His gaze is drawn back to the familiar headscarf, the sprinkling of pale flowers on a blue background. It is exactly the same as his mother's, except the pale flowers of this one are being swallowed up by the dark stain that is spreading, and he knows that the head beneath it is crushed and that this woman will never get up.

The man has noticed the look on Jack's face. He has stopped digging and is staring at Jack again. 'She's here,' he says. 'I know she is . . .'

Jack tries to swallow, to clear his throat, but the words choke with the dust in his mouth. The man turns back, attacking the rubble even more frantically, and Jack wants to reach out to stop him, and he crouches down and puts a hand on the man's shoulder, but the man carries on scratching, and Jack can see that the rubble is turning black and the man's fingers are turning black, and Jack realises it is blood: the man's hands are bleeding as he scrapes and scratches at the rubble. And Jack wants to say sorry, sorry for the body in the rubble, sorry for taking the picture frame and the candlestick, but he just doesn't know how.

Suddenly, bizarrely, there is a knock at the front door, and a voice calls out, 'Mr Knightley? Mrs Knightley?' Jack stands as an ARP warden comes into the room. She too is smeared with dirt and dust. 'Mr Knightley?' She peers into the gloom, shines her torch across the ruins of the house until the beam lands on Jack, dusty and wild, a scavenger on the prowl.

'Who are you?' she asks. Then, spotting the silver still clutched in his hand: 'Put those down! How dare you . . .?'

'I was going to . . .' but Jack's voice tails off. There's no point in explaining. He is what he is. He does not have the kind of bravery or even the kind of words it takes to turn a life around.

'Get out!' she is saying. 'Go on! Out, you animal!' He dodges her blows, and scrambles to the window, dropping the frame and the candlestick as he climbs back out the way he came in, his cheeks burning with humiliation. He shakes his coat out and grabs hold of Betsy's small hand, and they're off again. He suddenly has an urgent desire to reach home.

Jack tries not to look at the things that loom out of the night. Is that an arm or a foot? An ARP warden picks it up. His eyes have a faraway look, as if he's trying not to see it either. Jack blinks, and through the swirling clouds he sees

Tommy – or it might be Vince – rifling through the outer garments of a legless piece of flesh. How has he never noticed this horror before? He closes his eyes, and the broken body of the woman, her head crushed in his mother's scarf, swims there. When he looks again, there is a lady without any skirt or shoes or stockings on. She is stumbling along the road, naked from the waist down, her charred skin lit by the flames of a thousand fires. And there, behind her, is Stoog, and he is rattling the bent and broken doors, searching high and low for whatever he can lay his hands on. Jack trips on, over a baby squashed and pulped in the gutter; beneath a bare tree, its branches adorned with limbs instead of leaves. And all the time the jangling bells of the fire engines and the crunching of the rubble underfoot and the cries for help and the dust filling their lungs so that he is choking on death.

Jack squeezes Betsy's hand tighter, pulling her on. They are nearly at Southwark Park Road when they catch sight of Stoog and the others again. Stoog is grinning. He has got what looks like a haunch of meat and some new boots. The other boys' bags are full, and they are carrying things too: Jack glimpses a stiff chicken, its feathers dull, its neck thin and long, a pair of gentleman's silk dressing gowns.

The all-clear siren is sounding, calling out across the city that the danger has passed. All over London people will be coming out of their shelters, wondering what they will find.

'What you got?' says Stoog.

Jack shakes his head.

'Nothing? But . . .'

Jack holds up his hand. 'Don't,' he says. A terrible, morbid feeling has settled in his bones.

Stoog grins disdainfully and moves off. The other boys follow. Their faces are speckled with grime; they are camou-flaged soldiers fighting their own battles. They melt away into the war-torn city before anyone can ask questions. Jack watches them go and is filled with disgust at what they have all become.

He and Betsy make their way home. Ash floats through the air, settling in their hair. Small flames still burn around them: wisps of light in the dark. The fires cast a creepy guttering light across Jack's broken neighbourhood. The high street is unrecognisable. Walls are missing. You can see right in to people's bedrooms. Clothes flap across the ground. Twisted metal lies everywhere. The moon is reflected in a mirror on someone's wall. A bed half hangs from a first storey.

The pub on the corner that marks where they turn for their road is a furnace, flames burning in every window. Clouds of black smoke billow from the roof into the sky. There are fire wardens everywhere, clutching their stirrup pumps, aiming their hoses at innumerable streaks of flame. Boys and girls younger than Jack, many of whom he knows, fill buckets of water for them. Others race around with wheelbarrows full of sand, which they tip on the flames. Girl Guides in their blue uniforms soothe the injured and carry water and blankets to the shell-shocked.

They almost stumble into a deep crater halfway down their neighbouring street. Jack starts to jog. Broken glass crunches and crackles beneath his feet. Betsy runs to keep up. But it is all right. The houses at their end are untouched. Their home is still there. The front door is still on its hinges.

His mother is behind it, chewing her lip. 'Where have you been?' she shouts as soon as they fall into the hall.

Jack hesitates for a moment. The relief that surges through him is quickly replaced by defensiveness. 'Down the Underground,' he says. No need to look at Betsy. She will always back him up. But their mother doesn't question them; that they are here and alive is enough. She kneels down and opens her arms and clings to them in the dark.

Outside, sirens still scream and bells still ring. The clean-up will continue all night. Inside, the three of them slump on the floor. Betsy is a ghost, her face and clothes so pale with ash, the dribble of dried blood a dark scar across her forehead.

Their mother leans her head back against the wall, a knot

34

of exhaustion. 'Enough is enough,' she says. She picks something out of Betsy's hair. She does not catch Jack's eye. 'It's just us left,' she says.

'Don't say it.' Jack clenches his fists.

'They're gone. Both of them. They're not coming back.' There has been no news of his dad or Walt. They did not return with the men from Dunkirk.

'You don't know that for sure,' says Jack.

'I do.'

They stare at each other.

'There's a special train leaving in the morning. Another round of evacuations. I've booked her on it.' She doesn't need to carry on. Jack's shoulders sag. He cannot fight any more. His mother is right. He cannot keep his sister safe. No one left in this smouldering city is safe.

Betsy's eyes widen as the news sinks in. She shakes her head and inches back towards the door. 'You promised,' she says. Jack cannot stand the accusation in her voice, her eyes. He stops her, clasping her tightly, smoothing her smoky hair, filled with the dust of the dead. He feels her knobbly shoulders shiver beneath his sore hands, and he feels the piece of glass from Cherry Garden Pier burning like a hot coal in his pocket.

They wake early to the scratch of metal on rubble as London clears away debris on top of debris. Jack's mother dresses Betsy in her only coat. Her shoes are so threadbare now that Jack shoves some cardboard into them to cover up the holes. He can barely look at his mother. He can barely look at himself.

His mother has written 'Betsy Sullivan, Drummond Road, London SE17' on a large white label. She ties it to Betsy's coat, as if she's a piece of lost luggage. 'I've done you lunch, my love,' she says. Her voice is almost a whisper. A tremor runs through it, but she has no more tears to cry. 'Jam sandwiches. And I made your favourite biscuits.' She has used their week's ration of butter and sugar for these instead of the stale bread she usually tries to get away with.

Betsy holds the bag with her food in it. Jack holds her little suitcase. His sister has been polished and scrubbed. She looks as tidy as if she is off to church. His vision blurs for a moment. Then he clears his throat. He must be strong for her. He takes her hand. Their mother hovers in the background. 'Right, you,' he says, struggling to force the words out as they scratch and catch in his throat. 'Let's go.'

They pass walls teetering on the edge of collapse, hosepipes and buckets of sand, burning gas pipes, curtains flapping in the wind in buildings that look like dolls' houses with their fronts left open. They pass the posters telling mothers to send their children away, people who look like they haven't slept for weeks. They look out for live wires, particularly where the streets are waterlogged. Everywhere there is the smell of sewage, and wet, charred wood.

At Paddington Station, Betsy is pushed and pulled into one of the many groups of children. They all have the same wide, staring eyes. Some of them are crying. Betsy bites her lip and swallows, but she won't cry. Jack feels his heart break. It actually breaks in two right there. He stands next to his mother. He feels her coldness. She is their mother, but she's a shell. She steps forward towards her daughter. 'Betsy love, I'm sure you'll be back by . . .' She cannot finish her sentence. The word 'Christmas' is too gay and bright and precious to exist at this moment. She tries to bend down and kiss Betsy's pale cheek, but she is split from her by the ample figure of a buxom woman in a tweed suit.

'Where are they going?' Jack asks the woman, who is checking off a list.

'We'll tell you when they get there,' she says, without looking up.

Jack smacks her clipboard, making a sharp sound. Now he's got her attention. 'Tell me now,' he says.

'You'll find out in due course,' she says, glancing at him as her lip curls. She is not intimidated. 'Now hurry along. You're only making it more difficult for your sister.' She is right. He

36

can see that Betsy's bottom lip is quivering. He lets her usher Betsy towards a group of children who are then herded down the platform by more women in tweed suits. Betsy doesn't even turn to wave goodbye, she just lets herself be carried away on the tide of other bewildered children. The battered gas mask box bumps against the back of her legs.

His vision blurs as she is ushered up into the train. The platform is an empty space, devoid of life as he is devoid of feeling. His fingers close over Betsy's piece of glass, and he feels the familiar rage trickle into his bloodstream. The woman with the clipboard is still here, ticking things off her list. He grabs hold of the top of her arm. 'You can't just send them off and not know where they're going,' he says, his voice rising. 'You wouldn't do it to your own kids . . .' He wants to crush her. He feels so impotent. The woman struggles to shake herself free, but Jack won't let go, and she makes a strangled yelp for help, and suddenly there are people descending on him from all sides, and his mother cries out and there is a policeman, his helmet bobbing above everyone's heads, his buttons a neat, shiny row down his front, and Jack's mother has a hold on the policeman and they are talking and pointing, and Jack's rage turns to fear. Would his mother turn him in? She has sent her only daughter away. Perhaps she will do the same to him. And he cannot take it any longer – the relentless inevitability of it all.

Jack does not stop running until he reaches Carl's door. He hammers and hammers, and eventually it opens, a narrow crack through which Mr Mills is peering. The man is not happy to see him, but Carl is there in the corridor, and he whispers quietly to his father, who eventually moves aside.

Jack does not care that his eyes are red and his grubby face is streaked with tears. He reaches out to Carl. 'Can I come?' he asks. 'Can I still come with you?'

And Carl pulls him inside, where it is bright and warm and he feels the weight of his friend's arm across his shoulder.

CHAPTER 3

Charlie

Charlie braces himself against the heavy swell. The Atlantic Ocean stretches mile after choppy mile in every direction – every crinkle in every wave could hide a U-boat. The first British ship was sunk out here in the North-western Approaches, just hours after Chamberlain's radio broadcast, and not much later than the sleeper train was pulling away from London towards Inverness all those days ago. It was an unarmed passenger ship, torpedoed as the evening meal was being served.

He scans the flight deck, flat apart from the island with its shiny black pom-pom guns. What a sight an aircraft carrier is! She carries the might of fifteen hundred men and more than fifty folded planes anywhere in the world, transporting them safely in her enormous belly like a battle-ready whale.

Charlie steadies himself again: even a ship this size bounces like a cork on these waves. The planes are being brought up on the lifts from below. This is what he's been waiting for. No more exams. This is the real thing. Squadron 843's stumpy Blackburn Skuas appear first. He scratches his head and runs his fingers through his hair. He's glad he's not flying one of these new fighter planes. Give him a good old-fashioned bi-plane and an open cockpit any day.

He shakes his legs and arms out to get the circulation going. His sheepskin-lined clothes are warm but cumbersome. He smiles to himself as he remembers target training. He has always been a good shot. Calm and steady, like his plane. And she may be slow, but boy, does she respond to his touch. He can make her do whatever he wants with the lightest pressure from his hands and feet. They can swoop and climb, turn and stop, bank, dive, soar, roll, loop the loop . . . although that's a court martial, of course – if you're caught.

'Either you're young and brilliant or young and stupid,' one of his instructors had said.

'A little bit of all three, I suspect, sir,' he'd answered, grinning. But he isn't. The one thing you can't call Charlie is stupid. He's sensible, and he can assess a situation in a split second. He knows what he's capable of and he knows what his plane's capable of. That's why the training was a doddle.

'Thinking about a pretty lady again, boyo?' says Mole, his words whipped away by the wind.

'You could say that,' says Charlie. And actually, he has allowed himself to think of the girl from the train, but not out here on the flight deck. Here, he needs to focus. He slips his arms into the Mae West, wriggling to make it more comfortable on his shoulders. 'Bloody thing,' he says. 'Too many damn straps and buckles and safety clips.'

'Mind your language in front of young Billy the Kid,' says Mole. He nods at the boy standing next to them. Bill is actually a little older than Charlie, but he seems younger without Charlie's breezy self-confidence. He is their TAG. The plane's telegraphist–air gunner. He is quiet and respectful. But then, he is only a lower-deck rating. He is also perpetually unflustered. Important if you find yourself in a sticky situation.

Bill smiles and makes a gesture like firing a gun with his hands, before he slips on his leather gloves.

'Come on, Billy. Let's do this,' says Mole. The Welshman has taken the Kid under his wing. He takes everyone under his wing. He's an astute observer, and has a gift for making people feel at ease. Both traits useful when you're the navigator in a cockpit flying at almost two thousand feet.

The fleet has received a distress call from an unarmed and lonely cargo ship two hundred miles away. It is being chased by a German submarine. It is too far for the fleet's ships to get there quickly, but the pilots will.

The airmen were immediately at the ready. They are always at the ready, whether they are standing by in the ready room or writing letters in the wardroom or asleep in their cabins. The flight deck crew indicate that the Skuas are good to go. Charlie says a silent prayer for them. There is ribbing in the wardroom about Charlie's squadron's old Stringbags, but out here on the wind-lashed flight deck, there is nothing but respect for each other.

Charlie shivers: part anticipation, part wind chill. There is no dread: this is what it's all about. At last he can put the training into practice.

'Number four crew, stand by to scramble!'

Charlie nods at Frank and Paddy – the other two squadron pilots – and their crew. The Fairey Swordfish have been run into place. They rise and fall at the far end of the ship. The flight deck crew unfurl their wings as the airmen lumber towards them like bears in their thick boots and Irvin jackets – but in a moment they too will be weightless, as graceful as the most delicate of insects.

Charlie can see the bombs strapped in racks beneath their plane. Mole and Billy disappear behind her wing and haul themselves up into the cockpit. Charlie nods at Tugger, solid and windswept on the deck. He reaches for the handholds, climbing up above the wheel, over the wing and into the front of the cockpit. He hands Tugger the crank handle, sits down on the parachute, clips himself in, yanks his goggles down, pulls his harness tight, starts his cockpit checks.

Tugger, his large body squeezed between a strut and the body of the plane, fits the handle into its hole and starts to turn, slowly at first, then faster. Danny, wedged further down, helps him. Through the howl of the wind Charlie hears the whizz of the motor. Tugger and Danny wind, faster and faster.

Their arms become a blur. Charlie gets ready with the throttle, mixture, switches, trim. He can tell from the sound that it's time to flick her into life.

With a cough and a splutter, the propeller starts to rotate. The men still crank. The smoke from the plane's engine belches out and is whisked away on the wind. The propeller is a spinning blur, just the paint on its tips visible, a yellow circle. Tugger and Danny can finally stop. They jump down on to the deck. Tugger runs around the wing to the rudder. Danny does the same on the other side. They lie on the struts beneath the tail fin, holding the plane steady as Charlie does his final checks. The legs of their overalls ripple and flap in the slipstream. The engine warms up to a throaty roar. Tugger and Danny can feel she's ready. They glance back at Charlie. Thumbs up. As one, they run to the wheels. The chocks are away. Charlie is free.

The deck stretches out in front of him. Beyond the deck, the sky and the ocean. The ship is head to wind, ready for take-off. The sound of wind and machine is thick in his ears now, and Mole's voice, through the rubber Gosport tube that links them together. 'Steer two six zero.'

'Roger, two six zero.'

Charlie opens the throttle and the Swordfish answers with a growl. He checks the revs, the pressure, the temperature. He gives the thumbs-up to the flight deck crew, and they're away, the world slipping past faster and faster, the wheels bumping. And then all is clear and smooth and they are dropping off the end of the ship and up, up into the sky.

'Steer two one zero,' says Mole in his ear.

'Roger, two one zero,' he replies.

Charlie has perfected his deck take-off, but every flight is like the first. The sky opens up before him as the ship disappears behind until it is a dot among the shifting waves. It is beautiful. Breathtaking. Nerve-wracking. Exhilarating. It is like nothing else in the world. The sea sparkles miles below. He fancies he sees the curve of the globe. He trusts his plane implicitly, as he trusts Mac and the Kid, Tugger and Danny, almost more than he trusts himself.

Mole starts to hum some ditty down the tube, Charlie catching parts of the tune before they are snatched away on the slipstream. The observer is always singing as he scratches away with his pencils and compass on the charts. Charlie has no idea how he manages to balance the boards and the rubbers and all the other paraphernalia, since he isn't really sitting down at all. It is only Charlie who gets a proper seat. The others perch on nothing more than a cross bar.

It is an hour's flight to the merchant ship. Nothing to do but enjoy it. He uncricks his neck, rolls his shoulders to loosen them up as much as he can in the cramped seat. The sky is a patchwork of dark and light. Visibility is good. The sun breaks out, and Charlie could be four years old again – on his first flight: there's the same roar of the wind, the rumble of the plane – and him, weightless, soaring into the endless sky, his father behind him, beaming with pride, his mother's face receding way, way below, creased with worry. His thoughts drift to the girl he met on the train. Olivia. Perhaps he could bring her up here one day. She is the kind of girl his mother would have approved of. Or at least, he thinks she is. He remembers his mother talking about families, and how she hoped that one day he would meet the right person, like she had. She had laughed, imagining herself as a grandmother. In his memory, they are stretched out on a picnic rug on the beach. His father must have been swimming in the sea. The air is warm, and he is lying looking up at her, and she is stroking his head, her curly hair a hazy halo of gold around her smiling face. He is not sure whether the memory is true or false. It feels real, but he must have been only five or six. The year before they both died.

Mole has stopped humming. 'Dead ahead.' The words bring Charlie back to the present. As usual, the observer's calculations are spot on, and already they are closing in on the merchant ship. Charlie pushes all thoughts from his mind. The world shrinks. As they approach, one of the Skuas flies past them, back towards the carrier. 'Must be low on fuel,' Mole yells down his ear. Charlie nods, concentrating. Ahead, he sees another Skua wheel around like an angry seabird. He sees the tiny bombs fall and the plumes of smoke and spray as shrapnel bursts from the sea where they land. It swoops in low – too low – next to the ship. As the mess clears, he can see that the plane is in trouble: smoke trails from its nose. Damaged by its own bomb, it splashes into the sea.

'Bugger,' says Charlie. 'Where's that U-boat?' All he can see is the merchant ship, a long and low smudge on the sea, her drab sides a dusky contrast to the red ensign that flutters at her stern. She is hove to, rocking in the waves.

'Must have dived,' says Mole.

Charlie loops around the merchant ship. He needs to assess the situation as quickly as he can. It looks as though some of the crew are still on the ship. But the ship's lifeboats are in the water – and full of crew waving at them frantically. There is a lot of debris around them, some of it from the plane that just crashed. But another plane is missing. Did that go down too? There are two yellow life jackets – the missing airmen? – swimming towards the merchant ship; a third bobs inertly on the waves. Charlie has swung the plane right back out to sea. He works the port rudder and they turn towards the ship again. They must be eight hundred yards away when, 'There! There!' Mole suddenly yells.

The submarine is rising. Its conning tower and gun break the surface first as water cascades off its back. Charlie's heart thumps. This is not a dummy run with pretend bombs. It's the real thing. He swallows. His mouth is suddenly dry. Time moves slowly. Second by second. His thoughts are clear as a reflection in a puddle on a still day.

It's all in the timing. He drops the plane lower over the water. Closer and closer. The submarine lies alongside the merchant ship, sleek and black. Wait, wait. Wait. Now! Charlie presses the button, and, as they pass over, the Kid starts to fire, *clack-clack-clack*, manoeuvring the gun into position. There is a thud that resonates in their chests as the bomb Charlie released explodes, and spray spatters the back of the plane.

Mole cranes his neck to see behind. 'Good shot, boyo,' he shouts. 'It's dived again. Won't go far. It's Germans on the ship. Five of them. Must have boarded before we got here.' Charlie knows the Germans will take whatever provisions and information – and British – they can and then scuttle the ship with their torpedoes.

He circles again. He can see the life jackets have reached the ship and are being hauled out of the water. The third life jacket still bobs near to where he first spotted it. The Kid keeps his finger on the trigger as he swings the gun back and forth, always ready. Sure enough, the U-boat resurfaces. Charlie goes in for the attack. This is their last bomb. He needs to make it count. Five hundred yards. His hand is on the button. 'Steady, boy,' says Mole. Four hundred yards. Three hundred. He presses the button. The charge dislodges from its bracket. Another thud resonates through their bodies and seawater spurts into the air as the bomb explodes. They can't see anything through the smoke and the froth.

'Spot on!' says Mole.

'Thanks for the shower,' says the Kid.

'You were beginning to smell.'

'That's it. We're all out,' says Charlie.

The sub is on the surface again. The German crew are scrambling to get off the captured ship and back to their submarine. There is a kerfuffle, and the British airmen leap off the ship and into the water, yellow blobs in the dark sea.

The Kid yells from behind, 'Take us in closer, Charlie. Let me have a go.' But Charlie doesn't dare. It's a mess down there. The submarine is trying to pick up her German crew, who in turn are trying to grab the British men from the water. Training doesn't prepare you for this.

Mole is in his ear. 'Here comes back-up, boyo.'

Frank and Paddy are here at last. But too late: the greedy shark has swallowed its German crew and its British prize. Charlie is relieved that he doesn't have any more bombs to drop. He doesn't want to make that decision. Frank and Paddy go in for the kill. But the submarine sinks back into the ocean with its catch. As a final goodbye it sends its own torpedo to take out the merchant ship. Charlie spots the track of the missile under the water but there is nothing he can do. The merchant ship flinches, spewing black smoke up into the air. Her back is broken, and, as dark clouds cascade into the sky, she too sinks deep into the sea.

It is as if she were never there.

Mole doesn't sing on the way back to the carrier. There is just the sound of the air rushing past, and the hum and rattle of their aeroplane. Charlie has kept his crew and his plane safe, but seeing a ship die leaves a bitter taste in their mouths. He tries not to dwell on the captured airmen, men whose hands he grasped only moments ago on the flight deck, who will either never wake again, or find themselves in an enemy camp.

They are about eight miles from the rest of the fleet, close enough to see the carrier in the distance, when suddenly Charlie hears Mole's breath catch in his throat. At the same time, Charlie sees it too.

'Forty-five degrees starboard,' says Mole.

Charlie presses the foot pedals to operate the rudder. The plane responds immediately. He dips the starboard wing. There is shadow, and above it a mark like a white scar in the water. Charlie feels a shiver of anticipation. There's no mistaking the track of a periscope.

The U-boat is heading straight for the rest of the fleet, approaching at a ninety-degree angle. It is almost close enough to attack. The British ships won't have seen it yet, but Charlie can't warn them: radio silence must be kept at all times in case the Germans pick their messages up. They have no bombs left, either. There's only one thing to do.

'Take me in!' yells the Kid.

Charlie doesn't even have to think about it. It's the only way they can alert the fleet. He feels the gunner's weight shift as he leans out over the side of the plane, searching for his target. The hunter is about to become the hunted.

Charlie has his own gun in front of him. Its barrel gleams gold in the afternoon sun. He drops as low as he dares, the plane's wheels almost skimming the dark crests of the waves. Charlie opens his gun. As they pass, the Kid lets rip. *Clack-clack-clack*.

'Diving!' says Mole, and, although the Kid fires a little longer, swinging the gun as they bank around, the U-boat has gone. In its place is a mass of seething green. They may not have done the slightest damage, but at least they have warned their ships that the enemy is on the prowl.

The aircraft carrier is now close enough to make out the tiny figures on the high deck. She is still sideways on to the U-boat, the worst position to be in if you're about to be fired at. But she is beginning to turn. The three airmen look down over the edge of the cockpit. At the same moment they spot the telltale streaks of white under the water. The submarine has fired, but the carrier is still turning, turning, and she manages to swing her great mass head-on to the submarine, and the torpedoes pass either side of her and safely into the empty water behind.

At once, the destroyers that have remained with the aircraft carrier go on the attack, like a herd of grey sea elephants rounding on the enemy. The sea is churning foam as they drop their charges, and the air is bursting with noise that dies away as the ships stop. They wait. Charlie's blood pumps in his ears.

The sea settles back to a ripple, and then the submarine slowly breaks the surface. Its conning tower has been damaged. White horses break against its monstrous sides. But it is broken. Charlie sees men jumping into the water.

Charlie needs to land: he is very low on fuel. The carrier

signals with its lamp. The Kid signals back. The great ship turns head to wind. Her wake is a foamy ribbon fluttering out behind her. Charlie approaches alongside. He glimpses the pink faces of his fellow sailors looking up as they pass. He swings the plane one hundred and eighty degrees, lines himself up, considers wind speed, direction. The flat of the landing deck stretches before him. He can see the white stripes. The metal wires strung across it. The batsman with his ping-pong bats. He slows the engine right back. The ship slices through the water ahead of him, the V of the waves spreads out, ever increasing.

He pulls a lever on his right to lower the hook beneath the plane. The batsman holds the bats out level. He is on line. About fifty yards to go. He drops the tail. Nose up. It is just the deck and the plane, the batsman, and Charlie. And then he is over the deck, the batsman gives 'Cut', and, as the plane's wheels make contact, the crew lurch against their harnesses and bounce and scrape as the arrester hook tugs at the wires that slow the plane down, and they finally come to a stand-still. Charlie unclips himself. His legs are stiff as planks of wood.

Mole squeezes his shoulder. 'Top landing, boyo,' he says.

The plane's propellers slow and stop. They clamber out, back on to their version of solid ground, the steady, humming mass of their aircraft carrier. He has grown accustomed to the rumble of the engine and the rush of the air. But now there is the sound of the sea and the Tannoy and the shouts of men. The ship is manic with activity as the other Swordfish come in to land. The flight deck crew clear the way as they manoeuvre the planes back towards the lift.

Charlie heads for the island. He removes his helmet and goggles as he goes. His legs are coming back to life. He is desperate to pee, but he has to report to the captain first.

Captain Turnbull is a man of determination. He acknowledges Charlie as he approaches, but keeps his head cocked to the side as he listens intently to the pilot of the Skua that returned earlier and to Paddy, who has made it here already. The captain's eyes are bright above the black bags. He has a shock of white hair, although he must be in his mid-forties – about the same age as Charlie's father would have been. And Charlie is the same age as his father was at the beginning of his own generation's Great War. Life gone full circle.

'Nice work, pilot,' says Captain Turnbull as Charlie reaches them, and the other pilots nod a welcome.

'Thank you, sir,' says Charlie. He ruffles his hair up with his fingers, where it has been plastered to his head beneath the leather helmet.

'Your first operation and our first prisoners-of-war,' says the captain, indicating to the destroyer that is picking up the men from the submarine. 'And not a casualty among them. Not from the U-boat, or among our fleet, thanks to you.'

'Thank you, sir.'

'Keep it up and you'll go far.'

'I hope so, sir.'

'Shame about that merchant ship.'

'Yes, sir.'

'We lost four men. Two dead. Two prisoners.'

'That's right, sir,' says Paddy.

'Attacks are getting worse.'

Paddy nods. 'They are, sir.'

'You think they were part of a coordinated effort? Or just a bit of luck?'

'Hard to tell, sir. The sea is chock-full of them at the moment.'

They all gaze towards the destroyer. Charlie imagines the Germans being hoisted on board, their heads hung low. There is no honour in being captured.

'It seems that your beloved Fairey Swordfish may not have had its day, FitzHerbert,' the captain says, still looking out of the window.

'Certainly hasn't, sir.'

'Could indeed be our secret weapon against these U-boats.'

'Yes, sir.'

'Pass my thanks on to the rest of your crew.'

'I will, sir.'

The captain turns back to the other men and his charts. Charlie is dismissed.

Back on the blustery deck, Mole and the Kid are also staring out at the destroyer as the last of the Germans is transferred on to the ship. Charlie knows it will be the U-boat commander, the eagle of the Third Reich glinting on his peaked cap.

'Dry clothes and a stiff drink, that's the order of the day, boyo,' says Mole.

'Just my tot'll do me,' says the Kid.

Charlie starts to undo his coat as he follows Mole to the wardroom. He slaps the Kid on the shoulder on his way past. 'Good job today, Billy,' he says. The Kid nods and grins. 'Now go and tell everyone how you were responsible for taking Britain's first prisoners-of-war.'

'I will. Thanks, Charlie.' The Kid disappears off to his own mess deck.

'First POWs, eh?' says Mole. 'Now that calls for a party.'

There are great celebrations throughout the ship that night. Below deck, the men cram into their messes. Once the rum lies warm in their bellies, they don't notice how cramped everything is. The air grows warmer, and the atmosphere lighter. The cooks slap extra food on the airmen's plates.

In the wardroom, Charlie and Mole drink gin with the rest of the officers. Lieutenant Commander Widdecombe, the squadron commander of 686, will write to the captured and dead men's families in the morning. For now, they will focus on the positive. Flying is what they were born for, and this war will show the world what they are capable of. Charlie's thoughts drift to the girl on the train. The men mistake the flush in his cheeks for booze, but really it is because he is remembering how Olivia had walked down the carriage, tucking her hair nervously behind her ears as she followed the waiter who was trying to find a spare table for her to sit at. But of course there were his cadets, lounging oafishly across the seats, ogling the poor girl and making inappropriate remarks until he had brought them into line. He could hardly blame them: she was extremely attractive. Charlie had been momentarily lost for words before inviting her to share his table, and breakfast had somehow been an intimate affair, even among the clinking of plates and cutlery, and the stares of his giggling charges in their crumpled uniforms. And then there had been the fantastic luck that she was going to stay with Nancy, of all people. Her aunt, his godmother. If that isn't fate, he doesn't know what is. He hadn't been able to resist writing to both her and Nancy, to tell the latter what a delightful girl she had coming to stay, and to tell Olivia how much he enjoyed meeting her. He smiles to himself as he dares to contemplate her writing back.

He feels Mole's arm around his shoulder. 'Now you're definitely thinking of a pretty lady,' the Welshman says, his flushed face inches from Charlie's. Charlie nods, grinning back, and Mole clears his throat and starts one of his songs. Charlie can feel the music vibrate and rumble in his chest as he places his own arm around the observer's shoulder. Side by side, they are an odd couple: the tall, angular Englishman and the short, dark Welshman. They have been flying together for almost six months, more time than Charlie has ever flown with anyone before. He is called Mole because of his habit of staring at the charts so closely that his nose almost touches them. But of course, his vision is perfect really.

Their shipmates believe the Swordfish are their guardian angels. And Charlie has to admit, they do look like angels up there, floating and weaving through the sky. And Olivia, with her golden hair and her pale blue eyes, is an angel too. The drink warms his belly and the music fills his head as he leans back and gently glides away into the clouds.

50

CHAPTER 4

It is only a few days later, his hangover barely cleared, that Charlie hears the shocking news that a British aircraft carrier has been torpedoed and sunk off Ireland, with few survivors and more than five hundred dead. The men's grief is deep and unfathomable, like the ocean they feel cast adrift on. Everyone knows someone who died. The Kid is distraught. He has lost a close friend from his home town. They joined up together. There are boys and men, sailors and pilots, telegraphists and signalmen, photographers and marines, stokers and plumbers, cooks and gunners, mechanics and joiners and sailmakers – all gone, along with two entire squadrons of Fairey Swordfish. It could so easily have been Charlie's ship.

The Admiralty is nervous. They cannot afford to lose another aircraft carrier: bad for morale, bad for publicity, bad for the coffers. Charlie's ship has orders to withdraw from submarine patrol. The men are dismayed. They would like nothing better than to avenge their brothers. They hear that the submarine that attacked her has escaped and that the German Kriegsmarine are elated, boasting of their success. The sailors fume and mutter below deck. But orders are orders. When you're in the Royal Navy, you do what you're told.

Tonight Charlie's carrier is returning to the naval base at Scapa Flow. As they approach, Charlie's eyes take in the gentle peaks of the Orkneys. Waves rush out in front of the ship as the land appears and disappears with the rise and fall of the ship. One minute it's there, the next all he can see is the sky.

51

They negotiate the trench of Hoxa Sound, the only part deep enough for the aircraft carrier's draught. The channel leads them to the shelter of Scapa Flow, the natural harbour nestled beneath mainland Orkney and protected by a chain of islands.

Hills rise out of the mist on either side. Ahead, a line of wooden buoys floats along the top of the water: the boom defence. The nets lie like hidden curtains beneath: interlaced circles of metal designed to prevent submarines getting in, and to snag enemy ships. Tugboats pull the booms out of the way, and the aircraft carrier slides in. Everyone breathes a little easier: they are safe.

Another battleship heaves into view, standing out proudly in contrast to the wilderness. A thrill runs through Charlie when he sees her. She is an important part of the Royal Navy's history, launched in 1914 at the start of the Great War, and, although she is too slow to keep up with the more modern ships in the fleet, she is ideal for training – this is where the boys he escorted up here on the sleeper were headed. The ship holds a special place in Charlie's heart: his father served on board as first lieutenant towards the end of that Great War.

They drop anchor about seven hundred yards from the older ship. The heavy chain rushes out of the hawsepipe with a rattle and a splash, and plummets to the bottom of the harbour. The men get ready to relax. Some prepare for a night of cards or building models or listening to the radio. Others will go ashore to stretch their legs. Charlie is surprised to find a letter delivered into his hand. Hope leaps in his chest like a fish. He opens the envelope slowly, savouring the rarity. His eyes scan down the page, across the spindly words that fall over each other until they get to the end: Olivia. The girl from the train. He props his back against the wall, stretching out his legs across his bunk as he settles down to read.

The letter makes him smile. He loves the description of her journey from the station to Taigh Mor. He knows that road well. It is one of his favourite journeys, winding its way through the Highlands, passing only the occasional cottage, the tops of the hills almost touching the sky, the burns glimmering in the distance, the sudden smattering of hardy, ragged sheep or a lone red deer. It is a journey back in time.

He is delighted to discover that Nancy has lodged Olivia in the little bothy down by the loch. He wonders whether she knows that her uncle did that bothy up as a wedding present for his then young wife before the last war, and how special it was to the pair of them. He has no doubt that the place will work its magic on her. There is something so charmingly naïve about her letter. She has been cosseted and kept from the real world. He can't help feeling excited at the prospect of her learning to love Scotland as he does.

What he would give to be there now. To lie in the silence broken only by the murmur of water on shingle and the rustle of the trees, instead of the hollow clanking of his ship and the thoughts and voices of so many men. Ironically it is only a few miles around the coast, but it might as well be a thousand miles away.

Charlie resists the urge to hold the letter to his nose, to breathe her in. Can it really be only ten days since they met? And now she has replied. Things couldn't be better. He rests his head back against the cabin wall. Life is good. His first goal was to fly, and now that he's doing it, the rest of his dreams will follow. Suddenly his future is something that is tangible, ready to be plucked in all its shining glory as soon as the war is over.

Night is drawing in and the light is fading. The aircraft carrier's signal lamp winks its message to ask whether they can join the men on the battleship for a few drinks. Charlie is bursting with energy. He feels as though he could do anything. He joins Paddy and Frank, Mole and some of the other officers who want a closer look at the veteran ship. They motor across the black water of the harbour. The movement of a small boat is completely different to that of the aircraft carrier; the smell of salt water and the sloshing of the waves more powerful. The sea glints where the small light on their launch catches the ripples.

Although the old battleship – like all ships – is in blackout, Charlie can just make her out in the twilight: the pom-pom guns next to the funnel, and the huge fourteen-inch guns at the front trumpeting up to the sky, the lifeboats dangling on their davits like hanging baskets. The sound of the water changes as it slaps ineffectually at her sides.

'Boat ahoy!' Someone shines a light down on them. They blink up at it, unable to see anyone behind the brightness. An officer is there to greet them. He grabs Charlie's hand firmly, gripping his forearm with the other hand. 'Welcome aboard,' he says.

It does them good to see new faces. The officers relax into a catch-up, trading stories of German reconnaissance and squeezing each other for news of home and where they might be sent next. Charlie wonders whether his father ever sat in this same wardroom, among the chink of glasses and the hum of men.

'Any on-shore entertainment here?' asks Frank.

'Not unless you like sheep,' says one of the officers, a man with a long, narrow nose.

All the men laugh, but Charlie says, 'I love it up here. Think I might buy a place one day.'

Mole grunts. 'Not on a sub-lieutenant's pay, you won't,' he says.

'I won't be a sub-lieutenant for ever,' says Charlie.

'No,' says Mole. 'Knowing you, you won't.'

'Don't tell me,' says one of the older officers, with a wry smile, 'you've got it all mapped out: captain, commodore, admiral?'

Charlie looks down at his drink. The liquid sloshes against the glass. 'Doesn't everyone want to progress?' he says quietly.

'Life never turns out how you expect,' says the man with the narrow nose.

'I do know that,' says Charlie, thinking of his dead parents, feeling a lump in his throat and desperately trying not to let it escape into his mouth.

The older man is leaning forwards: 'I had it all mapped out

too. Pipe. Slippers . . . And look at me now. Back on a bloody ship, faced with another war.'

'Isn't it your duty—' Charlie starts to say.

'Duty? Duty! Don't talk to me about bloody duty. I did my duty last time around . . .'

'Leave him alone, Bruce. He's only a youngster.'

Charlie is sweating. It is partly the whisky, partly embarrassment, partly anger. He grips the tumbler in frustration. He's not that young. He's twenty, the same age as his father was at the start of the last war, and he's already doing things that boys can only dream of.

Bruce downs his drink, sighing as he tops up the glass again. 'No offence, old boy,' he says, rubbing his hand across his eyes and settling back in his chair. 'I'm just a weather-beaten old fool, and you're right. I'm glad we've got a bunch of optimists to see us through . . .'

To Charlie's relief, the conversation is brought to an end there, as a rating knocks at the door to ask if the officers need anything further. Charlie recognises the freckle-faced boy immediately as one of the batch he escorted up here on the train. He gets to his feet and crosses the wardroom. 'Summers, isn't it?' he says.

The boy nods, his cheeks colouring. 'Yes, sir.'

'How's it all going?'

'Very good, sir.'

'They treating you well?'

'Of course.' Summers shifts nervously from foot to foot.

'Is it all you thought it would be?'

'And more, sir.'

'I gather your training class is coming over to our ship tomorrow, to get a taste of life on an aircraft carrier?'

'I believe so, sir.'

'Well, I'll look out for you, then. Send my regards to the other cadets who travelled with us, won't you?'

'I will, sir. Thank you, sir.' Summers nods, still red-cheeked as he disappears away down the corridor.

Charlie feels as though he has reasserted some authority. He turns back to the men in the room, dusting down his jacket. 'Probably time for us to get back,' he says. 'It's been a long few weeks.'

Back on board his own ship, Charlie stands on the flight deck for a moment before heading down to his cabin. The harbour is so quiet that he can hear the capital ship's boatswain's mate piping down. The piercing notes echo across the water like a strange bird's cry. Above him, the sky starts to shimmer. There is a line of sparkling luminescence in the sky, a ribbon of undulating neon pulsing over the ships. At the edge it is aquamarine and blue, and the stars still twinkle in the darker velvet sky around it. The Northern Lights. Instead of coal-black, the sea is beginning to glimmer luminous green. It is a moment of wonder, like receiving a letter. Charlie wonders if Olivia is watching them too: they are connected by this inky water that bleeds into the nooks and crannies of the northern shores of Britain.

Mole puts an arm around Charlie's shoulder. 'Don't take it to heart, boyo. It's been a hell of a week.'

'What's wrong with aiming high?'

'Nothing at all. But you should remember there is more to life than just this. I know you've had it drummed into you by that fancy school you went to.'

'Don't they teach you the same at grammar school?'

'Yes. But I also know you need more than that for a happy life.'

'You mean, a wife and family? Like you.'

'Exactly. Man cannot live by bread alone . . . there's drink and women and singing . . .' Mole starts to sing. It's a song that Charlie recognises as 'Calon Lân', one of the Welshman's favourites. The notes bounce across the harbour and out towards the hills. As his voice fades, so too do the lights in the sky, and once again they are left in silence and darkness. Charlie feels a deep hollow in the pit of his stomach and with surprise he realises his eyes have filled with tears. Must be the whisky. He leaves Mole on deck and heads for the isolation of his cabin.

Charlie is woken by a loud bang. It is 0104 in the morning. The night is black as coal. He stumbles to the door of his cabin. A signalman trots along the corridor. 'It's the battleship, sir,' he says. 'Some fuel or ammunition gone up in the bows.'

Charlie nods. Through his porthole he can hear a faint tinny voice. Probably a message on the ship's Tannoy system. 'OK. Thanks, Walker. Let me know if they need help.'

'Will do, sir.' Walker jogs back along the corridor, his feet reverberating through the metal tunnel.

Charlie turns back to his cabin and closes the door. He isn't concerned. After all, this is a naval base. They couldn't be safer. He has almost reached his bunk when there is another almighty boom. There is no mistaking that noise. It is an explosion – and a large one. He opens the porthole and sees flames across the water. He grabs his clothes, his boots, and runs up on deck still clambering into them. He pushes past the crowd of men to the rails. The battleship is listing like a drunk. Everyone is shouting at the same time: 'Away lifeboat's crew! What else can we do? Hurry!' Charlie runs for the tender they used only a few hours ago. But it has already cast off with Frank and a petty officer to go and help. The aircraft carrier has switched on her searchlight and aims it at the water where the vast ship is now floundering, almost flat on her side.

Men and boys are scrabbling from every part of her in desperation. They are sliding down her hull, jumping into the water, crying out from where they are trapped inside. Fierce white flames rip out of the vents and portholes as there is another echoing blast. Suddenly the ship heels further, the weight of her guns pulls her over and under and she vanishes from sight, sinking towards the mud of the harbour floor, with so many men still screaming from within. The bitter stench of cordite stings Charlie's nostrils. The sea thrashes with survivors and debris. Cries. Flames. Frank's tender joins a converted drifter moving among the objects in the water. The drifter has managed to rescue several people. More clamber at the sides to be hauled in by their friends. They cry out in terror. Other bodies float face-down in the water. A few of the men strike out for land. It is less than a mile's swim. The sea is an oil slick. Deadly and viscous. There is smoke everywhere.

Charlie helps transfer the rescued men from their own tender on to the deck. Many are wearing only their night-clothes: vests and pants. They shiver uncontrollably. Their skin is covered in oil. Some are burnt. Their skin is blackened, blistered, bubbled. Some of them die there and then on the deck. The oil has coated their lungs and they can't breathe any more. Others whimper and cry out. The legs of the men who slid along the hull of the ship as she went down are shredded: the barnacles have ripped into their skin. Their teeth chatter with cold and shock. Among the faces of the survivors Charlie cannot find one that he recognises – not Bruce or the officer with the narrow nose.

At four in the morning they give up looking for survivors. The sea is ominously quiet. There is no life left upon its dark and indifferent surface. 'Any sign of Summers?' Charlie says to Frank when he hauls himself back on to the ship. 'Summers? With the freckles?' Frank shakes his head, tries to say some-thing, but it comes out as a gurgle. Charlie gets him a drink and a blanket. 'Come on, Frank. Have some of this.' He holds the drink to Frank's lips, but before he can drink, Frank turns and retches violently. 'They were stuck in the gangways. We could hear them. They couldn't get out . . .'

For a moment Charlie hears again the voices of those boys and men who cried out as they sank and the icy water filled the corridors and they scrabbled to get past each other. It was too crowded and dark and they were half asleep or in a night-mare, and they gulped great mouthfuls of air, and then water, until they were silenced for ever.

They give the survivors whatever clothes and rum they can find. No one knows what caused the explosion, although there are rumours that the impossible has happened and a U-boat has sneaked like a wolf into the lambing shed. More than eight hundred men have drowned within yards of them. Many were only boys, asleep in their hammocks. It is impossible to comprehend. They were supposed to be safe. Charlie sits in the yellow light of the wardroom in silence. Tonight he has stared death in the face and he will never forget it. It doesn't matter how old or experienced you are. In the eyes of death, all men are equal.

That a German U-boat managed not only to infiltrate the impregnable Scapa Flow but also sink an iconic battleship is a devastating blow not just to the Navy, but to a nation that believed it ruled the waves. The men fret about the families and friends they have left behind in the towns and cities, the villages and hamlets of home. The odds of war are stacking up against them. The Germans have pushed relentlessly on, into France, the Netherlands, Belgium. Sometimes it feels as though the Navy is all that stands between the enemy and Britain.

Charlie's aircraft carrier is assigned a new captain as Captain Turnbull is promoted to commodore, his expertise needed elsewhere. Captain Pearce is a mean little man, cross that he's been called back from retirement; already fed up with the constant demands of life at sea, particularly on his weary old bones. He had imagined his life would end differently, preferably in the garden with his prize dahlias, but another war has put paid to that. He has no experience of flying, and the pilots cannot stand him. Worse, he believes the Fairey Swordfish to be outdated relics of the past: he cannot see their advantages. He makes them fly in the most terrible conditions, unaware of the finely-tuned capabilities of individual pilots and planes. He sometimes makes them fly without their accompanying plane guard, which means a downed crew would be left to fend for themselves in the water. The carrier is deployed to the African coast to search for a German commerce raider that has been causing havoc. Captain Pearce sweats and grumbles about the heat. Then they escort a damaged cruiser back to Britain, ending up a few months later – and after the turn of the new year – back at a windswept Scapa Flow. The captain shivers and moans about the cold. They say goodbye to the Blackburn Skua squadron, who are left – to their delight and everyone else's envy – to add to the defences in northern Scotland.

The only joy at this joyless time is another letter from Olivia. Charlie thinks longingly of a visit to Loch Ewe, but there is not time to get there overland for a day's leave, and Captain Pearce won't allow them longer: they have been assigned to the Mediterranean fleet for exercises. He consoles himself over the weeks by savouring every word that she has written. It sounds as if she is settling in, as he knew she would. His mouth waters when she talks about how rationing doesn't affect her because she has milk and butter and fresh eggs in exchange for helping on the Macs' farm, and later there will be honey from Mrs Ross's bees. She has been preparing the ground for vegetables in the walled garden under Greer's beady eye, and the house-maid, Clarkson, has been teaching her to forage for young shoots of nettles and wild garlic. There is even talk of trapping rabbits.

Charlie's aircraft carrier is called back from exercises soon enough, and near to Scotland: it is to make up part of the large British fleet trying to prevent the Nazis from taking Norway. The Germans are pushing into Scandinavia, creeping closer to Britain every day. The first British civilian is killed: a young man the victim of an air raid on Scapa Flow. Charlie shudders: his anxiety about Olivia's safety rises. He has received another two letters from her, and they are fast becoming the only things he has to look forward to, apart from the hours spent flying. He rereads the letters daily. They warm him up and pour a little colour back into the grey and white world of snow and ice that is life on the Norwegian Sea. She is expert at painting a picture of the landscape. When Charlie closes his eyes, he can see the liquid gold of autumn bracken, the spring riot of red and orange and white magnolia, rhodo-dendron and azalea, the gnarled silver alder trees all hung with pale green lichen and the changing colours of the loch.

Conversation on board often turns to home, and now Charlie feels he can join in. Mole talks about his young son and wife. Billy wants to get back to his childhood sweetheart. They gently tease each other. Mole and Billy quiz Charlie about Olivia, and he smiles and tells them to mind their own business, but that she has hair the colour of the rising sun and eyes the colour of the morning sky, and they laugh and say he hasn't got a hope in hell: he's fallen hook, line and sinker.

The Norwegian campaign is fought furiously on land and at sea. The Norwegian ports, tucked inside the folds of their magnificent fjords, are taken and lost, and taken again. Navy warships engage in constant battle with Nazi destroyers. The snow-covered hills are either obscured by smoke or lit by flashes of gunfire. The sound of heavy artillery booms across the sea. The icy waters are full of the wrecks of ships from both sides. The British, the French, the Polish, struggle to halt the enemy. The men on the ground fight viciously. They are hampered by heavy snow.

Olivia's letters turn yellow, and the ink begins to fade. It doesn't matter: Charlie knows them off by heart. He keeps them close. They will protect him from harm. The squadron's morale is low, not least because of Captain Pearce. The captain briefed them earlier in the ready room, his face devoid of emotion. 'If Hitler gets control of the Norwegian coast, he'll be able to reach our supplies coming through the north Atlantic. And he'll be able to reach Britain more easily. This is an important moment, men: the first airborne torpedo attack from a carrier of the war. You are history in the making. Let's not make a hash of it.'

Their target is a German battlecruiser in Trondheim Fjord. Taking her out would be a substantial blow to German morale, and give the Allies a valuable boost. But they all know it is too early to fly – they will not be able to see the target until there is at least a little daylight. They should wait for another hour. But there is no telling Captain Pearce.

The Swordfish take to the skies. The sun has not yet risen. Below them is darkness; above the stars glitter like thousands of candles. It is confusing, disconcerting. Usually it is lights that twinkle below them, and darkness above. For a second Charlie's brain is muddled. It feels as if he is flying upside down. He is tempted to right the plane. He checks the faintly glowing instruments in the cockpit again. He has to trust them. Night flying is all about trust: for the engineers who keep the instruments working, to the pilots who keep the planes flying, and the observers who find their way home. Charlie has heard of pilots getting confused, spinning upside down and losing control in similar conditions.

'Did you see that?' Mole asks.

Charlie shakes his head. He was too busy concentrating on the needles and dials and numbers around him.

'Starboard,' says Mole.

Charlie senses the Kid move, and picks up the shift in tension too. Could it be the German ship? Could something that large manage to slip so silently across the sea? Easily. But he can't see anything. The wind rushes in his ears. Is that the faint pale mark of waves breaking behind a ship? Or a trick of the light? Captain Pearce's words ring in his ears. They must not fail. There's nothing for it. Mole unpacks a flare. Charlie gives him the thumbs-up. The safety and hum of the darkness is theirs for a moment longer, and then *phshshshsh*, Mole drops the flare and it falls downward, a spiralling comet of light heading into nothing, nothing, and then suddenly streaks of light explode into the air around them, followed by a barrage of gunfire.

'Bloody hell, Mole!' Charlie dips the plane sideways and lower, swinging through the hail of ammunition.

It is not the battlecruiser. It is a German destroyer. It will have to do – they have blown their cover now. Charlie steadies the plane through the flak and lines himself up for a torpedo run. The cockpit is lit by flashes of tracer fire. It gives him some sense of direction, but as he looses the missile, he has no idea whether it has found its mark.

'Just get us out of here,' says Mole.

'Damn,' says Charlie, partly because he knows Captain Pearce will be disappointed, and partly because there are two neat holes in the fabric of the plane near his right elbow, where bullets have passed straight through. If she was made of metal, she'd have been blown apart. As it is, she is flying, but something doesn't feel right.

'You all right, Mole?' Charlie shouts behind him.

'Fine, boyo. You just get us home safely.' Mole reads him the correct course, squinting in the orange glow of his tiny lamp. They will be there in sixteen minutes.

Charlie doesn't want to let them know that the plane isn't responding properly. But then, he doesn't need to. Her juddering and balking do the job for him.

'What is it?' Mole asks. 'Propeller? Fuel tank?'

'I think it's the port wing,' says Charlie.

Mole peers into the dark. 'Can't bloody see,' he says.

The problem is getting worse. The plane dips on her port side. They all lean to starboard, trying to right her, but it's just a reaction, it won't do anything.

'Hang on,' says Mole. Charlie feels him jiggering around with something. It's his chart lamp. Mole tries to light the wing, leaning out of the cockpit as far as he can. 'Pin's been blown out. The wing is folding.'

It makes sense. The wing rattles and jangles ominously.

'Shit,' says Charlie.

'No need for bad language, boyo,' says Mole.

'Will we make it?'

'Depends if it folds.'

The way it's shaking, Charlie thinks folding is pretty likely. The weight shifts again in the cockpit behind him. Mole starts to hum, but the noise isn't coming through the Gosport tube: the notes are drifting out into the night.

'What are you doing?' Charlie asks.

'Never you mind, boyo,' says Mole.

Charlie can feel vibrations beneath his feet. He tries to look

63

behind, but he can't see anything. He hears Mole say something to the Kid, and the noise of a clip clicking on to something. He senses Mole stand up, the balance of the plane changing. The wing is juddering now.

'Mole? What . . .'

'You just fly, boyo.' The voice is almost in his ear. Fingers appear next to him in the cockpit. The Welshman has clambered out on to the wing.

'Get back in . . .' But Charlie's words are pulled into the slipstream. He can just see one of Mole's arms wrapped around one of the metal struts.

'You're a fool,' says Charlie, but he knows Mole can't possibly hear him above the screaming of the wind and the rumble of the engine. He concentrates on keeping the plane balanced, checking the instruments, sensing the plane, as if it's part of him. The extra weight on the wing is pushing it down, but still the plane is coping, and then suddenly it feels right again. Mole edges back into the cockpit, toppling in sideways with a thud. He gives a whoop of delight and bursts into song.

Charlie starts to laugh. He can hear the Kid laughing too. They are all laughing into the night air with a mad joy at being alive. The plane is still coughing and spluttering. Her engine must be damaged too. But he trusts her. She will get them back safely.

As they reach the ship, Charlie flashes the red light on his starboard wing twice, followed by the green light twice. The ship signals back, and the faint path of guiding lights comes on. He has done this landing a hundred times and it makes no difference in the dark. He looks for the batsman's signal. The lights on the bats are dim but legible. The plane gulps and spits, and when they land he can hear and smell the petrol spewing out of her.

The propeller chokes to a standstill, and Tugger's face materialises out of the gloom. 'What have you done to her?' he asks. 'And the hell's this?' Tugger points at the running repair that Mole has done. Charlie walks around to inspect it, for once glad to be back on solid ground.

The Welshman has used his bootlace to tie the pin back in. It's pretty heroic. He will dine out on it for months.

'She'll be all right,' says Mole. 'If anyone can fix her up, it's you.'

Tugger suddenly steps back and salutes, and Captain Pearce appears behind Charlie. In the dim dawn light, his eyes are cold and hard, his lips thin and his eyebrows bristling. 'Wrong bloody ship,' he says. 'What did you think you were doing?'

Mole and the Kid and Tugger stand there, eyes glazed, faces expressionless. Charlie's cheeks burn. 'I know that, sir,' he says. 'But once . . .'

'And you've damaged the plane. Reckless. I've a good mind to send you home for reassessment. God help us, if you're the best we've got . . .'

'It was impossible to see out there, sir . . .'

'Don't you bloody answer back! You're an idiot, and that's it. I will have to report this.' He turns and stomps back to the bridge.

Charlie swallows in the silence. 'Don't listen to him,' says Mole. 'He's a bitter old fool who should be in a flowerbed.'

'Preferably six feet under it,' says Tugger. 'And don't worry about the plane. She'll be fine.'

'We did good, Charlie,' says the Kid.

But the captain's words wound Charlie deeply. He is not used to falling foul of those in charge. He feels diminished. Only one person doesn't see his faults: Olivia. Her letters are a lifeline to cling to in turbulent water. He clings to them all the tighter.

CHAPTER 5

Olivia

Olivia sits on a bench at the station. The heat is already almost unbearable. Her pale green travelling outfit is crumpled and creased. She fans herself with her hat. The din of people and trains arriving and departing has died down. Trucks and cars, horses and carts, troops and families have been and gone, churning up the dust, making it twirl in the warm air before it settles back in a thin layer over everything. In a way she is glad that she is alone, no longer at the mercy of the wandering eyes and nudges of strangers, like the impertinent ratings on the train who had frightened her with their whispering and pointing. She wishes Charlie, the officer who rescued her at breakfast, had got off here too, but he changed for the train to Thurso, taking his raucous charges with him. She feels comforted as she remembers his protective arm ushering her to safety, the aura of confidence. And then she smiles once more at what turned out to be a wonderful coincidence. Charlie's godmother her aunt? Funny how one chances across these connections, but perhaps not so unusual among her class.

Olivia reaches to fiddle with the bracelet at her wrist, a nervous habit, but then her heart sinks as she remembers that she has lost it, and tears prick at her eyes. She feels so vulnerable sitting here on this bench in the middle of nowhere, travelling on her own for the first time, no handsome officer to protect her now. The fact that she has lost the one treasure that she owns makes her feel all the more so. Perhaps she left it at Stoke Hall, but she is sure she can remember clicking the delicate clasp together and pulling her cuff down over it yesterday morning. Maybe it came loose during the panic when the faulty siren went off at the station. And then there was that boy with the wild eyes . . . but that's unfair – the kind of thing her mother might say. He only helped her find her way to the Underground. No. She must have left it at home. The thought of home, and her bedroom, with its pretty bedspread and her favourite lamps with the hand-painted flowers twisting up their stands, and Jasper, her old teddy bear, on the mantelpiece above the fireplace, and Nanny, who always knows what to do, and all the other familiar things she loves, sends a hot, thin tear sliding down her cheek.

She hears a cough and looks up, wiping her face with the back of her hand. The stationmaster is looming over her. 'Are you sure I can't call someone for you, miss?' he asks.

'Absolutely,' says Olivia. 'My aunt will be here any minute.'

He looks disbelievingly up the empty road. 'Perhaps you got the wrong day, miss.'

'I don't think so,' she snaps at him, immediately regretting it, but she is hot and tired and worried.

'Maybe she's driving slowly. To save on petrol.'

Olivia nods and tries to sit up straight and look as if it is a perfectly normal thing to be sitting outside a train station on one's own.

Eventually a small car materialises slowly out of the haze and draws to a lazy stop outside the station. A sprightly old man with silver hair and a dour expression clambers out of the driver's seat. His eyes narrow when he sees her, and he tips his head.

'Lady Bowman?' he says, with a strong accent.

The stationmaster appears again, and the driver becomes more animated as the two men exchange pleasantries in a language that Olivia does not recognise while the porter packs her cases into the back of the car. Olivia waits for them to finish. It takes a while; neither man appears to be in a hurry. The sun gleams on the car's shiny black paintwork, the polished chrome of its radiator and the spokes of its wheels. She fans herself with her hat, and tries to look composed. At last the man is ready to go. He climbs straight into the driver's seat and leans across to do the passenger door from the inside so that she must pull it open for herself. He sweeps a length of twine and a box of fishing weights on to the floor at her feet, where there is already a pair of galoshes and a rain hat. The car smells of rotten fish, and when she turns to look behind her, there is a creel dripping seawater all over the back seat; a straggle of grassy seaweed caught in the netting glistens at her. She shudders and faces forwards again, leaning her head against the side window.

The journey to Poolewe takes almost four hours. Four hours, and they pass not one other human being. Just a few lonely crofts tucked away in the folds of a hill here and there. The fine morning has become muggy, the air heavy, crackling with energy. Olivia stares at the scenery passing by: great bleak spaces of wilderness, long empty expanses of water. Her clothes stick to her, damp against the leather of the seat. In the back, there are small pale deposits of salt where the seawater dripping from the creel has dried. The driver does not speak. He stares resolutely at the road ahead, occasionally grunting when they bump over a particularly deep rut.

Olivia's mind wanders. What an exhausting few hours she's had. From the thrill of the station and air-raid siren, to the boy with the wild eyes at the station, and then Charlie, so handsome in his uniform, so gallant, off to protect the seas. Well, if he can face the Nazis, she's sure she can face some Scottish solitude.

She sticks her hand out of the open window. Beyond her fingers, the desolate emptiness stretches on forever. She closes her eyes. The breeze pushes at her arm, cools her skin, blows in her hair. It reminds her of climbing out on to the roof at home, the view so different to this one: the neatly rolled grass court where the rabbits crouch, flashes of brown and white in the long grass at its edge; the cedars with their stately, sweeping branches; the cobbled stable yard with its bell tower; the pale dovecote next to it; the mottled doves, half-pigeon now, circling above.

At last they turn through an ornate pair of iron gates and bump along a potholed drive at the end of which is a large white house. Taigh Mor. Olivia scrambles out on to the gravel, glancing up at the smart black windows, and then across the lawn that sweeps down to an enormous loch surrounded by hills. The front door is wide open, but instead of Aunt Nancy appearing, Olivia is greeted by an elderly servant with hair that was once black but is now peppered with grey.

'Your aunt sends her apologies,' says the servant. 'But she's a wee bit tied up with unexpected visitors. She says Munro's to take you down to the bothy, and she'll be there as soon as she can.'

Olivia stares at the maid blankly.

The man who she assumes is Munro grunts as he opens the trunk and starts to unload the cases, handing two to her, by which she understands that she is meant to carry them.

'Shouldn't we leave them here?' she asks.

'Oh no,' says the maid. 'You'll be needing your things.'

'You mean I'm not staying in the house?'

'No, no. Didn't I say? You're in the bothy. You're very lucky. She doesn't usually let anyone stay down there.'

The maid disappears back into the house. Olivia's bottom lip trembles. Munro looks her up and down with disgust. She digs her nails into her palm. She won't give him the satisfaction of seeing her cry.

She traipses after him down a dry, rutted track covered in wispy, pale grass that soon becomes a tunnel flanked by twisted rhododendron bushes beneath thick woodland. The house disappears behind them. The air is cooler here, and birds and other creatures call warnings to each other as they trudge on. Olivia's fingers ache, the blood squeezed out of them by the handles of the bags. A layer of dirt attaches itself to her shoes. They will soon be ruined.

Eventually, they emerge into the sunlight on another lawn that ends only a couple of hundred yards away at the shore of the loch. To their left is a small white cottage, bright beneath the dark Scots pines of the woodland behind.

Munro puts the bags down on the stone steps.

'Is this it? Is this the bothy?' she asks.

'Aye,' he says. 'You go and have a look around. Take your time. We've plenty of it.'

Olivia climbs the steps. The door is propped open with a large pebble. Inside, it is cool compared to the thundery heat outside. It smells of flowers and the sea. Along the sills are old shells, stones, sea urchins, and driftwood that have paled in the sunlight over the years. To the left is a small sitting room that looks out towards the loch; on the right is a tiny kitchen warmed by a large range stove, and a bedroom that is just large enough for a bed and a dressing table, also with a view of the loch. Someone has blown the dust from the kettle, there are fresh sheets on the bed, the cupboards are filled with food, and the windows have been flung open. At the back of the cottage an old lean-to has been converted into a lavatory accessible through the kitchen; the other half acts as coal shed and wood store.

The entire cottage is smaller than the folly at Stoke Hall.

Munro is still standing on the steps, staring out towards the loch. The only sound is the rasp of water on the shingle and the whisper of wind in the leaves behind the bothy. What Olivia would give to hear a familiar noise: the whistle of the groom, or cook shouting in the kitchen, or Pike banging the gong for tea. She makes a noise, a half-strangled sob, and Munro turns to look at her, his eyebrows knitting together. He clears his throat. 'Where would ye like to start?' he asks.

'I don't want to start anywhere,' says Olivia.

70

'Would ye rather fish?'

'No,' says Olivia. 'I don't want to fish. And I don't want to stay in this hovel. I can't understand what I'm doing here. I just want to go home.'

He watches her without blinking, and then slowly shakes his head as she runs past him and back up to the house.

Olivia stumbles through the front door and across the echoing hall, wildly trying every door to every empty room until she finds the occupied one. It is a large drawing room with French windows opening out on to the lawn and grand views of the loch, the sea a sliver of silver beyond it. And there at last is her aunt, head bent over a table, deep in conversation with a couple of men. As her niece enters, Aunt Nancy looks up, a smile breaking across her face. 'Darling girl,' she says. 'So sorry. We're just wrapping up here . . .'

Olivia stops, suddenly self-conscious. She smooths the creased pale-green coat and pats her blonde hair. Her hat is lying somewhere on the floor of the bothy. She is out of breath, and aware that she is not entirely decorous before these men.

Her aunt bustles out from behind the table, extending her arms and clasping Olivia's face in her hands. 'Look at you! You must be exhausted. Have you found everything you need?'

'I . . . Well . . .'

'Did Munro show you how to light the stove? Don't you love it? It's my favourite place in all the world. So special . . .'

Olivia swallows, aware that the men are watching her. 'It's just,' she says. 'It's just . . . so . . . so lonely.'

'Such bliss.'

'But couldn't I stay here? I'd so love to catch up with you . . .'

'There'll be plenty of time for catching up. I can't wait to show you about the place . . .'

'But I really don't want to stay down there. Isn't there a spare bed here?'

Aunt Nancy's smile is beginning to look a little worn. 'There just isn't enough room at the moment, what with Commander Shaw and Brigadier Worthington here.' The men nod apologetically. 'And more arriving tomorrow.'

'But I'm your niece!'

'And these are my guests . . .'

'But what will I do? There's no one to help me . . .'

'There's Munro . . .'

'I don't think Munro wants anything to do with me . . .'

'Hush, hush.' Her aunt is holding up her hand. She ushers her out into the hall. 'Now what exactly is the problem?' she asks.

Olivia starts to list. 'There's no bath.'

'There's a tin bath in the shed.'

'How am I meant to fill it?'

'From the tap.'

'You mean with a bucket?'

'You're jolly lucky there's running water. I had it put in especially for you. We used to have to fetch it from the burn.'

'There's no electricity.'

'Did Munro not show you where the oil lamps are kept?'

'I don't know how to light a fire.'

'Munro will show you.'

'I don't know how to cook.'

'Then it's about time you learnt.'

'I want to go home.'

'You can't.'

'I'll take myself.'

'The station is at least a twenty-four-hour walk . . .'

'Surely Munro can give me a lift?'

'No one will give you a lift. There'll be petrol rationing soon, and besides, your mother has asked me to keep you here. Now pull yourself together. You're making a scene. I can't think what my sister is doing bringing up a creature with no idea how to think or do anything for herself. Do you know what I was doing at your age?'

Olivia does not reply.

'I was driving ambulances in France for injured and dying men. You think living in a warm cottage by the side of a loch, where your family have sent you to be safe, is a hardship? I could tell you things that would fill your childish slumbers with nightmares. I could tell you how I watched your uncle bleed to death before I could get him home. And now here you are, in his home, safely. I do not want to hear such nonsense again. Now stand up straight and behave as a woman of your standing should. With a bit of bloody backbone and some good grace.'

Olivia swallows, shamefaced. She has only met her aunt a couple of times. She had been fooled into thinking that she was like her sister, Olivia's mother, a quiet and kind, gentle person. But this steely creature whose young life was forged in that Great War is nothing like her. In the dark of the great hall, poor, dead Uncle Howard stares down at them through the gloom, handsome in his olive-green army uniform and peaked cap, painted into a frame from which he will remain for ever twenty-five years old.

Aunt Nancy pats her shoulder. 'Now,' she says. 'I've said my piece and, as far as I'm concerned, it's done and dusted. Come and have some tea and meet the brigadier and commander properly.'

Olivia hopes her cheeks will stop burning before she re-enters the drawing room.

After that first afternoon, Olivia resigns herself to this temporary new life. There is no time to mope: Aunt Nancy is determined that her niece will be useful, helping in the garden and on the farm now that all the young men have rushed off to join up. She soon has Olivia digging for potatoes with Greer the gardener, hauling creels in and out of the water with Munro, wheeling manure, drying seeds, not to mention plucking pigeons with the maid and cook, who she now knows as Clarkson. Her time in the bothy is spent reading through the cobwebbed copies of books on the shelves, learning by trial and error how to cook, how to keep the greedy stove going, and how to light a fire in the sitting room, how to wash her own clothes, how to refill the oil lamps, to make her own bed.

Then the first letters arrive from Charlie, and Olivia is hugely grateful to him, for her aunt seems to warm to her a little. She really doesn't need Aunt Nancy to encourage her to write back to the young officer; she enjoys it, writing letters as though Charlie is a diary, a confidant. For although she is busy, she is terribly lonely. Her aunt is always preoccupied with visitors and paperwork – something to do with joining the FANYs again, as far as she can glean from Munro – and the local schoolchildren – of which there are only a handful – are all half Olivia's age. The other neighbours are kind, but they are not companions, and she still does not speak Gaelic.

The letters she receives back from Charlie are her only friends in those long hours of loneliness. And they make Olivia appreciate her own situation all the more when she reads about conditions on his ship, and how he keeps a sense of humour about the horrible cockroaches that invade, capturing and racing them against each other. Of course she has no idea where he is, but she shuffles closer to the fire when he writes of the snow and ice, and how he has to be winched out his pilot's seat after a flight, his hands stuck like claws until someone brings him a steaming cup of cocoa.

As the days pass, Olivia's truculence begins to ebb. The world slows to the lazy chewing of one of the cows that watch her with liquid eyes from beneath their thick, curly brown hair. Munro has indeed taught her to fish, and how to catch shiny green prawns in the rock pools. She is captivated by things she never knew about: baby starfish no bigger than a fingernail, seals lumbering across the rocks, the sudden flash of a pine marten's creamy chest.

She speaks to her mother on the telephone once a week, but she does not miss home as much as she thought she would; somehow the pull of the breeze sweeping in off the loch and down from the hills is hard to resist. Take today, for example. It is one of those blustery autumn days, the weather as changeable as her moods can be. This morning she was eating corned beef from the tin while the rain lashed against the window as she tried to play patience in the yellow glow of an oil lamp. Now she is following the tumbling, churning burn that careers down the hill behind the farm between the thick, sodden bent heads of bracken. She sticks to the rocky bits, using the boulders as steps. When she looks up, she has to narrow her eyes as the rain drives into them. When she looks back to the loch, far below, only the pale foam of whipped-up water delineates dark grey water from dark grey sky. She is drenched to the bone.

She is looking for Mac, who farms behind Taigh Mor. One of his sheep has got stuck, and she has been sent to help. She finally spots him, a small green figure in a flat cap crouched on the rocks like moss. The sheep is still stuck. The farmer isn't surprised to see her there. He doesn't even glance up. But Olivia is growing used to the quiet, calm manner of the locals – and in a situation like this, there's no time for pleasantries. The banks down to the burn are steep here, carved into the hillside over thousands of years. The sheep has slipped and got wedged between some rocks. It is in an awkward position, about level with Mac's head. It bleats in their faces, a loud, raspy, aggressive mixture of fear and confusion. Its musky fleece is heavy with the rain.

Mac shouts above the crash of the water, his voice thick and lilting like the burn in calmer times. She is quicker to tune in to the inflections now. 'I cannae get behind, lassie,' he says. 'We need to tie a rope.'

Olivia looks up at the steep rock. The rain streams down her face and drips off her nose. Mac points further up, jabbing with his finger. The sheep gets noisier, the sound a hoarse bark. 'You want me to climb up there and throw the rope down?' she says.

Mac nods and gives her the rope. He looks so small and wrinkled, like a walnut. She heads away further up the hill, past a craggy rowan tree that marks a deep pool, and to the boulders above. Her feet slip with every step, and she has to be careful not to catch her ankle in one of the uneven, bottomless holes. It is steep, and for a moment her head spins. She is in the right place: from here she can see the top of the sodden sheep and Mac's flat cap. She crawls out on to the rocks. They scrape into her knees, cutting through her flannel trousers. She lies down and inches forward to look over the edge. Mac and the sheep are directly below her. There is nothing to grab on to, just the weight of her body holding her to the ground. Her heart thumps against solid rock. She dangles the rope down. It takes a few goes, but she manages to feed it in behind the sheep, and Mac disappears to scrabble for the end underneath the creature. He reappears, gives her the thumbs-up, and then she throws the other end of the rope down to him and scrambles away from the edge, her hip bones grazed against the rock.

By the time she gets back, Mac has tied the rope around the sheep. They each take the rope in their hands and begin to pull. The rope burns, but, with a struggle and a grunt, the sheep is freed. It rolls on to the ground for a moment, a bundle of legs and wool. Then it stands up and trots away with a dismissive bark.

'Ungrateful creature,' says Mac, and they both burst out laughing, wiping the water from their faces, unsticking their feet from the squelching mud.

'Will it be all right?' Olivia asks.

'Thanks to you, lassie.' Mac smiles, and she can see his eyes are brilliant blue in the leathery face.

In the farmhouse, Mrs Mac says, 'Stay for something to eat, won't you?' She offers Olivia a slice of cake and a cup of tea. She drapes a towel around Olivia's back and rubs at her scraggy hair to soak up some of the rain. The simple movement touches something deep in Olivia. It is nice to be mothered.

'Hard work out there without our boys,' says Mac.

'I think the girl will do just as well for now,' says his wife.

Olivia smiles, pleased. 'Where are your sons?' she asks, her mouth full of fluffy sponge.

'Moved away. Got wee ones of their own now,' says Mrs Mac.

Mac lifts a picture down from the mantelpiece. 'There we go,' he says. 'Callum and Angus and their wives and our three grandchildren, Mary, Hamish, and wee Gus. Taken in the spring.'

It is a fine picture. Callum and Angus are in their uniforms, their wives looking at them proudly, the children at their feet. 'When will they next come to visit?' asks Olivia.

'Och. We won't be seeing them for a while,' says Mrs Mac. Her lips are set in a thin line. 'Silly boys. They're back with their regiments. They'll be off to France any day soon.'

'Now, now,' says Mac. 'We don't know that for sure.' Olivia is surprised to see that his hands are trembling as his cup rattles on its saucer.

Olivia drops in to Taigh Mor on her way back to the bothy. The rain has cleared, and now the bracken is shining yellow and orange beneath trembling aspen leaves that flash and flutter gold in the breeze. There are four shiny black cars parked on the drive in front of the house, all polished to perfection, the rain pooling in small puddles like ink on their bonnets. Leaning against one corner of the large house are four men, chatting and smoking cigarettes. The smoke curls white into the air. They stop to look at Olivia without interest as she crunches across the gravel, before turning back to their conversation. In the distance, the pale sea reflects the pale sky.

As usual, the heavy front door is open. Olivia walks slowly in. Like her own home down south, it is cool inside, but the wooden floors are bare of rugs, and the furniture is dark and dusty. There are antlers all over the walls, spiky and forbidding, and she suddenly longs for the light and airy bothy. Uncle Howard's eyes follow her along the hall, still unused to seeing a youngster in the house. Olivia's skin tingles; she is suddenly aware of her damp clothes, her tangled hair, her muddy boots.

There are nine men with Aunt Nancy in the drawing room, all with their backs to her. One of them seems familiar, with a jocular round face and a cigar, but he is probably simply a returning visitor, of which there seems to be a steady stream. Olivia would dearly like to know what goes on at these meetings, but has to be satisfied with evasive explanations about her aunt doing her bit for the war effort and reminding Olivia proudly of her role in France in the last war – which inevitably leads to memories of Uncle Howard and the end of the conversation.

'Come in, darling. Come in,' says Aunt Nancy, motioning at Olivia. Olivia points at her filthy feet, but Aunt Nancy shakes her head. 'Don't worry about those. These floors have seen far worse.' She introduces Olivia as her niece, and Olivia is sure she glimpses a flash of disapproval as the men take in her mud-stained trousers and unkempt hair, but they are too polite to say anything before turning back to help themselves to one of Clarkson's home-made biscuits.

'Dreadful news,' says Aunt Nancy. 'It was the bloody Nazis that got into Scapa Flow. Can you believe it?'

'You mean . . .'

'Yes exactly. Those poor boys . . . Torpedoed! Charlie was up there too.'

'How awful!' Olivia's hand goes up to her mouth.

'No, no. Don't worry. He wasn't on board. But he was in the harbour. All those poor souls. You must write to him.'

'I have.'

'I mean carry on. It's our duty to bolster the morale of men who are away fighting. Letters mean more than you can ever realise. Your Uncle Howard lived for them . . .' She peters out. The men stir their tea awkwardly.

The round-faced man clears his throat and takes a puff on his cigar. It is clear that he wants to get back to business.

'Well, you'd best be off then, darling,' says Aunt Nancy. 'I'm sure you have plenty to do.' Olivia turns to leave, knowing when she is dismissed. 'Oh' – Olivia stops, her hand resting on the doorframe – 'and don't be alarmed if you see more ships in the loch. Scapa Flow is obviously compromised, and these chaps need somewhere else to hide their ships.' The men stare at her. 'Hush, hush, of course,' says Aunt Nancy, putting her finger to her lips.

On the track back to the bothy, Olivia breathes in the autumn air. Out here, no one cares what she looks like. She makes the most of it, splashing through puddles that are orangey-brown, the colour of peat. On her right she is dwarfed by vast umbrellas of gunnera, still holding water from this morning's storm. On her left, ancient rhododendrons line the steep bank, their twisted branches and trunks an impenetrable tangle. A myriad of birdsong echoes through the plants. At the end of the track, the view opens out again into the vista she has come to love. There is the bothy on the edge of the wood, its knobbly stone facade bright white against the autumn fire of yellow and orange and red. The bright flowers that surrounded the cottage in the summer are no longer colourful but drooping with seed heads of all shapes and sizes. The lawn that runs down to the beach is still lush and green. The loch is calm, just the dark breath of a sudden breeze rippling across it. As she reaches the steps of the bothy, some seagulls fly up from the water with worried cries, the droplets from their legs fracturing their clear reflections. Startled, Olivia turns to see what has frightened them, and, as she does, she catches sight of something that – even with her aunt's warning – makes her breath snag in her chest. On the other side of the island, where the fishing fleet shelters by the village of Aultbea, a vast grey mass of metal rises out of the water. It is a British destroyer. Next to it, the fishing trawlers are mere specks.

Olivia takes in the heavily armoured bridge, the fat funnel, the mast like a crucifix reaching up to heaven, the spiky gun turrets, the guns that seem to be pointing in every direction and from every part of her. This is what war looks like: cold and grey and forbidding. She shudders and goes into the bothy, closing the door firmly behind her for the first time in weeks.

CHAPTER 6

At first the ships come and go without incident. Olivia gets used to them gliding silently into the loch, tries not to let their presence disturb her. But then, in early December, German mines punch a hole in a battleship at the mouth of the loch. Olivia is awake when it happens, lying in bed, a pale light pencilled around the window frames, a chill breeze blowing through the open window, while she is as warm as one of the eggs beneath Mac's chickens. A boom, and she is out of bed and pedalling to Aultbea, where worried locals try to send her home again, but not until she has seen the divers go down in their suits to inspect the damage. She wants to write to Charlie about it, because it is frightening to think that the Germans must know there are ships here now. But of course she can't.

Nor can she write about the special pass she has been given to show she is allowed to be here, for Loch Ewe is now Port A, a secret base, the perfect place for the Admiralty to hide their ships. Or the plane that passes low over her one afternoon when she is out checking fences for Mac. Or the black puffs of flak in the air beneath it, and how – a second later – the thud of the anti-aircraft guns that are now positioned at the mouth of the loch reaches her ears. It is an eerie, ominous blast that echoes in the gullies behind her, sending a shower of snow from the branches of small trees nearby, and on up the glen. The plane growls on, and she is frozen to the spot until it is over her, quite low – low enough to see the pilot seated inside – low enough to see the black cross painted beneath its wings. She is sure she sees the pilot raise his hand in greeting, and then the plane passes over the peak and dips out of sight.

After that, she makes an effort to traipse up to the big house every day to listen to the news on the tortoiseshell wireless, and to talk to Aunt Nancy, who seems to know more than the authoritative voice of the BBC broadcaster. She hears how Norway is lost, and she wonders if that was where Charlie was, and where he will be sent next. Chamberlain resigns, and Churchill takes over. With Norway secured, the Germans turn their attention to a massive assault along the Western Front. They push the Allies back and back until they are trapped along the north coast of France, on the beaches and in the town of Dunkirk. Olivia hears about the miracle of Dunkirk, how so many men are delivered safely home across the Channel. She picks up whispers that Charlie might have been involved. She wonders whether the Macs' boys, Callum and Angus, are among those that were saved. She lies awake at night, staring into the dark, knowing that Britain is all alone.

Olivia is in the echoing hall at Taigh Mor, talking to Mother about how Stoke Hall is now being used as a barracks for hundreds of soldiers. It is early summer and, with the Nazis occupying the Channel Isles, the threat of invasion is once again a reality. Hard to believe on such a beautiful summer's day. As usual the large door is wide open, the sunlight from outside banishing some of the gloom from the vast room. The silhouette of a man throws a shadow across the door. For a moment Olivia doesn't recognise him, but when she replaces the receiver and sees the features fall into place, there is Charlie, tall and tanned, in his uniform, and looking every part the war hero. It is strange – like meeting an old friend who she somehow doesn't know at all. She isn't sure whether to embrace or shake hands, but he takes charge, bending down to kiss her cheek, and she feels his uniform prickly against her skin.

She hides her hands behind her back, suddenly conscious

that her fingernails are ingrained with dirt. But Charlie is looking at her feet in amusement. These days she doesn't bother with shoes when it's warm – she grew out of her old ones ages ago, and there is nowhere to buy more. She borrows whatever she can find from Aunt Nancy's boot room when she needs to. Her feet are thick-soled, and she thinks nothing now of running over rocks and gravel.

She blushes and looks up at him. 'I'm afraid I've grown rather wild,' she says.

'I think it's rather charming,' he says. There is something different about him that she can't put her finger on: a sadness or an emptiness behind his smile.

'Aunt Nancy will be thrilled that you're here.'

'I certainly am,' says her aunt, appearing behind her.

Charlie grins. 'Lady M.' He stoops to kiss her and she holds his face in both her hands as though admiring a child.

'It's so good to have you home,' she says, ushering him and Olivia into the drawing room.

Charlie strides to the French windows and looks out at the ships on the loch. 'How many are coming in now?' he asks, his voice suddenly sharper, more officious.

'A lot more. It could become a useful place for convoys to congregate.'

'Any permanent site?'

'On its way. Should be up and running by this time next year. For now, officers are messed at the hotel or here. Others are billeted with various people – wherever there's room.'

'What about the mines?'

'We've had no more problems . . .'

'I heard there'd been a U-boat?'

'Dealt with immediately.'

'We've also had the Luftwaffe over,' says Olivia.

Charlie looks anxiously at Aunt Nancy. 'I hadn't heard about that.'

'It's nothing to worry about,' says Aunt Nancy. 'Just reconnaissance. There are far more dangerous things going on

83

elsewhere. Please don't look so worried, my dear. Scapa was a terrible, terrible tragedy. But it won't happen here. Now how about going for a swim? It's lovely out there.'

Charlie looks as though he's going to say something else, but then turns to the windows again. Beyond the warships, the water is sparkling seductively. 'We can still swim?' he asks.

'Of course!'

He takes a deep breath and exhales, as if banishing bad thoughts. Then he turns back to face them, the frown gone from his face. 'Good idea,' he says. 'I'm boiling and filthy from the train. It took an age.'

'I'll take you across to Firemore,' says Olivia. 'I'd like to put out some lines anyway.'

Charlie grins. 'Who is this?' he asks Aunt Nancy. 'Certainly not the prim girl I met on the train last year.'

'I'm not prim!'

'I'm only teasing. But you are quite different.'

'So are you.'

Charlie glances at her and then down at his feet. 'Yes. I suppose I am,' he says. He is not smiling any more.

Firemore beach is on the south side of the loch, a long horseshoe of reddish golden sand. Charlie insists on taking both oars, while Olivia throws the creels and lines over the side, the muscles in her brown arms tensing with effort. When she has finished, she hangs over the edge, enjoying being rowed by someone else for once. She sees silver slivers of sand eels dart beneath the boat, and dangles her hands in the water, leaving glittery trails. The loch is calm and the air is warm; the heat makes her light-headed. Two oystercatchers flit past, black and white against the pale water, their distinctive peeping whistles ringing out across the loch, their orange beaks and pink legs vivid against the blue sky. They flash their white underbellies before turning and sweeping back around, the white V on their backs and the white stripes down their wings in perfect symmetry. She wants to ask Charlie whether he flew at Dunkirk, but the words won't come. The familiarity of their letters doesn't seem to translate when he is actually here, in front of her. She closes her eyes, the world a haze of unanswered questions behind her eyelids.

Charlie suddenly stands, setting the boat rocking. Before she can tell him to sit down, he has unbuttoned his shirt, taken off his trousers, and leapt overboard, his pale body distorted beneath the water. He breaks the surface, his hair flashing in the sunlight, sleek against his head. 'Are you coming in?' he asks.

'What about the boat?'

He laughs. 'She'll be fine. There's not a breath of wind, and the tide is on the turn,' he says. 'Chuck the painter over the side and let her go. I'll grab her in a minute.'

Olivia needs no further encouragement. She slips off her shorts and pulls her top over her head, already dressed in her bathing costume. She throws the end of the rope into the water and leaps over the side with a whoop, scattering the fish and sending glittering droplets into the air.

The change in temperature makes her draw her breath in sharply when she emerges. She slips under the water again. Relishes the coolness, the translucent green, the muffled sound of Charlie's voice above. Then she breaks the surface again, and everything is bright and clear. She can just touch the bottom. Her toes scuffle along the cold sand, trying to get a purchase. She joins Charlie and grabs hold of the side of the boat, helping to tug it in to shore, their legs kicking out beneath the hull. His arms are strong and thick next to hers; the water glistens like dew drops on the blond hairs.

They drag the boat up on to the beach. It shooshes along the sand, leaving a groove. The tide is out and the beach is vast. They are the only creatures on it, apart from some sand-pipers that fly up and settle further away, whistling to each other as they go. Charlie's skin is pale where it has been covered by his uniform. His chest is smooth and hairless.

They soon dry in the heat of the sun. They eat sandwiches

while sitting on the sand, digging their toes through the warm, dry top layer into the cool damp below. Afterwards, they explore the beach, turning over heavy stones to look for crabs that burrow secretively away from them. Olivia climbs a mound of rocks and surveys the loch. The water is cobalt blue further out, turning to emerald green as it grows shallower. To the left she can clearly see the open sea, the hills at the mouth of the loch gradually sloping into it until there is nothing, just endless ocean. It is easy to pretend the smattering of ships and the pillboxes aren't there.

Charlie calls out and points at a round shape like a brown balloon bobbing on the surface of the water. Olivia spots it just as the seal disappears from sight. 'Oh!' she says, disappointed.

'It'll come up again,' says Charlie. 'There!' It is much closer this time. Close enough to make out the mournful black eyes and mottled head.

'Sing to it,' says Charlie. 'That's what they say. If you sing to them, they come closer.'

'I'm not going to sing to it,' says Olivia self-consciously, then laughing as Charlie starts to sing, 'God Save Our Gracious King', and the seal watches them both, bemused, before disappearing again.

'You've scared it away,' says Olivia.

But Charlie is undaunted and carries on, tunelessly. The next time the creature comes up, it is a bit closer. So Olivia joins in, and they stand there singing as the sun beats down and the sandpipers feel braver and rush closer on their tiny legs, and the minutes stretch and mould into hours, and war and the cold ships that lie on the other side of the island are far from their minds.

Charlie is insistent that he teach Olivia how to shoot. He borrows an old air rifle from the gunroom at the back of Aunt Nancy's house. Uncle Howard's shotguns and rifles line the walls neatly, like sentries on duty. The room smells of gun oil and leather.

He hands her the gun. 'Practise first,' he says. 'The principle is the same.'

Olivia holds it awkwardly while Charlie rigs up paper targets outside. The targets seem tiny, but Olivia is beginning to learn that she likes a challenge. Her first few shots are way off the paper, but she quickly gets her eye in and it turns out she's pretty good. Soon she is just a hair's breadth off the centre. Charlie nods as he watches her break the rifle and feed another silver pellet into it. She snaps it shut, aims and fires. There is a tiny hole in the bull's-eye. And again. She hits it four times in a row.

'I guess you've either got it or you haven't,' she says, smiling.

'All right, all right,' says Charlie, laughing. 'Let's try with the proper rifle.'

The sporting rifle is much heavier. Olivia lies next to Charlie on the ground. First he demonstrates how to put the safety catch on. Then how to lock and unlock the bolt, and where to lay the smooth, pointed bullets. She takes one and slides it into its chamber.

Charlie shows her how to steady the gun. 'Use my arm, if you need to,' he says. He pulls the rifle up and into her shoulder. The cold stock touches her warm cheek.

'Feel there?' he says. 'Where the stock sits comfortably?' She nods.

'Now, when you fire, you squeeze the trigger. Don't pull it. Just squeeze.' He holds his hand over hers to demonstrate. 'This rifle will have more of a kick than the air rifle. So make sure you hold it in.' She can feel his breath on the tip of her ear.

'Line up the sight like you usually do,' he says. She drops her head. Looks along the top of the barrel. Adjusts the position until the marker sits between its dip.

'Fire when you're ready. But only if and when you're a hundred per cent ready, with a clear, true shot.'

She pulls the trigger and there's a zipping noise and the rifle kicks back against her shoulder. Charlie gets to his knees, squinting at the target: there is a neat hole ripped just on the edge of the bull's-eye.

'Looks like you'd give my gunner a run for his money,' says Charlie. Olivia grins. 'Seriously, though.' Charlie's brow furrows, and he sits back on his heels so he can look at her properly. 'This could be useful if things get sticky.'

'I don't think I could shoot someone, if that's what you mean,' she says. 'Not even a Nazi.'

'I hope it won't come to that, but you might get short of food. It sounds ridiculous now it's summer, but once winter comes again I think rationing will really bite . . .'

'We're stocking up. We've been pickling and bottling like mad.'

'But there are many more people living here at the moment – and you'll need fresh meat once it's too cold to fish. Get Mac to show you which deer need taking, and you'll have fresh venison.'

'Mac's given all that up.'

'He may have to change his mind.'

She sits up too, dusting the soil from her elbows. 'Do you really think things are going to get that bad?' she asks.

'I'm sure they will. The Germans are in the north of France. They're in the Channel Islands, for God's sake. It's only a matter of time before they strike.'

'Sometimes it's hard to believe that anything will happen. All we've had here are a couple of ineffective mines and some fly-pasts. You know, Mother said she'd heard it called the "phoney war" in London.'

The colour drains from Charlie's face. 'Is that what you think?' he asks.

'No,' she says. 'I suppose I've been lucky, that's all . . .' Olivia is startled by the sudden change. His eyes have clouded to a turbulent green. His whole body is tense. He starts to walk away.

'Charlie . . .' she calls out after him. He doesn't turn to look at her, just carries on walking, his back straight, his hands gripping the rifle, knuckles white. She has to jog to catch up.

'I'm really sorry,' she says. 'I know you've had a terrible time . . .'

'You don't know anything,' he says. 'You're just a child.'

'Then tell me?' she says. She rests her hand gently in the crook of his elbow. He slows a little, and then sits on a fallen tree. Olivia sits next to him. The bark is old and spongy, crumbling a little beneath their weight.

'I couldn't,' he says. 'It's not the kind of thing a girl like you should hear.'

Olivia leans against him, and he puts out his hand and she holds it in hers. 'I'm here if you want to,' she says quietly. They sit in silence for a long time, while the branches of the trees creak and rub above them.

A week's leave is over quickly. Charlie has shown her his favourite spots. He has taught her how to build a small fire on the beach to cook her catch on, finding the driest leaves and hearing them crackle as they catch and burn. He has taken her up to the string of freshwater lochs, and to the places where the golden eagles glide on thermals high above the hills. The osprey nest was not used this year – possibly because of all the commotion around the loch, but it meant they could get a bit closer to examine the great heap of twigs and branches. Sometimes, in the evenings up at Taigh Mor, she catches him staring at nothing and glimpses that darkness or hardness again in his eyes. But she doesn't pry.

She tries to be cheerful on his last day, but she knows she will miss having him around. His case is packed and he is getting a lift to Inverness with some of the other returning sailors. 'Thank you,' he says, taking her hands in his.

'For what?'

'I've had the best leave ever. Like one of the summers of my childhood. Swimming. Shooting. Fishing. Heaven.'

'Do you know where you're going next?'

He shakes his head. 'But I do know I'll be back as soon as I can next get leave.'

She kisses him on the cheek. 'Be careful, won't you?' she says.

'You'll write?'

She nods. 'Of course,' she says.

'In that case, I can do anything.' He stands up straight, smoothing his sleeves down, every part the young officer. The light bounces off the stripes on his sleeves, but the cap throws his face into darkness.

With autumn comes terrible news from down south as the Luftwaffe begin to attack London and beyond, night after night. The RAF struggles to keep them at bay. Returning home is out of the question. Mother tries to keep her tone light on the telephone, but Olivia can hear the buzz of exhaustion beneath. Stoke Hall is so close to the coast, there could easily be a stray bomb – or even an intentional one. There was a furore recently when two parachutists were seen landing in the Fir Wood, but the soldiers who are now camped out in the gardens went to investigate and found the two German airmen dead. The thought of those two dead men – German or not – dangling among the dark and spiky conifers, puts her own inconveniences to shame. She stops moaning about the security checkpoints that have sprung up at all the roads coming into or leaving the area – Gairloch, Achnasheen, Inverness. There is even one at Laide, near Mrs Campbell's shop, where Olivia is sent to stock up on tea for Aunt Nancy, which the shopkeeper marks neatly in their ration books. And now more ships begin to arrive at the loch – this time a hotchpotch of merchant ships, refuelling before setting off on their long and treacherous journeys across the ocean. Sailors and soldiers begin to outnumber locals significantly.

The news from Charlie is intermittent. It seems he does not have time to write, and each long stretch without a letter is accompanied by a fear that there will be never be another one. But Aunt Nancy tells her not to worry, making a passing reference to Fleet Air Arm pilots helping the RAF over London.

'Charlie will be fine. He's extremely accomplished. You just keep writing. Give him something to look forward to,' she says.

As the nights draw in and winter approaches, the fish supplies dwindle. Olivia thinks it is time to take Charlie's advice. 'I'm too old to take you up there, lassie,' says Mac, pointing at his creaking knees and swollen knuckles. But Olivia soon works him around.

Mac is impressed by Olivia's marksmanship and her quiet respect. They walk and climb and inch for miles up into the hills that turn from purple to gold and russet through the autumn. Olivia learns how to throw a piece of torn heather into the air to determine which way the wind is blowing. She learns how to track, and how to avoid a herd. She learns their habits, where they like to shelter, where to eat. She learns how to use a spyglass without it catching the light. She learns how the fog distorts sound and distance. She knows when a mist will settle and when it will clear. Together they crawl and creep for hours, above the clouds, across peat bogs and through the heather, and over boulders and up glens, only to turn back if the stag is too fine. Mac teaches her to hunt the frail, as well as poor quality and weaker beasts. Thistle, the old stalking pony, is brought back into service. Olivia slowly gains the pony's trust, and when she shoots her first stag and Mac grallochs it, she learns the fine art of balancing a stag across the pony's stalking saddle. Mac hangs the beast in the large, cold game larder. He butchers it himself, swift and deft despite his arthritis.

The Macs have a sailor billeted with them, a steward who has never tried venison before, but is keen to sample anything that hasn't been salted or dried or stewed within an inch of its life. He chews on the meat thoughtfully, nodding his head and licking his lips. 'I think this would go down well in our messes,' he says. 'Could we buy some? Our men are always clamouring for fresh meat.'

The idea snowballs. Word spreads around the ships, and Olivia is soon inundated with orders, from sailors, soldiers, and Wrens. She is worried about what Aunt Nancy will say, but her aunt is thrilled that she is showing initiative. 'And Clarkson could do with some decent meat to serve to the officers we have billeted here,' she says. She even takes the time to show Olivia how to write the orders in a ledger and keep a note of the money coming in and going out. It is the longest amount of time she has spent with Olivia since she arrived. 'Watch those men,' she says. 'Don't think they won't try for a bargain just because you're a girl.' But Olivia is as canny as anyone, and she turns it to her advantage. She finds the men are keen to talk, and even keener for a smile. Many of them have been away at sea for weeks and miss female company.

Mac is delighted: he gets a cut, and Olivia starts to offer his eggs and milk too. They turn more of the garden over to growing vegetables. Other locals offer what they can: last year's jam; Ben Munro's apples; Mrs McLellan's chutney. Mrs Campbell comes in on the business, always happy to receive more supplies for her store – particularly when the roads are blocked with snow and she is running low. Olivia learns how to drive Aunt Nancy's ancient Austin and, each week, she transports whatever she hasn't sold directly to the ships to Mrs Campbell's shop. By late autumn, they even have a buyer from Edinburgh, who bumps along the single track road from the city once a week to collect venison or lobsters for his restaurant.

It is deep winter, and fresh meat stocks are running low again. The stag-hunting season is over, but there are plenty of hinds to be taken. Olivia is up and out of the house before dawn breaks across the loch. There is no need for a torch: the snow that settled overnight has turned the world luminous. Something crackles away into the undergrowth, startled by the crunch of her feet on the path, in turn setting a bird fluttering and flapping through the branches above. Then silence again. A world muffled by snow. Beyond the trees, the loch: grey and silent as the ships packed with sleeping men. She has grown to love this time in the morning, the only time there is true peace and quiet these days. The roads are empty once again and she can slip into the hills unnoticed.

Her pass and gas mask and ID card are gathering dust on the dressing table in her bedroom. She has no need of them; she knows how to get past the checkpoints and guards, crossing between Gairloch and Poolewe undetected by following the low road along the shoreline like the other locals. And there are no checkpoints up in the hills. No one would be foolish enough to cross them without local knowledge.

The hills are where she is headed now. She cannot see them, but she can sense them looming in the darkness ahead, steady and solid, unmoving and unmoved by the world's turmoil. By the time she gets to the farm, the sky is beginning to glow aquamarine as dawn breaks. The tack room is empty. A faint orange glow of embers breathes among the ash as she opens the door to retrieve Thistle's saddle. The pony comes straight to her now, letting her slip on his head collar without a fuss. She adjusts the stalking saddle, holds her hands under the pony's mane, where he is warmest, and presses her face against his shaggy grey fur, breathing in the horsey smell.

She leads him out over the cobbles. The snow is dirty here, trampled with mud and grit. The pony snorts, clearing his nostrils into the chilly air. His bright dark eyes peer out at her from beneath his ragged forelock. She glances down at herself, pleased at how her camouflage has turned out. She has butchered her aunt's debutante dress, sewing it into a new outfit that covers her clothes so she is white all over. Underneath she has on her woollen jumper and the flannel trousers and knee-length socks that she always wears to keep herself warm. She has used the arm of an old fur coat to make a cosy scarf for her neck. The rifle sits cold and heavy across her back as they trudge away from the farm.

Now it is morning. The loch is a mirror far below. The snowy peaks, jagged and bright, reflected in its surface. Down nearer the shore, the trees stand out against the white, the prickly and black conifers, and the twiggy and twisted leafless winter trees. The shoreline is a smudge of orange, just beginning to show beneath the melting snow. From here, the loch is so large and shining that it is easy to misread the size of the ships that lie on its surface.

The hills sweep up out of the ground ahead of her, their tops still wreathed in cloud. But the sky is blue, the heavy snow clouds have moved on, and it will be a fine day. She follows the burn, a glimmering crack, the water sparkling like a necklace of diamonds among the softer white of the fresh-fallen snow. By the time she reaches the rowan pool, she has worked up quite a warmth. The rowan tree is hung with frosted particles like sugar icing. The only sound is the beat of tiny wings as some snow buntings fly up, white like rising snowflakes, apart from the flash of black on their wings.

She leaves Thistle by the tree, tied to a boulder. He is also well camouflaged: only the tips of his grey tail and his unruly mane – and his knobbly knees – standing out. His neat little black hooves are hidden, sunk into the snow. She sets to work in the silence, her brow furrowed in concentration. She reads the tracks: the delicate Ys of the birds busily criss-crossing all over the place; the long oval shapes of a hare; the solid shuffle of a grouse; the stealthy holes of a fox. The snow is yellow in places where an animal has peed. There are dark holes where rabbit droppings have steamed through to the ground.

She has to be careful. The snow has drifted deeply in places, hiding crevices and cracks in the ground. She comes across the multiple tracks of deer not much further up. They have sheltered in the lee of the hill, where the boulders make a natural cave. The wind seems to have shifted, possibly because of the lie of the peaks above her. There is less snow on the ground, more for the deer to eat. She creeps forward. Peers

94

beyond the next boulder. She cannot see the herd – but she can see a stag. Either the hinds are around the corner, or they have scarpered and this is a lone male. She crouches, inching forward on hands and knees to get a better look. The stag is about four hundred yards away from her, in a dip across a narrow part of the burn. Still no sign of any hinds. Her rock is slippery. She moves carefully, hoping she won't cause a vibration that dumps the snow above on top of her.

The stag snuffles at the ground. Suddenly it lifts its head. Its nostrils dilate. Olivia stops and drops flat, her cheek scratching against the hard crust of snow. She slowly lifts her head. The stag is staring at something she cannot see, in the opposite direction. He is magnificent: all muscle and searching eyes and flared nostrils. His ears swivel. His neck is thick and shaggy. There is the black scar down his flank. He flicks his tail. The tips of his nostrils move, in and out, twitching, smelling, searching for whatever it is he thinks he's heard.

As the stag turns and springs away, a loud crack whips out across the snow and Olivia sees the animal stumble awkwardly as if he has been hit, but then his feet find the ground and he is off like the wind across the hillside and down the pass and deep into the crags and contours of endless wilderness.

Olivia's heart races with him. For a moment her mind is blank, and then she wonders who else could be up here in the snow and the wind? And who would go for a stag at this time of year? Or a stag like that at any time of year?

She doesn't dare move. She doesn't want anyone to spot her. She strains to see anything against the glare. And then she spots something: a figure wading through the snow, dark against the sparkling crust. Olivia presses herself as flat as possible down on the rock. She wants to see who it is, but she can't. They are still too far away.

The figure draws slowly closer, hampered by snow. As it approaches, Olivia holds her breath: she doesn't want the vapour to give her away. She can't see his face, but it is definitely a man. He looks at where the stag was. Glances around. He looks down at the ground again. He paces around, shaking his head and pulling his arms tighter around his body, rubbing at his shoulders. His clothes are flimsy, too thin in this cold. A sudden gust dislodges some snow from above her and the movement makes the man jump. He stares in her direction, his body rigid. Waves of fear course through her body. Surely he will see her. But now he is hurrying away as fast as he can. She lies still until the desperate figure is out of sight, feeling the cold and damp seep into her knees and elbows. By the time she dares to move, she is stiff as new leather. She pulls herself up and then slips and scrambles back down the hill as quietly as she can, not wanting to look back, half-expecting the man to jump out at her. She is relieved to see Thistle still there, his eyes half-closed, unaware of her panic. There is some comfort in his presence, but not much. As they stumble and trip down the hill, she keeps glancing over her shoulder. But there is no sign of anyone else.

It takes almost two hours for her to reach the farm. Her clothes are now damp with sweat, and Thistle is fed up with being pulled, digging his feet into the ground in protest. The fire in the tack room is leaping in the grate, warming the backs of the men who are seated at the table, cupping hot mugs of tea laced with whisky from the bottle that Mac keeps behind the old dresser. As soon as they see Olivia's face, they slam their mugs down, the sound marking an end to their easy conversation.

'What is it?' Mac asks.

'There's someone out on the hill.' Mac frowns, his blue eyes sinking into the leathery face. 'With a gun,' she adds. The men scrabble to their feet, chair legs scraping on the flagstones. Someone runs to fetch Ben Munro, who arrives on his bicycle, dressed in his Home Guard uniform and carrying a rifle. Olivia repeats what she has seen. The men discuss in Gaelic. Mac collects two more rifles and a shotgun, talking to his wife quietly in the doorway of the house.

'Off you go now,' Ben Munro says to Olivia. 'Run home. Stay indoors until you hear otherwise.'

'Don't you want me to come and show you?'

'Och no, lassie. It's no place for a young lady up there.'

'But . . .'

'Go on, now.'

Olivia watches the men tramp up into the hills, small, steady, determined. She feels a sudden stab of anxiety for the pathetic creature she saw out there. She turns for home as the men fold into the hills as if they are a part of them.

Hours later, when the only sound on the hill is the trickling of water back towards the loch, Ben appears at the bothy. 'We couldn't find anything,' he says. 'It's been snowing, and a herd has trampled right through there.'

'I suppose he's hiding somewhere,' she says, thinking out loud.

'No, no. Whoever it was is probably sitting by a nice warm fire somewhere towards Gairloch.'

'You think it was a local?'

'We've had poachers for centuries. I'm sure we'll have them for centuries more. Your aunt is nae bothered. And nor should you be. There's plenty to go around.'

'But he didn't . . .'

'Look,' says Ben, 'whoever it was will be long gone. No one can survive out on those hills in these temperatures. We'll stay vigilant, but keep off the hill for a wee while. Find yourself something more ladylike to do. Mrs Munro is still looking for more people to help knit scarves for the troops . . .'

Olivia nods, but she has no intention of doing such a thing. She would rather be captured by Germans than join the knitting circle.

CHAPTER 7

Winter finally turns to spring, and Thistle can be let out into the small paddock behind the farmhouse while Olivia cleans out his stable. She rubs the pony down in the yard, watching the dust dance in the bright, cold sky, running her hand along his flank as he blows in her hair. She slips the head collar from his shaggy head, untangling the thick mane where it catches in the buckle. Thistle shakes his whole body, from his velvety nostrils to his broad rump, a huge shudder of relief. Then he wheels around and races off across the field, head down, bucking with freedom, searching for the patches of grass that lie temptingly in the sunshine.

Back in the stable, clearing the dirty straw, not for the first time Olivia wishes there was a light so she could see better. There are three other stalls, empty and bare, and beyond them a load of old feed bins and farming implements. She doesn't like to venture back there, where it is dark and dingy and hung with curtains of dusty cobwebs. She is shaking the clean bedding out when she hears a strange noise above the rustle of dry straw, and her heartbeat quickens. She stands still, head on one side, listening in the silence. 'Is anyone there?' she says. There is no answer. The hairs on her skin start to prickle. She grabs the pitchfork. There is a swish of movement again. A rat? She peers into the gloom, takes a step closer. She doesn't dare go right in. The sunlight is on her back. It cannot penetrate further. She squints, leans forward, pointing the pitchfork into the darkness.

There is a faint sound: 'Pleez . . .' It is so quiet that she has to strain to hear, which means she can't scream as a shape begins to evolve in the shadows, a shape that turns out to be a person holding his hands up above his head. 'Pleez,' he says again.

'Don't you come any closer,' she says, jabbing the fork in his direction.

He stops there, half hidden. He is desperately thin. His top is grimy, and his trousers are torn down one side and stained with dirt. His feet are bare. He smells of stale sweat, filth, and fever. She would have thought he was a tramp, if it wasn't for the unmistakeable insignia stitched on to the right side of his jacket: the eagle of the Third Reich, the Nazi swastika clasped in its claws. She remembers the two dead parachutists swinging in the Fir Wood. She thinks of Charlie's letters and the poor men who never come back. 'Pleez, *Fraülein*,' he says again. He rests his puny arms on his head, too exhausted to hold them up, surely too exhausted to harm her.

Still, she keeps her distance. She indicates that he can drop his arms. His thin face contorts into a grimace, and she notices that one of his eyes is swollen shut.

'Who are you?' she asks.

He says something she doesn't understand, but then stops as he starts to cough, a rasping, phlegmy sound that rattles in his chest and makes him double over with the effort. 'Shh,' she says, holding up her finger and moving a little towards him. 'Shh.' He tries to stop, swallowing the coughs behind his hand as he collapses wheezing to the floor.

Olivia doesn't call for Mrs Mac. She is surprised to find that she isn't scared. He may be German, but this emaciated creature is no threat, and she remembers well the look on the men's faces when they set off in pursuit of him. Which reminds her. Gun. He must have one somewhere. She makes the shape of a gun with her hand. 'Revolver?' she says. He scrabbles backwards into the dark.

'No. I'm not going to shoot you,' she says. 'Your gun?'

He shivers, uncomprehending, staring up at her from his one good eye.

She runs to fetch a torch from Mrs Mac, telling her she plans to do a full spring clean. When she returns, she shines the light around the back of the stable, picking out the shadows of the old feed bins, buckets, ropes, shovels, all covered in a thick layer of dust, shed from animals and hay over the years. The German is huddled right back into the far corner, a shadow within a shadow. He has made a bed from some old straw, with a pillow – his life jacket – stuffed with more. Apart from the grubby clothes he is wearing, there is a leather jacket and some decent-looking boots, which are lying on their sides.

She can hear the breath bubbling in his lungs. She knows he needs warm clothes, decent food. She is fascinated and repelled. His puffy eye is weeping. He moves towards her and she backs away. He slumps into the corner, dejected, coughing, too weak to move. She immediately feels bad. 'I'll try and bring you some clothes,' she says. He doesn't look at her. 'And clean water.' He still doesn't look at her, and then the cough starts barking in his chest again. There is a noise out in the yard. The German looks up at her, his eyes wide with fear. Someone is calling her name. Olivia puts her finger to her lips and then backs out into the light, leaving him alone in the darkness once more.

Olivia visits the German when it is safe to do so, sloshing the rancid water he had been drinking out on the cobbles and replacing it with fresh, borrowing a bale of fresh straw to spread out for him, removing the old straw when she is mucking out the pony. She lugs warm water in a bucket, leaving him to peel off his filthy clothes and scrub at his filthy skin. She finds some clothes that must have belonged to Uncle Howard in the dressing-up box at Taigh Mor. Eccentric, but at least they are clean and warm. She takes the man's uniform and buries it far away, deep in soft peat. Once the grime is washed off and the sickly pallor has faded from his skin, she can see that he has hazel eyes and mousy-coloured hair.

At first they struggle to communicate in broken English, using hand signals and pictures drawn in the ground to clarify meaning, like a child's game of charades. Slowly, Olivia learns that his name is Hans, and that his plane was shot down at sea. Somehow he managed to drift to shore and climb up into the hills. He has a revolver, but no bullets: he used the last the day he tried to shoot the stag. He missed because of the damage to his eye. He followed her tracks back to the stable and hid, surviving on a mixture of stale pony nuts and the occasional foraged vegetable from the walled garden. He is twenty. The same age as Charlie.

Hans lets her clean the bad eye with salt water, drawing his breath in sharply as she dabs at it. The eyeball was punctured by a piece of Perspex from the cockpit of his plane, and although Hans managed to pull it out, and the eyeball itself seems to have healed, the shard also cut the skin at the corner, and it is this that has become infected. Olivia washes it every day, but the skin remains hot and swollen, and she knows that Hans's temperature is high. She raids the tack room, finding an old bottle of iodine, the brown glass marked with skull and crossbones. She dabs it on the wound, feels Hans's body go rigid, sees his eyes water with unshed tears. She remembers how painful iodine is even on grazed knees. She stops, but he indicates that she must carry on. Tears come to her own eyes, because he is so very brave and he does not make a sound. She cleans it this way every morning and evening, until at last the wound stops festering and starts to heal, and now the cough begins to clear up, and finally colour returns to Hans's pasty cheeks.

The fear of discovery grows less with each day that passes, and as they both relax in each other's company, that corner of the stable becomes almost like home. They play cards: Pelmanism and rummy. Hans picks up English a lot more quickly than Olivia has managed to pick up Gaelic. He has a gentle, shy smile and calm manner. He is the complete opposite to what she's heard and read about Germans. She feels

101

guilty for liking him, but then why shouldn't she? They can't all be bad, can they? Olivia wonders how many of the Wrens and soldiers who career around the loch have ever met a real German. Is it just the uniform that gives the enemy away? Or is it something deeper?

Hans shows her the crumpled photograph that he keeps in his pocket. She studies it in the crack of light that slopes in through a missing tile in the stable roof. It is a picture of Hans, his mother and younger brother. A shaggy mongrel lies with its head on Hans's foot. The little brother is wearing leder-hosen, a serious expression on his face. Hans is smiling in his Luftwaffe uniform. His mother's arm is linked through his and she is looking up at him proudly. She is wearing a flowery dress. She looks no different to Olivia today. In fact, Olivia looks more Germanic with her pale eyes and blonde hair. Hans gazes sadly at the photograph before putting it carefully back into his pocket. Olivia thinks how similar they are; both in a place they never intended to be; both isolated from friends and family.

'What is your home like?' she asks.

'My home town is Dresden,' he says. 'It is very beautiful. Many old houses. Much history. Very different to here.'

'It sounds like London,' she says.

He nods. 'It also has a big river. The Elbe. We live near it. I like to walk my dog there.'

'I'm not sure it would be very safe walking a dog in London these days . . .'

'So sad,' he says. 'I would like to visit London one day.'

'If there's anything left . . .'

He clicks his tongue, shaking his head as if he cannot believe the world. 'I will help rebuild it,' he says. 'I will be an archi-tect when this is over.'

'Is that what you always wanted to do?'

He nods. 'My father has – had – an architect business in Dresden.'

'What is he doing now?'

'He is a captain in the Kriegsmarine.'

'No!' she laughs. 'Mine is too . . .'

'Let's hope they never meet.'

Spring begins to warm the air, and soft new leaves unfurl on the trees as the days begin to lighten. Up in the hills, the stoats start to lose their creamy winter coats, their faces and backs turning russet brown again. Somewhere a cuckoo is calling. The sound gladdens Olivia's soul: it means summer is approaching. The wind drowns out the sound of traffic on the road. As she battles to hang the washing out on the blowy line, the sheets snapping and cracking against her, she almost forgets why she is here – and how once she had not wanted to be.

What with preparing the ground for planting vegetables, and being able to fish for salmon and brown trout again, with negotiating with kitchen staff or directly with the men on the ships, she has less time to spend with Hans. She brings him books from the bothy to read when he dares to crawl closer to the stable door. 'I must thank you for all your kindnesses,' he says.

'Anyone would have done it.'

'I know that this is not true.'

'Well, you don't seem too frightening to me.'

'I am certainly not the ideal of the Reich's *Aryan Herrenvolk*.'

'I'm hardly the ideal daughter, let alone British subject . . .'

He smiles, but the smile quickly crumbles. 'It is strange that you are on one side and I am on the other simply because of where we are born.'

'We call it a quirk of fate . . .'

'Like whether you are rescued by an English girl . . . or lose your life in the sea . . .'

'Looks like fate has been good to you . . .'

'Perhaps.' Hans holds a hand over his good eye and squints towards the light.

'Is it any better?' says Olivia.

He shakes his head. 'It is not painful,' he says. 'But the sight is blurry. Like flying in fog.'

'Maybe it will improve with time . . .'

'No. I fear it will be like this for ever, and I will never fly again. This is something I cannot bear.'

'I know someone who would understand that.'

'You have a friend who flies?'

'He lives for it . . .'

'I hope he never suffers this . . .'

'What do you think you'll do instead?'

'You mean until the war is over? I will be forced to work at a desk. Or in a prisoner camp . . .'

They sit there in silence for a moment, both trying to see into an unforeseeable future. Olivia throws the cards at him. 'Let's stop being morbid,' she says. 'Look on the bright side. It means you won't have to drop any bombs on me . . .'

He smiles. 'Now who is being morbid?'

She laughs. 'Imagine there was no war, and we met at a party . . . What would we be talking about? Music or something . . .'

'Ah,' says Hans, his face lighting up with memories. 'Now music is something we Germans can certainly be superior about. After all, we have given the world Brahms, Mendelssohn, Handel . . .'

'Hang on . . . I think we can claim Handel as one of our own . . .'

'How do you figure this?'

'He's an honorary Englishman. He loved it so much over here that he ended up staying . . .'

'Things were surely less complicated in those days.'

The days lengthen. More hours of daylight mean more chance of discovery. As much as she wants him to stay, she has to persuade Hans to move on. 'You won't be able to hide for much longer,' she says. 'More people are arriving every day. They've commissioned an official naval base at Aultbea now.

104

And you must leave before the winter comes again. Do you have somewhere to go?'

'There are places,' says Hans. 'Places of sympathy.'

Olivia holds her hand up to stop him. She doesn't want to know in case anyone ever asks and she feels obliged to tell them.

She draws Hans a map of how to cross the hills without nearing a checkpoint. She collects food over the weeks, and he stows it away carefully. 'You stand a good chance before the weather turns,' she says. 'And you might even pass for English, you know. You're speaking it really well.'

'I have the best teacher,' he says. 'Thank you.'

Olivia smiles, feels the tears prick her eyes.

More buildings have been erected at Aultbea, and a mass of Wrens have joined the soldiers and sailors who now throng the area around Loch Ewe. They sit behind the wheels of cars and trucks, at the helm of small boats delivering supplies and letters to the ships. They run errands. They man the offices. They drive messages to Inverness. They collect personnel. They move munitions. They are cooks, stewards, telephonists, radio operators. Two of the Wrens – Gladys and Maggie – often drive to the cottage to play cards or lie on the lawn outside. They are only a couple of years older than Olivia. She can't help admiring their uniforms, their strong sense of purpose. She grills them for information about life as a Wren. They laugh and tell her she should join. 'But I've still got almost a year before I can,' she says.

'It'll come around soon enough,' says Gladys, who is always immaculately turned out. She has kind eyes and a genuine smile. Her best friend Maggie is fiery haired and fiery tempered as well as curvaceous: she looks as if she's about to burst out of her uniform at any moment, the buttons straining at her chest. The three of them are lying on the lawn, soaking up the warm sunshine.

'We've been talking to your aunt,' says Maggie.

'You never told us you had a friend in the Fleet Air Arm,' says Gladys.

'What squadron is he in?'

'Eight-five-eight,' says Olivia. 'Fairey Swordfish.'

'Any idea where he is now?'

Olivia shakes her head.

'I wonder if he was involved in the Taranto raid. That was all Swordfish. Incredible, those old bi-planes . . . Who'd have thought it?'

'Wasn't Taranto the first all-aircraft attack by our Navy?'

Gladys nods. 'Not only that, they destroyed half of the Italian Navy's capital ships and gave us the upper hand in the Med . . .'

'I don't think that was Charlie's squadron,' says Olivia. 'Or if it was, I don't think he was involved. The Fleet Air Arm have been helping out over London.'

Both Wrens grimace. 'God knows the RAF needed them.'

They are silent for a moment.

'I take it he wasn't flying stringbags over London?'

'I shouldn't think so. And I'm sure he'd be offended if he knew you were calling them "stringbags" . . .'

'It's what we all call them. Said with much love . . .'

'Unless he's got no sense of humour . . .?'

'Actually, he has a great sense of humour.'

'Don't tell me he's handsome too?'

'Has he got a girlfriend?' Maggie primps her hair as if styling it in a mirror.

Gladys squints at Olivia. 'You're a dark horse,' she says. 'You never told us you were sweet on anyone.'

'I'm not! He's more like a brother . . .'

'That's a classic hedging line!'

'It's true . . .'

'Keeping him all to yourself, eh?' says Maggie.

'That's enough from you,' says Gladys. 'You've got Rob.'

'And Danny,' says Olivia.

'I don't believe you should focus all your efforts on one man.'

'We can see that.'

'And if you really are going to confine yourself to one – then you've got to try the goods before you commit. Otherwise you may be in for a lifetime of disappointment.'

Gladys shakes her head, laughing. 'You're incorrigible,' she says, pushing Maggie in the shoulder so that she falls back on to the grass.

'Don't you act all innocent with me,' says Maggie. 'I know you've enjoyed the odd fumble after lights-out.'

'I'm not quite in your league, though, am I?'

Olivia goes to fetch a jug of water, taking the opportunity to wind up the gramophone again and avoid the conversation. She suddenly feels foolish next to these liberated girls who know so much about relationships and men. Charlie is the closest thing she's ever had to a boyfriend, and she couldn't exactly call him that. He really is more like a brother. She enjoys his company, but she could never imagine . . .

She wanders slowly back out, sipping her drink, watching the others lean back on their elbows and look out across the loch. The swallows flit up and disappear into the eaves of the house. The gramophone scratches to a stop. Peace descends for seconds, but is broken by the drone of a plane. A Junkers 88 appears, a growing dot in the distance. They are such a common sight now that the girls just lie there, watching it approach. The planes usually circle the loch on reconnaissance and then disappear back to Norway again.

Suddenly Gladys jumps up and grabs hold of Olivia's arm. 'Inside! Now!' she yells as she starts dragging Olivia towards the cottage. 'Kitchen table!'

But Olivia resists, standing motionless, enthralled as she sees the first tiny charge drop towards earth. This is no reconnaissance plane. Maggie pushes her: 'Come on,' she says and Olivia starts to run, but can't help glancing back to watch the tiny bomb float down, down, and then explode among the ships on the loch. The bang of the anti-aircraft guns starts to fill her ears, tracer fire trailing up through the air. But the plane avoids the bullets and carries on. *Boom, boom, boom*, the heavy anti-aircraft guns go, almost drowning out the sound of the lighter batteries. The sound is deafening: there are guns positioned all around the loch now, and the noise echoes and ricochets around them. The ground shudders. But still the bomber flies on. It drops its next bombs: one near the school, and then one more as it flies on towards the hills.

'Mac!' Olivia says, because the last bomb looks as though it has landed smack bang on the farm. And Hans, she is thinking. And although her heart is racing and her legs feel like jelly, she runs back out into the open.

'Leave it,' says Gladys, but Olivia ignores her and races away to her bicycle.

As she draws nearer the farm, she meets Mac. 'We're all right, lassie. It landed in the east paddock. We're going up there now to have a look. You'd better go and check on the pony.'

Inside the stable Thistle is sweating and rolling his eyes, pacing around the stall, throwing his head up and down. But Hans is not there. His boots have gone, as have the saved rations and one of Uncle Howard's coats. All that is left is a word scrawled on a piece of paper – *Danke* – and his watch, which she later hides deep in a drawer like a guilty secret.

Olivia is glad that she no longer has to lie, but she is downcast too – losing Hans is like losing a friend as well as losing a bit of excitement in her life. For a while she keeps away from everybody, spending her time fixing old lines and hooks, sanding down the rowing boat and repainting it, renewing the clusters of corks she uses for buoyancy and markers in the water, cleaning Thistle's tack. And then one morning, the grim, flat shape of an aircraft carrier carves its way into the loch, and Olivia drops what she is doing and runs up to the house. Aunt Nancy is already out on the drive, waving at her. 'It's Charlie!' she says. 'They're refuelling. They'll only be here for twenty-four hours, but it's better than nothing. Do go and meet him! He'd be thrilled.'

Olivia cycles the six miles to Aultbea. At first, it's hard to make him out among the rest of the men in the launch as it gradually draws closer to the jetty. They are a blur of matching navy uniforms and caps. But then an arm goes up, and she can see Charlie's smile as he leaps on shore to the ribbing of his shipmates. Most of the men disperse to the hotel for drinks and relaxation. Charlie and Olivia hitch a ride back towards Taigh Mor, but have to walk the last bit from Tournaig, pushing the bicycle between them.

'Thanks for coming to meet me,' he says.

'You're only here for a short time. Got to make the most of it.'

They walk on in silence, Olivia glancing up at him occasionally. He looks tired, and there are faint lines across his forehead.

The last mile is downhill, and Charlie says, 'How about I pedal, and you sit on the handlebars?'

'I'm far too heavy.'

'Don't be silly. Come on. I could probably lift you with one arm . . .'

He makes a move towards her and she backs away, laughing. 'Don't even think about it . . .'

'Get on the handlebars, and I won't.'

Olivia arranges herself on the handlebars, giggling as she tries to keep her legs free of the front wheels and leaning some of her weight on Charlie behind her, who almost has to lean on her shoulder to be able to see past. The bicycle wobbles beneath her as Charlie finds his balance. 'Ready?' he says.

She giggles again. 'Ready.'

Olivia trusts Charlie enough to enjoy the rush of the wind catching in her throat, and the glimpse of woodland and rock and flash of water as they descend. She is happy to hear his laugh in her ear and to feel the comforting warmth of his shoulder supporting her back.

Clarkson has pulled out all the stops, and the dining table

is laid with a feast. There are three other officers eating with them, and Olivia's awkwardness returns as she sits at the formal table in her bare feet and tatty clothes. The chink and rattle of cutlery and plates seems old-fashioned and staid. She doesn't join in the conversation, but watches Charlie instead, noticing that the corner of his eye sometimes flickers. Whenever it happens, he tries to hide it with his hand.

'Did you hear about those spies that were apprehended at Portgordon station the other day?' says Aunt Nancy, before handing around the cheese.

'On the east coast?' says Charlie.

One of the officers nods. 'Pretty hopeless spies. Could barely speak a word of English, and their clothes were soaking wet,' he says.

They all laugh.

'Actually, we found an empty dinghy along the coast here,' says another officer.

'Luftwaffe?' Charlie asks, his eye starting to twitch again. Olivia passes the board on to her neighbour, suddenly not hungry.

'Yes. No sign of an occupant, but it does make you wonder how we can police the whole coast.'

'You don't think he escaped?' says Charlie.

The man shakes his head. 'I should think someone finished him off before he made it to shore – if he ever got into it in the first place.'

'Just killed a downed pilot in cold blood?' says Olivia. 'That's awful.'

The men go silent and stare at her as if only seeing her for the first time. Her cheeks burn.

'It's hardly cold blood,' says one of them.

'But I thought there were rules . . . Geneva . . .'

Aunt Nancy clears her throat. 'Time we all got on,' she says, folding her napkin before putting it on the table. 'Lunch has dragged, and Charlie must be desperate to stretch his legs.' She rises, and Charlie rises too, helping to pull her chair back.

*

On the way down to the bothy, Olivia says, 'Do you think it's right? Would you kill a man in a lifeboat?'

'Of course I don't think it's right,' says Charlie. 'But the truth is, you don't know what you'd do until you're faced with it . . .'

'Imagine if it was you in the dinghy?'

'Let's hope it never is.'

'Of course. Sorry. It's just so horrible.'

'It's war,' says Charlie.

'But they're only German, for goodness sakes. We were all being sent to German finishing schools only a couple of years ago.'

'It's not the Germans that are the problem. It's the Nazis that they're fighting for.'

'So not all Germans are evil and dangerous?'

He sighs, exasperated. 'I'm sure they're not. But the fact is, we are at war with them. They are the enemy. That's how you have to look at it.'

'But to them, we are the enemy. Does that make us bad too?'

Charlie's eye is twitching again. 'Let's stop talking about things you don't understand,' he says.

'But I'd like to understand.'

'There's no need to concern yourself with such things. Leave that up to us.'

'Who? The Navy?'

'All the armed forces who are protecting this country.'

'And all of us poor, helpless women.'

'I didn't mean it like that.'

'What did you mean it like?'

'I'm sad that the world isn't safe for you.'

'It's exciting.'

'Exciting?' He shakes his head. 'Sometimes you do sound very young.'

Cross, Olivia picks a piece of long grass from the side of the track and starts to pull it apart, strip by strip.

'I'm sorry,' he says. 'I didn't mean to offend you. Let's talk about something else?'

'You think that you know everything, and you don't,' she says, still tearing at the grass.

'Of course I don't know everything, but you're obviously thinking of something specific. What is it?'

'Nothing.'

'Don't tell me you've got a German stashed away somewhere?'

'Of course not.' She wishes she could stop the blush that is beginning to spread across her cheeks.

'What, then? What don't I know? Come on.'

She falters, clutching at straws, anything to throw him off the scent. 'I think Aunt Nancy could be a spy,' she says finally.

He throws his head back and laughs.

'Why is it funny? You should see the sorts of people who come and go. It's not all uniforms and brigadiers, you know. And she's so damn secretive sometimes.'

'Of course she is. She's working for the SOE.'

Olivia looks blank.

'You know – Churchill's Secret Army?'

Olivia still looks blank.

'The Special Operations Executive.'

'Doing what?'

'It wouldn't be secret if we knew.'

'I thought she was something to do with the FANYs.'

'She was. The SOE recruited a handful of FANYs from the last war. She's quite some woman, your aunt.'

'But what could she be doing secretly up here?'

'I assume it's something to do with getting men in and out of occupied Norway. She has a wide knowledge of this area, and the men who know these waters.'

'So she is a sort of spy?'

'I suppose . . .'

Olivia mulls things over in her head. 'I wonder if I'd make a good spy?' she says eventually.

'I doubt it.'

'Why?'

'Far too innocent and easy to read. Just like your letters.' He smiles at her.

She smiles back, but she looks away, in case he should see an image of Hans walking across the hills in one of Uncle Howard's overcoats there.

Charlie doesn't want to do anything for the rest of the afternoon except sit on the lawn in front of the bothy. He doesn't want to go out on the boat or up into the hills. Instead, they play cards and listen to the gramophone, but conversation is stilted. It is still easier to be familiar in letters than face to face, and Olivia is still aggrieved that he seems to regard her as so young and naïve. 'Are you sure you don't want to come up to the rowan pool?' she says. 'It's a lovely day. It might do us both some good.'

Charlie shakes his head, and his eye twitches. 'There's no time,' he says, frowning across the water. 'I'm going to have to get back to my ship.'

'Do you know where you're headed this time?'

He shrugs. 'Back to the Atlantic, I think. I don't care. I'm back with my squadron, that's all that matters.'

'Was London really horrific?'

He nods.

'Do you want to talk about it?'

He shakes his head.

'You should, you know. A problem shared . . .'

'Will you come and wave me off?' he says.

'Of course.'

They scramble to their feet, leaving the crumpled outlines of their bodies on the grass. They hitch a lift to Aultbea in the back of a Bedford truck, lugging Olivia's bicycle up into it so that she can cycle home later. At the pier, he takes her face in his hands and kisses her forehead, a paternal gesture. 'Make sure you look after yourself,' he says. 'Keep your rifle with you. Don't go near any strangers. Don't go into the hills. Don't go where people can't see you.'

'Look around,' she says. 'The place is crawling with Wrens and soldiers and sailors . . . not to mention Aunt Nancy. It's probably the safest place in the country. I'm much more worried about you.'

'Don't worry about me,' he says, pulling his hat down firmly. 'I'm invincible.' It is easy to believe looking at him now, no sign of a twitch. 'Just keep those letters coming.'

As he makes his way to the launch, Olivia cycles on to the end of the road at Leacan Donna. She drops her bicycle before the checkpoint, avoiding it by climbing up into the hill behind Mellon Charles. Behind her, the loch is pockmarked with ships. Instead of the cries of seabirds, the air is thick with clanking chains and the shouts of men and whir of motors. The tugs open the boom defence to allow Charlie's ship out into the wide ocean. Minesweepers trail their thick cables in the water as the aircraft carrier ploughs on. Opposite her, on the other side of the mouth of the loch, there is now a battery of anti-aircraft men, hidden in ugly concrete pillboxes cemented into the large boulders that tumble down to the water, where the seals used to sunbathe in the summer. She scans the sea, a crinkled expanse of liquid silver set beneath a granite sky, danger lurking beneath its waves. And suddenly she wishes it would all go away, and that things could go back to how they were, to the peace and quiet of a hidden loch, and an innocence that her family had tried to protect.

CHAPTER 8

Jack

Jack has seen plenty of ships before, but none like this one. She is of a bygone age: her smart black paint is spotless, her three masts are beautifully polished wood reaching up into the mist, ropes and ladders suspended between them like an elaborate spider's web. There is some kind of figurehead – a woman? It is hard to tell. The ship is so perfectly balanced and elegantly rigged that it looks as though if you snipped one of those ropes, the whole thing would come crashing down. Beneath her vast hull the turgid water of the Gloucester canal seems viscous, like oil. Behind him, the River Severn swirls and veers towards the sea.

The ship is a sea training school, running free three-month courses to turn boys into seamen. Jack and Carl are part of a sorry-looking group staring up at her from the towpath. The selection process did not seem too rigorous – a matter of convincing a man in a white coat that he could read and tell the difference between the colours red, green, and white. Merchant seamen are in much demand. If they pass, they should be guaranteed an apprenticeship on a ship. Jack could be travelling the world in a matter of weeks.

Carl hasn't asked about Jack's mum or Betsy since his friend arrived blank-eyed on his doorstep. Not even when Jack wakes in the darkness, trembling and sweating. In their world, it is

115

not unusual for families to disappear overnight. He has given Jack a change of clothes, but apart from that, Jack has nothing. He is not alone; he glances at the boys next to him. A couple had parents to wave them off back at the station, but most have the hangdog air that suggests they belong to no one.

There are about forty boys, a few the same age as Jack, some possibly as young as twelve, their limbs still gangly, their knees knobbly, as if they haven't yet grown into their bodies. In their ragged short trousers and stained tops, the jaw-clenched new recruits are a stark contrast to the naval officer's uniform of the men who collected them from the station. The younger of these two men – tall with grey eyes – is addressing them now. 'Welcome to Training Ship *Constance*,' he says. 'I'm Mr O'Brien. This is Mr Harker. We're the poor fools who are going to wrestle you sorry lot into seamen. Follow me.' He turns with a click of his heels and starts to walk up one of the two gangways that protrude stiffly from the ship, linking her to dry land.

'Quick march!' shouts the other man. He is red-faced and broad, his chest straining at the buttons of his jacket.

The new boys fall into a line behind O'Brien. The wooden gangway is narrow, so there is room for only one at a time. They follow him like stray dogs, heads down. If they had tails, they would be curled between their legs. Mr Harker brings up the rear. 'Step to it,' he says. His voice is laced with disgust, as though he finds himself doing something beneath a man of his qualifications.

Jack inhales the familiar smell of dampness, of being near water. He hears their footsteps shuffling along, feels the gangway bounce beneath his feet. He stops for a second to glance back along the canal, to the world he knows. Immediately, he feels something shove against his back. It is Mr Harker, whose red face and cold eyes are only inches from his own.

'If I say, "Step to it", then you step to it!'

Jack doesn't budge. 'Don't touch me again,' he says.

But Mr Harker will not be deterred. He prods Jack once more. 'You have a choice, sonny. Either you do what you're told, or you get off this ship right now and crawl back into the stinking piss-hole that you came from.' Mr Harker smiles, his mouth disappearing into his ruddy cheeks. He cocks his head and stands aside, indicating a space for Jack to pass and step back on to the path.

Jack is ready to elbow his way through, but Carl grabs hold of him. 'Where are you going to go?' he asks.

'I was wrong. I shouldn't have come. I'm not cut out for this.'

'You can't go back. You're better than that. It's time you did something with your life.'

He is right. Jack turns away from Mr Harker and steps on to a ship for the very first time.

A narrow door leads to a steep ladder. The boys descend gingerly, watching they don't bump their heads. They find themselves in a long, low room, with tables and benches down each side of it. Running along the ceiling above them are metal bars, with white hammocks slung between them.

'Welcome home,' says Mr Harker, pacing up and down, the tread of his boots determined on the polished wooden floor. 'This is where you will eat, sleep and live for the next twelve weeks.' He stops in front of Jack. His brown eyes are flecked with yellow. 'Or at least those of you who stick it out.' He prowls on. 'This is my mess deck. You're to keep it spotless. Otherwise you'll be up in front of the captain superintendent. Understand?' Everyone but Jack stares at their feet. O'Brien reads down his clipboard, and, calling the boys by surname, separates them into deck and catering. The catering contingent are marched elsewhere by O'Brien. Mr Harker indicates the hammocks, and snaps, 'Fall out and choose yourselves a berth.'

Jack and Carl make sure they are next to each other. On the other side of Jack is a boy with a large mole on his cheek; beyond him, a curly-haired boy with sallow skin.

'Take note of where your hammock is. It must be stowed properly every morning.' Carl catches Jack's eye and raises an eyebrow. 'Mr Harker?' he whispers. 'More like The Barker.' The boys try not to smile. Mr Harker is immediately bearing down on them: 'Something you'd like to share?' he says. Jack feels the anger simmer in his bones. The boys shake their heads, but The Barker sticks.

The Barker stalks off again. He stops in front of the boy with curly hair, using the end of the cane to lift his dark curls, shaking his head in despair. 'Fall in. After me. Quick march.' And the boys file after him, through the maze of corridors until they are pushed into another room where a couple of older boys are waiting.

First, they are made to strip, and then, one by one, their hair is shaved off, falling to the floor in clumps of blond, brown, red, black, where it lies in a sorry heap with their clothes. Bewildered, they stand, shorn and naked, while they are measured and poked and eventually handed new clothes: long trousers, woollen jumpers, tops, vests, pants, thick socks, and even a blanket. Jack clambers into the uniform, feeling the unfamiliar weight of decent material against his skin. He cannot remember when he last had new clothes to wear. He slings the extras over one arm, using the hand of the other to receive a sailor's cap and a pair of new plimsolls.

Barefoot, the boys return to the mess deck where O'Brien is waiting. He nods, pleased with what he sees. 'At least you look the part now,' he says. 'Ten minutes. Then you eat.'

The officers disappear, and the atmosphere immediately changes. The boys begin to talk, touching their own and each other's velvety heads, as if trying to remember who they are. It is dark outside now, and inside is dimly lit: the old gun ports have been turned into windows, but they have blackout screens fitted. Jack climbs into his hammock. It tips, but balances quickly. It is not comfortable.

'Not sure I'll be able to sleep without falling out,' says the boy with the mole on his cheek. 'I'm Si,' he adds, putting out a hand. He has pale brown eyes and an open face. He points at the boy who used to have curly hair. 'That's David.' David waves at them, revealing crooked teeth.

Jack ignores the proffered hand. He is not here to make friends.

'Take no notice of Jack,' says Carl. 'He'll be fine come tomorrow. I'm Carl, by the way.'

'Where are you from?'

'Southwark. You?'

'Highgate. Wish I was back there.'

'Why'd you come here in the first place, then?' says Jack, swinging himself back out of the hammock and landing on the ground with a thud.

'Why'd you come?'

Jack shrugs. 'Ask him,' he says, tipping his head at Carl.

'It's a good place to start. Gives us prospects.'

'Me too,' says Si.

'And it gives us a chance to have a pop at them Nazis,' says David.

'He tried to join the army six times . . .'

'Not my fault I'm too short to pretend I'm eighteen . . .'

'How old are you?'

'Sixteen.'

'Same.'

Another group of boys files into the room, making their way down the other side of the ship, where the hammocks are coiled up neatly against the metal bars. They are all smart in their neatly pressed uniforms. They are the last intake of recruits, and they hiss at Jack and the other boys across the floor: 'Ready to run home to mummy yet, new boys?'

'You look like you'll last all of five minutes.'

'They're down to the dregs now.'

Jack clenches and unclenches his fists.

Suddenly two ear-splitting notes fill the air. It is the first time they have heard the boatswain's call, and some of the new recruits jump, their hands flicking to their ears. The boys from London don't move. They are used to loud noises.

The sound has come from a small boy with a metal whistle in his hand. 'Like dogs,' whispers Carl.

The Barker and O'Brien appear again. 'Obey the last pipe!' yells The Barker. Then, shaking his head at their stupefied expressions, he adds, 'Cadets, demonstrate how to lash up and stow!' The previous recruits cross the mess deck, each choosing a new boy to show how to roll up their hammocks and tie them out of the way of the tables. 'Not so brave now, are you?' says Jack, trying to catch the eye of the boy who is demonstrating the seven evenly spaced knots.

'You'll shut up and watch, if you know what's good for you,' the boy whispers back. Jack digs an elbow into the boy's side, just as The Barker strides over, and, with barely a movement, jabs the side of his hand against Jack's throat, leaving him bent double and gasping for air. No one dares react. The other boys simply stare straight ahead.

The catering recruits march in bearing tea: bread and butter, and some kind of cold meat. The boys seat themselves at their allocated tables, mixed in with some of the older recruits. Jack rubs at his neck. Everything is done in silence until The Barker says, 'Grace!' The boys stand and bow their heads, and O'Brien thanks the Lord for the food they are about to eat.

Once the prayer is over, they sit down again. Carl starts to help himself, but a metal serving spoon is brought down hard on his knuckles by one of the older boys. 'Seniors first,' he says, piling his plate high. By the time it is Jack's turn, there is not much left. He isn't bothered; he is used to feeling hungry. Besides, his neck is still throbbing. He takes a slice of the meat and passes it on.

The boys stare at their plates until the call squeals again and they start to eat. Jack chews at the fatty meat, the dry bread, washing it down with the water. The only sound is the clattering of plates and chomping of teeth, followed by a rush to collect any leftovers.

Carl grunts. 'I'm bleeding starving,' he says. The senior boy gives him a dirty look and he shuts up.

When they have finished, the piper blows his call again and there is a cacophonous din as the boys start chattering while the plates are cleared away. The noise lasts for about four minutes and then the call blasts again. Silence. O'Brien says, 'Cleaning stations.' The boys collect buckets and mops and start to scrub at the tables and at the floor. They work silently. For the boy who finishes last, there is a flick of the cane from The Barker.

Once the mess deck is spotless, there seems to be time to relax. Jack watches from the corner while the others strike up stilted conversations, or stroke their bare heads, or fold and refold their new clothes into their wooden chests. A few of the boys simply sit and stare, too shell-shocked to do anything. Another pipe signals that it's time to unravel their hammocks again. Within minutes, the beds are swinging freely from the bars. They are marched down the gangway for ablutions. Jack has never heard the word 'ablutions' before, but it is obvious what this is. In a stone building beside the towpath, there are twelve holes in a plank of wood. Through the holes, Jack can see the tidal water of the Severn reaching up to wash the effluent away. There are a few small basins and some icy water. The boys strip naked, splashing the freezing water over their shivering bodies. They jog back to the ship in an attempt to warm themselves up. On board it is as cold as outside, the only heating supposedly coming through a pipe that is never more than tepid to the touch. Jack bunches himself into his hammock. He is so close to Carl that he can hear him breathing. Carl shifts and leans towards him. 'How's your throat?' he asks.

'Fuck off.'

'Shh.' The older boys tell them to shut up. It's a proper flogging on the quarterdeck for boys caught talking after lights-out. There is a faint movement from the water beneath the ship. They lie in a silence broken only by the occasional sniff.

It is the kind of quiet that Jack hasn't experienced for a long time. He struggles to keep images of home from filling the space in his head. He keeps his eyes open for as long as possible, staring up into the blackness, listening to the snoring and whimpering, until eventually he gives in and sleeps.

They are woken by the shrill scream of the reveille. It is still dark outside. 'Show a leg,' someone yells, and there is the sound of banging on the metal pipes. The boys' bare feet thump on to the wooden floor. Again, they file back to the toilet block, splashing cold water on their tired and puffy faces. The older boys shave. Everything is performed in silence until the right pipe is heard.

The Barker and O'Brien appear. 'Why haven't these hammocks been stowed?'

Si starts to say, 'We didn't know . . .'

'I don't want your life history. Just do it!'

The boys start to try and make sense of the tangle of knots and stow the hammocks in as tidy a fashion as possible. When they are done, there are two beds left hanging. Their occupants are nowhere to be seen.

From the corner of his mouth, Carl says, 'Must have sneaked out in the night.'

The rumour soon spreads down the line.

'Silence!' shouts The Barker. He points at the empty hammocks with his cane, and then at Jack. 'You! Clear them away. We don't want boys like that anyway.' He narrows his eyes at Jack meaningfully. Jack removes the hammocks, and O'Brien collects them from him. No one can recall the faces of the boys they belonged to. It doesn't matter. They are never seen again.

'Prepare for morning inspection,' says The Barker. The new boys get into line, facing the boys on the other side. The Barker walks past them, using his cane to point out a flap of something untucked here and a sleeve turned down there. 'Since this is your first morning,' he says, 'I'll let it go. But if there's anything amiss tomorrow . . .' The threat hangs like a noose in the air as he taps the rod against his leg.

The catering recruits bring cutlery and breakfast to the tables. Gloopy porridge steams in bowls. The older boys get jam. There are more thick slices of bread. It's the same as last night: grace, senior boys serving themselves first, and all in silence.

Almost before Jack has swallowed his last stodgy mouthful of gruel, it is cleaning stations again. A boy is assigned to polish each table. Another the metal bars. The Barker watches all the time, ready to strike somewhere soft and prominent if he disapproves of anything: behind the knee if they're standing, or on the knuckles if they're kneeling – even behind the ear if he can't reach anywhere else. When the mess deck is clean and sparkling again, and the boys are back in line, The Barker shouts, 'All hands on deck.'

The new boys fall in. Carl is in front, and Jack has to stop himself from pushing his friend out of the way in his scramble to get into the fresh air. One by one they come blinking into the fresh morning sunlight, a ragtag bunch of new recruits, slack-shouldered and feeling sorry for themselves. The deck is vast and smooth, the wooden planks worn from years in service. A chilly wind whines in the rigging. Si sniffs.

'Stop snivelling,' says The Barker.

O'Brien joins them. The boatswain's mate pipes. The boys line up against the rails at the side of the ship. There are more than a hundred boys up here: the entire ship's company. Beneath them the water is murky. Above them the ropes bang and tap eerily against the mast.

An older man appears. 'I am Training Officer Turner,' he says. 'You can call me Mr Turner.' He is a tall, thin man. The hair beneath his peaked cap is snow-white, as is his beard. His voice is clear and loud, carried on the wind along the deck into the ears of the cadets. Jack shivers.

Mr Turner marches up and down the deck in front of them. His boots make a firm, positive sound on the wood. 'I'm in charge of your general deck training. We'll be covering basic seamanship: navigation, steering, lifeboats, fire drill, survival at sea. By the time you leave us, you will be an asset to any merchant ship.

'You'll be divided into two watches. You' – he points at the boys who arrived last night – 'are port watch. You' – he indicates the older recruits – 'are starboard watch.'

The boys shift a bit. The wind bites at their hands and cheeks.

'Port watch: this morning you are on physical. Starboard: below deck.' Somewhere a bell rings, another signal. 'Left turn. Quick march.' Jack watches them file back down to the classrooms.

Port watch learn to swab the deck, half of them attacking it with brushes while the rest, including Carl and Jack, kneel, rubbing at the wood with a gritty holystone until their hands are chapped and stinging from the cold. The water seeps through to their knees. If they are too slow, The Barker snaps at their bare heels with a rope. Then they learn to polish the brass until it shines like a new penny. The bell clangs, and it's a run along the canal; another bell means parade, standing and moving in line like soldiers while the drill instructor yells at them. The next bell brings O'Brien to give them a lesson in ropework. He sits them in a row and demonstrates how to make a loop with a bowline and how a rolling hitch won't slip; the sheepshank to shorten a length of rope and the clove hitch to start lashing. The Barker advances with his cane when he notices the boys losing interest, but O'Brien holds up his hand to stop him. 'You'd do well to pay attention,' he says. 'A knot could be the difference between living or drowning.' The boys practise on a long piece of rope with their own little piece attached to it, a line of bowed heads deep in concentration. Jack soaks it up, finds the practical work begins to fill the empty space inside him. Soon he is as deft as O'Brien at splicing. And all the time, the bell clangs to mark a change in the half-hour.

By midday they are starving, and this time Jack makes sure

he gets a fair ration. Even this slop tastes good after the morning they've had. The afternoon is spent below deck, shuffling down the companionway to the classrooms on the lower deck. The officer in charge of most of their classroom activity is a bristly-looking man with a limp. He is called Signals Officer Scott. He is fair, and he explains things well – but Jack still struggles. The classroom never was his strong point.

Officer Scott introduces them to signals and how to identify the Pole Star. He scratches numbers and diagrams on to a blackboard. They cover some maths and science. In time, they will learn how to recognise different international flags and how to read an angle from a sextant, holding the telescope to their eyes and measuring the altitude of the sun above the horizon, how to work out longitude from the shiny and perfect chronometer in its little wooden box. They will get used to the weight of the Aldis lamp, and how to use it to communicate with another ship by Morse code, begin to understand the rudiments of meteorology and how to use semaphore: holding the flags above their heads, to the side, one up, one down – a strange folk dance performed by boys acting as men.

Although they have their favourite and worst lessons, there is one thing they all agree on: that they hate inspection, when The Barker arrives with his white gloves and checks for dirt and dust in the mess deck. If he's in the wrong sort of mood, he has a go at them for not breathing correctly. He is in that sort of temper tonight, running his finger along the bar, along the chest where Jack keeps his clothes neatly folded. He sticks his cane into the box, lifting out the trousers that Jack should have washed and pressed yesterday. Foolishly, he had hoped to get away with it, but the creases are almost non-existent, the material too soft and crumpled to have been laundered. As The Barker lifts them, dangling on the end of his cane, something drops to the floor.

Jack scrabbles to pick it up, but The Barker gets there first.

125

'Give it back,' says Jack.

The Barker examines it, holding it up to the light. It glints, green like the leaves in the park in spring. 'A piece of rubbish. I will dispose of it,' he says.

Jack moves towards the officer. 'Give it back,' he says, louder this time. He can sense the other boys holding their breath.

'Important to you is it, cadet?' He holds the glass in front of Jack's face. Jack tries to grab it, but The Barker snatches it away. Jack feels something burn like scalding porridge deep down inside him. He tries again to get it, but The Barker jabs at him, catching him on the temple.

Jack takes a step back, but his blood starts to pump. The watching faces recede and the world narrows. 'Give it the fuck back, you bastard!'

But still the officer won't. He leers at Jack, goads him, taunting him with the glass – with Betsy's piece of glass. And the thought of his little sister and his mother who he's tried so hard to forget rises up in front of him and the pain is so intense that he launches at The Barker with all his might, taking a swing, but The Barker steps out of the way and lands a blow beneath Jack's ribs, winding him momentarily. Jack springs back, then throws himself towards the man again, but instead of feeling flesh beneath his fist, he finds himself rammed up against one of the wooden columns by the throat, The Barker's face right up close to his, the man's breath warm on Jack's cheek.

Jack struggles, but the officer has him pinned good and proper. 'Is that all you've got?' says The Barker, his cheeks flushed brighter than usual, his barrel chest rising and falling. Jack struggles again, but he cannot move. He tries again and again until he is as weak as a baby, but the officer stands firm. Jack gives up, feels his shoulders slump, his own cheeks burning crimson.

But The Barker hasn't finished: 'What is it that you've got to be so cross about, cadet?' Jack doesn't answer. 'It can't be

126

because you've lost someone? We've all lost someone. It can't be because you're hungry. We've fed and clothed you.'

Silence. Jack avoids his eyes.

'Come on. Spill the beans. I've been desperate to find out ever since you arrived.'

Still Jack cannot look him in the eye. 'It's because . . .'

'What?'

'Because you treat me like shit.'

'I treat you all like shit.'

'. . . like I'm from the gutter.' Finally, he meets The Barker's gaze.

The officer shakes his head, and his grip relaxes as he releases Jack. 'I'm not interested in where you're from,' he says. 'As soon as you stepped on board this ship, you had no past. It's your future I care about.'

Jack stands, confused, looking around him.

'Now,' says The Barker, dusting himself down. 'I think you'd better sign up for next week's boxing match. You need to learn to control that temper of yours.' Before he goes, he presses Betsy's glass into Jack's palm. 'Hold tight to your passion, cadet. It'll make you a leader of men yet.'

Jack excels in the boxing ring. Finally able to focus his energy, he is one of the best boxers they've ever had. As he picks up the vocabulary of the sailor outside the ring – port and starboard, aft and fore, hull and keel, bulkhead and ballast – he learns to control himself inside the ring. He gets used to the clanging of the bell and the whistle of the boatswain's call. His life is divided into watches and meals, inspections and drills. The regime of the training ship breeds camaraderie, the new knowledge breeds respect – for themselves and for their shipmates. They want to help each other succeed. David and Si help Jack work out atmospheric pressure on a barometer, remind him which is longitude, which latitude; in return, Carl and Jack go over and over their knots until the boys can whip a rope's end in their sleep. He begins to feel a new emotion: pride.

And soon enough, they are the senior boys, helping themselves to the first dollops of rabbit stew, watching the huddles of new recruits with a mixture of amusement and relief. On their last day, O'Brien takes the boys for a farewell row. Wielding the long oars took some getting used to, but now each boy can sense when the person behind or in front dips his oar into the water and pulls. O'Brien sits in the stern, his hand on the tiller. There is purpose in their strokes, and within minutes they are slicing through the canal, their oars splashing in steady rhythm, past barges, dinghies, sailing boats tied up along the canal. They whistle at the women who man the longboats along the canal up to Gloucester and beyond. They are determined-looking women in dungarees, sleeves rolled up, who raise their arms in greeting, cigarettes dangling from broad smiles, bright headscarves nodding. They remind Jack with a wrench of his mother. Beyond the canal, the River Severn is wide like the Thames. Jack thinks of home. Can Betsy read yet? Is Stoog still thieving? Is Vince still fencing? Is Tommy a lookout for them, or for the firewatch? He begins to see where his life could have gone if he'd stayed.

When they return to the *Constance*, O'Brien accompanies them to the mess deck, where The Barker is waiting to say goodbye. 'I'm going to miss you lot,' says O'Brien. 'Reckon you're one of the best groups we've had yet. You're going to make fine sailors.' He turns to the older man. 'What do you say, Mr Harker?'

The Barker can barely manage a grunt. His red cheeks grow redder, and he tries to say something that might be 'yes', but it comes out half-strangled, and Jack can't help laughing. It starts as a kind of choke in his throat, and then his stomach and his shoulders are heaving. And suddenly all the boys are laughing. And Jack isn't sure, but he thinks he sees The Barker wipe a tear from his eye as he stomps away.

Someone has managed to secrete some home-brewed beer. The cadets pass it around, swigging from the bottles. The liquid

128

leaves a warm feeling in their bellies and a light feeling in their heads. Si puts his arms around Jack and Carl's shoulders. 'A fine pair of sailors,' he says, mimicking O'Brien's voice.

'Can't be a real sailor until you've got a tattoo,' says David.

'Says who?'

'Ask anyone.'

'How're we going to get tattoos?'

'I know how to do one,' says Carl. 'My dad taught me.'

'Do me one,' says another boy.

'Me too,' says David.

Jack nods. 'And me.'

'Let's get them all the same,' says Si. 'So we can recognise each other when we're old and wrinkled.'

'What'll we get?'

'A swallow?'

'A ship?'

'A shark?'

'A mermaid?'

They snort with laughter. 'I'm not that good. I could try something like a compass,' says Carl.

'A star?' says Jack.

They mull the idea over.

'I'm up for a star,' says Si.

'The Pole Star,' says David, 'so we'll always find our way home.'

They raid the ship for the things they need. Needle and thread from the cupboard with the sailmaker's kit. Some ink from the classroom. No one bothers them tonight: they will be gone tomorrow. Carl lights a match and burns the end of the needle to sterilise it.

'Where do you want it?' he asks.

The boys opt for the inside of their forearms. Jack draws the stars on their skin, and Carl digs the needle into their flesh. The alcohol acts as a painkiller.

Carl stands back and surveys his handiwork. 'Not bad. Now who's going to do me?'

*

129

It is their last hour. The captain-superintendent is congratu-
lating them. At their feet are their own canvas sea bags that
they have cut and stitched with the sailmaker. Jack is sure
he has grown by at least two inches since being here. He
stands tall, with his chest out, his eyes fixed ahead.

'Without men – yes men – like you, this country would be
in trouble. The Merchant Navy and the Royal Navy make Britain
the mightiest force on the sea. Between us we keep the planes
flying and the tanks rolling. We bring the fuel for the vehicles.
Why, we bring the vehicles themselves. Who is crossing the
Atlantic every second of the day? Who is bringing the food?
The ammunition? The troops? Us, that's who. And now you
will too, cadets. They're crying out for men like you to crew
the ships that keep the country going, and Hitler and his Nazis
at bay. I know you won't let us down. Make no mistake: your
training has been tough because it's tough out there. But each
of you is a credit to Training Ship *Constance*. I have faith that
you are Britain's lifeline. Our own king, George VI, has spoken
of it. Without you Britain will not win this war.'

After passing out, Jack is at last ready to face the past. He knows
that his life was on a downward spiral, dragging his sister into
its vortex. He heads for London to make his peace with his
mother, Carl by his side. The city of his childhood is still smoking,
still torn. His neighbourhood looks different through his
seaman's eyes. It is more damaged than he remembers. So
many vacant buildings, scorch marks around the shattered
windows, so many piles of rubble and debris, it is difficult to
see how things will ever be right again. Children climb among
the ruins, still looking for shrapnel, no doubt, still living on the
edge of existence. Jack feels years older, although in reality it
has only been months. He is not the boy who left here all those
weeks ago. He feels his clothes pressing against his skin, thick
and warm. He sees the ragged clothes and blackened feet of
the children around him, and flexes his toes in his boots.

Carl leaves him on Southwark Street, so he can visit his

own family. Jack heads for Drummond Road. He knows his mother will be pleased when she opens the door and sees him standing there in his new uniform. He can picture the wide look of surprise on her tired face. He can't wait to tell her what he has learnt – how one day he could become an officer. He wonders whether time away will have had the same result for Betsy – shown her how life can be. He smiles to himself as he imagines visiting her with his mother, maybe even tomorrow. How the three of them will be reunited.

He passes many gaps between the once-terraced houses that his neighbours used to live in. As he reaches his own house, he blinks and swallows. There is another empty space. His home is gone. He can see through to the backyard, where the hump of the Anderson shelter is still visible. But the house is not there. He walks between the inner walls of what used to be the living room and kitchen, stumbling on the uneven ground as he looks up and around in bewilderment. The fireplace, where his mother used to warm his clothes, is now just an exposed, blackened chimney. There is nothing left among the debris to say who once lived here, not even a shoe. Whatever was not destroyed has already been taken by the wanderers and pilferers, behaving as he would have behaved only months ago.

The shelter is dented and the door has gone, but someone has been tending some thin and sickly-looking vegetable plants. Jack hears a noise. For a moment, his heart leaps: a grubby girl is clambering over the rubble beyond the backyard. Betsy? But as he approaches, he sees that she is only a toddler. She looks up at him, her eyes empty and expressionless.

'Do you know what happened to the woman who lived here?' he asks. She shakes her head and steps back, stumbling a little on the uneven broken bricks. Still watching him, she sniffs, wiping her hand across her nose. The snot leaves pale streaks in the grime on her cheeks. Another child calls her name and she runs to him, tottering across the crumbled bricks. Jack calls out: 'Wait! Do you know what happened?'

The boy shrugs, holding out his hand for the girl to grasp. 'Bosch, in't it. Killin' everyone.'

'Do you know if anyone survived?'

The boy shakes his head. 'No, mister. We're not from round 'ere.'

'Where are you from?'

The boy grips his sister tighter and backs away. 'We're from where we're from, mister.'

'Do you know the Stoogleys?'

The boy shakes his head.

'The Taylors? Or the Browns?'

The boy shakes his head again and bends down to tug at a piece of timber he has spotted that might be useful. It is stuck fast and he gives up, turning back to eye Jack, who has started to knock on neighbours' doors.

Most of the houses are empty, their inhabitants away at work or volunteering or fighting, but Jack notices a curtain twitch at one window. He raises his fist and hammers on the door, watched at a safe distance by the boy and his sister.

'Sorry to bother you,' he says to the woman who answers. 'I'm trying to find Elizabeth Sullivan? Alfred Sullivan's wife?'

'Oh dear,' says the woman, nervously primping her hair, taking in the smart young man in front of her. 'Oh dear, oh dear.'

Jack's mouth is dry. 'I saw the house . . .' he says.

The woman leans out and glances up the street, as if hoping the house might have reappeared there. 'I'm afraid it was a direct hit, dearie,' she says. 'There weren't nothing left. We have to take comfort in the fact that it was so quick. Lizzie wouldn't have felt a thing.'

'How long ago?'

'Two or three weeks back. We've had a proper hammering, mind, so it's hard to remember exact.' She stretches out a comforting hand. 'Family, were you?'

Jack looks down at the ground as he nods. He cannot squeeze the words out.

'Glad she's got some family left. Poor Lizzie. Husband and oldest son missing doing their duty in France. Daughter sent to safety in the country, and the one son she had left, who should have been a help to her in her darkest hour, was a good-for-nothing little hooligan. Ran away. Upped and left her all alone.' She is warming to her theme, glad to speak of something other than the death of a neighbour. 'Mind you, he was always a bad one that. Not an honest bone in his body. We all told her he was a troublemaker, but she always stuck up for him. Him and his friends brought the neighbourhood right down. Wasn't safe to leave anything lying around . . . I suppose you can't choose your family – no offence meant, dearie – but if he'd stuck around and pulled his weight, maybe she wouldn't have been so tired that night and she might have got out of the house in time . . .'

He wants to say he's not that person any more, but the words won't come out. He never meant for his mother to die like that. Alone. He feels the bile rise in his throat, and he holds his hand over his mouth before turning to throw up.

The woman is shocked and hurries inside, slamming the door behind her.

Jack stands, wiping his mouth. The boy and girl stare vacantly at him from the other side of the street.

'What are you looking at?' he says. 'Scram. Go on!'

And they run through the ruins of his home, skittering away across the wasteland beyond like feral cats.

CHAPTER 9

The boys from Training Ship *Constance* disperse across the United Kingdom to seek work on board the merchant ships. It is not hard to find: enemy U-boats claim more victims in the Atlantic every day, but the supply chain needs to be kept going. Carl, Jack, David, and Si head for Liverpool. There is nowhere else for Jack to go now: the Merchant Navy is all he has.

The train stops and starts, pulling slowly away from the nameless stations, their signs removed to confuse the enemy. Jack does not tell Carl what the neighbour said, just that his mother is gone. 'At least Betsy will be safe,' says Carl, trying to cheer his friend up.

Jack nods. His shame is deep and painful, made more so by the fact that his orphaned sister must feel so alone wherever she is. He cannot help thinking that the woman was right, and that if he had stayed, his mother might still be alive. He wonders whether Betsy will think the same. 'Do you reckon anyone will have told her? Visited or written to her?' he says.

'Who knows. There's that many people scattered across the country . . .'

'How will I find her?'

'I'll help you . . .' He feels Carl's solid hand on his shoulder. 'Listen, don't blame yourself,' he says. 'There's nothing you could have done.'

But Jack stares into the distance, lost in thought. 'Maybe you can never drag yourself out of the shit-heap,' he says.

*

At Lime Street station, they ask directions to the Sailors' Home, where the Merchant Navy pool is. The porter points along the road. 'Look for the Pearly Gates,' he says. 'Can't miss 'em.'

It is not a long walk, although it feels it, with the weight of their sea bags on their shoulders. The city is another London: craters and rubble, twisted metal and broken glass. The sounds are of brushes sweeping and the coughing of hollow-eyed people living among dust. Jack is not alone in his loneliness.

The Home is an imposing building, with turrets above its four corners, and hundreds of windows reflecting the shattered city. It is so close to the docks that they can see the Mersey – a slippery eel, its skin glinting in the sun – and the masts of the ships coming and going. The sound of the cranes creaking as they unload cargo transports Jack back to happier days on the Thames docks.

The Home's arched door has an impressive decorated iron surround and gate that the four boys stand and stare at open-mouthed. There are golden mermaids and Neptune's trident, a latticework of ropes, and, at the top, great fish entwined with wheels and flags, bugles and shells, and topped with a king's crown. They hoist their sea bags up on to their shoulders again and make their way up the steps.

At the top, a group of seamen are pushing their way out of the door. The steps are wide enough for them all to pass, but when they see the younger men, they stop their chattering and start to sneer. One, a short, wiry man with a gruff voice and a surly face, eyeballs Jack. Jack braces his shoulder as the man slams into it. 'Watch where you're going, pretty boy,' says the man, stopping on the step.

But instead of squaring up to him, Jack moves away. 'Sorry, sir,' he says.

The sailor's friends cackle with laughter. 'Ooh, "sir", is it now, Mart?'

Mart breaks into a lurid grin. Half of his teeth are missing and his face is leathery and tough, scoured by sea winds. Without taking his eyes off Jack, he turns his head sideways and spits something brown that splats noisily on the pavement. 'I do like the polite ones best,' he says. Then he makes his way down the steps. His mates follow, still laughing.

'Come on,' says Carl, ushering them through the door. They find themselves in a huge hall with a galleried landing rising for five floors above their heads. Each landing is protected by painted iron railings. It is interminably noisy, the sound of footsteps and men calling and doors banging echoes through the air. There is the musty smell of an institution mingled with unwashed bodies and not helped by the fact that it is extremely warm due to the glass ceiling, which intensifies the heat and light of summer outside.

A thickset Irishman directs them to a room where they can register. It is cheap for a sailor to find a bed with breakfast included in the morning – there are numerous such places in every town or city with a port. 'Although the breakfast tastes like shite, and make sure you lock your door at night,' the man adds, his voice a warning. 'And if you go out, be sure to be back by ten. That's when we close the gates.'

The wood-panelled rooms are modelled on a ship's cabin: cramped, with an iron bedstead, a small table, and just enough room to put a bag down. The bathroom is communal, and there is a large mess room downstairs that reeks of inedible food. Every corner of the building is filled with growling seamen of all ages, sizes, shapes, and colours.

In a spacious room on the ground floor, the boys find the register where the jobs are given out. There is a long counter, in front of which is an impatient queue of men. Along the counter is wire netting, and behind it are two hassled-looking men.

'What's the netting for?' says Jack as they take their place in the queue.

'You'll see,' says the man in front, without turning around.

As if on cue, there's a commotion, and a swarthy man starts to rattle the metal, yelling at the men behind the counter. It is hard to make out what he is saying as he has a thick accent.

136

His hands and face are black with coal dust. It is clear from his actions that the man is extremely cross about the ship he has just come from. Eventually, after much rattling and shouting, he stomps out of the room, and the queue shuffles up.

Jack makes it to the counter first. 'Yes?' says the man on the other side.

'We're from Training Ship *Constance*,' says Jack, indicating at his friends, who squish in closer.

'*La-di-da*,' says a man behind them, the sweet smell of stale alcohol on his breath.

'That's enough,' hisses the man behind the counter.

The man with the rotten breath slams his fist against the netting next to the boys. It shakes and pings alarmingly.

'I told you to back off,' says the counter man. 'Or you won't be going through today.'

The sailor mutters, but retreats. 'What are you looking at?' he says to Jack.

The man behind the counter studies their papers, glancing again at the boys, then shuffles the papers into a neat pile and hands them back. 'You can all go through,' he says, indicating the next-door room. They thank him, but he hurries them on before more violence erupts, nodding at another man who guards the entrance to let them past.

There are three more counters in here: 'Firemen', 'Deck', and 'Catering', also protected by wire mesh. The boys head for the Deck counter. There are more men behind it, sitting and standing, checking papers and peering out at them from the shadows. The man behind the pen looks Jack up and down.

'Experience?' he asks.

'Three months on TS *Constance*,' says Jack.

The man harrumphs and runs his finger down a list in a large ledger. He stops by one of the names. 'The *Aurora* is looking for two apprentices,' he says. He looks up at one of the faces in the semi-darkness, the man nods slowly. He is puffing on a pipe.

137

Jack pulls Carl forward. 'My mate's from the *Constance*. In fact, we all are,' he says, indicating Si and David.

The man with the pipe leans forward and speaks in the man's ear. 'Only two apprentices, I'm afraid.'

'Oy. Take what you get,' says the man who was behind them before. 'Can't go making demands just because you've done some fancy training.'

Men lined up at the other desks start to mumble and stare at them. The man behind the counter continues to run his finger through the list.

'Apprentice and deck boy needed on the *Pluckston*.'

Si and David look at each other. Deck boy is a bit of a step down when you've put in all the training, but they'd like to stick together. 'Where do we sign?' asks David.

The man scrawls in his book. 'Papers?' He holds out his hand, checking their certificates as he finishes scribbling in his book. 'Right. Your first set of ship's articles, I believe. Check and sign.' The man hands them more papers. He points at a door marked 'Doctor'. 'Get the Doc to sign you off, and you're done.'

There is a wizened old sea dog with a mop of shaggy hair and a straggly grey beard already waiting to see the doctor. He grins at Jack, a gummy toothless smile. Another gnarly old man comes out of the doctor's room. As he passes the sea dog, he pulls the false teeth from his gums with a sucking noise and hands them over. The man swipes them over his top and slips them into his own mouth, sucking and clicking them into place. He raps on the door and enters. He reappears three minutes later and sidles away with his friend.

It is Jack's turn. He enters the room. The doctor is in front of him, a rotund man leaning over a desk. He holds out a hand without even looking up. 'Papers,' he says.

Jack hands the papers over. 'Drop your trousers,' the doctor says, pushing his glasses up his bulbous nose.

He gropes Jack's balls: first one, then the other. 'Cough,' he says. His hands are cold and clammy. 'Cough.' It is uncomfortable and humiliating, and Jack can't wait to get out of there. 'Open!' says the doctor, peering inside Jack's mouth. 'Well, pull your trousers up, boy,' he adds irritably. And it's as easy as that.

Jack spends an uneasy night listening to men calling to each other, and metal clanging, and footsteps ringing out. He is grateful for the advice to keep his door locked: more than once, it rattles. He does not want anyone to see him weep for his mother. If only he had stayed, he might have got her to a shelter. But who is he kidding? He would have been out on the streets with Stoog, and his mother would still have died in an empty house with no one to hear her cries. Betsy is better off wherever she is. Without him. He stares into the darkness, willing himself to forget her until the pale morning light glows in the frosted windows.

It is a relief to be down at the docks after breakfast, where business grinds on among the stench of coal and burning oil and the bombed warehouses. Small gangs of snotty children wander about or sit and watch the ships and the men come and go. There's no need for the boys to find an outfitter as they already have their kit from the training ship. Their articles don't specify they need anything more.

The *Aurora* and the *Pluckston* are moored within sight of each other, but they could not be more different. The *Aurora* is bright and clean. Her cargo is being loaded neatly by the stevedores into her holds, her crew is orderly and calm. The *Pluckston* is a grimy tramp ship. Her crew seem chaotic and bad-tempered, and there is much arguing over orders.

'Time to say goodbye,' says Si.

'For now,' says Carl.

David slaps Carl and Jack on the back. Jack clasps their hands and smiles, but he bites his bottom lip too. It is a wrench after so many weeks together, and as Jack watches them walk slowly away he has a terrible feeling that he will never see them again.

The *Aurora*'s hull lies deep in the water, the load line that shows she is almost full to capacity only just visible. Two men are dangling over the side on a ladder strung between a rope that is cleated to the deck. The sailors' backs are to the boys. They are painting the side of the ship with thick grey paint. The smell mingles with the stench of salt, burning, and sewage.

Suddenly they hear a voice. 'Aha! Fresh blood,' says a man in a peaked cap who is looking over the railings. 'You must be our new apprentices? Come aboard! Come aboard!' The cargo ship is very different to TS *Constance*. She is polished and scrubbed, but mostly metal, not much wood in sight. She has masts fore and aft, and a large funnel in the middle, behind the square bulk of bridge, where the captain keeps watch.

'I'm Russell. First mate,' says the man. 'Welcome.' He sticks out his hand. He is a genial-looking man, young, with a neatly-trimmed beard. 'You must be our new apprentices. Hope you last longer than the last lot.' He shakes their hands. 'You'll be needing the Bose, I should think. Bosun!'

'On my way,' a voice answers him from somewhere down below. They hear coughing and swearing, and then, 'Ah, the pretty boy, is it?' Jack's heart plummets as a familiar face appears on deck.

'You lot know each other already?' says Russell.

'You could say that,' says Jack. Carl throws him a warning look.

'Mart's our bosun. He'll show you to your cabin. Point out where everything is. Anything you're not sure of, ask him. Anything he's not sure of, he'll ask me. Although I think Mart knows more about seamanship than I ever will.' Russell tips his head in deference to the bosun.

With a sinking feeling Jack follows Mart into the belly of the ship. It is another sunny summer's day, and inside the ship is already warm and smells of hot metal. Mart mutters along in front of them, clearing his nostrils every now and then with a deep snort.

140

Jack is pleased to discover that he is sharing a cabin with Carl. The cabin is small, barely big enough for the three of them to stand in, but it has bunks and is positively luxurious compared with what they are used to. Mart is insufferably close, and Jack can feel the vibration as he clears his nostrils again. 'You might think you're the business, but you won't get no special treatment from me.' He snorts again. 'Last apprentices couldn't hack it.' He spits the words out like phlegm. 'One disappeared, the other pleaded to be let go. Not prepared, you see. Don't matter how much training you think you've had, the sea will pick out the lily-livered bastards from the true sailors sooner than you can say "Bosch".'

Jack ignores the bosun, hoisting his bag up on to the top bunk. Carl chucks his on the bottom. There is one chair and a fold-down table. There is a sink with a bucket underneath to catch the water. The porthole is painted black, but at least they can open it. There is no light bulb in the fitting. 'Hope you're not scared of the dark, my lovelies,' says Mart.

He sidles past them back out into the corridor. 'Best follow me if you want to know where everything is.' He leads them to the forecastle at the front of the ship, where her movement is most pronounced. 'Me and Grifter's cabin,' Mart says, indicating a tiny room with one bunk in it. He points at the other cabins as they walk: 'Able seamen Burts and Sheldon. And here's the firemen and greasers.' Two men scowl down at them from their bunks. The other berths are empty. They move past the chartroom, the master's cabin, the first mate's cabin, the mess room, the galley, the heads. 'Sparks and Chippy in there. Stokehold down there.' He indicates another ladder that leads below the waterline to the boiler room. 'Purser, steward, cook, galley boy.' Jack is beginning to sweat. The noise and the smell is different to *Constance*, more metallic and suffocating – as is the sensation of tidal water rather than canal beneath his feet. 'The Chief and his men.' Jack looks blank. 'Engineers, boy. Don't they teach you nothing on those fancy training ships?' Jack needs to get back on deck. The

141

heat, the dark, Mart's breath, all these men crammed into this ship are making his stomach turn.

They burst into sunlight moments later. Mart clicks his fingers and one of the seamen hands Jack a bucket. Jack holds his face over it, but Mart cackles and shakes his head. 'I want her ship-shape before we sail,' he says, as another seaman hands them some cloths.

There is a lot of it to polish, but polishing is something they've been trained for. They quickly get into a rhythm. Carl works behind Jack, rubbing, while Jack loosens the dirt first. Caustic soda has been added to the water to make the brass shine. Jack's hands sting and his nails start to turn soft and brown. They have almost finished when Russell appears. 'Nice work, boys,' he says.

Relieved, they sit back on their heels, admiring the golden sheen. But not for long. Mart hands them a pot of paint: 'Now paint them.'

'But that's black,' says Jack.

'Smart as well as pretty,' says Mart.

'But . . .'

'Just get on with it.'

The paint is thick and heavy. It makes Jack's head ache. Next they scrub the deck down and then check the limited woodwork, sanding down the scuffed bits, varnishing where needed. Occasionally, Mart swaggers past, inspecting their work and spitting over the side of the ship. 'Redo the paint on the load hatch. Oil these davits. Check the lifeboats. Stow those ropes. Not like that! What a disgrace.' On and on it goes.

Jack's whole body throbs, and his nostrils are burning. He glances at the bridge, wonders who might be in there, looking out. 'Fancy a break in the wheelhouse, boy? Go on then.' Mart hands Jack another rag. 'You can scrub the floor and polish the brass in there too.' Jack starts to remember The Barker with fondness.

*

142

They stumble to the mess, ravenous. It is a comfortable room, meticulously clean, and very warm. At one end is the galley. Vast silver cauldrons steam on the cooker. The cook is shaking something in a frying pan. The smell of food permeates everything. There is a galley boy who looks about the same age as Betsy, but who must be older, all arms and legs like a newborn calf. He bears the brunt of Cook's temper as he rushes about, wiping and cleaning, fetching knives and checking pots inside and on top of the oven. He also has to keep a load of water on the boil, ready to make cups of tea or to pour into buckets for washing things down.

The long table is laid with cutlery and mugs. There is even a white cloth spread over it. There is already a group of men sitting at one end, their forks clattering against their plates. When Carl and Jack enter the room, the men stop and stare at them, but only for a couple of seconds. They return to their food. They speak a language that the boys cannot understand. The galley boy indicates where they can sit. 'I'm Fred,' he says. He notices them staring at the men at the end of the table. 'Norwegians,' he adds as he puts their food in front of them. 'Same as the Old Man. But them's engineers.'

More men cram into the room as Carl and Jack greedily swallow their food down in lumps. It is strange being surrounded by so many men after being on the *Constance*. The voices are deep and gruff. There's no formality – no grace or silence or passing the plates along – as they shovel their food in and glug from their mugs and bang the table with their large fists. They have obviously sailed together before. Mart holds court in the middle, relishing every mouthful of food.

First Mate Russell enters the room. He doesn't sit down. The men stop eating and talking. Smoke curls up from their mugs. Russell smiles and nods at Carl and Jack. The men pick food from their teeth. Another man appears behind him: the man with the pipe from the shadows in the Sailors' Home.

'The Old Man,' says Fred in a whisper.

The master is younger than Jack imagined he would be.

His thick blond hair is slicked back. He occasionally draws on his pipe, the bowl glowing as he does so, lighting up his face before it plunges back into darkness. He is gaunt, the cheekbones pronounced, the eyes deep and unreadable. When he speaks, his accent is pronounced but easy to understand.

'Well done on passing your medicals, men,' he says. 'I am happy to have you all back. And welcome to our new apprentices. I am Captain Andersson. I trust Bose has sorted you out.' Mart glares at them. The boys nod. 'Now. Olsen's got a present for us all. Especially from the Ministry of War Transport, to help us on our way.' Excited murmurs. The purser appears with a bundle of clothes. Andersson continues: 'I'm sure you all want to know where we're off to, but you'll find out soon enough. I thank you for sticking with me. It means much.' He looks at Russell, who nods at him. 'Right,' he says. 'Sorry for an interruption. Enjoy your food. We sail at 0600 hours.'

He leaves the room.

Mart helps Olsen distribute the clothes. 'Looks like we've got ourselves some fine thick clothes to keep us cosy and warm,' he says, holding them up.

'Another Atlantic run?' says one of the engineers.

'Canada, for sure,' says another.

'Never been given woolly coats before.'

'Maybe they're finally showing a little appreciation.'

'More like danger money.'

Mart snorts and spits into his mug. 'None of that nonsense. I haven't lost a ship yet,' he says.

Jack tries his new coat on. It is heavy, and lined with sheep's wool. It certainly is warm – too warm for a summer evening below deck. There are also gloves, scarves, strange hats with only slits for eyes, and thick woollen socks.

'What's it like, Canada?' he asks.

'All right if you like the snow.'

'And wolves,' says one of the men.

'I'd like to see a wolf,' says Carl.

'You want to see a wolf, do you?' Mart hisses at him. 'I'll tell you about wolves. They're like the Nazis. They hunt in packs. And when the snow comes down and the wind is screaming and food's scarce on the ground, then they creep along on silent paws. You can't see them. But still they come and when they grin their grin is bloody and when they leap you have time only to glimpse the redness of their mouths and the blackness of their eyes and then – snap!'

He snaps his fingers, and Jack and Carl jerk back with a start.

Mart begins to laugh. It is a laugh that gathers momentum and becomes a throaty cackle. Some of the other sailors join in.

'Come on, now,' says Cook. 'No need to scare them on their maiden voyage.' And the men laugh again, and Mart spits into his mug.

'Make no mistake, boys,' he says. 'The wolves are out there, waiting for us.'

Jack lies open-eyed in the dark, trying not to think of his mother or father, or of Walt, hoping that Betsy is safe wherever she is, wondering how he will ever find her, and if he does, whether she will blame him for abandoning them all. He falls into an uneasy sleep, and it feels only minutes before Mart is shouting through the door: 'Show a leg, Peggies!'

Dawn is breaking, pale streaks of light brightening on the horizon. The dock is alive with noise. The very last of their cargo is being loaded. Mart directs it into the hold. Carl and Jack have removed the guardrail to make it easier to swing the crates on to the ship. They must remember to put it back again.

'What are we carrying?' Jack asks Burts, the burly man who he recognises as one of Mart's friends from the steps.

'Supplies. Boots. Coats. Wool. Military vehicles.'

'It's a bloody floating haberdasher's,' Mart says. He spits another brown glob over the side.

'What do the Americans need that for?'

'What's it to a couple of Peggies? Get on and stow those ropes.'

They set to work, heaving and coiling, battening down hatches. Burts lowers the derricks. Mart shouts orders. He seems to be in charge of everyone. Soon everything is folded and stowed neatly into its place. Carl hoists the ensign of the merchant marine, the Red Duster – the red flag with the Union Jack in the corner – and the Blue Peter flag, blue with a white square in the middle of it, that indicates they are about to get under sail.

'Stand by fore and aft,' says Russell.

The ropes are large and weighty and stiff in their hands. In the water below, the squat tugs beetle around, their pilots craning their necks as they concentrate on manoeuvring the *Aurora* into open water. They wear dark coats, grimy with coal dust. Their boats are rusty and worn, huge coils of rope lie curled on their decks. The tugs burp black smoke with the effort, but though they are small, they are also strong and have soon pulled Jack's ship into the less crowded water of the river, where the current runs faster.

The command comes: 'Let go tug ropes.' The deck buzzes with activity. The tugs drift away from the *Aurora*, their pilots waving and tipping their flat caps as they swing back to the docks. The *Aurora* releases a plume of black smoke as she slices her own passage across the Mersey, past the other ships coming and going in the shipping lane, as they head towards open water.

Nothing prepares Jack for his first day at sea. Not O'Brien or The Barker, not Mr Turner or Officer Scott. Not the mucking around in boats or lifeboat drill or any amount of knots. The bile of seasickness sits in his throat. Fred the galley boy is the worst: he vomits so much during the first two days that Cook makes him wear a bucket around his neck.

The only thing that keeps their minds off it is work, and

146

there is plenty of that. Jack and Carl are given the early-morning watch with First Mate Russell: 4 a.m. until 8 a.m. Then it's eight hours off, before watch again from four in the afternoon until eight in the evening. Then sleep until the early watch begins again. The clanging of the ship's bell divides their days into half-hours, just as it did on the *Constance*.

The *Aurora* slips quietly, efficiently into routine; Jack and Carl already a part of it. On Sundays they have inspection by Andersson, who appears in his dark peaked cap, which is usually a little skewwhiff. He checks the dust and polish, and examines their hands and feet. 'Someone's got to look after you,' he says in his clipped accent. His eyes are crinkled at the edges from where he squints into the sun as he sucks on his pipe.

Since no one is allowed to smoke on deck in blackout, the mess room becomes a smog of cigarette smoke. The men play cards amid the blue vapour, which drifts around them like wraiths, shovelling their winnings into secret places. It is August, and the sunshine feels relentless. It burns the moisture from the air, leaves salt stuck to everything, and makes their skin dry.

The men strip off their tops when they are down below and sit around the table scratching at their bare chests and their sticky hair.

'Like what you see, my pretty one?' Mart says when he notices Jack staring at the tattoos that are inked across most of his wiry body, briefly reminding him of another time, a gold-toothed sailor. Jack turns away. But Mart is in a chatty mood. 'Look here,' he says. 'You can read me like a book. This one's to show I've crossed the line.' He points at a green and black turtle swimming on his left shoulder blade. 'That's the Equator to those from the good ship *Constance*,' he adds. He lifts his right forearm to point at a blue anchor. 'This here's the Atlantic.' Most of the men have this. 'And this,' he says, pointing at a dragon curling its tail over his right shoulder, 'this is Ernie. He's a Chinaman.'

There are other marks too. A compass on his left bicep. The

words 'hold' and 'fast' across his knuckles. On one ankle he's got a pig, and on the other a rooster.

Jack touches the star on his forearm, aware of how minute it is compared to the bosun's. 'How long have you been in the Merchant Navy?' he asks.

Mart snorts. He looks around the men at the table. 'Merchant bloody Navy!'

The men all laugh. Jack turns red from the neck up.

'Only a navy when it suits 'em.'

'You youngsters don't know how lucky you are.'

'You lot with your new register and new clothes.'

'Mollycoddled, that's what I call it.'

'We're no more mollycoddled than anyone else,' says Jack.

Mart doesn't look at him, just carries on. 'Spoon-fed and spineless,' he says.

The heat is getting to Jack, and, combined with Mart's taunting, he feels the tension begin to rise. 'Say that to my face,' he says, pushing himself up on to his feet, the chair scraping across the floor, stopping all conversation.

In the silence, Jack hears Mart's bones crack as he too stands slowly up from the table. The bosun pulls himself upright so that he is almost as tall as Jack. Although he is skinny, he is as sinewy as a stray dog, his body as tight as a drum. His hard blue eyes glitter as they search deep into Jack's dark and furious ones. 'Are you really going to fight me, boy?' he says.

'You don't know nothing about me,' says Jack. 'I'm not spineless or spoon-fed.' He tightens his hands into fists as his heart thumps in his throat.

Mart leans forward. 'You are if I say you are,' he says, jabbing his finger against Jack's chest with each word. 'And if you raise a fist to anyone on my ship, you'll be off it before you can say "pretty".'

'Jack,' says Carl, a warning in his voice.

The bell clangs. A thousand images flash through Jack's head: of a bracelet, of his mother's disappointment, of his sister's wide eyes, of Stoog's raised fist, of The Barker's hand against his windpipe, of the people who have clothed and trained him, of a gold-toothed sailor who told him to change his life. He lets his fist drop. Mart snorts and turns to spit. 'Your watch, Peggy,' he says.

The *Aurora* steams up the west coast, through the Irish channel, between Ireland and England. This is the safest part of her journey – in home waters. Once they clear the north of Ireland, they will head out into open sea. Jack's red, raw hands begin to harden, as do his muscles, and he sleeps like the dead. His family have stopped visiting him in his dreams. It is as if he has let them go. The nausea has passed. He watches the world turn rainbow colours as the sun rises, and mythical creatures appear through the sea mist: dolphins break the water in silence, twisting and turning across their bow; stumpy puffins with their wide, colourful beaks fly past; gannets plummet into the sea, pale streaks beneath the water. Jack has only ever known buildings and brick and rubble, yet here pale yellow beaches are strung between shining black cliffs. The water slides past, now grey, now green, now blue. And in the distance, the peaks of Scotland are purple in the haze.

And then the land slips away until it is just a dot of clouds, until that too disappears, and there is only silvery water as far as the eye can see. Mart growls at them: 'Keep a sharp lookout for tin fish.' The threat of torpedoes increases minute by minute. The men mutter around the mess table. They are confused because ships heading to America or Canada usually head out westwards across the Atlantic, but the *Aurora*'s course seems to be taking them further north.

The waves become choppier. Routine becomes rhythm. They wake for the dawn. They keep watch. Jack feels a flutter of panic. They are alone on a wide, wide ocean. Staring so hard at the sea makes him cross-eyed. Occasionally they pass other ships returning the way they have come. Jack's stomach lurches every time before they confirm it is an Allied ship. He is ready to sound the alarm bell at any second.

149

When they are not on watch, Mart never lets up. He tests Jack on his meteorology, makes Carl go over his hitches. In the mess they fill themselves with steaming porridge and bread and marmalade. They scrub and polish the deck. They run any repairs, and if there's time, they play games on deck in the summer sunshine. As they draw further north, the hours of night shorten until there is barely any darkness. They are glad that the porthole is painted black. They shut themselves in and try to sleep, even though it is still bright outside. Their bodies soon adjust.

They don't come across the men from the stokehold much, apart from when they appear on deck with buckets of cold seawater to try to wash the coal from their faces. Their bodies are pasty in the daylight. Carl and Jack chip and scrape, wash and paint, sew and splice, as the men talk in their own language and cough the dust from their lungs. Sometimes Russell calls Jack to the wheelhouse and lets him steer the ship. But most of the time Jack is on deck, keeping lookout in the sun and wind and rain, following Mart's orders.

On the third day without seeing land, Andersson calls everyone to the mess. 'You will have noticed we are too far north to be making for Canada.' The men murmur. 'But we are going to make up a convoy. Just a convoy of a different sort.' Andersson sucks on his pipe. The smell of tobacco mingles with the smell of sweat and the stew that's cooking in the stove.

'Some of you will have guessed it already,' he says. 'We go to Russia, men. We assemble in Hvalfjordur tomorrow.'

A hush descends. The only sound is the creak and hum of the ship.

The west coast of Iceland rises bleakly from the water. In the background the mountains are sprinkled with snow. The *Aurora* steams into a fjord packed with ships: converted whalers, armoured Royal Navy ships, and merchant vessels from Canada, Belgium, Panama, America.

'I thought the Russians were the enemy?' Jack says to Russell as they stand on the deck and watch the land slide past.

'Not any more, my friend. Not any more.'

The morning after they arrive, the old man allows them to go ashore. There are plenty of boats ferrying crew from ship to shore and to other ships, where friends wait to play cards or dice. There is a rowing race going on: the coxes yelling and coaxing their men on, a crowd on shore and on the ships calling and cheering. Seals bob in the water between them, their inquisitive eyes appearing and disappearing.

The boys revel in the chance to stretch their legs and walk on land again. It takes a while for the ground to stop swaying like a ship. The locals avoid the incomers' eyes: Iceland has been occupied by the British, and there is an awkward tension in the air. Sailors from across the world roam around the Nissen huts: Africa, India, the West Indies, Eastern Europe, America, Canada, and China. The whiff of opium cuts through the smell of oil.

Andersson instructs his men to avoid the large beer hall, where fights are always breaking out. Instead, the crew from the *Aurora* climb up into the hills, which are green and open, with sweeping views. They follow a track along a steep canyon above a river. Warm pools steam into the cool air. They reach a waterfall that crashes down slippery rocks. Above them, white-chested birds squawk and fight. Small shaggy ponies trot past, foals in tow. Sometimes the ground is bare and rocky like another planet, a moonscape.

The engineers and some of the stokers are with them. They perch on the rocks. The Norwegians are pleased to be out in the open. Two of them don't speak much English, but the Chief breathes the air deep into his lungs and says, 'Fresh and clean. Like my homeland.'

'You miss it?' says Jack.

The Chief nods. 'One day I'll go back,' he says.

They watch the small boats ferrying men miles below around

the fjord. In the distance the open sea glistens. The engineers yawn and lie back, let the sun warm their pallid faces.

'You like our ship?' asks the Chief.

'Sometimes I think I'd like to be down with you lot in the warmth instead of on lookout.'

'Ha!' The Chief translates for the others. When they have stopped laughing, he says, 'You are so naïve. Just little boys. You come work with us for a day and see if you don't like lookout.' The other men nod and mutter in agreement.

'We cross the Atlantic safe for now. But we hear them waiting. All the time we hear them. We hear them explode out there under the water. It is luck. When it do come, we have no chance. We go up.' He raises his hand in the air. 'Boom! Like a magic vanishing trick. You will not find us. No one will ever find us.'

One of the stokers says, 'You think they survive longer in that water? That water is so cold. It turns blood to ice in a moment. Only difference between our death and yours is that we won't know about it.'

'You'll get a minute before your arms and legs freeze and turn black and your heart turns to ice and crumbles.'

'Ha! So poetic you Estonians,' says the Chief.

It's the first time Jack has really thought about what it might be like to go down on a ship. Mart has kept them so busy.

'What's Mart's story?' he says.

'Mart is good man. He keep us safe. He knows the sea better than any I've sailed with. He respect it.'

'Why else you think we stay on this ship? The Old Man and Bose, you couldn't get better.'

'You do what Mart says and you survive.'

'And the Old Man?' says Carl.

The Chief says something in his own language to the other men. They murmur their agreement. 'You'll all be glad of a Norwegian master when the cold sets in. If there's one thing we Norwegians know about, it is ice.'

*

The order finally comes to set sail. One of the merchant ships is Dutch, but the rest are British. They are surrounded by ships of the Royal Navy, prickly with guns: destroyers, minesweepers, anti-submarine trawlers – even an oiler.

Birds circle the convoy as it leaves the harbour. The sky is a mixture of deep blue turning to aquamarine as the sun grows stronger. The ships slide above their reflections on the glassy water. Birds fly up when disturbed, turning the air dark. Jack hears the beat of their wings against the air. He is glad to be moving on, with the throb of the ship beneath him and the groaning and creaking, and even Mart's barked instructions.

The *Aurora* has to stay in convoy with the other merchant ships, moving together in formation. This means that the entire crew from the stokehold up has to concentrate much harder. The bridge is a studious place of charts and checks. They watch the commodore's ship for its signals via flags run up its halliards, or flashes of its Aldis lamp. In the distance, the grey Royal Navy escorts slip in and out of sight.

They steam through the Denmark Strait, fierce and ragged Greenland to port, Iceland to starboard. Lumps of blue-white iceberg start to appear, snowy islands that are drifting all the time, covered in clusters of seabirds. The convoy alters direction to avoid them. Russell lets Jack steer, showing him how to compensate for the wind, how the side of the ship is like a sail, how the engine and speed affect their passage.

Towards the end of their watch, the mist has cleared and visibility is good. They glide on, over the silver water. Jack's eyes are sore from staring. He doesn't know what to expect, just knows that if he misses something important it could be the difference between life and death. He scans the water. Something catches his eye: a huge shape looming beneath the surface. It disappears for a moment, but then it is back, near the surface, grey and sinister. His heart starts to thump. He reaches for the bell and starts to ring it wildly. Mart and Russell come running. Jack points at the shape, and as he

153

does so, it rises slowly out of the waves and he hears a shooshing sound and a fine jet of water sprays into the air, the drops shimmering in the haze. Its black back glitters in the light, its tail flips up in a salute and then it dives.

'Worried it's going to shower us to death?' says Burts, and Jack's cheeks burn. He's never seen a whale before. Some of the other seamen start to laugh, but Mart silences them with a raised hand. Jack's heart sinks. He prepares to be torn apart by the bosun. But Mart says, 'You'd do better to thank the boy instead of laughing like a bunch of old women. You might be grateful for those sharp eyes one day.'

The men swallow their laughs and, ashamed, get on with what they were doing. He turns to Jack. 'Well done, son,' he says. 'Keep your wits while the world throws what it's got at you, and we'll all get home safe.' He would rather they rang the bell every time than left it too late. He knows better than most about the terrors of convoys. He has crossed the Black Pit in the Atlantic many times, where the U-boats congregate, ready to attack.

In almost perpetual daylight, the sky remains bright and clear and the sea empty. It seems the Germans are not expecting the British to send supplies to Russia. Mart spits over the handrail, watching the other ships around them. 'Reminds me of Dunkirk,' he says.

'You were at Dunkirk?' Jack asks.

'Near enough.'

'Bose is being modest,' says Burts. 'He took his brother's fishing boat over.'

'Twice,' someone else adds.

'You had someone there, did you?' says Mart.

'My dad and brother.'

'Did they get out?'

Jack shakes his head. Mart puts a hand on Jack's shoulder and squeezes. 'You've got to let it go,' he says. 'This here ship's your home now, and this crew's your family.'

The convoy reaches Archangel without incident. The land sticks starkly out of the water as they make their way through the White Sea. They unload their cargo among the sullen Russians on the dilapidated wharf. No one speaks on the docks. The soldiers watch them suspiciously. There is nowhere onshore for entertainment. The only amusement is to marvel at the women piloting their own ships, a novelty to everyone on board the *Aurora*. The crew is delighted when it is time to leave. Mart watches Russia recede into the shimmering sea. 'Congratulations, lads,' he says. 'You've just completed the first convoy to the Soviet Union. A big thank-you from that Commie bastard Uncle Joe, and a slap on the back from our own Mister Churchill. Now let's get home.'

CHAPTER 10

Charlie

Charlie's carrier is scouring the Atlantic for the pride of the German fleet. His spirits were restored a little by seeing Olivia – and Captain Pearce has moved on at last so they have a decent captain once again. But it has been a long stretch. Some of his squadron have been lost. You never become numb to it. But it does become a kind of normality. One of the hardest things is when a plane takes off and never returns. Not to know whether the men you were sitting next to in the officers' mess only yesterday have been shot down or miscalculated their route and run out of fuel, or whether the plane has failed . . . Sometimes he likes to think they've just flown away, on to another land where there is no war, no torpedoes, no gunfire. But of course, there is no such place, apart from in his memory.

The German ship they are looking for is the largest battle-ship ever built. Only two nights ago she scored a big Nazi victory, sinking a ship carrying more than fourteen hundred British men. Only three survived. She is a threat to every convoy bringing supplies across the Atlantic for hungry, bombed Britain, and she needs to be stopped at all costs. But the ocean is great and wide, and sometimes it feels as if they're chasing the impossible. The pilots fly day and night, scanning the waves, but still there is no sign. Lookouts are on edge.

156

Everyone is on edge. The ships are constantly zigzagging to avoid the U-boats. No one is sleeping. No one is speaking.

Charlie has returned for some well-earned rest, struggling out of his clothes and into his bunk. It feels as if his head has only just hit the pillow when the call comes to action stations. The ready room is packed with men. The air is stale and warm. At last there is news.

'She's been spotted by an American pilot.'

'How far?'

'Half a day.'

Charlie's heart quickens. Only an hour or so in a plane.

The CO points at the chart. 'Last spotted here,' he says. 'The plan is to attack from all sides. Draw her fire. Confuse her. We're sending the first squadron up now. If they're unsuccessful, then you'll go.' He nods at Charlie and Frank and the others.

They wait anxiously. Charlie cracks his knuckles. Frank and Mole argue about which homeland is better, Wales or Ireland. They play cards and wait some more.

The other squadron returns. Their attack has been problematic. Charlie's squadron is scrambled immediately. The weather is getting worse. The flight deck crew have brought all fifteen of their planes up from the hangar. They have unfurled the wings, and the great machines wait at the end of the deck in a herringbone formation, rising up and down with the motion of the ship on waves as big as mountains. Charlie's plane crouches among them. He can just make out the long torpedo slung beneath her undercarriage, wet and glistening with seawater. Spray pours across the deck in a torrent. The wind lashes his face, and the rain appears in undulating sheets. Up there, it will be colder, wetter, windier. But it is always a thrill going on the attack – and this would be quite some prize.

The clouds are low and ominous. The carrier rolls and bucks as they take off. A heavy northwesterly blows in fierce gusts. The flight deck is a glistening puddle. The Swordfish take off one by one, their outstretched legs lifting apparently without effort into the air, their bodies rocking from side to side.

157

Charlie is in the first formation of eight. Frank and Paddy are to his right and left. They signal to each other, arms extended, thumbs up.

'Right, boyo,' says Mole. 'Let's find this German *Fraülein* and show her what real men are made of.' The clouds are a dark rolling mass, their edges seeping into the sky in black wisps, like blood unfurling into water. It's going to be bumpy. The advantage is that they can fly above it for now, unseen by whatever lurks below. On they fly. The rain pours down on them. It drips inside the cockpit. It settles in patches on Charlie's legs. It works its way into his gloves, down his back, his thighs. It patters against his leather helmet. But up here, in control of his plane, the world makes sense. Charlie knows what is expected of him.

It takes them an hour to find her. As they approach the coordinates, Charlie's heart starts to pound. He dampens the fluttering in his belly and concentrates on the plane, the instruments, the torpedo. They know the ship is there before they dip below the clouds, because she starts to fire. And then the clouds part and she is revealed in all her glory, every inch of her covered in guns that have swivelled to face them. A torrent of tracer fire blazes against the storm clouds, flecks of light painting the way for the barrage that follows. She is the largest ship Charlie has ever seen. Larger than his aircraft carrier. And the guns . . . rows and rows of them hammering away like thunder, one after the other, *boom, boom, boom.*

Frank and Paddy drop away, falling off to the side. Charlie fights the instinct to pull his plane up higher, out of harm's way. He has to fly lower still, to get to the right level to send his torpedo on its way. Endlessly down, down.

'That's it, boyo. Hold her steady.' Mole's voice reaches his ears, calm and reassuring.

The rain drives straight into them. The wind rattles and blows, buffeting the plane. He tries to focus on the ship. She is enormous. He is a gnat buzzing at her. It seems impossible that he could so much as sting her.

158

'Hold her there,' says Mole.

Charlie swallows. His mouth is dry. His heart pounds in his throat. Frank and Paddy swoop from the same side as him. Wilson, Bob, all the others come in from the other side. They may be small, but they are mighty. The ship tries to take evasive action, but she is too large to avoid an attack from both sides. She swings one way and then the other. But the Swordfish swarm at her, together more powerful.

'Dive!' says Mole.

Charlie flies still lower and levels up. Now they are in danger from the waves lunging at them from below. The surface of the water is only a few yards away, the spray from the bullets splashes over them. The ship is firing everything she has. The noise of her guns is so loud that it drowns out the wind and the propeller and the blood beating in his ears. He feels shrapnel sting his cheek. He hears it clatter against the plane. He is surrounded by black puffs of flak. The rain mingles with the spray from the sea. His eyes sting. He is soaking. But the blood coursing around his body keeps him warm. Surely they are low enough to launch their torpedo. The world slows. The water rolls. The wind blows. The rain streams across the plane. Charlie's chest tightens. The guns batter and blast. Bright flashes of flame inside white clouds of smoke.

'Steady,' says Mole. The observer's voice brings the world back into focus. 'Steady.' He can feel Mole's weight shift and lean in the cockpit behind him.

'Now?' says Charlie.

'No! Not yet!' He glances over his shoulder. Mole is leaning right out of the cockpit, mad Welshman that he is.

'Wait . . .'

The battleship is firing. The rain is slapping into them, but it isn't rain, it's shrapnel. And then there is a great burst in the sea, and a fountain of water flies up in front of them as if a depth charge has gone off, and now the ship is firing into the sea in front of them, trying to knock them off course. They are looking down the colossal barrels of this monster

159

ship and the noise is tremendous and Charlie wants to press the button . . .

'Wait . . .'

They are almost within rifle shot of the ship. Charlie's vision is clear. He is so close that he is sure he will smash straight into it. The plane is taking a battering. 'Now!' says Mole. 'Let it go!'

Charlie presses the button and the torpedo is released from its clamp. The cylinder falls from the plane. It carries on forward, in the same direction they were travelling, as Charlie throws all his energy into turning. Mole and the Kid hold their breath. He can picture the faces of the men who are firing at him, intent, lips set in lines. They are shouting and pointing, and the Kid starts his firing, and the plane judders as she starts to turn, turn. They are alongside the ship, dwarfed by her. Charlie feels as though he could reach out and touch her. Waves are smashing against her side, frothing up into their faces. But the plane is turning, and the ship is falling away from them, and they are reaching safety, and he can see the other Swordfish also banking and their torpedoes have gone, and soon they will know if any of them has made any difference.

'It's a runner!' yells Mole. And he whoops with delight. And now the adrenaline kicks in and Charlie is ready to go again. But of course they have only one torpedo. They climb up towards the safety of the dark clouds. The German ship is firing at their friends. Charlie feels the anger rise. They turn and slope back down towards the ship, circling it like vultures. Another wave of planes has come in from the starboard side. The rest of the squadron. They swoop through the tracers and the flak, gliding low over the water, and somehow they too avoid the guns and drop their torpedoes and turn back out of harm's way. Charlie laughs out loud, cheering into the air.

The German ship is wounded. Not sure which way to fire, she is firing randomly at anything and everything. She tries to turn to avoid the torpedoes, but they are coming from all sides. They must have hit – must have.

*

After the noise and flames and smoke it is strange to be flying back over the grey, blank ocean, in the wind and the rain. Charlie has a moment to think. He glances across at the other planes. One, two, three, four . . . all eight of his squadron are there, skimming the waves. Relief floods through him. He relaxes his shoulders, eases his grip on the control column. He cricks his head from side to side, trying to loosen his neck, but it is too stiff, and he feels an intense pain in his right shoulder and a stinging pain in his neck and cheek. He presses his hand to the spot, and there is blood on the palm of his glove when he takes it away.

'You all right, boyo?' Mole shouts in his ear.

Charlie tries to nod, but the pain is growing and his head feels too heavy to move.

'My shoulder,' he says through gritted teeth.

'Can you make it?'

'Think so.' He tries to nod again, but he can't: it feels as if something is stabbing into his muscle.

'Any requests?' Charlie knows that Mole is trying to keep him engaged, but the pain is too much and he can't answer. It takes all his strength to hold the plane steady.

Mole starts to sing quietly. It's a tune Charlie instantly recognises. 'The Skye Boat Song'. Suddenly Olivia is floating next to him in the darkness. He clutches at the memory. He barely notices the gale, barely feels the plane tugging at his weakening arm. He bites down on his lip as the song fills his head. The deck of the carrier is smooth and glassy like the loch, and the lights guiding him in are stars on a summer evening, the green of the starboard light is like the gleam of the Northern Lights, and he just must land this plane on that deck or else he'll never see her again. He sees the batsman dancing. He feels the wheels touch the deck, the tug of the arrester wire. He feels the breeze across the loch. Then nothing.

'We got it, boyo. We bloody got it.'

The voice swims in his head, and for a moment he's not

sure whether he's still in the cockpit of the plane or not. It is pitch black and the world is moving, but as he comes around, he realises it's dark because he's in the sickbay and it's night-time, and the world is moving because they are back on their ship.

Mole is sitting next to him, smoking a cigarette. As he takes a drag, his face lights up. 'We left her going around in circles like a dog chasing its tail.' He giggles, and then puts his other finger to his lips. 'Keep it quiet. Not meant to be in here. Just had to make sure you were all right. And you are.' He giggles again. He leans forward, trying to whisper. There is an empty glass in his hand. 'The fleet finished her off. Took them a long time, mind. She fought bravely. In the end, they scuttled her. Not many survivors, I'm afraid. Typical Jerries. Heroic to the last.'

Charlie closes his eyes again. He saw those men only hours ago, fighting for their lives. Them or me. He remembers the conversation with Olivia on the track down to the bothy. 'How long have I been out?' he asks.

'Just over twenty-four hours. I'll go and tell the Kid. He's been hanging around since we dragged you in here . . . I'd only just sent him off to get some food.' Charlie hears Mole exhale as he rises out of his chair. He wants to ask the observer not to go. Not to leave him in the dark on his own. But it sounds stupid.

His chest is agony. He cannot move. 'My arm . . .' he says.

'Shush now,' says Mole from somewhere further away. 'You need rest. Thank the Lord you're still alive. I'll drink to that . . .' He hears a stumble and a curse, a snort of laughter, as the footsteps cross the room. There is a chink of light as the door opens a crack. The voice is even further away now: 'Welcome back, boyo.' The words are left hovering in the air as the door closes, and Charlie is left alone in the blackness.

He can't get comfortable. His skin is covered in a film of sweat. The cloying smell of fever lingers in his nostrils. He longs for the cool breeze of an open cockpit. When he moves, the sheets rasp like sandpaper against his body. The light hurts his eyes – either it is too bright or his lids are too heavy. He can't see anything. But he can hear: metal against metal, shrieking in his ears – someone stirring a hot drink. A voice drones from behind a mask. 'Not sure whether to operate. Might lose his arm if we do.'

No! He wants to cry out. Don't operate! But his mouth is too dry and he feels dizzy, so dizzy. It is like night flying, except he is not in control. He cannot lose his arm. How can he make sense of the world if he can't fly? He is a pilot. What else can he do? More sounds stab his nightmares. The tinny sound of the Tannoy, issuing instructions. Laughter – it sounds mocking. Footsteps walking, running. Whirring. Clicking. Banging. The hangar going up and down. Hands are touching him, moving him. Leave me alone, he wants to say. Get off me. Pain ripping into his body. The prick of a needle. A screech, like the plane's tyres, the wind in his ears, the world unfolding before him, the infinite sky above.

CHAPTER 11

Charlie is transferred ashore to a hospital in Kent – to a building that was once some grand hotel or home, but is now a stagnant pond of damaged men. Before long, the blood has stopped seeping from his shoulder and the smell of rot has gone. He's sure it doesn't need a dressing any more – fresh air would clean it up in no time. But the nurses insist. They have to have something to do. One of them is fussing over him, pulling the blanket up over his legs and trying to get him to sit back in bed. 'But I'm ready to be discharged,' he says. 'I'm absolutely right as rain.'

The nurse smiles. 'You'll be here for a while yet,' she says. 'That's a nasty wound. It did a lot of muscle damage. Lucky you didn't lose the arm.'

'Believe me, I've never been more grateful for anything, but being stuck in here is almost as bad.' The nurse shakes her head at him, but it's true – he feels as wretched as when he heard that his parents had died, rudderless, impotent. He wants to get back to his squadron as soon as possible; he has been separated from them once before, and those were the darkest, longest days of his life. He sighs and leans his head back against the wall, pushing the memory of that time back where it belongs, flinching as the pain rips into his shoulder again. It's all so damn monotonous: the meals and the nurses' rounds, the poking and prodding, and the doctor nodding his head. The nights are the worst. The snores and the whimperings remind him of his school dormitory, as if the exams and

164

the flight training never happened. He longs for the call of action stations, the thrill of flight, the sea air . . .

'Cheer up, Lieutenant FitzHerbert. You'll be out of here soon enough. Then you'll be wishing you were back with us.'

'I don't think so,' he says.

She smiles at him. She is middle-aged, matronly. Her uniform is starched and spotless. 'Why don't you try to think about something nice?' she says. 'Do your family know you're here?'

'I haven't got any family.'

'What about that sweetheart of yours? Have you written to tell her what's happened? Maybe she'll come and visit.' She offers him some paper and a pen from the table by his bed.

'How am I supposed to write with this?' He looks down at the shoulder.

'Try your left hand?'

But he's not going to do that. His writing would look ridiculous – malformed and childish.

A voice cuts in: 'Here, let me do the honours.'

'Mole! Thank God,' says Charlie.

'All right, boyo? Stop being grouchy to this poor nurse, and let's get something written to your lovely lady.' Mole pulls up a chair next to the bed. 'We'll lay it on thick. What a terrible injury. How brave you've been. She's going to love it.'

Charlie allows himself to smile. The squadron has been sent to an airfield in Kent while their planes are given a proper going over and the Admiralty sort their next posting. It means that Mole – and even Frank and Paddy – have been able to visit if they can get away. But Charlie knows they hate this stifling place too. No one in their right mind wants to be here among the disinfectant and kidney bowls.

'So tell me about operations,' he says. 'What am I missing out on?'

'You don't want to hear about all that. It'll only make you miserable.'

'It won't. I just want to get back.'

165

'It's not healthy, my boy. You need to think about something else for a change. As I've told you before, there is life beyond flying . . .'

'I know that.'

'So what plans have you made?'

'Plans? You make it sound like I've been written off. I'm going to be back up there with you as soon as they release me from this prison.'

'I can't wait for you to fly me into the jaws of danger again, but let's focus on Olivia for now. Have you asked her to marry you yet?'

'Don't be ridiculous.'

'Now's the time to strike, boyo . . . She'll find it impossible to say no when you're in this state.'

'I hope she'll find it impossible to say no anyway.'

'All I'm saying is you'd better get on with it. Girls are being snapped up left, right, and centre. I'm glad my Jeannie said yes before all this started.'

'Don't think you'd stand a chance now?'

'Not with all you handsome young pilots hot on my heels.'

Charlie is serious for a moment. 'Even if the time was right, I'm not sure I'd know how . . .'

'Doesn't matter how, boyo. Got to seize the moment. That's what I did.'

'Do you miss her?'

'Like I'd miss my right arm – no offence, chappie. I've loved Jeannie since we were kids. And now I've got my beautiful Alis . . .'

'She must be walking by now?'

'Walking and talking. I'm so proud of her I could puff my chest out like a cockerel and strut around this ward.'

'Don't do that or they'll have you in a strait jacket before you can say "cluck".'

'If I died tomorrow, I'd die happy – that I've been able to experience the feeling of being a father – there's nothing else like it. I'm telling you, you need to get on with it . . .'

'I think you're jumping the gun . . .'

'No, no,' says Mole. 'It's what we need. More love and more Alises in the world.'

'What if it's a boy?'

'You'll call it Mole, of course.'

Charlie laughs for the first time in ages – he is so unused to doing it that he can feel the muscles in his face stretch and contort.

'That's better,' says Mole. 'Now let's get writing. All I ask in exchange is "Cwm Rhondda" at the wedding, and me for best man.'

'What if she says no?'

'She's not going to, is she? Look at you. Young and handsome and wounded defending your country. Even I'm finding you hard to resist . . .'

Charlie laughs again and pulls his pillow out from behind his back so that he can whack Mole with it.

Once they've written to tell Olivia that Charlie is safe but in hospital, Mole leans back in his chair. The afternoon light sloping in through the windows catches his face and he suddenly looks tired – even old.

'So who are you flying with?' Charlie asks.

'Paddy,' says Mole. 'He's good.'

Charlie's eyes flick up to the ceiling in irritation.

'Not as good as you, of course.' Mole smiles. 'Fancy some of these?' He has managed to get hold of a couple of oranges.

Charlie shakes his head. 'I want to know what's going on out there,' he says. 'We don't get told anything.'

'You've heard about the Nazis doing the dirty on Uncle Joe, I take it?'

Charlie nods. 'Yes. That at least we did hear.'

'Well Uncle Joe's not happy about it, and Hitler's going to stamp and starve his country into submission.'

'Might as well leave them to it. They're as bad as each other. Both countries run by mad men.'

'Problem is, we need one of those mad men on our side. If Russia goes, the Germans can put everything they've got into taking us out. Ironically, the Commies are the only thing standing between chaos and civilisation.'

Charlie struggles to get his head around this. He is used to being told the Russians are untrustworthy Bolsheviks, mad socialists intent on destroying the world order. 'The whole world has gone crazy, and I'm stuck in here,' he says.

'It gets crazier still,' says Mole. 'I have it hot off the press that we're going to be supplying Stalin with munitions, with help from the Americans.'

'The Americans? They trust the Russians less than we do.'

'I think the point is that Russia can't survive without us, and we won't win the war without them.'

'And how are these supplies going to get to a country that's been cut off by the Germans?'

'There's only one way: through the Arctic Circle.'

'Is that even possible?'

'It'll have to be.'

Charlie shuffles into a more comfortable position. 'I suppose anything's better than sitting in this bloody ward,' he says.

'I wouldn't be so sure,' says Mole.

A week later, Charlie is finally discharged. He dresses slowly, ignoring the ache in his chest. He rolls his shoulders, looks down at his arms. His navy jacket is neatly done up. The white collar and black tie tidily in place. There is the proof of his new ranking in the extra golden looped braid around his cuffs. The doctor is sitting at his desk, surrounded by mounds of paperwork. 'You're not to fly for six months, lieutenant,' he says.

'Six months!' says Charlie, almost shouting.

'That's right.' The doctor is irritatingly calm. 'You've got to let it mend properly,' he says.

'But it's fine.' Charlie swings his right arm around in an arc, ignoring the stabbing pain.

'You're to keep it still as much as possible. It needs more time or it may never heal properly.'

'Are you sure? Is it possible to ask someone else?'

The doctor glares at him, pen poised above Charlie's papers. 'You could. And I could change my recommendation and suggest that you never fly again.'

Charlie pales, and settles his arm back into the sling. 'Sorry,' he says. 'I just want to get back to it.'

'You're bloody lucky, thanks to that surgeon on your ship. Wish they could all be like that. Don't waste your good fortune. Six months will pass in a flash – you never know, this madness might be over by then.'

Mole is waiting for him by the front door. 'Do you want the good news or the good news first?' he says.

'Six months, Mole! How can there be any good news?'

The Welshman puts his arm around Charlie's shoulders. 'Someone told the CO you've got a connection up in Scotland. You're being sent to help out at HMS *Helicon* until you're better.'

Charlie feels his insides flip over. The new naval base has recently been commissioned at Aultbea, and Olivia is the only thing that could ever have sweetened the blow. He gives Mole a lopsided grin. 'Guess I've got you to thank for that?' he says.

'As long as you keep your side of the bargain – I've got a great best man's speech lined up . . . but don't thank me quite yet, because we've got another treat in store . . .' Charlie sees Frank and Paddy waiting in the Land Rover. 'Hop in, boyo. We're taking you to London.' He winks. 'You need a bit of help in the love department, and we all know a wounded pilot is irresistible.'

Charlie steps backwards, the shock evident in his face. 'But you're married,' he says to Mole. 'Surely you wouldn't . . .'

'Oh no,' says the Welshman. 'I'm just after a few drinks. I'm pretty adept between the sheets already. I told you I've known Jeannie since we were kids. But you need to get some practice in if you're going to court this girl properly.'

Charlie looks at Frank and Paddy, who give him the thumbs-up. He sighs. He can't let his friends down, but he has no intention of being unfaithful to Olivia. He relaxes on the journey up to the city, settling back into the easy banter of the men who are like his brothers. They head to the West End, to Eddie's Bar, a popular haunt for naval officers. Wine flows freely. There are women everywhere. In the noisy, heady world of booze and flirting and dancing, it is like sitting in a sea fog. Mole buys the drinks. Charlie's shoulder throbs. Faces appear and disappear in the dim light. Men and boys enjoying small moments of freedom. The music is so loud that some-times Charlie can't hear what anyone is saying. It doesn't exactly matter. It is more about letting the alcohol work its magic: it is a relief to feel the fiery liquid trickle down his throat and take some of the edge off.

At a table in the corner some women are giving them the eye. They are pretty in a gaudy way, with brightly-painted lips and heavy, dark eyes, short dresses revealing tantalising stockings. The officers pick up their drinks and join the girls, who immediately start to cluck over Charlie's shoulder.

'Now's your chance,' says Mole, digging Charlie in the ribs. Charlie is grateful for the smoky, dim atmosphere; it hides his embarrassment. He sits on the other side of the observer, gripping his drink. The Welshman is the entertainer; he delights in an audience. The girls lean in and hang on his every word, giggling too loudly.

But the girl seated next to Charlie doesn't laugh. She has long dark hair and large solemn eyes. It may be the alcohol talking, but when she glances at him, he feels some unspoken connection flitter between them – neither of them wants to be here. Like him, she is young. But unlike him, she is really young. Surely she can't be more than fourteen. Her body is skinny, like a boy's. Her breasts are just small mounds, hardly there. Of course, it could be lack of decent nourishment.

Another officer plonks himself down on the other side of the girl, squeezing between her and her neighbour. He rests his hand carelessly on her shoulder, as if they are together, looking down at her, but not at her face, only at her barely formed breasts. Her lipstick is garish; her cheeks are bright with make-up. And she's probably had too much to drink. A child playing a grown-up game. Charlie's stomach turns. The officer laughs and pulls the girl up for a dance. She appears willing, but Charlie can tell there's resistance in every part of her body.

Mole nudges Charlie. 'Go on, boyo. She's obviously holding out for the injured pilot. *Carpe diem*!'

Charlie wants to say, 'Can't you see, she's a child?' But one look at Mole and Frank and Paddy, and he isn't sure they can see anything. They have been flying so hard that they are making the most of this night out, and their words are slurring, their faces glowing.

Charlie looks at the rest of the men around the table, eyes too bright, top lips sweaty. He notices the spiv in the corner, watching. He sees the girls looking at the spiv. He thinks of Olivia and her wild freedom. Her innocence. Her ability to do whatever she wants. He sees this girl, with her made-up face and her primped-up hair, the dress that hangs from her boyish hips and her flat chest. He pities this girl. He will play along for her sake.

He ruffles his hair, takes a swig from his glass, feels the liquid warm his heart and soul. He takes hold of the girl's hand. 'Sorry, but she's with me,' he says. The officer looks pissed-off, but sees the sling and doesn't argue. The girl is dead-eyed. She doesn't say anything as Charlie gently manoeuvres his right arm out so that he can use it, but her grip is tight as they move around the dance floor.

'Look. I only want to dance,' he says. 'Nothing . . . well . . . nothing else.' He isn't sure if she has heard him above the noise. But after a while, he feels her body relax a little. He can't think of anything else to say, apart from 'What's your name?'

He has to strain to hear her small voice above the sound of clinking glasses and music and chatter.

'Bluebell,' she says.

He looks down at her with raised eyebrows. 'Your real name?'

She smiles shyly, looking directly up at him. Her eyes are dark and wide. 'Betsy,' she says. 'My real name is Betsy.'

CHAPTER 12

Olivia

Another summer is coming to an end. The fruit is ripening on the trees: crisp round apples with impossibly red skin that deepens as the summer fades and autumn takes hold. The branches of the pear trees droop with the weight of their fat golden fruit. In the shrubs and hedges, plump blackberries hide between brambles. The vegetable patches are burgeoning with produce: carrots, potatoes, cabbages, broccoli, beetroot, and now the pumpkins are beginning to ripen and swell like fat bright stomachs. The sun stays up in the sky until late, bathing the loch in a warm orange glow, made all the brighter by the good news that Charlie is out of hospital. Olivia spends more time than ever outdoors, collecting blood-red rosehips to turn it into cordial rich in vitamin C with her sugar ration. She gathers enormous whelks, as big as her hands. Fish are bountiful in the warm sea, and business is brisk.

Today she is at Aultbea. She has sold a bucket-load of ling. It is early afternoon, and the loch is packed with clanking, anchored ships, the air thick with shouts and calls and whistles as sailors prepare for the evening. Small boats transfer men to and from shore, chopping and churning at the water. Olivia is slooshing the guts and blood from one of her empty buckets, leaning out over the side of the boat as it tips and rocks, thrown about by the motion of so many ships and people jostling for space. As she is drawing the bucket back out of the water, there is a crunch, and the rowing boat jerks sideways. She loses her footing momentarily, but manages to rebalance, cursing out loud at whoever has hit her, but letting go of the bucket as she does so. She tries to grab it, but her hands are slippery from the fish. Too late she realises that she has stupidly wound the rope tied to its handle around her left wrist and it is beginning to tighten as the bucket fills.

The bucket starts to disappear beneath the surface, its outline fracturing and distorting as it sucks murky water into its empty mouth. Now it is dragging at her, and, between trying to keep her balance as another wave slams beneath the boat, and trying to free the rope from her arm and berating herself for being so bloody stupid as well as the idiot who has steered into her, she cannot stop the panic from rising in her throat and she cannot think, and it's so tight now that the circulation is being cut off and she can't pull it up without toppling forwards and she really doesn't want to fall into the water because once she's in, she might not be able to get out.

She gasps, tries to call out, but the words don't come. She struggles with the rope, but it only bites into her flesh more tightly. She is being pulled towards the edge. Her breath comes in ragged spurts. The jetty is full of people, and there are more along the shore, and everyone is too busy chatting and laughing in the afternoon sunshine to notice what is happening. Her knife. She remembers her knife. She tugs it free from her pocket with her right hand but she can't open it. She fumbles at it, lifts it towards her mouth to use her teeth, but it slips from her grasp because her hands are still slimy. She tries to pick it up again, but her feet are slipping, and the side of the boat is digging into her knees when suddenly there is a shape behind her and someone is reaching out to tug the rope back towards her, and holding her within the circle of his arms, using his other hand to grasp her knife and hack at the rope until it breaks, and she stumbles backwards into the boat, landing against his chest, warm and solid.

It takes a moment for her breath to slow, to even out. Her arm is shaking – it feels as though it has been stretched – and there is a livid red mark around her wrist where the skin has been rubbed raw.

The body shifts behind her and they both struggle to their feet. 'Sorry,' says a voice. 'Came in faster than I meant to. Are you all right?'

For a moment, Olivia is speechless, just grateful to be free of the tightening rope. Then anger takes over. 'You nearly killed me,' she says, still flexing her fingers and watching the blood seep back into her hand.

'Actually I just saved you.'

'If you hadn't rammed my boat . . .'

'If you hadn't had a bucket tied to your wrist . . .'

'My bucket . . . It's gone . . . I'll never get it back now.'

'Look. Are you coming up or not?' The stranger has clambered on to the jetty and is now leaning down, his large, rough hand outstretched. Olivia hesitates for a moment and then grabs hold of it crossly. He pulls her easily up and next to him. Now she takes the time to glance up. He is so close that she can feel the heat of his body, his breath on her hair. He is gazing directly at her, his black eyes sending a jolt through her body. She almost feels that she knows this boy. Ridiculous. She tucks her hair behind her ears.

They stand there side by side on the jetty for a moment, and then the boy clears his throat. 'I'm Jack,' he says.

She blushes. Damn. Why does she always blush? 'Olivia,' she says. His arms and face are burnished golden brown by reflected sun. His chest is broad. She reddens further as she realises she was pressed against it only moments ago. She is still covered in hard flecks of scales and salt. She probably smells of fish. But Jack is looking at her as if she's the most special thing in the world. The water laps beneath them, green and alive, and the sun beats down, and she should turn away and head home, but it is only now that she realises they are still holding hands.

*

Another boy, shorter and wider than Jack, is approaching them. 'Hope I'm not interrupting?' he says.

Olivia drops Jack's hand and steps away, feels her cheeks burning again.

Jack is unaffected. 'Carl, meet Olivia,' he says, rolling her name slowly across his tongue as if he's tasting it.

Carl nods in greeting and then addresses Jack. 'Thanks for coming to get us,' he says. 'The others'll be along in a moment. We didn't get far. Maybe you can help us?' He turns to Olivia. 'We're here for a few days. What's there to do?'

'There's always lots going on,' says Olivia. 'There are dances, we've got two cinemas . . .'

'And what do you recommend?' Jack asks. 'What do you like doing?'

'I recommend you climb the hills. The views are incredible . . .'

'I bet they are,' says Jack, still staring at her.

'Here come the others now,' says Carl.

There are four men making their way towards them. They eye Olivia with amused interest, eyes flicking from her to Jack. 'Where's the boat?' one of them asks, his voice rasping like pebbles beneath water.

Jack indicates the launch that is tied alongside Olivia's boat. ''Scuse us,' says the man with the raspy voice. They will have to climb down into her boat to cross into theirs.

Olivia stands aside, watching as they leap down, steady even though the small vessel rocks with their weight. Jack lingers next to her. 'See you tomorrow,' he says. It is a statement rather than a question.

'I don't know where I'll be . . .' she is saying, but he is already hopping down after his crewmates, his bare feet making no sound. He balances for a moment on the gunwale of his own boat, looking back at her over his shoulder until Carl pulls him in as it chugs to life. Olivia watches the boat make its way out past the sleek, grey Navy ships and on to the new rabble of merchant ships that are kept separate. She tries to make out which ship is his, but it is impossible, and all she can do is watch until he is lost among the towering hulls and fat anchor chains slimy with seaweed.

Olivia wants to try for flatfish in the small bay out beyond Cove. It is a secret place that Charlie told her about, but never had time to show her. It didn't take her long to find, and has become one of her favourite spots, hidden away from the multitude of eyes and ships that now infest the loch. She digs out the trident from the shed. It is a fearsome-looking weapon with three pointed, barbed spikes on the end of a pole. She lashes it to her bicycle and sets off, her empty fishing bag slung across her back. Cove is about five miles away, along a bumpy track that hugs the south side of the shore. She flies downhill with her feet off the pedals, the air catching in her throat and making her as breathless as when she thinks about Jack, her heart skipping with the excitement of promise, and she has to stop herself smiling. Above her a purple blush is spreading across the hills as the heather comes to life.

As she passes Firemore Beach, she spots two boys in the road. She comes to a halt, dragging her bare feet on the stony path, sending dust billowing into the air. It is Jack and Carl, who must have been exploring the beach. Olivia feels the heat in her cheeks – glad she can blame it on the exertion. It is as if her body has decided to act all on its own, without listening to her brain. 'Can't keep away?' she says, her voice casual but her heart pounding.

'Nope,' says Jack. 'Where are you going?'

'I'm on my way to stock up on fish. I sell them in the afternoons. You can catch me later at Aultbea, if you want . . .'

'We could help you now,' says Jack.

'Oh no,' Olivia says, shaking her head. 'I can't give away my secret hunting ground . . .'

'Can't believe there's anywhere secret around here.'

'There are plenty of places if you look hard enough. And that's the way I want to keep it.'

'We'll follow you.'

'You're not allowed beyond Cove. There's a checkpoint.' The sentence hangs in the air like a challenge. Jack raises an eyebrow and smiles. Olivia stands up on her pedals, pushing herself away along the road. 'See you at Aultbea this afternoon,' she shouts over her shoulder. She lifts her hand in a dismissive wave as she cycles on, but her heart is racing and a broad smile is spread across her face.

Before it peters out, Olivia comes off the path, hiding her bike among the peat hags. A little bit further are a couple of bell tents where the anti-aircraft regiments are living. She scrambles away and over the rocks behind them like one of Mac's sheep, invisible to the half-naked men shaving in the burn that runs down on to the road. She continues along the coast until she can descend to a pristine beach – white and untouched. Electric pink thrift and mustard yellow lichen brighten the soft grey of the bare rocks, which are still cool underfoot.

Olivia takes in the empty beach and smiles to herself. She uses a box with a glass bottom to spot the fish, which are camouflaged on the seabed, just throwing up a telltale cloud of sand as they flutter off. She wades out up to her thighs, the water touching the bottom of her shorts and making them stick to her legs. Jagged pinnacles rise dramatically on either side of the bay, as though the cliffs are breaking up. Rocks throw indigo shadows beneath the jade water. The sand kneads the bottom of her feet. She focuses on the box in her hand; the trident poised in the other. All that exists of the world is the view through the glass. The water is crystal clear, just the odd thread of dark seaweed tumbling gently over the rippled sand below. She moves as slowly and imperceptibly as she can, the trident at the ready. Her bicep begins to ache. She sees a shape in the sand and brings the trident down in a flash. She knows she has got it before she lifts it flapping out of the water. It was a perfect strike.

She holds the trident up above her head. The fish struggles on the end, gasping for air, its body flipping and flopping in the sunshine. She wades ashore. Shoals of tiny silver fish dart away in front of her. She dispatches the fish with a sharp blow and slips it into her fishing bag, ready to go again, when she spots Jack and Carl making their way across the beach.

She is half-annoyed that she has to share the beach, half-pleased that he has made the effort.

'Hope you're going to catch more than that,' says Jack. 'We're a hungry crew.'

'It's harder than it looks,' says Olivia.

'Let's give it a go.'

'I'll be fine right here,' says Carl, throwing himself down on to the sand and lying back to sunbathe.

Jack laughs, and, bold as brass, removes his top, pulling it off over his head and aiming it at Carl. The muscles in his shoulders and arms are strong and smooth in the sun. They wade out into the sea. The water in the shallows is as warm as bathwater now. Olivia glances over at Jack. His brow is furrowed in concentration. He moves slowly and gracefully in the water. His arm is steady. A vein pulses in his neck. His forearm is as brown as hers. She sees his muscles flex as he plunges the stick down into the water.

'Got one!' he says. Olivia can't help grinning too: he seems so pleased with himself. 'First time I've ever caught anything.'

'We'll have to celebrate then. You must eat it here and now – fresh as it possibly can be.'

'What – raw?' He makes a face.

She laughs. 'No! We'll cook it. I'm not a Neanderthal.'

They wade back to the shore, the water rolling down their legs like rows of pearls. Olivia unhooks Jack's fish and whacks it over the head.

'Can I see?' says Jack.

'Your fish?'

'No.' He points.

'My priest?' she says.

'Priest?' He laughs, a deep, rich sound that makes her heart lift. 'Doesn't look like any kind of priest I ever heard of.'

'It's what you call something you hit a fish over the head with.'

'Strange thing to call a killing instrument.'

'Ever sat through a long sermon?'

He laughs again. 'Never sat through any sermon,' he says. He runs his finger down the knife. 'O.J.B.'

'My initials. My aunt gave it to me. It's also a knife,' she says, taking it back and showing him how to unfold it.

'Beautiful,' says Jack. But he is looking at her and not the knife.

Olivia builds a fire with driftwood that Carl and Jack have collected from the shoreline. The wood is dry as paper. It catches instantly and crackles, the flames leaping up, almost invisible against the sky, bending and distorting the beach with their heat. When it has died down to an orange glow, Olivia whittles some fresh wood and spears Jack's fish, laying it between some longer branches pushed into the sand. Jack watches her all the time, dark eyes unreadable. Yet she doesn't feel uncomfortable, just as though every sense is on fire.

When Jack's fish is cooked, Olivia passes it to him. Their hands touch. She feels the heat in his fingers. He starts to flake the white flesh of the fish from its skin, shoving it into his mouth.

'You want some?' He offers it in his fingers. She shakes her head. She is too breathless to eat.

They lie back on the sand. The sea is a soft blanket of green. A white-tailed eagle soars through the thermals above them, the tips of its large wings like elegant palm fronds. In the distance, ships come and go in the haze like ghosts.

Later they catch nine more flatfish between them: not a bad haul. The day has passed quickly but the sun is still warm even as it melts into the sea. The tide is coming in, fingers of water reaching out for them.

'Won't someone be missing you?' Jack asks.

'Not likely,' says Olivia.

'My mum was always on at me to get home.'

Olivia turns on her side to look at him. 'Where's home?'

'London.'

'Is your mother still there?'

Jack stares into the sky. Carl's eyes are closed, but she can tell that he is listening too. 'You don't want to hear about her. Tell us about your mum . . .'

'I think she's too busy saving people to care about what I'm up to . . .'

'Oh dear, poor lamb.' He pushes her shoulder. 'What about your dad?'

'He's away at sea. He's a captain in the Navy.'

'A captain? I never met a captain's daughter before.'

'Do I live up to expectation?'

He glances across at her, looks her up and down. She enjoys the way his eyes linger on her skin. He nods slowly. 'Yes,' he says, 'I reckon you do.'

'What does your father do?' she asks. The question is automatic – something built into her – but as soon as she has said it, she feels foolish. She doesn't want to make him feel awkward – and anyway, out here, in the hills and on the beaches, it doesn't seem to matter where you come from.

'He's a corporal in the army. Or he was . . . He was in France . . .'

'I didn't mean to pry.'

He peers out towards the horizon, narrowing his eyes. 'Missing presumed dead is the fancy term,' he says.

'I'm sorry.'

'Could happen to any of us,' he says. 'Your dad. Me . . . Death don't mind – we're all the same to him.' He starts to stand. 'We'd best be getting back,' he says, brushing the sand from his legs and shaking it from his top.

'You enjoyed learning to harpoon?' she asks, relieved to lighten the tone.

'Not just that.' He stares at her in the fading light, the pink glow in the sky reflecting in his dark eyes. There is a hunger about him that is both threatening and exciting.

Olivia tucks her hair behind her ears. 'If you'd like, I could teach you how to catch from a line tomorrow,' she says. Her heart is pounding again.

'I'd like that,' he says.

They make their way back to Firemore in comfortable silence. In the warm twilight, Olivia feels as though the beach and the rocks, the hills and the loch, are somehow part of her, and she of them, and when she glances across at Jack, it feels so right that he should be here, as if he too is already a part of her. She waves goodbye to the boys and pedals home in the luminous dark, feeling less lonely and more whole than she ever has. Somewhere along the shore, a lonely curlew calls, an eerie shriek that skids and bounces across the water, but Olivia is too wrapped up in her thoughts to notice.

The next morning she is out on the springy lawn in front of the bothy, checking for weak points in a fishing line and attaching more barbed hooks at various points. As she searches among the chalky necklaces of sharp barnacles for bait, Jack appears. Her stomach flutters, but she carries on smashing the limpets from the rocks, skewering the slippery molluscs from their shells, and threading them on to the hooks.

He helps her to drag the old red rowing boat down to the water's edge. The hull scrapes on the shingle. The paint is peeling in places, and the wood inside has been bleached by the sun. Olivia removes her socks, tossing them on to the lawn. Jack helps push the boat out. She gasps as the chilly water touches her warm feet, feels the pleasing roundness of the pebbles massaging her soles. Jack hops in at the same time, and the boat dips and bobs and turns slowly on the water.

'Here, let me,' says Olivia. 'I know where the lines are.'

'Let me. You can direct me.' She doesn't argue.

'Haven't been in a rowing boat since my training ship,' says Jack.

'That must have been a change from London.'

'It sure was.'

'A bit like school?'

'Better. Hard work, but I made some good mates, and I learnt more than I ever did at school. Now I've got a good job. I'll be an officer one day. Might even be good enough for the likes of you . . .'

Olivia colours. 'You already are,' she says.

'We'll see.'

He pulls the boat deftly and fast. They skirt the edge of the loch. She indicates for him to stop by the corks that mark her lines and pots. The long lines are weighted down by stones, smaller lines with hooks at the end dangling off the main line like socks on a washing line. The sun is not yet high in the sky, but Olivia's face is beginning to tingle and her skin feels taut and dry where the salt water has evaporated. A black-headed gull sweeps through the air, its deep orange-red beak open as it squawks crossly at them.

She starts to pull the first line in. The seawater drips on to her bare legs, leaving fine white sprinkles of salt when it dries. The first two hooks are empty, but Olivia can tell by the weight and movement that there is something further along. As the third hook draws in closer to the boat, she sees a flash of gold and then a pinkish-red fish is twisting on the end of the hook, its pale belly flashing, oversized fins flapping like wings, bulbous eye staring. It makes a horrible croaking noise like a frog as she brings it into the boat.

'Don't touch it!' she says. But the warning is too late. Jack drops the fish, sucking his fingers. It has sharp spines on its back and its gills. He thrusts his stung hand into the water, hoping the coolness will ease the burning.

'Are you all right?'

'Don't stop,' he says. 'There's more . . .'

He's right. They keep pulling the line in. The next two fish are more streamlined and a golden colour, with a protruding lower jaw and huge dark eyes. 'Pollock,' says Olivia.

She clubs each fish over the head in one deft movement,

killing it instantly. Then she starts to gut them, hanging over the side so that the entrails are washed into the water, before slipping them into the bucket. Almost immediately there are three gulls clamouring above them: a black-headed, and two larger black-backed, cawing and squawking and yelling at each other.

When they have finished, Olivia rebaits the hooks and drops the line back into the water for tomorrow. She turns to Jack, who is still sucking his finger. 'Let me have a look?'

He holds out his hand and she makes a show of examining it, enjoying the feel of his warm, dry hand in hers. 'I think you'll live,' she says.

'You'd better hope so,' he says. 'Us Merchant Navy boys are indispensable.'

'I don't doubt that for a second.'

'King George himself has said so.'

'I'm sure.'

The water buffets the little dinghy, and Jack pulls the oars in, resting them on the rowlocks. He lies back on the thwart, his head resting on the gunwale, his feet up on the opposite side, soaking up the sun. The loch is emptier today. Another convoy must have moved out. The remaining ships are far enough away not to encroach on their world. A cormorant bobs nearby, a sleek, Z-shape on the water.

'Listen,' says Olivia.

'To what?' says Jack.

'Exactly.'

They look up at the bright blue sky, the three gulls squawking overhead. The water kisses the bottom of the boat as they bob and drift. Around them the hills slope away to the sky. From this position, Olivia can almost pretend the loch is empty again, no ships squatting behind them, just the open sea.

'What made you join the Merchant Navy?' she asks.

'Had to join something. Too young for the army. Too dumb for the RAF . . .'

'I'm sure that's not true.'

'I haven't had what you'd call a good education.'

'The war put a stop to all that?'

'Oh no. I was long gone. Everyone stops at fourteen. Didn't you go to school?'

She shakes her head. 'We had governesses.'

'Governesses?' He laughs.

'What's so funny about that?'

'It's proper fancy having a teacher come to your house.'

'I couldn't help it. My parents hired them.'

'Only time my parents met my teacher was when I was in trouble.'

'Is your mother dead too?'

He nods.

'I'm so sorry.'

'It's not your fault.'

'Do you have any brothers or sisters?'

'My brother's missing. But I've got a sister. She's safe.'

'Whereabouts?'

'I don't know,' he says, his face clouding over. 'One day I'll find her.'

Olivia thinks of her mother at home, her sisters in London, her father at sea. She cannot imagine not knowing where her family is, being anchorless.

Jack sits up and stretches. 'Come on. I thought we had more fish to catch?'

Olivia gathers the line from a bucket and says, 'If you row straight and at a steady speed . . .' She starts to trail the line out behind the boat. There are feathers and hooks and weights tied at intervals along it. Olivia holds the line in her hand. As Jack rows, they chat: about food – how delicious sausages used to be, and sweets, and how war makes you appreciate that kind of thing more. 'I reckon I've learnt more in the last two years than I ever would at home,' says Olivia.

'Me too,' says Jack. 'I'd never been on a ship before . . .'

'Me neither!'

'This isn't what I'd call a ship . . .'

'It must have been a bit of a shock for you?'

'I guess you could call it that. I'd seen plenty. Just not been on one. I used to work on the docks.'

'You're making me feel useless. I've never worked in my life.'

'What about now? All this?' He points at the fish and the hooks.

'It's not exactly work, is it?'

'None of us would be able to work if we couldn't eat.'

'I hadn't thought of that . . .'

It is so good to be able to talk to someone her own age about life and the future. But there's more to it than that. She's never felt this alive, this receptive to how another person thinks and feels, as though they are finely tuned in to each other.

Suddenly she feels the familiar tug on the line. 'Here!' she says. 'Hold this.'

Jack lets the oars rest as he takes the line from her, feels the sharp pull.

'Let's keep it in for a few more seconds in case it's a shoal.'

When they pull the line in, there are fish on four of the hooks. The green and black pattern on their backs glitters like mother-of-pearl in the sunshine. 'Mackerel,' says Olivia. She yanks her knife from her pocket and quickly sets to work, dispatching the first fish and slicing it open.

Jack watches in quiet amusement, leaning back and resting his elbows on the gunwale. 'You're really not afraid to get dirty, are you?' he says.

'Why would I be?'

He shrugs. 'I thought someone like you would be all snooty and proper.'

'I'll show you snooty and proper. I don't think you gutted your fish yesterday? Didn't want to or didn't know how?'

'Didn't know how . . .'

'Oh. I thought someone like you . . .'

He laughs and holds up his hands. 'All right . . .'

'Anyway, if you're going to eat it, you should be prepared to gut it.'

'So show me.'

They work in companionable silence. He has to shuffle up closer to her because of the knife being attached around her waist. Olivia feels the muscles in the top of his arm tighten against hers as he works. Occasionally their brown legs bump against each other.

She shows him how to slice the knife into the fish's belly. The guts spill out, soft and warm, and they tug them from the fish's body and let the sea swill them away, where the gulls splash on them with delight.

The days are shorter now that autumn is coming, but the trees around the loch are still covered in leaves, and they glow green and orange in the setting sun. They row back across the coloured ripples. 'Are you with anyone?' says Jack.

'A man, you mean?' Olivia blushes and shakes her head. With a stab of guilt, she thinks of Charlie, but he does not make her pulse race and her heart sing.

'Good,' he says, and she laughs because he is so direct and that is so refreshing.

They have reached the steps of the bothy. 'This is me,' she says.

'Nice place.'

'I manage to squeeze in.'

'Should think so too. You should see the cabin I share with Carl. This place is almost bigger than my home in London. And that was me, my sister, my brother, my mum, and my dad living there.'

'When you put it like that . . .'

'What's your home like, then? Don't tell me . . . A palace . . .'

'Not exactly . . .' She thinks of the twelve bedrooms, the rambling kitchens, the long corridors, the billiards room and the conservatory, the boot room and the morning room . . .

'I'm teasing again,' he says. 'You can't exactly help where

187

you come from. Of course, I have to say that, else you wouldn't give me a second look,' he adds.

She laughs and shoves him in the shoulder. A breeze pushes her hair across her face. She reaches up to tuck it behind her ears, but Jack does it first. It is a gentle movement, and it makes her heart flutter. Who cares where you're from, she thinks, if my skin feels on fire every time you touch it. He lets his hand rest on her shoulder and then fall down her arm, leaving a trail of warmth.

'There's a dance tomorrow,' he says. 'Do you want to come?'

She doesn't even pause before saying, 'Yes.'

He walks down the steps and grabs hold of his bicycle. 'Until tomorrow,' he says.

'Tomorrow . . .' She stands out on the step for a long time after he has disappeared into the twilight, dangling the bucket of fish from one hand and steering the bicycle with the other.

CHAPTER 13

Olivia digs out a blue dress that brings out the colour of her eyes. Although she has grown taller since she first came here, she has also lost weight, so the dress fits perfectly. It feels strange not to be in shorts or trousers: girly and somehow vulnerable. She is still barefoot.

Jack is waiting for her at the jetty where they first met. She can see the beach is lined with men and women in their naval uniforms drinking beer out of jam jars, passing them from one to another. Everyone is in high spirits. She wonders if she'll see Gladys and Maggie, but there's no sign of her friends, although there are plenty of Wrens about.

It is not dark yet, but there is the beginning of the magical glow of dusk. Jack tucks her hair behind her ear like he did before, but this time letting his hand stroke the side of her cheek as he does. She puts her hand up to his and cups her palm over it, feels the strength, the heat. He offers her his arm and escorts her into the wooden hut from where music is spilling into the night. Inside, there is a man playing the piano, and two Wrens are singing. The room is packed with people dancing. The atmosphere is friendly, welcoming. Carl waves at them as they enter. He is already on the dance floor.

Jack takes Olivia's hand and they squeeze into the throng. The steam from all the bodies warms the hut. She has forgotten what it's like to dance. It is another kind of freedom. She relaxes into Jack's arms, enjoying the moments they have to move closer because there are so many people, or when he says something she can't quite hear. She can feel the strength in his chest and stomach, strong but compliant, as if their bodies might melt into one. Around them, it is not only Gaelic that Olivia doesn't understand. There are men of all nationalities here, united by the music.

When the reeling starts, the atmosphere becomes more boisterous. Olivia is good at reels: she once had a governess who insisted she learn. They line up for Strip the Willow – a long row of men on one side, women on the other – Olivia laughing at Jack's protests, insisting that she will teach him as they go along. She links her arm with his, ready to spin, when three Royal Navy officers, resplendent in their uniforms, swagger in from the hotel next door. The atmosphere immediately changes; some of the crowd mutter and shake their heads. One of the incomers spots Olivia. 'Can I have this dance?' he says, taking hold of her elbow. She wants to tell him to get lost, but she senses this might be a bad move. She raises an eyebrow apologetically at Jack and takes the officer's hand as the rest of the crowd relaxes.

Jack steps back and watches from the side. The officer pulls her close. She pushes him back. There is no call to be close in a reel. His breath smells sickly, of alcohol and cigarettes. His hands are sweaty and holding her too tightly. As they spin, he brings her towards him again and this time she shoves him harder away. He tries to pull her back against him but suddenly Jack is there. He puts a hand on her shoulder. 'Can I have my partner back?' he says.

'She's not yours . . .' says the officer.

'She came with me . . .' says Jack, and there is anger in his voice as they square up to each other.

'Then I think the lady is confused by which week to come dancing,' says the officer. The two friends that he arrived with draw closer. The skin on the back of Olivia's neck begins to tingle.

'I don't,' says Jack, circling.

'Royal Navy dance is next week.'

'So why are you here, then?'

The men are close – too close. In the background, the music is still playing, but no one is dancing. As she glances around the crowd, it is only now that Olivia realises that she is surrounded by merchant seamen.

The officer throws the first punch, but he is drunk and Jack is fast and easily steps out of the way. Jack jabs back so hard that the officer stumbles backwards, clutching at his nose. When he takes away his hand and sees the blood that has trickled into it, the officer launches again at Jack, but Jack is already poised to lash out. The officer's two friends step forward, but Jack is too fast and avoids them easily, keeping the first officer in sight. Carl makes a move towards the men, to shield his friend from their advances, but Jack doesn't need help. His second blow lands in the same place as the first, and, as the officer staggers backwards again, his friends both come at Jack, but Carl is in the way and there is a scuffle and a shout, and for a moment there is a melee of arms and fists. Then suddenly a loud voice calls out from the silent crowd, and Olivia turns to see Charlie striding towards them. 'What the hell's going on here?' he says.

'Charlie!' says Olivia, surprised but not entirely relieved. 'What are you doing here . . .?'

'Looking for these three . . . But more to the point, what are you doing here?' Charlie asks, his jaw clenched.

'I'm with a friend.' She points at Jack, who is eyeballing the officer, whose blood is still seeping from his swollen nose.

'Well, say goodbye,' says Charlie. 'It's time to go.'

'I don't want to go . . .'

'You have to . . .' Charlie takes hold of her upper arm.

'I don't have to do anything.'

Charlie grits his teeth. 'I don't think you realise, but tonight's dance is for the Merchant Navy.'

'I do realise. Now get your hands off me.' She is aware that Jack is watching, still bristling with rage.

'Do as you're told.'

Olivia feels the hot flush of embarrassment and anger spread across her cheeks. 'I'm not a child, Charlie,' she says, shaking her arm to try to free herself from his grip.

Now Jack steps towards them, smoothing his ruffled hair. 'She asked you to leave her alone,' he says.

'I'm not sure what it has to do with you.' Charlie's eyes flicker disdainfully at Jack, and then back to Olivia. It is as if he is trying to get her to understand some secret code, but she does not feel the connection.

'She's here with me, that's what.' Jack is trying to get Charlie's attention, but there is a blur as the injured officer launches himself at Jack from behind, and Jack falls forward, hitting the ground with the officer on top of him. He is floored only momentarily, then he is back on his feet and taking a swipe at the officer, who goes down properly this time, clutching his stomach. And now Charlie lets go of Olivia and tries to apprehend Jack by grasping him around the chest, but Jack is broader and stronger than Charlie, and easily twists free, turning to thump Charlie as hard as he can, which just happens to be on Charlie's bad shoulder. Charlie gasps and doubles over, his face white as his freshly pressed officer's shirt. Carl steps in again and this time he holds Jack back. And now the whole room is silent once more, all eyes on the kerfuffle, all minds wondering what will happen next.

Charlie helps the felled officer back up through gritted teeth. The four naval officers glare at Jack and Carl. Charlie is still pale, and Olivia feels a twinge of pity for him, but Jack is there, breathing heavily, and she finds herself crossing the floor to stand next to him.

Charlie and the injured officer lean on each other and begin to make their way to the door. Charlie stops by Olivia. 'Have you gone mad?' he asks. 'These are not the kind of people you should be consorting with.'

'Don't be so pompous.'

'What would your parents say?'

'I don't care. I'll live my own life, thank you very much.'

Charlie shakes his head in disappointment as Olivia threads her arm through Jack's in defiance. She cannot bear the expression on Charlie's face.

'I hope you know what you're doing,' says Charlie.

'I do,' says Olivia. And then all she can do is turn her back on her friend as people trickle slowly back on to the dance floor.

Early the next morning Aunt Nancy swoops into the cottage. 'I've got Charlie sitting at home looking as if the world has come to an end,' she says.

'That's a bit over-dramatic when you think there are people dying out there,' says Olivia.

Her aunt closes her eyes and takes a deep breath, opening them with a cold, hard stare. 'He says there was a spot of bother last night,' she says.

'He should stick to his own business and stop telling tales.'

'Olivia! How unkind. The boy dotes on you. He was looking out for you.'

'I don't need looking out for. I was only dancing.'

'Yes. I heard.'

'Why do you say it like that? Am I not allowed to dance?'

'I don't mind that you were out dancing. It's who you were dancing with.'

'Because he's not an officer . . .'

'There are rules and regulations that we must all abide by . . .'

'Perhaps if you met him . . .'

'I will not meet him. By all accounts, he's a vulgar young philistine, and certainly not good enough for the likes of you.'

'A vulgar young philistine! He's got better manners than you and Charlie, that's for sure.'

'Starting fights, behaving in such a rough manner . . .?'

'He didn't start it! If you must know, it was a fine, upstanding member of His Majesty's Royal Navy that started it . . .'

'Provoked, no doubt . . .'

'No! You're utterly wrong. Just because he hasn't got a

country estate or a title or the right number of stripes on the right sort of uniform, doesn't make him guilty . . .'

They glare at each other for a moment. Aunt Nancy looks Olivia up and down, and then she finally says, 'It's my fault.'

'What's your fault?'

'That you're a wild girl with no manners who needs to be taken in hand.'

'Rubbish.'

'I thought it would do you some good to have a bit of freedom. I hadn't realised you weren't ready for it. I've been distracted . . . You need to go home. Before you turn completely feral.'

'You said I'd done well – selling food and keeping accounts.'

'It was meant to help you grow up, until you are old enough to do something truly useful.'

'It is useful.'

'Maybe. But you can't sell fish here for the rest of your life.'

'Why not?'

'Don't be ridiculous. There are expectations. And being a fishwife is not one of them.'

Olivia rolls her eyes. 'God, you're all such snobs . . .'

'Perhaps we are. But one day this war will end, and you'll start a proper life. Get married . . .'

'This is a proper life.'

'It's not. A girl like you can't live here.'

'Why not? What about you?'

'It's different. My life is over. Yours is just beginning.'

'You can't make me leave.'

'I can.' Her aunt turns to go. 'I spoke to your mother this morning and booked the tickets. You're going in three days.'

'But I thought it was too dangerous at home? That's why I was sent here in the first place.'

'That was when no one knew what to do with you. You're older now, and it's time you did something worthwhile instead of swanning around here.'

'But you wanted me to become more independent . . .'

'Independent, yes. Without regard for your position, no.'

Olivia is shocked. Shocked that her aunt can be so forceful. Shocked that her aunt thinks she's so terrible. Shocked at the thought she might have to leave Loch Ewe. Shocked that it's leaving Jack that hurts more than anything. Everything is suddenly so complicated. Tears prick her eyes. 'I won't go,' she says. 'You can't force me.'

'Oh, believe me, I can.'

Olivia watches her aunt disappear up the track. Across the loch, the ships turn and twist with the tide. Behind her, Jack pokes his head into the hall. 'All clear?' he asks.

Olivia turns. His hair is tousled, and he still looks half asleep. He grins and they both start to laugh, but then Olivia feels as if she might burst into tears. 'Did you hear?' she says. 'She's sending me away.'

He walks to her, barefoot and bare-chested. He enfolds her into his thick arms. She can feel the life pulsing through his body. He buries his face in her hair. 'I've got to go too,' he says. 'My ship's leaving the day after tomorrow.'

'Where?' she says. It seems so unfair. They have only just met. There is so much to learn about this quiet man with the dark eyes. It is as though someone has tantalisingly allowed her to experience the most exquisite happiness, and now there will be nothing but pain.

'Back south to take on more cargo.'

'And from there?'

'Wherever the waves take me.' He grabs hold of her arm and pulls her close. 'So let's make the most of what we've got.' She pushes him away, as if pushing away the pain that is separation, but his arms are strong and solid and he does not let her go.

He follows her into the kitchen and watches her making tea. She has got used to his eyes on her, drinking her in. The hunger in them makes her feel like something precious.

The sweet, hot liquid revives her. She feels hope trickle back into her bones. 'We could run away,' she says.

195

He shakes his head. 'No. Running away's no good.'

'Is that what you did?'

'Yes.' He frowns.

She sits next to him, their arms and thighs touching. It's as if they are part of the same person. 'Will you tell me about it?'

'If you promise to cheer up.'

She smiles and pushes gently at his shoulder. So Jack tells her about Betsy and about his mother, about leaving them at the station, about the ruin of his home. 'See? If you run, you might never get the chance to say sorry,' he says when he gets to the end.

'I don't want to say sorry to them. They're pigs.'

'They're just trying to look after you.'

'I don't need looking after.'

'I want to look after you.'

'That's different . . .'

They sit quietly for a bit, listening to the wind rattling in the Scots pines, and the occasional muffled cry of a bird, or a man from the loch.

Then Jack says, 'There's something else I need to tell you.'

Olivia says nothing.

'They're right,' he says. 'I was a low-life. I used to nick things and sell them on. I tried to stop, but it was good money and things were hard . . .'

'I understand,' says Olivia. 'I do.'

'But it wasn't just little things. And it wasn't just from people who could afford it. I . . .'

Olivia holds her finger to his lips. 'Shh,' she says. 'It's in the past. You're not like that now . . .'

He shakes his head. 'It was still wrong,' he says.

'We all do silly things when we're desperate.'

'I can't imagine you stealing . . .'

'Or running off with complete strangers . . .?'

She smiles at him, and he reaches out and tucks her hair behind her ears. 'They only want to protect you. And I can

196

understand that. So should you. I am different to what I was, but you're still too good for me.'

'Nonsense.'

'I want you to know everything. Even my past. I want you to like all of me. Not just who I'm trying to be now.'

Olivia takes hold of his hand and presses her lips to it. Usually men do not seek her approbation. They assume it. 'I'm so spoilt,' she says. 'I've never had to go without anything.'

Jack takes her back into the circle of his arms. 'You're not spoilt,' he says, 'just lucky.'

The next two days are the most thrilling she has ever spent. The fact that people are trying to keep them apart pushes them even closer, and the excitement of avoiding everyone makes their time together all the more intoxicating. They vacate the bothy and, taking a few essentials with them, set up base near the pool by the rowan tree. Olivia loves the way the burn shifts and changes on its journey down the hillside: fast and frothy rapids here, shady limpid pools there, a trickle, a torrent, white and foamy, dark and peaty. From here they can look back down across the loch, to where the ships sit on the water, to the island and beyond, to where the sun glimmers on the open sea, and then to the Hebrides, shrouded in a hazy mist like a far-off land from a fairy tale. They are far removed from everyone – the soldiers, Wrens, officers, ratings, her aunt, Gladys and Maggie, Charlie – the whole damn lot of them.

Because they cannot row out on to the loch without being caught, they raid the walled garden at night, pulling up carrots and sneaking plump tomatoes from the greenhouse, enjoying them all the more in their shared furtiveness. They go to where Olivia knows that the best mussels hang in thick clusters on the rocks between succulent branches of seaweed. They collect the largest ones, smoking them against burning embers until they open to show the fleshy orange bivalve inside. They savour the smoky, salty flavour, spitting the tiny gritty pearls into their palms when they find them. They roam the beach at Gairloch, looking for the telltale signs of cockles buried in the sand and hoping to glimpse the dark fin of a porpoise rising out of the water. And they follow the sheep into the hills, to where plump brown grouse cackle like ducks and whirr up into the air in front of them.

On the second night they hide in Hans's old place in Thistle's stable. It is a wild night, and they are glad of the warmth of the straw and the roof over their heads. In the morning, all of the barrage balloons that were set up by the recently arrived regiment have been damaged in the high winds, floating flaccidly to the ground. Mac has managed to purloin one – the material is perfect for covering his haystack. He is coming back into the yard when he spots the two of them, dipping a mug into one of his milk churns, savouring the sweet, warm liquid as it drips down their chins.

'Hey,' he shouts, 'Lady McPherson's looking for you.'

Olivia and Jack drop the mug and run – back up to the rowan pool, their legs weak with effort and laughter as they stagger up the burn.

It is warm for late September. Almost as hot as a summer's day. Olivia is aware of the heat radiating from their bodies, but the water in the pool is sparkling and fresh. 'Shall we?' says Jack, and before she can answer, he is unbuttoning his shirt. She can see most of his chest already. His dark eyes are locked on hers. She starts to unbutton her shirt too. His is off now. His muscles contract as he moves his arms, and she sees the tattoo of the star on his forearm. She longs to reach out and touch his chest. He undoes his belt, his trousers. She pulls off her shirt, starts on her trousers too. Her heart is pounding. They stand opposite each other in their underwear. He is already stripping off his pants. She undoes her bra. Lets it fall to the stony ground. He yells and starts to run towards the water. She steps out of her pants too and runs after him. The skin of his bottom is as white as the moon that hung in the sky earlier that morning. He reaches the water and keeps on going, straight in, yelping and laughing and splashing. She is right behind him. She gasps as the icy water hits her warm skin. He splashes water over her. It soaks her hair, her face. She does the same to him. The sunlight catches in the drops of water, and it's as if they are standing beneath thousands of jewels that reflect and catch the sun's rays and the green of the moss and the brown of the peat and the blue of the sky and the pink of their skin.

Later, they lie on the heather under the rowan tree, a blanket half draped across them both. Jack takes Olivia's knife and starts to dig into the trunk. He carves their initials – JS and OB – and Olivia laughs and takes the knife from him, trying to add a heart that looks more like a V. Jack kisses her arm and they lie back again and watch the small wisps of cloud float across the sky between the feathery fronds of the leaves, and marvel at the soft warmth of each other's skin.

They have been lying there for a while when Olivia sits up. 'Did you hear that?' she says. There is a sound – not natural – a misplaced rock knocking against another one. Jack sits up too. There is definitely someone coming. They struggle to grab their clothes and pull them on. Olivia is grappling with her trousers, trying to do them up, the colour flooding her cheeks when a short, wiry man and a taller, stocky one come into view.

Jack relaxes, smiling at the newcomers, placing a confident arm around Olivia.

'What are you doing here?' he asks.

But Mart isn't laughing. 'You're a fucking idiot,' he says.

Jack's arm drops, leaving Olivia feeling exposed, despite the fact that she has managed to dress.

'You need to come now,' says Carl.

'What's happened?'

'You haven't got time to question, boy,' says Mart.

Jack snorts. 'But I haven't done anything . . .'

'That's not the way they see it.'

'Who sees it?'

'Lady Wotsit here's family.'

Olivia steps closer to Jack, finding confidence in being near him. 'We haven't done anything wrong . . .'

'That may well be the story as you see it, but there's all sorts of accusations flying around, and I've got to get this boy out of here or he'll be for it. Your people are threatening to involve the law, and I've got no sway over that.'

'My people? They're not my people . . .'

'Them's more your people than ours. Now if you want to help your boy, you'd best let me deal with it in my way. Jack, your stuff.'

Jack looks from Mart to Carl, and then to Olivia.

'The Bose is right,' says Carl. 'This is serious. I was there when they came looking for you.'

Jack is caught between the men who are his family and the girl he has fallen for. He looks from one to the other. 'It's not a choice,' says Mart.

'But it's not fair . . .' says Olivia. She can tell he is torn.

'If you want to know about fair, you should try being on an unarmed merchant ship at sea, missy.' Mart spits on the ground.

'But let me explain to them . . .'

'It's too late for that. Now show me a way down this bloody great mountain before I change my mind and leave you to it.'

Mart and Carl have brought the launch to the bothy to avoid the crowds on the jetty, where Charlie and Munro are looking out for them. Mart hisses at Jack to hurry, manhandling him towards the water. Olivia runs to the bothy first and then down the lawn and into the water after them, the water splashing up and soaking her trousers, slowing her down. She grabs hold of Jack, feeling the warmth of his body so different to the cold of the water around her legs, crushing him tightly against her as if she can imprint herself there. She doesn't care that Mart is staring.

Jack stops and holds her there in his arms. He looks into her eyes, frowning. 'I'll find you,' he says. 'When things have calmed down.'

She presses into Jack's hand the piece of paper that seems so flimsy compared to the tearing of her insides. 'Write to me. Tell me where you are.'

He takes the paper carefully, frowning at the letters. 'I'm not much cop at writing,' he says.

'I don't care. Just send me a time and a place, and I'll be there,' she says.

Mart pulls Jack away, his pinched face serious. Carl half smiles goodbye, his eyes apologetic. Jack does not take his eyes from her as he sits in the bows of the boat. She watches as they motor out to the ship, and when the launch is a dot and she cannot make out his face any more, she runs up to the cottage as fast as she can, her breath coming in ragged bursts.

She starts to pack, dragging her dusty cases out from beneath the bed, throwing her clothes into them. Her old shoes lie in the corner of her bedroom. She tries them on. They are far too small for her now. She can barely remember fitting into something so small and dainty. They are part of her old life, like Jasper, and her travelling clothes, and the felt hat and the gloves. They are remnants of the past, tight and constricting, like the feeling in her chest. They are dead to her, like the flowers on the table in the kitchen.

She is startled from her anger by the sound of knocking on the open door. Charlie's shadow falls across the corridor.

She shoots him a look of fury. 'I'm surprised you can show your face around here,' she says, folding her arms.

'I was worried about you,' he says. Olivia laughs dismissively and turns back to her packing. 'What was I to think?' he says, following her inside. 'You disappeared. He could have hurt you.'

'He would never hurt me.'

He places a hand on her shoulder and she shakes him off, turning to face his disappointment.

'Look. I'm not blaming you,' he says. 'It's not your fault that you've been misguided.'

'Misguided. What the hell's that supposed to mean?'

'I mean that you haven't met many people like him . . .'

'Like what?'

'He's different.'

'Why? Because his parents aren't titled?'

'No.'

'What then?'

'Because he's got a history. You can't trust someone like that.'

'You mean because he's *a commoner*?'

Charlie's laugh is short and brittle. 'You don't know anything about him.'

'I do. He's told me about his past.'

'And left out the juicier bits, I imagine.'

'He didn't actually. He told me warts and all, and I understand he's not perfect.'

'Not perfect? I don't know what he's said to you, but you just can't trust a man like that.'

'He might have had a hard time when he was younger, but he's fought to make things good.'

'So good that now he just steals milk and vegetables. Mac saw you . . .'

'That was my idea . . .'

'God, you're still so naïve. People like that don't change. It's in their blood.'

'And you're so rigid. Haven't you ever done something you regret?'

Charlie pauses for a moment. 'No. I haven't,' he says.

Olivia rolls her eyes and slams the top of one of the cases shut, struggling with the buckle in her anger. 'Let's hope you never do, then . . .'

Charlie pauses for a moment, sighing. 'Regardless of what he has or hasn't done,' he says, 'what about your parents? What do you think they would say?'

'Who cares? It's not their life. It's mine.'

'But they want what's best for you. Can you imagine what your father would think? What would they talk about when you all had dinner together?'

'I don't know. Ships. Don't be so bloody stuck-up.'

'I'm not. I'm being practical . . . It's your future.'

'And I can choose to spend it with whoever I want . . .'

'You can't. It doesn't work like that . . .'

They are silent. In the hush, Olivia can hear the rush of wind in the leaves outside and the whistle of the oystercatchers echoing across the loch.

'Things are different now,' she says finally. 'I'm different.'

'What about when this is all over?'

'You think it will go back to the way it was?'

'I don't know . . .'

'Well it won't. I won't . . .'

She stands there, defiant. She knows what is expected of her, but she knows something has changed, too.

'I'd better get on with my packing,' she says.

'I'm truly sorry that you're going,' he says.

'You should have thought of that before you went running off to tell Aunt Nancy.'

'I really thought I was doing the right thing.'

He looks so wretched that she cannot hold his gaze. 'Goodbye, Charlie,' she says.

His green eyes scan her face, but find nothing to hold on to there. He steps towards her and kisses her on the cheek. She remains immobile, her cheekbones hard, her lips cold. He walks to the door.

As Olivia watches his straight, proud back, she suddenly feels exhausted. It is so much easier to be angry at him. 'I'm sorry, Charlie,' she says, her voice a whisper. He doesn't turn. Just keeps on walking. The sky has turned a luminous peach colour and the grass on the hills around the loch takes on a soft tone. It is the start of the rutting season. The hills echo with grunts and roars. Somewhere two stags are fighting, their antlers clashing and clacking as the shadows begin to lengthen.

CHAPTER 14

Charlie

Charlie's disappointment hurts more than his injury ever did. He couldn't have been more pleased when his CO told him he was being posted to HMS *Helicon*, and he couldn't be more upset by how it has turned out. He cannot understand the madness that seems to have taken hold of Olivia. To become so involved with someone so unsuitable. He feels a stab of shame at how he has behaved, but also a genuine lack of understanding at how she could possibly see that she has a future with a man like that. He tries to push the situation from his mind and convince himself that it is simply that – a moment of hysteria that will pass once she is back among her family and has time to think rationally.

He is now billeted with Aunt Nancy, who agrees with him, partly blaming herself for letting Olivia forget who she is. Although the house is full, he has never felt lonelier, no matter how hard his godmother tries. Sometimes he wanders down to the bothy, but only shadows and the faint whisper of laughter linger in its dark corners. He spends more and more time at the Navy base, taking his meals there while the Naafi girls give him extra portions of food in the café, fussing over his shoulder which has had to be strapped again since the fight. But it is not their attention he craves. Once again his thoughts turn to his squadron. He needs to get back to them, to where he fits and knows what is expected of him, to feel the power and confidence of his plane, where the world is black and white and there is no grey.

Four long months pass, and he's still not fit to fly. Christmas has been and gone. Today is a crisp winter morning. The sky is the palest blue. The hills are clear and solid outlines, the leaves on the ground perfectly painted in frost. They sparkle, as if someone has painted them with sugar: every tiny crystal carefully placed overnight. The silhouettes of the leafless trees are lacy patterns, the thicker branches dissolve into thinner branches until they are a mass of wispy twigs. A fat pale moon sits in the perfect blue sky, a ghostly porthole to the heavens.

Charlie is on his way to the Navy base. Two hooded crows caw into the sky, their wings long black claws. He shows his pass to the guards and makes his way to the main office.

'Charlie!' An austere man with a kind voice greets him. 'How's the battle wound?'

Charlie laughs. 'Fine,' he says. 'Just the odd twinge when rain's on its way, but Mole will be pleased we've got our own personal meteorology office when we fly again.'

He follows Commander Denham into his office. From here they have a good view of the loch.

'I saw the convoy got off early,' says Charlie. 'Murmansk?' After the success of the first convoy last summer, there is one heading to Russia every few weeks.

The commander nods. 'Should be a successful run. They've got a decent escort and it's winter out there. Dark most of the time. Jerries won't be able to find them,' he says. 'Damned cold,' he adds. 'Although' – and here he rubs his hands together and blows on them – 'not exactly warm here either, is it?'

Charlie shakes his head. 'Any news of my squadron?' he asks.

'I understand they're back in Kent,' says the commander. 'Moved there a few days ago.'

'Do you know why?' says Charlie.

'Word is they're expecting the German ships at Brest to make a dash for home through the Channel.'

'The Nazis are mad enough.'

'They certainly are,' says the commander.

Charlie heads for his own desk. The hustle and bustle of the base calms him. From his window, he can see the water moving in the loch beneath the ships and the sky. It is almost like being on board a ship, except the ground is still and solid as a rock.

He leans back in his chair and stretches his legs out in front of him. His shoulder throbs. He's not sure how much longer he can take this.

Gladys appears. She also misses Olivia, but has become a good friend to Charlie. 'Tea?' she says.

'Lovely,' he says. She sits down opposite him.

'So how are you getting on?'

'I'm bored.'

'How can you be?' she says in mock horror. 'We've got car crashes and alcohol injuries, accidents on exercise and fly-away balloons . . .'

'It's not quite the same as flying . . .'

'I know,' she says. 'It must be frustrating.' She has a kind smile, concerned, but not patronising. She is attractive, with creamy skin and long eyelashes. Her dark hair is pinned back neatly. She is almost the opposite to the wild, unruly Olivia. 'Why don't you see if you can get to Kent?' she continues. 'While your squadron's land-based, I'm sure they'd be glad of your help. I know we have been.'

'Are you trying to get rid of me?'

'Not at all. I just think you'd be happier with them – and that can only help your recovery.' They chat for a while longer. Charlie enjoys her attention, the way her eyebrows knot in concern, the feel of her hand on his shoulder, the slight gap between her front teeth. For a moment, he is warmed, but then he glances across the water and sees the cold grey water and the craggy rocks and the spiky shapes of bare trees, naked and sharp in the winter sun.

*

Charlie arrives in Manston in early February. The airfield has suffered heavily from raids by the Luftwaffe, but tonight all is quiet. Conditions are not good for flying, and he can see the familiar shapes of their Swordfish lined up across the airfield. They are covered in a delicate layer of snow, like icing. He smiles to himself. It is like seeing old friends.

Charlie walks into the Fleet Air Arm's hut and the men cheer. His spirits are immediately lifted further as he soaks up the warm and fuggy atmosphere that is so much a part of his life. There is much banter about Charlie avoiding active service and holidaying in Scotland, and how he'll have forgotten how to fly, all taken in the good humour that's intended. The men fill him in on recent operations, comparing tallies and telling him he has a lot of catching up to do. Charlie feels more relaxed than he has done in months. He is back with his family.

Inevitably the conversation soon turns to wives and girl-friends.

'How's that young Olivia?' says Mole. 'I take it you're not engaged yet, else you'd have asked me to prepare my speech?'

'I've moved on,' says Charlie, not wanting to go into details. 'There's a nice girl called Gladys . . .'

But Mole knows Charlie better than that. 'What's happened, boyo?' he asks. 'It was all going so well . . .'

Charlie explains about Jack and the fight and its aftermath.

Mole whistles through his teeth. 'You've made a bit of a pig's ear out of that one, old chap,' he says. 'But I'm sure she'll come to her senses. She's young and confused. She'll soon see you for who you are. Part of your charm is that dogged belief in right and wrong.'

'I think that's exactly what she doesn't like about me.'

'You can't help it. Must've been drummed into you at that school you went to.'

'So you agree? You think I'm small-minded?'

'Not small-minded. A little unforgiving perhaps.'

'In what way?'

207

'Take this Jack. Maybe he's not as bad as you'd like to believe.'

'She's all but admitted that he used to be a petty criminal.'

'*Used* to be.'

'He's still different. He's not like us.'

Mole barks with laughter. 'Perhaps the world is changing. I bet you couldn't imagine being close to someone like me before all this business.'

'It's not the same.'

'It's a little the same.'

'You've had a good education.'

'I went to a grammar school.'

'Exactly.'

'But without this' – he points to his uniform – 'we would be moving in different circles.'

He is right, and Charlie knows it.

'No need to look so miserable, boyo. I'm not trying to make you feel bad. You're a good man. Just try and be a bit more forgiving. Put yourself in other people's shoes. Think of the Kid here. He's pulled himself up by the boot straps. You've just never spoken to him about it.'

It's true. Charlie knows nothing about the gunner. There is little opportunity to mix, and if he's honest with himself, he's had no inclination to. Mole thumps Charlie on the back. 'Enough of all this anyway. How about a drink, boyo?'

Paddy, who is now commanding officer, holds out a beer.

'Thanks,' says Charlie. 'None of you joining me?'

'Can't. We're on standby,' says Paddy. 'They reckon the Bosch will try and slip through under cover of darkness.'

'It'll be like the battleship all over again. Attacks from all sides,' says Mole.

'You'd better pray you don't end up like me,' says Charlie, tapping his shoulder.

'Not planning on it.'

Paddy deals some cards at the table. 'You know it's the same battlecruisers that did for our boys in the summer,' he says.

'All the more reason to make sure you take them down, then.'

'We will. Don't you worry.'

'We could be off any minute,' says Mole.

'Some party,' says Frank, gazing at Charlie's beer.

Charlie relaxes in the glow of the oil lamp, bantering with his squadron while they wait for their orders. It is good to be home.

But the Admiralty are wrong: the Germans don't make a break for it that night, and the crew are momentarily stood down. When the message finally comes through that the Germans are in the Channel, dawn has broken and snow swirls across the runway.

'Men, get ready. The balloon's gone up,' says Paddy.

'But it's daylight,' says Charlie.

Frank also looks concerned.

'Sorry, men. We're the only ones available,' says Paddy. 'More RAF fighter planes on the way. They'll meet us here.' But there is no sign of them in the brightening sky.

Charlie wants to go up, but Paddy is having none of it.

'But you need extra pilots.'

'I know, Charlie. But you're officially on leave.'

Mole stands and stretches, then starts to collect his flying kit. 'Don't worry, boyo. We can handle some cruisers.'

'It's not just some cruisers. It's a whole fleet! Not to mention the air cover they'll have.'

'Listen. You can't claim all the glory,' says Paddy. 'There's still work to be done.'

'Stop acting like an old woman,' says Mole. 'Have another drink. We'll be back before you finish it.'

The Welshman is flying with Paddy. The Kid is flying with Frank. Charlie watches his friends clamber into their boots and their warm coats, their hats and gloves. He follows them out into the bitter air. He sees the ground crew swarm across the frozen airfield to attend to the planes, easily identifies the shapes of Tugger and Danny. They have already been busy digging the aircraft out of the snow and running the engines on and off to keep them warm. The white ground is speckled with footsteps. The fighter planes are due to rendezvous here any moment. The excitement is so thick in the air that Charlie can feel it fizz in his veins. He would give anything to go up with them.

Billy, Frank and Paddy all slap Charlie on the back as they pass. Mole stops in front of his friend, clapping Charlie on both arms with his padded hands. Then he holds a clenched fist over his heart as he starts to sing 'Calon Lân'. Charlie can't help smiling. 'Go on,' he says. 'Get on with you.'

'I don't ask for a luxurious life,' says Mole. 'Just a happy heart, boyo.' Then he turns too, to pad away through the snow.

Charlie watches the eighteen men clamber up into their planes as the flakes bite and spiral around them. The wing commander is watching too. 'Damn fighters should be here now,' he says.

'If they're not, it'll be bloody suicide.'

They watch the six planes trundle along the runway, one after the other, following the path that has been cleared by the men on the ground. Paddy leads the way. Mole must be chuffed that he is flying with the CO. Charlie does the checks in his head: *fuel, brakes, wind speed* . . . The planes head down the runway, faster and faster. One by one they take wing. Charlie feels the lift of the plane, the familiar blow of the wind. He can almost hear Mole humming. The Swordfish circle above the airfield. 'Where the hell are these Spitfires?' he says.

The wing commander shakes his head. 'I don't flipping know.'

At last they see the shapes of the fighter planes appear out of the cloud, compact and deadly.

'Thank God. But I make it only ten.'

'Me too.'

'Where are the rest?'

'On their way?'

'Will they wait for them?'

'Any news?' the commander shouts inside.

A voice calls back. 'Nothing.' The commander shakes his head.

Charlie bites his lip. Maybe they will wait a few more minutes. But the planes are turning for the Channel, and Charlie sees Paddy's arm go up, and he knows they are on their way. The CO must have decided there wasn't time to linger.

'Maybe the other fighters will meet them en route. Otherwise . . .' There is no need to finish the sentence. The clouds have swallowed the planes. The two men on the ground salute a sky that is empty but for snowflakes that whirl earthwards. The runway is fast becoming covered in snow, and the footprints of Charlie's friends slowly fade, until they are no longer visible at all.

Charlie waits with the wing commander in the warmth of the mess room. It is the longest wait of Charlie's life. But he would rather wait for ever than receive the news that finally comes in. He tastes the salty bile of nausea rising as the wing commander pieces together the information. He hears how Paddy led the squadron with his usual fearlessness into a sky black with Messerschmidts. How the other RAF planes never arrived. He can picture the Luftwaffe gathering in swarms to dive-bomb the Swordfish, slow and graceful beneath, and the courageous Spitfires attacking back, an air battle like never seen before. He hears how the aircraft fought and clashed and tore at each other. How the Swordfish flew on towards the German ships. How the might of the German fleet turned their guns on his squadron as it flew in low over the sea. He can see the Kid and Joey and the rest of the gunners firing at the German planes from the tails of the Swordfish. He knows how the air was thickened with the screams of engines, the smoke of the flak, the tracer, the bullets. And still the

Swordfish flew on. He hears how the three battleships – along with six destroyers, forty flak ships and two hundred fighter aircraft – opened fire, and how his friends were wounded and bleeding, their wings shot away as black smoke bled into the sky and pieces of their beloved Swordfish were smashed apart. But still they flew on. They flew on until their planes were blasted into fragments, fracturing, spinning and spluttering into the sea. It took twenty minutes for the entire squadron to be blown apart. Not one plane survived.

In the pale, chill light of day, Charlie sits with the wing commander, their eyes hollow, their hearts heavy, their voices flat. 'Have they recovered anyone from the sea?' says Charlie.
    'Sounds like they've got Wilson and Joey.'
    'What about Paddy?'
    'Not a chance. His plane was obliterated.'
    'Frank?'
    'Didn't make it.'
    'Billy?'
    'No.'
    'Mole?'
    'I'm sorry, Charlie. He hasn't been found yet.'
    Five men in all are pulled from the sea.
    There is still no sign of Mole.

A few days later, the observer's body is discovered on the marshes. He was twenty-eight years old.

Mole's wife Jeannie and young daughter Alis are in the front pew of the chapel at the naval cemetery. The child is dressed in a coat of deep red with matching beret – a slab of colour among the black of mourning. She grips her mother's hand, and her little face is solemn as she watches her father's coffin, solid and dark beneath the flowers. Charlie hears footsteps as Mole's father walks slowly to the pulpit. 'No father expects to give an address at his son's funeral,' he says. 'But I am

212

honoured to celebrate the life of my youngest boy. Martyn was born in a force ten gale with a smile on his face, and that's how he approached the world . . . Whatever it threw at him . . . He lived life to the full and always with a song in his heart . . .' Charlie remembers his last conversation with Mole. Perhaps they might not have chosen each other as friends without the uniform, but here he is united with Mole's family in grief. What is it that makes us so different? he wonders. We all feel pain. Mole's father's pain is etched across his face so intensely that Charlie cannot bear to look. Instead he focuses on the stained glass behind the altar, the colours dull against a cold February sky.

Outside, making small talk with the other mourners, Charlie feels a small hand tugging at his. It is Alis. 'Do you know my daddy well?' she says, looking up at him.

He crouches down. 'I do . . . I did. Very well.'

'How do you know him?' The slope of her nose and her quick smile are her father's. It is a comfort to know a part of him is still here.

'We flew together.'

'Can I come with you next time you fly?'

'Why do you want to do that?'

'Because my daddy's an angel and we can find him up there.'

'I'd love to take you, but I don't think I'd be allowed . . .'

She nods, practical. 'Then will you say hello to him next time you go up?' she says. 'And will you sing to him? I don't want him to be lonely.' He nods because he cannot trust himself to speak. He feels her small hand, warm on his cheek. 'You mustn't be sad,' she says. 'My daddy wouldn't want you to be sad. And my mummy says that if I'm sad, he will know, and he'll be sad too.' Charlie wipes his hand across his eyes. There is a soft drizzle beginning to leave a sheen on his jacket and settling like mist in Alis's hair. 'See?' she says.

*

Later, as they lower the coffin into the ground, Mole's older brother sings 'Suo-Gân', his voice ringing out across the graves as the new widow picks up Alis and buries her face in her daughter's hair. The little girl remains serious, but when she glances at Charlie, she smiles. And even though the wind is crying in the trees that surround the cemetery, her smile gives Charlie hope. The breeze carries the smell of the sea up the River Medway, and, way up high, a lonely seagull wheels, a pale shape appearing and disappearing among the clouds like a ghost.

The pain of losing his squadron sits heavily in Charlie's soul, but every time it threatens to overwhelm him, he remembers Alis – so full of assurance that all will be well with the world; not bitter or sad. At last he is allowed to fly again. He is posted to RNAS Machrihanish to reacquaint himself with deck landings and the recent alterations to the Swordfish. He also needs to get fit, for being desk-based has taken its toll. Cross country and athletics soon turn the extra weight into muscle. It is indescribable joy to be flying again after so long. Soaring on a cloudless day or juddering between the clouds and the rain, with the feel of the wind on his face and the sound of the old engine in his ears, it is easy to believe as Alis does that his friends are up here, in the great wide sky, keeping watch.

Before long Charlie is sent orders to regroup with his squadron – the survivors and some new men – on an escort carrier at Lee-on-the-Solent. He travels via London. With a couple of days' leave he is able to meet up with Gladys and her boyfriend William, a Navy lieutenant, at Eddie's Bar. It is good to be out with friends, enjoying a drink and soaking up the atmosphere, particularly knowing that his next posting is about to start.

Gladys kisses him on both cheeks, her face fraught with concern. 'I was so sorry to hear the terrible news about your squadron,' she says. 'What brave men. You must be so proud of their awards.'

214

'We're all proud of them,' says William, firmly pumping Charlie's hand.

Charlie nods, and smiles sadly as they sit down. Every survivor has a gallantry award, and those who died had a mention in despatches. Paddy received the highest military award: the Victoria Cross. 'It's a bit galling that I wasn't part of it,' he says.

'We all feel like that,' says William. 'Our time may yet come.' He disappears to find some drinks.

Gladys leans towards Charlie, so he can hear her above the din. 'Did you hear about Olivia?' she asks.

Charlie shakes his head, the familiar feeling of shame at how he behaved pricking at his chest.

'She ran off and joined up with us – the Wrens. We all kept schtum about her age. She's flourishing. You should really get in touch with her.'

'I'm not sure she'd want to hear from me.'

'Of course she would. You're her friend. Her good friend . . .'

'Does she ever mention me?'

'We all do when we reminisce about those halcyon days at Loch Ewe.' She smiles as she says it, and he can almost hear the oystercatchers' piping call and see the sunset bright on the hills.

'What happened to us?' he says. 'I never meant to fall out with her . . . I acted like an idiot. I was just so worried . . .'

'I know that. She does too. Life has moved on for all of us since then.'

'Is she still seeing . . .' He realises he doesn't know the boy's name.

'Jack? Yes.'

Charlie leans back in his seat. 'I'm glad she's happy.'

'Actually, she's terribly worried at the moment: he's due on the latest Russian run.'

Charlie grimaces. He has heard reports of life on those icy convoys – far worse even than Norway. 'I still can't quite believe we're doing them,' he says. 'I mean, Russia of all places . . .'

'Strange, isn't it . . . But needs must. And they've been more successful than predicted so far.'

'Stalin's an ungrateful bugger, though. Moans when they don't get through – as if it's their fault rather than the bloody Jerries',' says William, returning with the drinks and placing them on the table.

'This must be something like the tenth one we've done?'

'More like the seventeenth,' says William.

'I remember talking about it with Mole . . .'

Gladys reaches out and touches his arm. 'You must still miss him like mad.'

'This is the last place we visited together.'

'I'm so sorry. If I'd realised, I would have arranged to meet somewhere else.'

'Don't be sorry. It's good to remember them.'

'I met him here a couple of times,' says William. 'Quite a character.'

Charlie nods, enjoying the memories as they reminisce.

It is very late, although the bar shows no sign of emptying. The night has worked its magic and the three of them are red-cheeked and merry. Gladys and William are all over each other, and talking about leaving, but Charlie is just getting into the swing of it. He is trying to persuade them to stay when he spots a dark-haired young girl who he recognises arrive, and start to make her way with her friends across the room. The group draws lots of admiring glances, but the girl notices Charlie almost immediately, and smiles when he waves at her.

She approaches their table, hanging back a little when she sees he is with Gladys and William.

'Betsy, isn't it?' says Charlie, standing up and welcoming her. She nods, but doesn't come any closer. 'It's good to see you again.'

William coughs. 'We'll be off now, then,' he says. Gladys rises and starts to straighten her jacket.

216

'I'll catch you up,' says Charlie.

'Or not,' says William, eyebrows raised.

Charlie ignores the comment, bending to kiss Gladys goodbye. 'You take care, Charlie,' she says.

'Nice to meet you, Betsy,' says William, and Gladys nods briefly at her as she passes.

When they have gone, Charlie motions to the seat next to him. 'Sit down,' he says. 'Let me get you a drink?'

Betsy grins and starts to unbutton her coat.

Betsy and Charlie talk. Or Charlie talks mostly, while Betsy listens. Remembering Mole has also made him remember his friend's request that he try to be more open-minded. He will start here. He will find out what drives a young girl like this to do what she does. Besides, he is enjoying the attention, and she laughs and smiles in all the right places until he feels as though they have become friends. The group of girls she arrived with grows rowdier, and there are plenty of young men vying with each other for the last dance, and it is good to feel part of it, part of the raucousness, the testosterone, the life.

As the bar staff shoo the last of the revellers outside, Charlie finds himself accompanying Betsy and her friends to a dingy house on Old Compton Street. Their footsteps echo on the pavement, the men's sure and steady, the women's neater, faster. They giggle as they trip and bump into each other in the darkness. His companions wink and grin at Charlie as they climb the stairs, but as soon as Betsy closes the door to her small room, Charlie says, 'I hope I haven't given you the wrong impression, but I don't want to do anything.'

Betsy gives a short, disbelieving laugh. 'Why are you here then?'

'I don't know. I wanted to make sure you got back all right. I was having fun.'

'We can have more fun, if you want.' She levers off her shoes, rubbing her feet as she sits on the bed next to him.

'I just want to talk.' He is struck once again by how young

217

she is. She starts to slip her dress from her arms, exposing her bony shoulders. She leans towards him, placing a provocative hand on his chest, but he pushes her gently away. 'I mean it,' he says.

'I'm clean,' she says, frowning slightly.

'It's not that.'

'What then? If you don't want it, you'd best get out. I could be earning . . .'

'I'm sorry. I didn't mean to offend you . . . If it's the money, I'll pay anyway.'

She raises an eyebrow, and he digs into his jacket for the cash, handing it over and watching her stuff it into a box inside the chest of drawers.

'Come on,' he says, holding up the blanket from her bed and placing it around her shoulders as she sits next to him. She huddles into it, like the survivor of a shipwreck. The two of them shuffle backwards until they are both sitting against the wall, leaning their heads against it.

'What do you want to talk about then, pilot?' she asks.

'Tell me what your life was like before the war?' says Charlie.

He immediately senses the change in atmosphere as she clams up, her lips becoming a thin line as if to stop the words falling out.

'All right,' he says. 'Not what your life was like, but what did you like to do? I liked walking. And playing tennis.'

'I wouldn't know what end to hold a tennis bat.'

'Racquet . . .'

'Whatever.'

'There must have been something . . .'

She looks upwards, as if she might find the answer printed on the cracked ceiling. Then she says, 'Mudlarking. That's what I liked. Still do it nowadays, given half the chance.'

Charlie raises an eyebrow and looks blank.

'Down by the river,' she says. 'Looking for things. All them bits of other people's lives washed along on the tide. Never knowing what you'll find.'

218

'Your fortune?'

'I'm not that naïve.'

'I can see that.'

'So what did you do before all this?' She points to his uniform.

'School, then training.'

'You was training before the war?'

'I always wanted to fly. It's all I'm good at.'

'Like this is all I'm good at.' She smiles then, properly this time, the harshness dropping from her face and her mouth softening.

They chat for a while longer, Charlie surprised by how easy it is. There is less of the nuance and unspoken meaning that he is used to when talking to women of his own class. He doesn't have to watch what he says. With a twinge of guilt, he wonders whether this is how it is for Olivia and Jack.

Outside, there are doors slamming and people calling. Charlie stretches. His legs are stiffening up, but he is enjoying being able to speak so freely. 'What about once the war's over?' he says. 'What do you think you'll do then?'

'I'll meet Prince Charming and live happily ever after . . .' The bitterness has returned to her voice.

'You might . . .'

'I won't. Love don't exist. Not for girls like me.'

'That's not true.'

'You said yourself, you don't want me.'

'You're too young. It's not right.'

'I'm not too young.'

'How old are you?'

'Old enough. Eighteen.'

'I don't believe that.'

'I can be however old you want me to be.'

'Don't do that.'

'Do what?'

'It's like a barrier comes up . . .'

'Why are you here anyway?'

219

'I told you. I wanted to talk.'

'Have you ever slept with a woman?'

Now it is his turn to put up a barrier. 'I asked first. How old are you really?' he says.

'I told you. Eighteen. I was ill when I was a baby.'

'I'm sorry to hear that.'

'Let me cheer you up.'

He laughs, fending her hand away. 'You never stop?'

She sighs and leans back again. 'You really don't want to?'

'No.'

'I'm tired.'

'Sleep, then. I'll look out for you.'

'I don't need looking out for.'

'I know that, but I'd like to.'

Charlie stays for a while longer, his head tipped back against the wall, staring up at nothingness, listening to Betsy's breathing grow deeper. She is lying down, curled into the blanket, her head on the pillow. Outside he can still hear the music from bars along the street. He stretches across to peer behind the blackout blind, sees that dawn is breaking. Trying not to disturb her, he edges off the bed and moves to the door.

'I hope you'll come back,' says Betsy sleepily from the bed.

'I'll come back,' says Charlie. 'I'm a bloody good pilot.'

'I don't mean just back from wherever you go. I mean back to see me.'

'I will.' He means it. Even in the cold light of day, with his mouth tacky from last night's alcohol and the blood sluggish in his veins, it feels good to be wanted.

CHAPTER 15

Olivia

Olivia had no intention of catching the train that Aunt Nancy had booked. Instead she heads for a Wren training establishment near Glasgow, where Gladys has put in a good word for her. The interview and medical are a cinch to pass, and Olivia is soon immersed in her training, suffering the blisters from her squeaky new shoes and the red welt where the rigid collar digs into her neck. The trainees' huts are in the grounds of a tumbledown castle that houses the naval officers who are also based there, training to navigate landing craft. Not only are the future Wrens kept busy learning to march and drive, but they also have to look after the men in the crumbling castle, lugging buckets of coal up and down the uneven stairs, cleaning the narrow windows, and scrubbing the stone floors, as well as laying out the officers' pyjamas and even polishing their shoes. Some of the other women suffer terrible homesickness, and some leave because such physical work is too much for them, but Olivia takes it all in her stride: the last few years have prepared her for hard graft, and anything is better than capitulating and heading back home.

It seems fitting to Olivia that she, a Navy captain's daughter, should end up in the Navy, but it isn't the only reason that she joined. Despite what she tells Gladys and Maggie and anyone else who asks, she does hope it might somehow bring her closer to Jack, perhaps because some Wrens do plot shipping movements, but also simply from being associated with the sea. In the rare spare moments that she has, she thinks of Jack, of where his ship will take him, and whether he will be safe, and how much she longs to hear from him. She begins to worry that Gladys won't forward his letters, chewing her nails down to the quick, but Gladys is true to her word, and a letter finally appears. Olivia reads and rereads it, a slice of happiness in her chapped hands. Of course there is nothing to tell her where he has been. The censors have seen to that. But it does say that he misses her and that he looks forward to seeing her whenever they can both manage to get leave. She tells him about her training, gives him her new address, feels closer to him because of her new connection with the ships.

Whenever there is a lull in duties, she scans the newspapers, searching for news of merchant ships that have gone down, hoping she will not see the *Aurora* listed in the columns. She reads with horror about the disastrous Channel Dash and the loss of the squadron of Fairey Swordfish, but remembers with relief that Charlie is still not allowed to fly. She wonders whether she should write to him, but decides it might give the wrong impression – and besides, she is still angry with him.

She has, however, kept in touch with her mother, mainly to keep her on-side, but also because she feels a twinge of guilt, although not enough to toe the line. Olivia fills the pages of her letters with details of daily life, avoiding the subject that neither of them wants to discuss, and her mother responds in similar closed fashion, writing about the slow trickle of staff away to do their bit, and the steady arrival of people employed in the businesses of war. The grooms and the houseboys joined up long ago. The butler is part of the Home Guard. Nanny has left for the NAAFI. In their place, the brown tents of the military are scattered across the lawns, and, in the lodge at the bottom of the drive, there are land girls who have turned the meadows where once Olivia picnicked among the cowslips and the harebells into deeply ploughed furrows ready for crops. Only Pike, the cook, has remained to help run the kitchens and laundry.

Olivia clips the fasteners shut on her suitcase and looks around the poky hut for one last time. Outside, the rain falls in sheets and the next bunch of trainees march past. Her training is at an end and she is to be posted to RNAS Yeovilton for her apprenticeship. She has some leave to take before then, and at last it seems there is an opportunity to meet up with Jack again. Not only has he managed to get a week's leave too, but he is able to rejoin his ship when it refuels afterwards – of all places – in 'our place on the lakes' for its next convoy. She had to read that line again. Loch Ewe. It must be fate.

Olivia has already written to Aunt Nancy, telling her that she wants to apologise for her behaviour in person and to spend some last happy hours at Taigh Mor before heading south. She knows her aunt does not harbour a grudge, and is secretly pleased that her niece has finally knuckled down and done something useful. She also knows that she must speak to her mother, both as an olive branch and a covering of her tracks.

She heads to the room that houses the switchboard operators and persuades one of the girls to allow her to make the call. She can imagine the solid telephone ringing on the desk in her father's study, the sound echoing through to the neighbouring rooms.

Eventually Mother answers, the relief evident in the tone of her voice as they start a stilted conversation, Olivia letting her know of her plans, and Mother allowing her nervous chat to run away with her. 'It's probably for the best,' she says. 'You wouldn't recognise it at home. We've had to roll up the carpets in the hall, but now the floorboards are all scuffed and scraped. There are far too many men quartered in the house. The officers are using the music room as a mess, and the ballroom is stacked with ammunition boxes. And I tell you, there are marks on the panelling in the library that look suspiciously like bullet holes. The lake looks like a mud pit, and the banks are ruined; they whizz all over the place in their tanks. And I've had to ban them from the rose garden. Someone blew the head off my cherub! Still, it's better than being a hospital . . . Or a prisoner-of-war camp . . .' She peters out. Olivia can hear the men shouting drills and parade in the background.

'So tell me how you're getting on?' says her mother. 'It's been so lovely having your letters. Did they ever find out how old you are?'

'No. It was only a matter of weeks anyway . . .' The line fizzles and crackles in the silence between them. 'But thank you for not causing a fuss . . .'

Her mother sighs. She sounds deflated. 'That's fine. Although I do wish you'd waited until all this . . . silliness had passed.'

'What silliness? I wanted to do something useful. Isn't that what you've all been on at me about? Didn't you say I needed to grow up?'

'That would include getting over this inappropriate infatuation.'

Olivia grits her teeth. She knew her mother would not be able to help herself. 'He's not some fever I can get rid of,' she says. 'I'm in love.'

'You cannot be in love with someone so unsuitable.'

'Perhaps if you met him . . .'

'I am absolutely not going to meet him. By all accounts, he's thoroughly dangerous.'

'That is rubbish . . .'

'And what about Nancy's godson? She had such high hopes for the two of you . . .'

'I don't want to go over this again.'

'Why are you so determined to ruin your life?'

'I'm not ruining it. I'm living it.'

'It seems to me that you're not yourself at the moment.'

She can hear the frustration in her mother's voice, but she is sick of being compliant. Of being expected to be compliant. 'How would you even know what "myself" was? You haven't seen me for almost three years.'

'That's unfair. Everyone in the country has had to make sacrifices. Besides, you seemed so happy . . .'

'I was . . .'

Her mother is silent for a while. 'I wish your father were here,' she says.

'*Plus ça change.* He never is.'

'That's what life is like for someone married to a man in the Navy.'

The remark is pointed. 'Perhaps I have to find that out for myself.'

The train she joins from Glasgow to Inverness is very different to that first train she took from London three years ago. There are hardly any women and no children in the carriages: it is mainly men sleeping propped against their neighbours' shoulders in the corridors, oblivious to the bumps and shudders of the train, as well as crammed in the compartments, three or four to a berth, some even in the luggage racks. The carriages are blacked out, and the only light is from a faint blue bulb. The men who are awake play cards, squinting to see. The air is fuggy with smoke; everyone is smoking these days. The train stops often because of bomb damage to the line or to let another train pass. Olivia keeps herself to herself. The men are too tired to take much notice of another woman in uniform.

At Inverness she catches a ride to Poolewe, making it through the checkpoints with ease. She still has her pass, and now that she is returning in a uniform, she barely needs it.

Aunt Nancy's home is bustling with the usual Wrens and dignitaries. The only place that is empty is the bothy. Aunt Nancy will give over any of her buildings to strangers apart from that one. 'But of course you can stay there, my dear,' she says. 'I'm so glad we've all moved on. I knew you had it in you.' She touches Olivia's cheek. 'And I'm so proud of you in that smart uniform. See you tomorrow? For lunch?'

'Maybe. I'd like to go into the hills, and out to the bay, and to see Mac and Ben. It'll be my last chance for a while.'

'I understand, dear. Enjoy your yomps. I'll be here if you need me.' And she turns to help a woman with some logistical question. It is as if Olivia never left.

Olivia runs up to see Mac. Mrs Mac is still in her element, baking and washing and looking after the sailors who come to them as if they are her own boys. Olivia apologises for stealing milk from them all those months ago, and Mac whistles through his teeth while Mrs Mac gives her a squeeze and mutters something about true love. Thistle is in the paddock. He nuzzles her gently. She checks the back of his stable, but of course Hans is long gone. She wonders whether he ever made it.

The only thing that seems to have changed is the bothy: it feels empty of warmth, light, and laughter. She collects some coal and gets the stove going, opening the windows to shift the stale air. The shells along the sills are dull beneath a film of dust, and there are cobwebs strung across the corners of the rooms. Something has knocked soot down the chimney, and it takes time to sweep up the gritty mess. She wanders down to the water. The loch is still black with ships. The garden is overgrown: Greer is busy enough in the walled garden and beyond. Olivia picks some delicate blue forget-me-nots and places them in a vase in the kitchen. A faint breeze blows through the open window, bringing with it the smell of salt and seaweed. The sound of the oystercatchers whistling across the loch reminds her that she is finally home.

It doesn't grow dark until very late. She lights a fire, losing herself in the flames. At almost midnight there is a knock on the door. She goes to it, her heart in her mouth. When she opens it, Jack is standing there, looking down at her, taller, broader than she remembers. His thick dark hair is matched by prickly stubble on his cheeks.

226

He enters the cottage awkwardly. Olivia takes his coat to hang on a peg. She feels odd, out of sync. She wants to throw her arms around him, but it wouldn't be right. Jack shows her the new badge he wears on his lapel. It is a knotted rope around the initials M and N. There is a crown on the top with sailing ships. It is made of brass and designed to fit in a buttonhole. He is very proud of it. 'To show we're pulling our weight,' he says.

'As if anyone could think otherwise.'

'You'd be surprised. We've got no uniform. People put two and two together and get five.'

She is glad she has changed out of her own uniform.

In the kitchen, Olivia makes tea. 'It'll be a bit like before,' she says. 'We won't be able to go out on the loch. Aunt Nancy doesn't know you're here.'

'Which means I get you all to myself,' he says, pulling her close, and at last she can sink into his arms.

Jack is exhausted. This is the first week's leave he has had in almost a year. There are new, faint lines across his brow and at the corners of his eyes. He has turned from green apprentice to old hand on the endless round of convoys – to America, Canada, Gibraltar, Africa. 'I don't want to talk about it now,' he says. 'I'd much rather hear what you've been doing.'

She knows not to press him. With a pang, she remembers the change in Charlie, the creeping shadows in his eyes. Jack falls asleep on the sofa. She finds a blanket and lays it over him. She sits on the floor and stares at him sleeping there, his face relaxed, the skin smooth and young again.

They are up and out of the cottage by five thirty. Jack is used to being on watch, and Olivia is too excited to sleep. The arctic terns are back, skimming the water, their slender white tails streaming behind them like sea swallows. Jack and Olivia spend the week wandering over the hills, revisiting the places they went when they first met. They see the seals out on the

227

point, curled into crescents, fanning their tails in the air. They watch the gannets diving into the sea, their wings folded back as they hurtle into the water with a splash. They forage for wild garlic, and cook it on the beach. At low tide, they search for purple glistening fronds of edible dulse seaweed in the secret bay. It is the safest beach for them to be on: away from prying eyes, and almost impossible to get to.

Olivia asks her aunt if she can dig up some vegetables this time, taking more than she needs and hoping that Aunt Nancy will put it down to her being extra hungry after living on naval rations. They spend as little time in the bothy as possible, worried that Jack might be discovered, only going back to warm some water to wash in.

Jack watches Olivia stir his clothes in the pot she has heated on the stove. 'Reminds me of my mother,' he says quietly.

Olivia keeps on stirring, the smell of the soap flakes filling her nostrils.

Jack carries on. 'That and the candles,' he says. 'There was always a candle burning because we never had pennies for the meter. I like the way a candle makes things look better than they are.'

'You mean the light?'

He nods. 'It makes everything warmer. And you can't see the damp and the mould. Maybe that's why I like it here so much.'

'Because of the candles?'

'Because it reminds me of my family.'

Olivia leaves the clothes to soak and walks over to where he is sitting. She reaches out to stroke his hair, and he leans his head against her stomach. 'You miss them,' she says.

He lets out a long breath. 'If she wasn't using it for washing our clothes, then it was for washing us. We put the tin bath in front of the fire. Betsy hated going in it, but I loved it. It meant it was Sunday, and that school was the next day.' He pauses. 'I missed school when I left. We used to get milk there. And food at dinnertime.' Olivia kisses the top of his head.

'And then the baths stopped too. We didn't have enough money for coal. We washed in cold water, but our feet and hands hurt like they were bruised.'

'Chilblains?'

He nods.

'We were hungry a lot. That made the cold worse. It's hard to get warm on an empty stomach.'

Olivia does not know what to say.

'My mum often went without, so as me and Betsy had a bit of food. If we got one meal a day, we were lucky.'

There is a long silence, punctuated only by their breathing – his heavy and fast, as if reliving the past; hers light and shallow, not wanting to distract him from his memories.

'I started stealing to help.'

'It's understandable,' she says. 'You were desperate.'

'After Walt went, we couldn't afford new clothes. Betsy used to wear a pair of Walt's old socks as tights. We held them up with suspenders, but they were always falling down and she was always yanking them up again.' He smiles at the memory. 'My mum made new clothes out of my dad's old ones. She cut them up and sewed them to fit . . .'

'She was resourceful . . .'

'It didn't feel right wearing my dad's clothes. I still hoped he would come back . . .'

'I know,' she says, pressing him into her, willing some of the bad memories to be absorbed into her own body.

'She used a sewing machine,' he says. 'Not just for our clothes, but for others on the street too . . .'

'That must have helped . . .'

'It did. But she bought it with money I gave her from things I'd thieved.'

Olivia kneels down in front of him and takes his face in her hands. His eyes are black, impenetrable, glittering in the candlelight. She forces him to look straight into her own. He looks so ashamed. 'Enough,' she says. 'You did what you had to. The important thing is you got yourself out of that situation. That's real strength of character and I think you're amazing.'

They take a couple of blankets back up to the rowan pool as they did before, making a bed of the soft moss, the smell of peat in their nostrils. They catch snatches of the men on the loch below singing and calling to each other, and of music playing, the sounds drifting out across the water and up into the hills where they lie. It is another dance by the hotel.

Olivia traces Jack's tattoo with her index finger, enjoying the feel of his skin against hers as they watch the sky turn from pale blue to indigo.

She hears his voice echo in his chest. 'I've got a feeling this one's a Russian run,' he says. 'We're assembling in Reykjavik.'

Olivia senses something – a deep fear they have been trying to avoid, a darkness like the sun being blotted out for ever by an eclipse. He has told her about the convoys he has sailed on, about the cold of Canada and the heat of Africa and all the places they have delivered supplies to around the world. And he has also told her how the Russian convoys are the ones that strike the coldest fear into the sailors' hearts. 'I thought the *Aurora* was a lucky ship?' She tries to sound bright and confident, but she has to force the words from her throat.

'So they say.' Olivia moves her head to rest it in the dip below his shoulder, breathing in his warm, safe smell. They listen to the trickle of the burn. They watch the stars come out, one by one, pinprick holes in a threadbare blanket.

'The Germans know what we're doing now,' he says. 'They've taken out more and more of us in the last few trips.'

Olivia doesn't know what to say. There is nothing comforting about heading into the path of the enemy.

'I don't want to go again,' he says.

She rests a hand on his chest, feels the heart beating inside beneath the flesh and bone, just like her own. 'I don't want you to go either,' she says. There is no doubt in her mind.

She wants to be with Jack, and she gives herself whole-heartedly to him on the hillside as the grey loch glints like cold steel in the moonlight below.

The day before Jack's ship is expected, they are clambering down on to the secret beach, when Olivia stops dead in her tracks. Jack follows her gaze. There on the rocks, where the burn dissolves into the sea, is an otter. Jack doesn't spot it until a second one appears from the water, its wet fur catching the sunlight. The wind is blowing inshore, and the creatures aren't aware of them.

The otters chase and skip and bound and hop after each other, racing along the shoreline and back to the burn, diving in, twisting, turning, bounding out again. Sometimes they are such a tangle of white chests and webbed feet, bristly whiskers and beady eyes that it is hard to tell where one ends and the other begins. But as soon as they notice Jack and Olivia, they stand up on their hind legs before diving into the water together, in perfect symmetry, noses first, thick tails behind.

'They're the first I've seen here,' says Olivia, exhaling at last. 'That is most definitely a sign of good luck.' She squeezes Jack's hand.

'How's that?'

'You should know. It's tradition: an otter protects against drowning. You're going to be fine.'

Jack pulls her close. 'If we're talking of luck,' he says. 'I want you to have this.' He draws a gold chain from his pocket and holds it up in front of her. There is a pendant on the end that flashes green in the sunshine.

'It's lovely,' she says, catching the pendant in her hand and holding it up to the light, looking at the star glinting at its centre. 'It's very unusual. What is it?'

'It's a piece of glass,' he says. 'My sister found it.'

She lets it go and it swings from his hand. 'You can't give me that,' she says. 'It's too precious.'

'You're precious.'

'Where did she find it?'

He winces. The memory is painful. 'Cherry Garden Pier. It was our favourite haunt on a Sunday . . .'

'What did she look like?'

'Me. Only smaller. Skinnier.' He smiles as he remembers. 'That was the last time I saw her properly happy,' he says.

'Keep it until you find her.'

He shakes his head. 'Please take it,' he says. 'I had it made for you especially.'

She stretches up to kiss his cheek. 'It's beautiful,' she says. 'Thank you.'

She turns to let him fasten it around her neck. Then she unties her knife from around her waist. 'It's not quite in the same league, but I want you to have this,' she says.

'Won't you need it?'

'You can return it when you come back.'

'I will.'

'Promise.'

'I promise.'

As they climb back over the hill, and the loch spreads out below them, Jack spots a familiar shape on the water. The *Aurora* is here.

CHAPTER 16

Jack

They hold each other all night, their arms and legs intertwined, each trying to ignore the fact that the ship is out there, crouching on the loch. Olivia drifts off in the early hours, but Jack can't sleep and he can't say goodbye. He leaves before Olivia is awake. He looks at her soft face in the pale morning light. The worry is gone. The skin is smooth and brown. She breathes gently against the pillow, her lips slightly parted. He kisses her cheek. He doesn't think there can be anything softer and more beautiful than her skin.

He creeps into the hall with his clothes in his hand and dresses. He quietly opens the door and glances back into the bothy one last time. There is a pain in his chest that he could do without.

He clicks the door to and grabs the bicycle. He is at the jetty in no time. The early morning sun falls across the hills that he has come to know so well. Delicate wisps of clouds touch their peaks. What he would give to be going back up there today. He can almost smell the heather and the bog myrtle.

He persuades one of the Wrens to take him to the *Aurora*. As they draw near the ship, he sees she has a new gun above her stern. She is very low in the water; her holds already packed. There is a whistle and a shout as he approaches. Carl leans over the side and waves at him. Jack is pleased to see his friend's face.

Apart from a couple of new men, including a gunner, the *Aurora*'s crew is the same. The Old Man is in the wheelhouse studying a chart, running his finger across the grids and boxes. He nods at Jack. There is no hanging around. They have refuelled and are due to set sail within the hour.

They travel to Hvalfjordur with three other merchant ships and a small naval escort. On the way, the escort spots a floating mine and blows it up. After the peace of the hills, the explosions and gunfire, and the fountains of water and billowing cloud set Jack's teeth on edge. An empty feeling opens like a hole in the pit of his stomach. It gets worse as they steam up the familiar fjord four days later. The jagged, snow-topped hills are the same, but on the water there are more – many more – ships from all over the world, and particularly America. The ragged Stars and Stripes – battered from the journey across the Atlantic – flail in a biting wind above the small and rusty, dark and dirty workhorses of the seas. All the ships are low in the water, and as the *Aurora* draws closer Jack can see why: above the rammed holds, many have trucks, tanks and even aeroplanes lashed to their decks.

This time only Captain Andersson and First Mate Russell are allowed to leave the ship. They meet the commodore and captains of the other vessels on shore to discuss the route, signals and formation of the convoy. Many of these ships have been here for weeks, and the mood is edgy. There have been fights and incidents with the Icelanders. The American sailors have been consigned on board. Frustration and rage hang like clouds around their ships: they have made it all the way from home, and across the Black Pit, and now they are stuck on board, tripping over each other, desperate to stretch their legs and see something other than uniforms and insipid food. The men are sick of the sight of each other.

Jack and the rest of his crew are happy to stick on board and watch as more ships chug into the fjord. They have been through so much together – things that no friends or family would understand. Besides, it keeps them away from the ugly rumours and whispered news about recent attacks on the Russian run. The previous convoy lost eight merchant ships. The Admiralty don't even want this convoy to get under way while there is still the perpetual light of the Arctic summer. But the politicians win, and the order comes. Jack and Carl have just started the first dog watch. The sky is grey. Jack tries to count the ships that are leaving with them, but when he gets to twenty-six, he gives up: the two columns stretch as far as he can see and well beyond. The Stars and Stripes now fly alongside the red flag of Russia with its golden sickle, the blue cross of Norway, the blue and red stars of Panama, and the Dutch – and of course the Red Duster of the British merchant marine.

At the front of the convoy the commodore sends his messages through the flags and signal lamp, the next boat repeating the message, and the next and the next, until they all receive the order to speed up or slow down or change direction.

As soon as they are out of the fjord, the sea starts to surge and swell. The sun disappears. In its place comes a steady battering of sleet. The stream of ships begins to form up nine abreast in four rows. Their British, American and Russian naval escort forms a protective ring of firepower. Jack glimpses anti-aircraft ships, submarine trawlers, minesweepers, corvettes, destroyers – they've heard there are even British and Russian submarines. There is almost one warship for every merchant ship. The Navy men stand to attention at their bows, rows and rows of peaked hats beneath the pale steam streaming from mighty funnels. The light reflects off the water, off the ships, off their guns, their depth charges, their rockets.

'What cargo have we got?' Jack asks Carl.

'Guns, medical supplies. Ammunition.'

'Let's hope not too much of that.'

'A few tanks too.'

'There's more than five hundred tanks between us,' says Mart, who is leaning over the handrail, watching the ships churn through the waves. 'And two hundred fighter planes.'

'I heard three hundred,' says Burts.

'And thousands of trucks.'

'Jesus! No wonder there's such a big escort.'

'Sounds like everything the Russians need to win the war.'

Although they know they are bound for Russia, it isn't until the Old Man confirms it that the reality sinks in. He addresses them in the mess, sucking on his pipe and running his fingers through his hair. 'I won't lie to you, men. This will be tough. But take heart – we are better protected than ever. The *Aurora* will make it. You know she will.' The men mumble and nod in agreement. But Jack's heart is in his boots, and his mouth is dry.

The ships stumble and grope their way through an impenetrable fog. The wind barrels through, but it won't shift. The muffled crunch of a ship running aground is drowned out by the shrill whistles of ships trying to steer clear of each other. Jack pulls his duffle coat tight and blows on his hands. It is already freezing.

The fog clears. The ships settle into their formation, keeping speed. Jack's eyeballs ache on lookout. A thin crust of ice like melting snow lies across the sea. The commodore's vessel hoists another flag. The message is relayed from ship to ship. 'Attack imminent.' Jack strains to see and to hear, scanning the sky and the waves, his heartbeat racing. The convoy moves as fast as it can, but the merchant ships are heavily laden and not one is built for speed. They don't have the sleek, sharp lines of the Navy ships. The convoy can only go as fast as the slowest ship, a steady eight knots. The Navy ships chivvy them along, worried hens trying to keep their chicks safely under their wings. They signal faster, slower, this way, that way, in a constant exchange of flashes and clicks.

Jack cannot see to the other edge of the convoy. There is

no clear water, just a block of ship after ship moving purpose-fully onwards. And then another fog comes down again, and he can barely see beyond the *Aurora*. For a while they feel more relaxed, cloaked from the Germans. The ships trail fog buoys from their sterns, desperate to stay in formation and not risk a collision. Jack can just make out the fountain of water spraying up behind the ship, a streak of pale grey in the gloom.

While the creeping, crawling cape of fog swirls around them, they have to slow down and zigzag more. All Jack can hear is the clang and rattle of the *Aurora* and the clicking of her signal lamp. Their course is constantly altered. There is less room for manoeuvre between Norway and the ice pack. The escort signals the commodore. The commodore signals the convoy.

Jack knows they're constantly being watched. The hair on the back of his neck tingles. It is only a matter of time. Grabbing some hot food in the mess, they hear the grim sound of the escort depth-charging somewhere far off to starboard.

'U-boats,' says Mart.

'You're telling us,' growls an engineer. 'The noise down there is so loud: we put cloth in our ears to block it out.' Jack remembers their conversation on the climb to the waterfall. He is glad to get back out on deck, however cold it is.

The fog starts to lift. Through a gap, a Focke-Wulf plane appears as if from nowhere. It swoops over them. They have no time to react. But the clack of its machine gun is half-hearted before it disappears again. There is no doubt that it will send more.

The U-boats harry them, but the escort keeps them safe, seeing off the attackers, keeping the convoy together. The ice floes grow larger: green, blue, and white sculptures smoothed by fierce winds dot the sea. A line of black from a ship's funnel is like an arrow pointing the way. The signal goes up from the commodore: 'Make less smoke'.

They swing around the north of Iceland. New escorts arrive.

237

If ships could swagger, then these ones do. Jack hears music playing from their loudspeakers. The confidence warms him. He lets his gaze run across the ack-ack ships to the side of the convoy and the anti-submarine trawlers at the front. With this much firepower, surely they will make it.

The alarm bells start going, calling a warning to each other across the water. U-boat in the vicinity. As if they need reminding. The growl and boom of depth charges and guns' replies.

The sun spreads across the sea, making it look like molten silver. Now it never goes down: it is perpetual daylight. Even at midnight, Jack can feel the sun on his skin. It makes him think of lying under the rowan tree with Olivia. He longs to be there again. If only to sleep. He aches for sleep. They all do. But brief respite, catnaps are all they get.

Jack's ears are filled with a new sound: the constant buzz of German reconnaissance planes, lazily circling like buzzards. They remain out of range of the escort's guns. One plane circles so many times that a ship signals with its lamp to ask the pilot to fly the other way and stop making everyone feel dizzy. The plane slowly turns and continues the other way.

As soon as one German plane is low on fuel, another arrives to take its place. It is only a matter of time before the bombers appear. Mart keeps his crew working all the time. They scrub and paint and polish. They splice and check and double check. They try not to think of loved ones. They pass debris in the water. Deflated life rafts, wood, metal. There is no sign of life.

The light is dazzling. The world shimmers. Banks of fog appear to starboard like long low clouds. They disappear just as quickly. The ships in the convoy grow and shrink like images in the hall of mirrors at a funfair. One minute they are tall and thin; the next they are long and flat; sometimes they appear to be upside down. Mirages distort and flicker. Jack feels as though he is dreaming. His thoughts wander. He doesn't know if it is four in the morning or four in the evening.

The ice pack stretches away to port, thick, heavy, endless, sparkling, white.

The U-boats send out long signals, calling the Luftwaffe in. The reconnaissance planes shadow them. The alarm bells start up again. The sky darkens. And finally the Heinkels and the Junkers come. The naval ships retaliate; black puffs of flak fill the sky. It sounds as if every ship is firing. But still the bombers come, darkly swarming over the convoy, and two of the merchant ships are hit, great columns of smoke rising into the air. The wounded ships fall back. The others can do nothing except hope that the rescue ships at the rear will help. No one is allowed to stop when in convoy, even if there are men calling and screaming in the water.

A cool mist offers some respite. Unseen, planes drone above it. Jack's mouth is parched. *Buzz, buzz, buzz.* He would prefer to be able to see them. In answer, the mist clears. A fresh wave of torpedo bombers comes from behind. One of the planes flies up the line of the convoy, every ship firing at it until it somersaults into the sea. The ack-ack ships chase the bombers away, but they still manage to drop their torpedoes. The deck crew see the white streaks below the surface. They wonder if it will be their engine rooms next. Speed picks up to ten knots.

There are more planes on the next attack. They fly past the escort, through the barrage of guns, and dive at the convoy. Bombs float through the air, splashing into the sea. Torpedo tracks spiral through the clear water. The merchant ships struggle to avoid them. Jack sees the telltale sign of another damaged ship: the plume of smoke billowing into the sky. He can't tell which ship it is. The escort fights back. More planes spin into the sea. A German pilot swoops down and lands on the water, scooping up the survivors standing on a downed plane's wing. The Allies cannot help acknowledging such bravery.

The world is unreal. Jack squints. His head throbs. An

iceberg is another ship. A ship is a building. The white tip of a wave is a tinfish speeding past. When he isn't on watch, it is impossible to sleep. It is too bright. He is too anxious. And there is that constant drone of the German planes watching them, following them, reporting back to base.

They are north of Bear Island. The planes still shadow them. But today the Americans are ebullient. It is Independence Day. They hoist fresh, bright Stars and Stripes. Music drifts across the water. There is dancing. Jack and Carl look at each other. They don't mention it, but they are both thinking of the last time they danced. On the shores of Loch Ewe, with pretty girls on their arms and solid ground beneath their feet. An American ship signals that Independence Day is a holiday to be celebrated with large firework displays. 'I trust you will not disappoint us,' it adds.

The sky soon darkens again. Bombs above, torpedoes below. The sound of retaliation is ferocious. Every gunner is at his gun: the pom-poms, the Oerlikons, the Bofors, the Lewis guns. The sound pounds in their ears. The Luftwaffe fly in fast and furious. Planes dive into the sea. The noise and the acrid stench of burning remind Jack of London. The sun is blotted out by great swirls and clouds of dense black smoke. The Russian tanker is hit. It lags behind. They are astonished to see female crew manning the guns in retaliation, and working hard to put the fires out.

Another German pilot lands to rescue his fellow airmen. They fly safely away from the chaos, leaving behind a sea glistening with multicoloured patterns of oil. But the convoy is in an optimistic mood. They have seen off another attack. They are perfectly protected, and more than halfway to Russia, heading into the Barents Sea. Spirits are high. The afternoon is bright and clear. Jack allows himself to think of Olivia briefly. Of her bright smile up in the hills. Of swimming in the rowan pool. He is ready for the next attacks.

*

240

Jack and Carl are just coming off their watch. It is eight in the evening. The sun is still bright above them, on its endless tortuous circuit. Jack is looking forward to some food, hoping it will dampen the dull fear scrabbling inside him. As the boys make their way along the deck, they hear shouts from across the calm sea. There is confusion. Burts says, 'What are they doing?'

Someone else yells, 'Hey! Come back!'

The boys peer across the glassy water, screwing up their eyes against the glare. Jack rubs at his eyeballs. Looks again. It can't be true. Around the convoy, it appears that the escort is peeling away, one by one, at speed.

The crew stand on deck astounded. 'Where are they going?' asks Burts. There is panic in his voice. 'What's happening?' There is panic in everyone's voices.

Everyone apart from those on watch is called to the mess. Andersson comes to address them.

'Men, we have received a most important signal. It tells us to scatter and proceed at speed to Russia.'

'Scatter?' says Mart.

'What do you mean?' asks the Chief.

Andersson pulls on his pipe and repeats: 'We are to make our own way to Archangel.'

'Without an escort?'

'I believe this is right.'

'Why?'

'I can only assume that the Kriegsmarine is on its way.'

The men glance at each other. They whisper the name of the largest and deadliest ship in the German fleet. It is enough to make them clench their hands together, in fear and prayer. Cook's pots clatter and bang in the galley.

Andersson nods slowly. 'We will head for ice.'

'There must be eight hundred miles still to go.'

'Can't we try and stick with some of the others?'

'No.' Andersson rests his pipe in his hand. 'The order is to disperse. This we have to do.' He stands. 'Chief? Some speed, please.'

The Chief nods. He will get the best out of his men. He always does.

The same conversations must be going on aboard every merchant ship in the convoy. The ships are in disarray. Some are going in circles. The last of their naval escort disappears in a south-westerly direction, a pip dissolving into nothingness.

Mart spits into the water. 'Must be where them Nazis is coming from.'

'They'd better get them.'

'They will.'

But Mart's confidence can't help the creeping dread working its way along the deck: they are all alone in a sea full of U-boats. They are as close as they can be to the German-occupied airfields of Norway. The German fleet is on its way. And they are as good as unarmed.

'We're sitting ducks,' says Burts.

'Not for long,' says Mart, nodding his head towards the funnel, which is beginning to blow more smoke from the Chief's engines.

Jack still feels dazed. 'I can't believe they've abandoned us, the bastards,' he says.

Mart takes him by the neck and slams him against the mizzen mast. 'Don't let me hear you speak like that again,' he says. He sniffs long and hard. 'Those boys is just following orders like the rest of us.'

The merchant ships flash and signal at each other. 'See you.' 'Good luck.' The *Aurora* sets her own course, picking up speed as she goes. Now that they aren't following directions from the specially adapted compass of the commodore, they have to use their own. It swings and fluctuates. They are too near the North Pole to trust it. The ships quickly lose sight of each other. Before long the *Aurora* is steaming as fast as she can through hazy sunshine. Around her all is quiet.

Jack prays for cloud, fog, anything to cover them and the

foamy line of their wake until they can find somewhere safer. But where is safe out here on the lonely sea? As they head north-east, the sea becomes a patchwork of thin ice stretching for miles. Beyond it is the ice pack, impenetrably thick. On they steam.

The U-boats watch below the waves, waiting for their moment. Andersson takes the *Aurora* as close to the ice pack as he dares. They don't want to get stuck in an ice field, but this is as far away from Norway as they possibly can be, and at least the deadly U-boats – painted white especially in this Arctic region – can't attack them from the port side, can't surface in the thick ice, or fire at them between the hulking icebergs. The ice clangs and scratches and bumps at the hull. A terrible fear settles over the ship. They are sure the Germans are everywhere, beneath them, behind them, next to them. The men spot things that aren't there. Waves look like battle-ships. Ice looks like periscopes. Seagulls look like planes.

Andersson doesn't sleep. He keeps watch in the wheelhouse, inspects the charts. He orders the crew to hang anything white – sheets, tablecloths, vests – over the ship to disguise it against the ice. A snowstorm blows up. The men grab fitful sleep while they can. For hours they see no other ships. They wonder how many of the others have survived.

Jack rings the alarm bell. The plane is on the horizon. Easily close enough to spot them, it arcs slowly through the sky and disappears, a black dot receding into nothing. Far away to the east, a pall of black smoke rises into the air and then along. Another plume drifts to the south – and another. It is as if the sea is bleeding into the sky. Jack's insides are a lead weight. In the radio room, Sparks relays the distress calls from their fellow ships to the bridge. The *Aurora* bumps and grinds against the thickening ice.

When it happens, it is a shock. Jack is just changing on to watch, and there is a crunch that goes through his body as the *Aurora* rolls and shudders. At first he thinks they have hit an iceberg, but then black smoke begins to billow into the sky. The world grows dark. The ship bucks again. Burts screams. There are men in the water. Men Jack has lived with for more than a year. Men who are his family. The sea is on fire around them. He tries to help Mart release a jammed life raft, using Olivia's knife to hack at the rope, but he can't stay upright because the whole deck is tipping, tipping, and now the ship is rising straight out of the water above him. And soon he'll be in the water with the fire and with the bodies and he mustn't breathe; he doesn't want to let oil get into his lungs. But his feet are slipping and the water is coming towards him and he tries to move back, to grab on to something and – is that Mart? And where's Carl? The sky is so blooming bright, but he can't see anything because of the smoke and something is stinging his eyes and there are too many men shouting and screaming and he can hear himself calling for Carl but he can't hold on any more and the ship is gone, the *Aurora* is folding and sinking, just her stern left sticking up above the water and he knows he's going into the flame and debris and ice but he promised he'd survive. He promised.

Jack hits the water, and the breath is knocked from him as if he has hit concrete. Freezing liquid splashes into his face, into his ears, into his eyes. The air above him is thick with black smoke, and the sound of explosions and yells mixes with the roar of the sea. His hands are numb. His mouth is slick with the oil that is spreading across the surface. He retches, then gasps for air, but water fills his lungs and he gags again. A wave smashes into the back of his head and he is underneath. Sounds are muffled here, but he can still make out the shouts of his friends, the whoosh of fire, the sharp zing of bullets. He tries to propel himself upwards, to force his head above the water, to try and suck at the oxygen above. But his legs are uselessly numb. He is suddenly launched skywards and he gulps at the air, but it is full of fumes and smoke and he chokes again. The planes above are still hammering at them, strafing the water with bullets and charges that splash into the sea all around, exploding out of sight. He barely cares any more. Someone unrecognisable is flung past, a saggy, pale face empty of life, pummelled by water and thrown against the floating, sinking, broken parts of their ship. There are men everywhere: confused, scared or face down, as if searching for something beneath the frothing sea. They move up and down, side to side, but their movements are not their own. They have become playthings of the sea, tossed about like seaweed.

How long has he been in the water? Ten seconds? Twenty? What was it that Mart always said? One minute was goodbye to your feet? Two, and goodbye world? Or was it three? He glimpses flashes of things: rags, limbs, a comb, a mug all bob past; close one second, they disappear and reappear further ahead or behind him. Blackened cheeks, melted skin, lumps of flesh mixed with ice and debris. There is no order, no sense in what he sees. He could be back on the streets, running past the limbless and the dead. Water splashes into his nostrils: freezing, salty, it scrapes at his eyeballs. His mind slows. The noise and the smell and the cold recede. He sees his father and brother before they wore khaki, sitting at the kitchen table, laughing. He sees his mother drying her hands on her apron, her dark hair loose and curling against her shoulders. His sister is there too, limp with sleepiness, curled against him in the chair, solemn and trusting, in the time before she grew so scared. And he sees Olivia on the hill. Her fearless eyes are the colour of the early morning sky. Her skin is smooth and brown. Her smile wide and kind. He hears the oystercatchers calling to each other across the loch, but he realises it is men shrieking to be heard above the thunderous, crashing noise. Another explosion, and he sees the silhouette of a lifeboat and then something whacks into the side of his head. He knows this should hurt, but he is numb and the world is black.

*

Olivia is very close to him now. He tries to reach out to her through the grey-green, angry water – but he can't. She smiles and her blue eyes flash in the dark, but he blinks and it isn't her. It is Betsy, cold and alone, her scared, dark eyes melting into the darkness. He shuts his eyes one last time. Olivia. He can feel the richness of her hair, gold like the sinking sun. He can hear her voice like the burble of the burn where it falls into their pool on a lazy afternoon. He strains to make sense of what she is saying, but it is impossible above the spray and the foam and the guns and the screams. Then all noise is sucked away, and he slips after Betsy into the icy, empty, infinite dark.

CHAPTER 17

Charlie

Charlie has been with his new squadron for long enough that the dynamic is comfortable. He has spent a lot of time in the air, and the pain has eased, although there is not a day that he doesn't miss Mole and Billy in the plane. Tonight his carrier is back in Lee-on-Solent, and the men have a chance to relax at the base onshore after gunnery practice.

It is a humid early summer evening. Beyond the blocks of hangars and the flatness of the runways lies the Solent – pale grey beneath an overcast sky. In the distance Charlie can see the Isle of Wight, dark and low in the water. He is nursing a drink with his new observer in the impressive old building that houses the Fleet Air Arm wardroom, on the southern edge of the airfield. Ned is short and stocky, with a mop of unruly ginger hair. He is a fine observer, but he is not Mole. The two of them are soon joined by more officers: you are never alone for long. The newcomers are mid-conversation, one of them shaking his head and saying, 'What a bloody disaster . . .' as he places his drink on the table and pulls back a chair without even glancing at Charlie and Ned.

'Madness,' says the other, also sitting down.

'They actually say that the admiral is mad. Something wrong with his brain . . .'

'Shh.' They nudge each other as they suddenly notice

Charlie and Ned; they do not want to be caught being dis-
respectful about their seniors.

'Don't mind us,' says Charlie.

'Have you heard the news?' says the first man.

'What news?'

'About the latest Russian convoy?'

Charlie shakes his head.

'Terrible affair. Order came in to scatter. Escort left and
didn't go back.'

'Not all the escort,' says the other officer. 'Some rescue
ships stayed . . .'

'So what happened?' Charlie asks.

'What do you think?'

'Nazis starting taking them out one by one.'

'It's a complete fiasco.'

'Don't know why they don't take you lot with them,' says
the man, pointing at Charlie's wings. But Charlie has already
slipped out into the night.

Charlie manages to reach Gladys on the telephone in the radio
room at RNAS Yeovilton, where Olivia has been drafted since
passing her training. Gladys confirms his fear, that Jack's ship
is missing.

'You should come and see her,' says Gladys. 'Really. I think
it would help.'

'I'm not so sure . . .'

'I am. She's not in a good place at the moment. She won't
even eat.'

The phone crackles in the silence. Whatever has happened
between them, Charlie knows better than anyone the devas-
tation of losing those you care about.

'Just come,' says Gladys.

Charlie travels overnight to Somerset. Gladys escorts him to
Olivia's hut. This is a world of concrete, grey and hard. Nothing
lives here: the base is a vast expanse of dreary asphalt runways

set in a flat basin and surrounded by Nissen huts and hangars. Charlie takes in the lowering sky; there is a threat of rain in the air – fat, dark clouds moving slowly towards them, preceded by a warm, damp wind. In the background planes land and take off: circuits and bumps. He remembers them well, for this is where he trained four years ago. Four years! It seems like a lifetime.

Inside, the hut is as drab as the world outside. There are fourteen metal beds, fourteen chairs, and seven chests: half for each Wren. Olivia is alone, sitting on her bunk, fiddling with the pendant on her necklace, turning it over and over between her fingers. Her skin is pale – no longer weathered by the Scottish elements. But it is not just the pallid colour that marks a change in her. She is thin – too thin – and there is a haze of illness about her, a sheen to her skin. She is utterly different to the girl he remembers, who radiated health and vitality. It is only a year since he last saw her, but she has aged, and a light has gone out.

Gladys hangs back by the door. 'I'll come and get you for lunch,' she says, before turning to make her way back across the windswept base. Olivia stands and allows Charlie to fold her into his arms. She seems to fit so perfectly there.

'I'm so very sorry,' he says. 'I've chased up what I can. All we know for sure is that the *Aurora* definitely went down.'

'Do you know if she managed to launch any lifeboats?' she asks.

Her hope is so strong that he can almost touch it. He does not want to encourage it, but he wants to stave off her falling into the abyss for as long as possible. 'Not yet. The Russians and the British are searching for survivors. But there's not much news coming through, I'm afraid. It's under strict embargo.'

'Oh Charlie. Will you keep on trying?' Her eyes are red from crying, and hollow from lack of sleep, but she is still beautiful.

'I can't promise anything . . .' he says.

249

'Thank you.' She hugs him again and he briefly rests his face in her hair. She smells of despair, sweet and sickly.

'What a terrible business,' he says.

'Why did they abandon them?' she asks.

He sighs. The entire Navy was sickened by the news. They all feel it: from the lowliest stoker to the highest admiral, from the most ancient of veterans to the freshest recruit. It turned out that the German fleet wasn't on its way, and the merchant ships were left defenceless in a place that is hard enough to get out of if you're armed to the teeth. A bitter shame runs through the British Navy like a wire snare, threatening to choke. 'It seems as though they were expecting an attack by the cream of the German fleet.' He can feel her face, damp and hot, against his chest.

'But why didn't they go back when they realised it wasn't coming?'

'I think some of them did, but it was too late. I know they would have done what they could. Every one of those men would have wanted to stay and help. But we have to follow orders . . .' Even as he says it, he can't help thinking it sounds unsatisfactory.

'Oh God,' she says, her bottom lip trembling again. 'I imagine the Nazis are having a field day . . . Those men have nothing to protect them . . .'

'There's always hope . . .'

'Hope?' She sounds bitter when she says it. 'That's what I always used to say. But what hope is there? If he has escaped the torpedoes and bombs, the cold will get him . . .'

'Please, Olivia . . .'

'Do you know how long men survive in the water out there? Seconds . . .' She starts to sob.

'Stop torturing yourself.' Charlie's voice is loud and strong; he needs to be firm. 'Getting in a state won't help him.' Olivia pushes him away and collapses back down on her bunk, but at least she has stopped crying.

He lowers his voice. 'Look,' he says. 'You've no idea what

might be happening. It's a big old ocean, and these men are made of strong stuff.' He perches on the wooden chair at the foot of the bed. 'I'll do my best to find out what I can. But they're going to keep as quiet as possible over this one. It's a blow to the morale of all at sea, let alone the public at home.'

She sighs, a sad, long sound. The tears still glimmer in her blue eyes. She lays her hand on Charlie's arm. It is small and pale on the dark of his sleeve. 'Thank you for coming,' she says. 'Really. It means a lot.'

'That's what friends are for.'

'I'm sorry I didn't write to you about your squadron.'

'It doesn't matter.'

'It does. I was too wrapped up in my own world . . . And after we argued . . .'

'Forget it,' he says. 'It's in the past. Let's start again.'

'I'd like that.' She wipes her eyes with her hands. 'Look at me,' she says, her voice stronger as she tries to smile up at him. 'I must look frightful.'

He shakes his head. He thinks she looks fragile. 'I promise you it gets better,' he says.

'Does it?'

'It might not feel like it now, but yes. The sun keeps on rising, and you'll stand up and dust yourself off, paint on a smile and get on with it.'

'I can't help thinking that if he's gone, I'll never get over it.'

'Perhaps. But you will learn to live with it.'

'Have you?'

He nods, thinking of his parents, and of Mole and Frank and Paddy, and realising with surprise that it's true.

Gladys appears at the door. She makes her way towards them both.

'Is there any news?' Olivia asks.

Gladys shakes her head. 'No. But it's lunchtime.'

Olivia's shoulders slump. 'I'm really not hungry,' she says.

'You must eat.'

'I can't seem to hold anything down.'

'Come on,' says Charlie as brightly as he can. 'No point in worrying until we know for sure. And you need to keep your strength up. What good will you be to anyone if you're ill?'

Olivia rises from the bed reluctantly, and Gladys hugs her friend's arm tightly as she propels her into the greyness outside.

Charlie follows. The rain is beginning to spit on to the asphalt. He tilts his face up to the darkened sky, feeling the drops, cool and fresh on his skin. He takes Olivia's other arm, and together the three of them cross the air station.

After Charlie has visited Olivia, he heads to London for the night. He is pleased they have patched things up, but the feeling of guilt over how he behaved has been replaced by a new feeling: envy. He had hoped that she might forget Jack, but it is now evident that she won't, and he cannot help feeling jealous that she has shared such intimacy and understanding with someone – that she is so bound to another person. The jealousy is partly of Jack, but also of the intensity of her feelings. He wants to be wanted like that, to share a longing, to taste that hunger.

He has an urge to find Betsy. He hopes she will be at Eddie's Bar. He peers into the darkness, scanning the faces of the people that he passes. It is busy tonight, and he is almost ready to give up, when she suddenly appears at his elbow, her eyes shimmering in the dim light. 'I've been looking out for you every night since you last came,' she says.

He smiles back at her. 'I don't believe you. That's fifty nights or something.'

'It's true,' she says, pushing gently at his arm.

'That's good to hear.'

They find space on one of the plush benches that run alongside a table, squeezing in next to a woman who is lighting her cigarette from her neighbour's, the glowing ash outlining her fur coat and the waves of her curled hair. On their other side is a couple so engrossed in conversation that their lips are almost touching. No one takes any notice of the newcomers. The table is littered with glasses and bottles and jugs and cigarette cases. On the other side of the tables, many of the chairs are turned towards the dance floor, and people come and go, resting their tired feet and downing their drinks before joining the dancers again.

'So where have you been?' says Betsy, tipping her head close to his ear so that he can hear her above the music.

'All over the place. Mainly the Atlantic, though,' says Charlie, pouring some wine.

'How long have you got off?'

'Only tonight.'

'You look tired.'

'I am. I've just had to visit a friend to give her some bad news.'

'Someone missing?'

He nods. 'A sailor. Ship's been sunk and no idea whether the lifeboats were launched. Searching for anyone out there is like searching for a piece of ash in a bonfire.'

'Won't they have sent a signal or something?'

'No. A distress signal is as likely to be picked up by a Jerry as a friendly.'

'You can't just lose someone . . .'

'I'm afraid it happens all the time. It's one of the hazards of the job. Ships disappear. They burn to nothingness. They sink and leave only an oil slick. No bodies. Nothing . . .'

'You think he's dead, don't you?'

'Yes.'

And as he says it, he knows that's exactly what he believes, and he feels so wretched that Olivia is going to be hurt, and so wretched for still wishing that it was him she was missing.

Betsy downs her drink, lays a hand on his arm. 'Who will tell me if you get lost at sea?'

'I won't get lost.'

'I hope not.' She is looking at him as though he is the only thing she cares about in the world, and it makes him feel so

253

good, that someone cares, that someone might miss him as much as Olivia misses Jack.

He feels his cheeks redden as she moves closer. He can sense the shape of her small breasts through her dress. He tries to quench the desire that is rising inside him by moving away, but she shuffles closer. And the thought flows through his mind that life is too short not to give in to desire, and even as he allows her hand to drop to his thigh and her lips to find his, he hates himself for allowing it, but he is also all too aware that these could be his last days on earth, and what's the point of living if you don't experience what living is about? Around them, the music steps up a gear, and the people dance as though they do not want tomorrow to come.

CHAPTER 18

Jack

When Jack wakes he can't open his eyes. They are encrusted with salt. It is everywhere: scratching at his eyeballs, cracking his lips, rubbing his skin, sticking in his hair. The movement of each wave crunches into his throbbing bones. Shadows flicker behind his gummed up eyes. Someone cradles his head and gently dabs at his eyelids, then pushes a cold mug against his lips. 'Only a sip, mind.' The cool, clear liquid trickles into Jack's mouth; absorbed by the salt, it barely makes it to his throat.

Eventually, he sees that he is lying under a canopy in the forepeak next to another man. There is room only for the two of them – and barely that. Jack pushes himself up on an elbow and squints into the brightness. The lifeboat is packed. The men sitting around the edge lean against each other, their eyes tight with fear and exhaustion. Jack scans the faces: Burts, the Chief, Grifter, and Fred, the galley boy, have made it. There is no sign of Mart or Andersson or Russell. There is no sign of Carl. The light hurts his sticky, sore eyes. The Chief bends down, blocking the sun, turning the world dark. He hands Jack a biscuit. It is tasteless, dry and salty. Jack can barely chew; his mouth is tacky with crumbs.

'How long?' he croaks, the words rasping and clutching at his throat. His voice sounds like a stranger's.

'Two days,' says the Chief.

Jack crawls from beneath the shade, and another man immediately takes his place. Tired hands help haul Jack up and slot him into the new space on the wooden plank. He is grateful that they are jammed together. There are pins and needles in his legs. He is not sure he could hold himself up alone. He runs a shaky hand over his head: someone has stitched it up crudely.

The crew have already got the boat in order. The Chief and Burts take readings and study the chart that they have crudely drawn up to the best of their knowledge. One group pulls on the oars, while another bails water from the bottom of the lifeboat. Someone steers, and after a turn resting beneath the forepeak canopy, they rotate on lookout, wedging themselves in against the mast so they can more easily brace against the waves. Each man looks forward to his rest beneath the canopy – which isn't exactly a rest because every time the boat slams against the water it jars their bones – but it is the only time they are able to stretch their legs and keep out of the relentless sunshine and sea spray.

'Where are we headed?' says Jack.

'There are islands,' says the Chief. 'North of Russia.'

'If we make those,' adds Burts, 'someone will find us.'

'Let's hope it's not the Kriegsmarine,' says Grifter.

Fred whimpers. It is a sound that reminds Jack of Betsy during the night raids.

There is always water in the bottom of the lifeboat, however hard they bail. At least the action keeps Jack's body warm. But his feet are constantly cold. A hunger of the sort he had forgotten begins to eat away at his insides. There are a few biscuits and some tanks of fresh water, but not enough to keep fifteen men alive for long. There are cigarettes. There is a rifle. Everything is cold and everything is damp and covered in salt. His life jacket rubs and chafes at his body.

Another forty-eight hours and the men stop worrying about

the Germans attacking and start worrying about the cold and the hunger. Jack sees now why Mart growled and spat like a tomcat to keep them in order. Some of these men have been in prison, most have had no other job than that in the merchant marine. It's as tough as a life on the street. A man with a neck as thick as a carthorse discovers a cask of whisky. 'Let's drink it,' he says. 'It'll warm us up.'

The Chief shakes his head. 'No,' he says. 'It won't warm. It will only kill you.'

A squabble breaks out. More than one man wants to drink. 'Who're you to tell us what to do?' they say, desperation in their eyes.

'He's the only officer here,' says Burts.

'He's not even British,' says the man.

'What's that got to do with it? He's still ranked. Same as us.'

'I'm not taking orders from no foreigner.'

'Who would you take orders from? Who's next?'

'It's the boy,' says Burts, looking at Jack. Hard as it is to believe, he is right. Not one officer apart from the Chief made their boat.

Jack shakes his head. 'It's the Chief. He came down on our ship. He's one of us.'

The Chief holds up his hand. 'Let them do it,' he says. 'They'll see.'

The men pass the bottle around the boat. Three of them swig at it. When it gets to Fred, he stares at it before looking at Jack and then back at the bottle, which is shaking in his hand. He cannot stop shivering.

'Go on, son,' says the man with the neck. 'It'll put hairs on your chest.'

'Warm your cockles,' says another, snorting with laughter. Fred looks apologetically at Jack and then lifts the bottle to his lips. The men chant as he drinks. The bottle goes around again. The same men drink. Jack tries not to watch. At least Fred's teeth have stopped chattering. The Chief gazes out to sea.

As the night progresses, the drinkers become more rowdy. Jack pretends to sleep, but he keeps his hand on Olivia's knife. When it is their turn to row, the men strip down to their vests, their pale skin steaming in the cold night air. When it is Jack's turn to row, their faces swim in and out of his vision, leering at each other, babbling nonsense until eventually they quieten, their heads lolling with the swell.

In the morning the Chief shrugs. 'I told them,' he says. 'It warms you on the inside and you forget about the outside.'

All four of the drinkers are dead, their bodies pale and stiff, so cold from their alcoholic slumber that ice crystals have formed in their bellies. Jack helps to remove their clothes as Burts whispers a prayer. They tip the cold, heavy bodies into the sea. Fred is lighter than the rest. He was only fourteen. Jack huddles closer to his neighbour.

'More food for us,' says the Chief.

'Might as well have been the rest of us,' says Grifter, gazing back at the wake of the boat, where the dead have long since disappeared.

'What you say that for?'

'What's the use in us drifting about here? We won't get paid for it. Our pay stopped as soon as we was sunk.'

'You're wrong. That's changed. They promised to pay us even if our ships do go down.'

'You think a country that abandons us cares about what it promises?'

'I'm not even from your country.'

'Look,' says Burts. 'Andersson was a good captain. I'm sure he's made provision.'

'It's not him that decides. It's the company that owns the ship,' says Grifter.

'What are you saying? Because he is Norwegian, he can't look after us?' says the Chief.

'Stop talking shit.'

'Who's talking shit? You're the stupid one.'

258

Grifter pulls a knife. 'Don't call me stupid.' The rowers stop rowing. Everyone stares at Grifter with the knife.

The Chief flicks his fingers. 'Come on, then.'

Grifter slashes the air in front of him. 'I'm warning you . . .'

Some of the men start chanting, egging them on as Grifter lurches to his feet and lunges, but, as he does so, Jack stands and grabs hold of his arm. 'Enough!' he says. The boat rocks wildly. Grifter's knife is caught in the air between them, but Olivia's knife is against Grifter's throat. 'I said enough!' Silence. All eyes on Jack, glittering in dark faces. 'We've got to pull together. Or we'll never survive.'

There are no blankets. Only dead men's clothes. Jack lets the gunwale slam deep into his back as the boat bumps up and down. Olivia's knife sits like a stone in his pocket. It comforts him to feel as if she is near, though he barely dares to think of her because when he does, he feels as though he might break. He knows Mart went down trying to help release a lifeboat for his men. He knows Andersson went down with the ship. He swallows. 'Does anyone know what happened to Carl?' he says.

'He pulled you in,' says Burts.

'So he's here? On the boat?' Jack looks around, confused. He knows his friend's face isn't one of the weary and haggard, bearded men frowning back at him. Burts glances at the forepeak. It is only then that Jack realises the other person he had lain next to under the canopy has not moved during their regular rotation. Jack falls to his knees and crawls forward. The figure is wrapped in heavy, sodden clothes. Jack tries to find the place where the face is. He finds hair. The skin is black and charred. The eyes are shut. There is a faint noise, the wheeze of an injured animal.

Jack works slowly, gently. He finds the shoulders, the feet. He works his way up the forearm. There is a clear patch, free from the melted, raw skin. Jack can just make out a badly drawn star tattoo.

Carl's burnt body is the worst thing he has ever seen or smelt, but Jack knows he needs to clean it and stop infection setting in. He sets to work, peeling away the soggy, salty clothes as carefully as he can. Carl says nothing. But afterwards, when Jack has managed to clean the worst bits and dress Carl in the spare clothes, he is sure he feels his friend squeeze his hand.

The weather changes constantly. One minute it is fine and bright, as if they are bobbing along on a holiday. The sea is calm and flat, the air pure and clear. The next moment, the sea swells and they are smashed from all sides, disappearing into the troughs of churning waves so it feels as if they are under water, only to rise to the top of the next peak. It is exhausting. Their bodies are covered in bruises. They tie themselves to any part of the lifeboat that they can. Jack remembers teaching David and Si their knots. He would do anything to be back at training school again. He understands why men like The Barker must find the strength to hold a crew together against whatever is thrown their way.

The wind squeals through their bodies and the tears freeze to their faces. The relentless thudding against the waves makes their bones ache, their eyeballs roll. They mumble and mutter, brief prayers, poems, ramblings. One man calls to his mother. They rub whale oil into their sore skin, but still it prickles and stings, and the tips of their fingers turn white as if they've been dipped in lime. Jack pushes against the gunwale, pressing it into his spine, concentrating on the pain, anything to keep him alive. He allows himself to picture Olivia, but only briefly. She is his strength and his weakness; the image of her keeps him going, but also brings the tears choking into his throat. Every few hours, he checks over Carl's body, helps his friend sip his ration of water, swallow his biscuit. Carl seems no worse, but he is no better either. Jack whispers in his ear, tells him it will be fine. That they are near land. That help is on the way.

*

260

In a blizzard, Jack opens his mouth, hopes the snow will quench the thirst, but the flakes are salty like everything else. Even beneath the canopy, they settle in his hair, on his shoulders. The shape of Burts appears and disappears. The snow swirls around them and they close their eyes against its bite. The wind moans and wails like a child. They bail and row and relieve each other hour after hour. Burts does not move from his lookout. When it is time for him to swap, Jack crawls from under the canopy, stretching his legs out for one last time, enjoying the sensation of the muscles and ligaments bending and lengthening. He pulls himself up and shakes Burts on the shoulder. 'Burts,' he says. Burts doesn't move. Jack shakes him again. Burts is solid, unmoveable. He has frozen to the spot. Three of them work hard to unwedge the body from between the mast. Snow has settled on his beard and eyebrows, frosting his face, making him look like an old man, only now he will never grow old.

As with the others, they undress Burts and bury him in the deep, taking his papers and the letter to his wife from his pocket, sending him on his way with a quiet prayer. Jack has to remind himself that this is not Burts any more as he slips into the sea, and the grey sky turns pale pink as the snow clouds clear.

The men begin to argue and fight over rations. Jack doesn't dare sleep in case someone steals what remains. Grifter hovers in front of him with his knife flashing in the pale light, but Jack is immediately awake and on his feet, shoving Grifter into the bottom of the boat, one hand around his throat, the other grabbing the knife. Grifter cries. They all cry.

Grifter is on watch when a ship materialises on the horizon.
Jack struggles to speak, his lips are so cracked and swollen. 'Friendly?' he says.
The rest of the men are suddenly alert. They force the words through their chapped and bleeding lips. 'Is it German?'
'Is it the Navy?'
'Are we rescued?'

Grifter shakes his head, trying to see. 'I can't tell,' he says, as the ship draws closer. Jack hasn't the energy to be scared. What can they do anyway? They can't outrun a battleship.

'Is it firing?'

'What's that in the water?'

'Torpedo?'

'Sit down!' yells Jack, as the boat tips.

'It's American!' says Grifter.

'It's from our convoy,' says the Chief.

'We're saved.'

The merchant ship is soon alongside, flashing its hello. The men's relief is only momentary. The sailors yell down at them, in accents that remind Jack of the pictures he used to sneak into in London. He tries to grab hold of the scrambling nets on the side of the ship but his fingers are numb, so he grabs at the rope with his arms as if he has no hands. The men are all talking at once.

'Shut up!' says Jack. 'I can't hear.'

The men fall silent, each craning their necks up at the Americans.

'You'll be better off where you are,' a sailor shouts down at them. 'The Germans are on to us. Our convoy's given Hitler something to crow about. He's determined to take us all out.'

The horror of the situation sinks in. The men in the lifeboat avoid each other's eyes.

'He's right,' says the Chief.

'Let them go,' says Grifter.

'But it'll be warm.'

'And dry.'

'There'll be food.'

'Let go. We're better off in here. No one will torpedo a lifeboat.'

The boat is rocking ominously as half the men try to grapple with the others who are scrabbling for the net. 'Sit down,' says Jack. But the men aren't listening. They are using their sore hands like claws to try to pull themselves up, scraping and kicking at each other in their attempt to leave the boat.

Jack resists the urge to join them. He knows the Americans are right, but the disappointment is like a punch in the stomach. Still he can't let go of the net.

The American shouts down again: 'We'll send a message. Let your Navy know you're here.' Still, their hands grip the net. One man is almost on it, one leg dangling. The lifeboat tips. Jack reaches for the rifle. A warning shot might stop the panic.

Then something hits him on the shoulder. Things are dropping from the sky. 'Bread!' someone says. And the men collapse back into the boat with their arms outstretched and Jack unhooks his hands from the net and holds them upwards too. The rolls plop into the boat and into their arms. And now no one is holding the net – they are grabbing the bread rolls and the ship is steaming away, the sailors calling 'Good luck!' as they disappear as quickly as they came.

The bread is manna from heaven, soft and sweet, but after a few bites, Jack's stomach starts to gripe, and his mouth is too dry and blistered to eat any more. He looks around. It is the same for all of them. He stuffs the bread into his pocket; he will give it to Carl later. 'We should save it anyway,' says the Chief, collecting the bits that are left and sealing them away. But it's fresh water that they really need.

Jack turns his attention to his feet, which are so swollen that he has to have his boots cut off. Most of the other men have already done this. His socks are damp and clinging to the lumps that were once his toes. As he leans down to massage life into them, a noise fills his ears and the men start to shout. A plane is hurtling out of the sky towards them, probably on the trail of the American ship. The Chief tries to fire the rifle, but it is too damp and his fingers are too cold. The plane dives at them, and the men scream, and all Jack can do is fling his ruined boots at it as it banks away, teasing, melting into the sky in the direction of the merchant ship.

*

Once again all they can hear is the sea. It is too much for one man. He simply gives up, falling awkwardly forward over his knees. No one says anything as Jack helps to remove the clothes. It takes hours to do it, as if he is half-asleep. Every button saps more strength from his body. It takes his last ounce of energy to tip the corpse over the side and into the sea. This time he feels nothing as it is sucked into the darkness. He slumps on the bench, exhausted, every inch of his body aching with effort.

It has been eleven days. They have lost six men. There are nine left. They pass the last of the fresh water around like holy wine in the two metal mugs. Most of the survivors are too weak to help or even feed themselves. The stench of urine and death burns Jack's nostrils.

The Chief is on watch, staring out across the dazzling water, squinting, glaring. He can barely keep his eyes open. Suddenly he shifts, pulls himself more upright. An energy sparks off him, radiating out to the men huddled around him. 'I see something,' he says.

Jack stands, wincing as his feet take the weight of his body. The men on the oars pull and pull with their last ounce of strength. The boat creeps slowly towards it. It is hard to tell. It could be a cloud or a ship . . .

'Land ahoy!' Jack fingers the knife in his pocket. Hope thaws his insides. Strangely, he feels like laughing.

The men row close enough to the shoreline to search for somewhere safe to land their boat. It is continuous rock, bleak and craggy and harsh. They are all on lookout, hanging over the sides of the boat. A rock could tear a hole at any moment and they are too weak to swim.

'There,' says the Chief, pointing at a sheltered bay. They steer inland, hear the rasp of the rocky beach against the hull of the boat. Jack is one of the few that can still walk. He clambers into the water, collapsing as his feet hit the ground. Seawater soaks his legs, his waist, his arms, but land feels good beneath his sore soles. He is surprised by how much he wants to live. Slowly he stands, shaking with the effort. Pins and needles bite at his muscles. None of them has walked for twelve days.

Jack helps lift and drag men from the lifeboat up the shore and away from the sea. Carl is the last. The Chief helps carry him gently to where the men are already beginning to build a fire. Those that are able to crawl, and stumble around the beach, searching for driftwood. First, smoke trickles up into the air, and soon flames crackle. It barely gives off any heat, but it's something. The men stare into it, each one thinking of fires at home. Jack is thinking of his first day on the beach with Olivia, cooking the flatfish. The memory makes his mouth water.

Some of the survivors hold their fingers and toes by the flames, trying to encourage the warmth into them.

'No!' says the Chief. 'Slowly. Or you will get rot.' He shows them how to massage and rub their feet.

'Do as he says.' Jack's words are an order, and no one argues.

The Chief points inland, to the bare rock and the snow. 'Who's coming?' he says. Grifter steps forward and Jack nods.

The three of them clamber slowly to the top of the cliff, slipping and stumbling as their sore feet give way, or the shingle crumbles beneath them. Jack prays that they will see something – a wood or a village – even a field – when they reach the top. But there is nothing apart from a barren landscape of stone and boulders that rise into rocky hills riven by ice and snow. A desolate wind howls in his ears. Behind him lies miles of Arctic ocean. No person could live here. There is no food. There is nothing. For a brief moment, he wishes he had died when the *Aurora* first went down.

The three of them slump to the ground. They don't dare look at each other. As they sit there, gazing down at the ragged bunch of men scattered across the beach below, Jack suddenly realises that there *is* something else, a familiar sound cutting through the whistle of the wind, conjuring up images of another place, another time. 'Birds!' he says.

The Chief and Grifter twist their heads from side to side. 'He's right,' says the Chief, pointing. They push themselves up on to their feet again and start to follow the coast. The cliffs rise higher and higher beneath them until they are confronted by a squawking, wheeling barrage of seabirds scrabbling in and out of their nests in the side of a sheer drop. For the first time since their ship went down, the men smile at each other, their blackened faces folding and cracking awkwardly with the effort. Grifter begins to pull a bundle of string from his pocket. It is so absurd that they start giggling. Jack snaps Olivia's knife open and they cut some lengths. Together they find a good place to lie above the cliff, the smell of bird shit making their eyes water. Jack and Grifter dangle their nooses over the edge of the cliff as the Chief gives them directions. The bickering and squealing birds remind Jack of his classroom before Mr Morgan appeared in the morning.

The Chief is giving Jack the thumbs-up and yelling his name, and he pulls the noose tight and feels the heaviness at the end. He drags the string upwards and on the end is a black and white seabird, thrashing and squawking. But Jack is ready with the priest: he bashes the bird on the head hard and fast and it goes rigid as it is stunned, convulsing, the feet sticking straight out as if it's trying to land, and its eye glitters at him and then the lid comes down over it and the bird stops moving. It is dead. Jack feels nothing for it: he has seen enough death over the last two weeks.

They do it again. And again. Until they have seven large birds, whose warmth leaches out of their bodies as quickly as it returns to the men's. They are pleased with themselves, carrying the dead birds by their necks down the hill, surprised at how heavy they are.

The men on the beach set to work plucking the creatures and, as the feathers float around them, they stoke up the fire. They gut and roast the birds, turning them on spits. The smell again reminds Jack of Olivia's secret bay. But the birds aren't like the fish they caught there: their flesh is tough and salty – and there is barely any of it. Seabirds are not fattened for the table.

Afterwards, they feel like stretching out to sleep, but Jack fears he will not wake if he allows himself to rest. 'We'll try for water again,' he says. The three of them set off with two water tanks from the boat.

They follow the coast. They don't want to walk inland, where they have heard foxes barking; it is so exposed. Eventually they find a trickle of a stream glistening down over the cliffs. They fill what they can. On the way back they notice rabbit droppings among the bird tracks along the tops of the cliffs. They spot the skull of a reindeer, its antlers broken on one side. The Chief points at a large track imprinted into some soft ground nearby. 'Polar bear,' he says. They walk faster.

As they clamber back down to the beach, Grifter says, 'We can't move the men again.' He's right. Most of them are unable to walk anyway. They sit bedraggled and crumpled on the seashore. More exposure at sea would surely kill them all. They organise the survivors into groups and watches as they would at sea – some to collect wood or water, some to catch seabirds, some to stoke the fire, and someone to remain always on lookout. With the sail from the lifeboat, they build a make-shift shelter and another fire. Jack makes sure that Carl is nearest the warmth. He concocts the comfiest bed he can out of clothes they have managed to dry. With warmth and food and water, his friend is even able to sit up on his own. But he needs medical help urgently. They all stare at the boat, wonder whether to burn it too. No one wants to get back into it, but it is possibly their only means of escape.

CHAPTER 19

Olivia

Olivia's anxiety about Jack affects her sleeping and her eating, manifesting itself in an overwhelming nausea, particularly in the mornings. To keep her mind occupied, she throws herself into work. She now considers herself a fully-fledged Wren: it is second nature to swab the deck instead of scrub the floor; a bed is a bunk, and her room a cabin. She has learnt the basics of signals and how to de-clinker a boiler, which is no different to cleaning out the stove in the bothy. She has even had to run across the airfield dragging a kite for the pilots to practise their target skills. There is no official time to mourn one missing sailor among the many, and it is hard to mope when you're meant to be on parade or sorting the laundry for a hundred other women. She feels a small surge of pride when she glances at her friends – women like her who were once good only for marriage, but can now repair an engine or operate a radio or load a torpedo as well as any man.

While she is learning, as Charlie predicted, to live with this new, emptier reality, the nausea does not subside, and now comes a creeping suspicion that she dares not confide in anyone yet – not even Gladys. She hopes that she is wrong. She hopes that she is right. The thought almost brings the tears flowing again, but she is all cried out.

Some of the Wrens fly – taking aerial photographs on

training ops or during target practice – or even piloting aircraft themselves, ferrying men and moving planes from airfield to airfield, but Olivia yearns for the sea. 'You should apply to join a boat crew,' says Gladys. 'With your experience, you'll have no problem at all.'

So that's exactly what she does, and when her apprenticeship is over, she is transferred to Plymouth. The boat crews take on basic harbour duties: delivering mail, transferring injured men ashore, or carrying messages or men on leave. Olivia is already adept at wending her way across a harbour, manoeuvring between the other ships and boats and buoys and chains and moorings. When the harbour is full, she motors out to sea, where the swell is larger and she has to keep her wits about her. She delivers ordnance Wrens to check the guns, and she helms for the Wren signals officers and the mine-spotters.

The men tease the Wrens as they are loaded into the launch, but the women have their respect by the time they reach the shore. Many of the sailors have not seen a woman for weeks. Olivia is used to dealing with the barracking from her days selling fish at Loch Ewe. But instead of bare feet and legs, now her uniform is trousers and shirt, the rounded hat set at a jaunty angle on her head. In driving rain, she wears an oilskin that glistens with water. Even as her freezing hands grip the towrope, she is glad she is not taking notes in an office or deep in an underground bunker, plotting the shipping traffic. Out here, she can feel the sun and rain and wind on her skin while her boat forges through the ever-changing water. And as she turns her face to the sky, she wonders whether Jack is doing the same, and it is hard not to let the sadness overwhelm her then; it's as if part of her heart has been torn from her body and the bit that is left is an agonising, raw thing that keeps beating even though she wishes it wouldn't. She wishes it would just stop. And then she remembers the life that she now knows for sure is growing inside her. The fear for Jack is compounded by the fear for her future. Her family might forgive her for falling in love with the wrong sort of man, but would they ever forgive her for the shame of an illegitimate child? Could she go through this without telling them? And how could she go through it alone? She has heard of girls getting rid of unwanted pregnancies, but how could she even contemplate getting rid of it when it might be the only part of Jack left in the world?

But of course, it isn't the only part of Jack left in the world, and, as the days pass, and Olivia feels more and more distant from her own family, she finds herself wondering about Jack's sister. Betsy could be a friend, an ally, her new family. Even if Jack is never going to return, his sister is out there somewhere. They could support each other through these dark days. She must find Betsy and tell the girl what has happened to her brother.

The problem is that there is nowhere that holds official records of when and to where children were evacuated. It is as if the most important thing was to get them to a place of safety first and ask questions later. Children from cities all over the country – Liverpool, Bristol, Exeter, London – have been tucked away into remote corners of Britain, their parents eventually receiving a letter, but no central organisation carrying the details. However, Olivia is determined. She learns that she might have a chance of tracing a child if she knows the name of their school. After that, it's a matter of contacting the different schools in Bermondsey until finally she traces a class with an Elizabeth Sullivan to a village in Devon called Cheriton.

One free morning, Olivia travels north into Devon from Plymouth. Cheriton is a small village beyond the bleak tors of Dartmoor, where the hills turn green and lush once more, and the soil is rich and red. The roads are narrow and banked by steep hedges overgrown with nettles and vetch and criss-crossed by Jack-in-the-hedge and cleavers that she remembers sticking to her own sisters' clothes when they were children.

270

Disturbed by the passing vehicle, birds flit in and out of holes between stunted roots and brambles entwined with stitchwort flowers like white stars and threaded through with the pink of red campion. Beneath the Devon hedges, it is easy to get lost, particularly since the road signs have been removed in case of an invasion.

The village is a cluster of thatched cottages gathered at a crossroads and set among rolling fields ripe for harvest. There is a pub and a shop and a church. The school is a long, low thatched building with wooden columns propping it up. It is good to be out in the countryside, with the smell of soil and grass in her nostrils and the sound of sheep bleating and birds singing in her ears. As Olivia walks towards the school, the strange noise of children chattering and laughing emanates from the playground. She is filled with nervous apprehension at the prospect of meeting Jack's sister for the first time.

But the school has no record of an Elizabeth or Betsy Sullivan having attended.

'Are you sure? I was told by her old school in London that they came here.'

The headmistress is a kind-looking lady with hair greying at the temples and small glasses perched on the end of her nose. 'I'm afraid it was rather chaotic,' she says. 'The children went with whoever turned up at the church to help. I have got a list of all the evacuees who now attend our school, of course. And her name is definitely not on that list.'

'Could she have come and not gone to school?'

'It's possible. We do have some remote families here. Perhaps one of the farms out beyond Sandiford?'

'Is there anyone I can talk to about it?'

'Mrs Batcup might remember. She's our churchwarden. She helped pair children up.'

'Would you be able to point me in the right direction?'

'Of course. Hers is the house next to the pub. Honeysuckle Cottage.'

*

271

Mrs Batcup's cottage is tiny, the thick thatch bearing down on it, pushing it further into the ground. Olivia's heart sinks when the old lady opens her door: Mrs Batcup is as bent and crooked as her house, as if the weight of the world is on her shoulders. But she is deceptively spry, and her eyes light up when Olivia asks for her help. 'Of course, my lovely,' she says. 'Come in. It's nice to have company. Ever since my Reggie died. Don't get me wrong. It's a wonderful friendly village Cheriton, but nothing beats a cup of tea and a good chinwag with a new face.' The old lady points to an armchair where a cat is curled up. 'Just push her off,' she says.

Olivia lifts the cat on to her lap, enjoying the feel of its soft fur and cosy warmth. It stretches and flexes a paw as it re-settles and starts a low, rumbling purr. 'I'm looking for a particular evacuee,' says Olivia. 'They have no record of her at the school.'

'Poor little things. Turning up here with hardly a stitch on and us heading into a proper winter. Makes me feel shivery thinking about it.'

'There was a girl called Betsy – or Elizabeth – Sullivan. I'm trying to track her down . . .'

The old lady places the cup of tea on the small table next to Olivia, stirring milk into it with her rheumy hands. 'I'm afraid I haven't got any biscuits to offer . . .'

'Don't worry . . . This is lovely . . . Thank you . . . I was just hoping you might remember this particular girl?'

Mrs Batcup sits in the chair opposite, her eyes bright and inquisitive. 'They were all terrible pale and quiet, you know. Not like our own children, rosy and full of life. It made the heart bleed to see them standing there, tears not yet dried on their cheeks. Most of them had never been out of the city before. Imagine that!'

'Did you ever learn any of their names?'

'Of course, dear. I had a list. I hoped they would all come to Sunday school.'

'Do you still have it?'

The old lady shakes her head with incredulity. 'Of course. It's in the church.'

'Can I see it?'

'There's no need. I remember the little girl you're looking for. Betsy Sullivan. She was worst of all. Quiet as a church mouse. Didn't say a word. We thought there was something wrong with the poor girl. We thought she was a mute.'

'Do you know where she went? Was it a farm?'

'Oh no. She wouldn't have lasted two seconds on a farm. You need to be fit and strong to get through a winter out there. She went to the Roses that live in the pub.'

'Next door?'

The old lady nods. 'I had to take her there myself because Mrs Rose never turned up at the church.' She shakes her head in despair. 'And them with all that room . . .'

'So why is she not at the school?'

'Oh dear, oh dear.' The old lady twists her gnarled fingers in her lap. 'She ran away. Missed her mammy, of course. Poor little mite.'

'Will the Roses know where?'

'Don't 'spect so. They keep themselves to themselves. Outsiders, you know. Only moved here at the start of the war.'

Mrs Rose is reluctant to talk until she realises that Olivia is not an official or a relation of Betsy's – and then she lets her tongue run away with her as she dries glasses and rearranges them on the shelves behind the bar. 'She was bloody awful,' she says. 'Wild as a sparrow hawk and twice as vicious. Didn't say a word. Scratched and bit and clawed at us when we tried to clean her up. Ungrateful little wretch. And us taking her in out of the kindness of our hearts.'

'Why didn't she go to school?'

'We thought she wasn't right in the head. She never said a word all the time she was here. Didn't see no point in sending her to school.'

273

'So what did she do?'

'Like I said, we tried to clean her up. Can't have something looking like that working in our pub. It'd put all the customers off. But she wouldn't let us touch her, so we only let her do cellar work. We do have our own kids to look after, you know.'

'Would they know a bit more about her? Might she have talked to them when they were in bed?'

Mrs Rose leans on the bar and her lip curls. 'She didn't share their room. Who knows what she might have done to them? I wouldn't have slept a wink wondering if she might have attacked them in the night. No, no. She slept in the cellar too.' She sees the look on Olivia's face. 'She liked it down there. It's warm, and she was alone. She didn't want to be with us. I didn't have time for her histrionics. It's hard enough running a business in this war, without having to deal with someone else's filthy little urchin.' She starts polishing the top of the bar with the tea towel.

'So did she give any idea of where she was going?' says Olivia.

''Course not. One morning she just wasn't there.'

'Did she have any money?'

'I doubt it. Her family never responded to the letter we wrote to tell them where the child was. The idiot creature couldn't even do that herself. I don't believe she could read or write. No doubt her mother was the same, and that's why she never sent us the money she owed us.'

'Her mother died.'

Mrs Rose rubs at a particularly stubborn stain. 'I suppose that's why they shipped the little hoodlums out to us in the first place.'

Depressed, Olivia returns to her duties in Plymouth. The weather darkens with her mood. The sky is overcast, and a fine drizzle patters on the metal and concrete world that surrounds her. It is fitting. The world is crying. She has known people who have disappeared, who will not be coming back again. But she has never felt a loss like this, exacerbated by the loss of a girl she never even knew. How can an entire family disappear and leave no one to mourn for them? She presses her hands to her stomach. There is no doubt now: she is nine weeks pregnant, and she takes comfort in the fact that a part of Jack is still here, and that it is her secret to hold on to in her most despairing hours.

She has been on duty for fifteen hours, but she can't bear to go to sleep yet. It is the same every day; anything to avoid a moment of stillness, to prevent the horror gathering in her mind. She is not the only one: there are always parties on ships, on shore, on submarines. Young men making the most of life in the strange world of unlit harbours, while the girls they will leave behind paint over their desolate insides, dancing that little bit more wildly, staying out that little bit longer, living twice: once for themselves and once for those that won't be coming back. Life is too short. You have to grab what's left by the throat.

She finds Gladys and another friend, Julia, crammed into their small cabin with a few other girls getting ready to go out. The Wrens are, as always, making the most of what they've got: starch for face powder, mixing their lipstick with water to make it last longer, or using beetroot juice to stain their lips instead. Olivia uses shoe polish to make her lashes look thicker.

Before they bluster out into the Plymouth night, Olivia's CO asks for a word. 'You've shown yourself to be a valuable member of boat crew,' he says. 'I'd like you to know that I'm going to recommend you become an officer.'

'Thank you, sir.' She smiles: moments of pride can be held on to during the dark times.

'I know it all seems a bit rushed, but you've shown yourself to be more than apt, and we're in need of good people . . . Have you got a particular position in mind?'

'I have. If it isn't too presumptuous, I'm interested in

becoming a boarding officer, sir.' She has heard about the new directive from Trade Division. The shortage of men means that Wrens will soon be delivering confidential orders direct to masters on merchant ships, among other things; ships like the *Aurora*.

'I thought that might be the case,' he says, flourishing some papers. 'I've already written it down.' CO Shepherd prides himself on understanding his charges. 'There's a course starting in a couple of months. It could be a tough gig. You'll be stepping into men's shoes and some of them may not appreciate it.'

'It'll be no worse than dealing with you lot.'

He nods and smiles. 'Good luck.'

'Thank you, sir.'

Overhead, the bombers drone out across the Channel. Later, she will try not to count them back in again.

The officers' training course is at Greenwich Naval College. Olivia is pleased to learn that the CO has also recommended Gladys and Julia. They will all be in London together, staying at a flat in Pimlico that Gladys often uses, lent by some friend of a friend; accommodation in the city is scarce. The rooms are spartan, too many people passing through to make a mark. Someone has tried to grow lettuce on the windowsill, but has forgotten to water it and the soil has shrunk away from the sides of the pot, while the leaves have withered.

Charlie has sent Olivia his congratulations and a message that he has a forty-eight-hour pass and would she like to go out to dinner with some friends of his. He has been such a rock that she does not want to turn him down, and besides, now the awkwardness is a thing of the past, she is looking forward to the company of an old friend. When he arrives at the flat, Gladys and Julia giggle like schoolgirls, while Olivia shakes her head and tells them to behave. She is always a little surprised by the effect he has on other people, even though she can see he is handsome, in a boy scout kind of way.

He follows her up to the kitchen and she pours him a drink. Gladys and Julia are getting ready to go out in the other rooms, and Olivia has no choice but to do her make-up in the kitchen while Charlie drinks whisky out of a teacup. 'Supper at the Empire Hotel with Spencer and Alice Stafford,' he says. 'He's an old friend of mine from school.'

'Is he Fleet Air Arm?'

'God no. Something to do with politics. But I thought we could both do with some cheering up. And I couldn't think of anyone else to ask.'

'Thanks, I think.'

He smiles and then frowns, his green eyes seeking hers. 'They did find more survivors the other day,' he says. 'But no Jack Sullivan.'

She knows how unlikely it now is that Jack has survived, but it still tears at her insides. She looks back at Charlie, forcing her voice to be cheerful. 'Let's forget that for now,' she says. She can see what an effort he has made to glean any information for her. She knows he is trying to make amends, and she doesn't blame him any more: her family would no more approve of Jack whether he was a vicar or a murderer. 'Let's not talk about it today,' she says. 'Let's just have fun.'

She smooths her uniform, for once relishing being in a skirt again, feeling feminine. She has unpicked and reworked the stitching so that it looks positively tailored. Charlie watches her.

'Not exactly glamorous, is it?' she says, suddenly self-conscious, smoothing her shirt into her skirt, hoping there is no outward sign of the child growing inside her.

'You look better,' he says. 'Healthier.'

She blushes, painfully aware of the reason for this.

'I still can't get used to you girls in uniform,' he says. 'Let's hope you're not swearing and spitting like men next . . .'

Olivia laughs and tips her make-up bag on to the table, rooting about for the tiny stump of lipstick that she has left.

Too late, she realises that something else has fallen out at the same time.

'What's that?' says Charlie, reaching across to pick up the watch.

She freezes, not sure what to say.

'It looks German? Where on earth did you get it?'

'I . . . I found it,' she says.

He stares at her, shaking his head slowly as realisation dawns. 'The dinghy?' he says in a whisper.

She nods.

'But we talked about it. Why didn't you tell me . . .?'

'It was too late by then. He'd gone . . .'

He puts the watch down on the table and looks at it in disbelief from between his fingers. 'God,' he says. 'That was bloody stupid of you. You could have been taken away.'

'I know.' Her voice is small, ashamed.

'What possessed you?'

'I'm not sure. I was . . . lonely. He seemed so vulnerable.'

'Bloody hell.' He smooths his hair back with both hands, then wipes his hands down his face. 'I don't know what to do. I should report this.'

He is silent for a while. Then he rubs at his face again, shakes his head as if he can't believe it. 'Bloody Germans.'

'He reminded me of you. You're the same age . . .'

Charlie looks at her as though she is a stranger. 'He could have gone on to spy. To kill our own people. Jesus. He could have . . .'

'He didn't. He wouldn't. I know he wouldn't. He had a dog. He wanted to be an architect. He was . . . nice.'

'Nice!'

She feels wretched. He paces up and down the tiny kitchen. Then he sighs, straightens his shoulders. 'Don't look so miserable,' he says. 'It's done now. Hopefully he's dead. Or back in Germany, and not . . . God . . . spying or something . . . And let's pray he's not languishing in a cell somewhere while MI5 try to get him to cough up the name of whoever helped him . . .'

278

'What would they do to me?'

'Hang you?'

'Oh, Charlie.'

'Look,' he says. 'It's not going to come to that. Let me take it. If anyone asks, you don't know anything about it. It's rather a nice watch, actually. Quite a trophy. And it still works . . .' He twists his arm so the watch catches the light. 'This way, if the truth ever does come to light, I can counteract by saying I found the watch, and you're innocent . . .'

'You can't do that.'

'I don't want to hear any more about it. We'd better get going.'

'But . . .'

He holds up his hand. 'Not to be mentioned again.'

The hotel is famously built of thick concrete, supposedly able to withstand anything – including Nazi bombs. It could not be more different to the kind of accommodation they have both grown used to, with its ornate columns and drooping chandeliers, the intricate rugs and the heavy, pelmetted curtains. The waiters are as smart as the guests, who include decorated officers of all military persuasions, politicians, and even well-known entertainers, all carrying on as if there were no sandbags or craters or people queuing for onions just yards from the imposing front doors. As they walk through the foyer, Olivia feels completely out of place. Charlie seems to sense it and puts out his elbow so she can link her arm through his. She is glad of the support. The other women waft through the rooms, their shoes clipping crisply across the marble floor.

Charlie and Olivia are escorted to a table where the Staffords are already seated. Charlie introduces Olivia as Spencer stands, bowing slightly and smiling at her. He is dressed in a dinner jacket. 'Charmed,' he says, taking her hand in his and pressing his lips to it. 'I visited Stoke Hall once. Shooting with my father years ago.'

'I'm sorry. I don't remember.'

He laughs. He has neat little teeth and a hint of puffiness around his chin. 'I wouldn't expect you to. I must have been about eight. I do remember it's a fabulous place, though. So sorry to hear it's been requisitioned. We managed to hold on to ours. I should think your gardens are in a dreadful state.'

'I think my parents offered . . .'

'Still. Won't take long to fix it all up again once this business is all over . . . Now. This is my wife, Alice,' he says, indicating the woman seated at the table. Alice's earrings sparkle and flash beneath her immaculate hair as she inclines her head in greeting.

Charlie pulls out Olivia's chair, and she sits, taking in the spotless lines of gleaming silver cutlery.

'You could have made a bit more of an effort, old boy,' says Spencer to Charlie. 'Uniforms are so bloody dreary.'

'And a dinner jacket isn't?' says Charlie.

'I think it's rather charming,' says Alice, fingering her necklace and letting her eyes roam over Olivia's body.

'Maybe you should join,' says Olivia, forcing a smile while she shrivels inside.

'Join what?' says Spencer. 'Are you a WAAF or a FANY?'

'Neither,' says Olivia. 'I'm a Wren.'

'Ah. A Jenny Wren. How lovely.' He addresses his wife: 'I don't know why you don't join up. You'd look very fetching in that.'

'I'm not sure I've got the figure for it,' says Alice. 'Suits the more boyish. No offence,' she adds, putting a gloved hand over her mouth.

'Champagne?' Spencer nods at the hovering waiter, who pours the golden liquid into their glasses, where it fizzes and bubbles enticingly.

The food is exquisite, and there seems to be an endless supply of it. The decor is fabulous, the furnishings so sumptuous that they seem unreal. Spencer advises the Ministry of Labour. His is a world of politics and money, something that might once have been familiar to Olivia, a fact that makes it all the more alien to her now.

Olivia twists the stiff, starched napkin beneath the table. She may feel out of place but she won't show it. Her palms are sticky and she longs to loosen her collar. She takes a deep breath and tries to engage in the conversation among the clinking crystal and chatter from the other diners, sipping slowly at the champagne, shaking her head when the waiter tries to top up her glass. Then suddenly, before the main course is served, and while Spencer is droning on about the National Service Act and reserved occupations and Alice is delicately sipping her wine, Charlie leans sideways, his shoulder bumping against hers, and whispers, 'Fancy going somewhere else?'

She looks at him, unsure whether he is serious. But his eyes are shining as brightly as Alice's jewels, and one of his eyebrows is raised. She grins. 'Most definitely,' she says, pushing herself away from the crisp white tablecloth, and leaving her napkin crumpled on the plush velvet chair. Charlie laughs too and holds out his arm as their hosts look up at them, their mouths half open. Then they turn and race for the doors, and out into the safety of the darkness of London at night.

It is not far to walk to Soho. Charlie and Olivia giggle most of the way, remembering their hosts' surprised expressions. 'I'm sorry,' he says. 'I hadn't realised what a bore Spencer was. He was quite a laugh at school.'

'I wonder if it's us or them who have changed?' says Olivia.

Eddie's Bar is full of familiar faces and uniforms. Charlie buys Olivia a gin cocktail and she relaxes into the drink and the music and the dancing. She has never seen Charlie like this: so gregarious. But then, she has never really spent time with him among other people. Everyone wants to talk to him, or to dance with him, or to buy him a drink, and all the time he is the perfect escort, making sure she is topped up, and introducing her to anyone she doesn't know. She feels a lightness that she has not felt in a long time; for once, she is not painting on a brave face or distracting herself: she is actually enjoying herself.

She stretches out her legs, feeling the warmth of the room wash over her. For a moment she cannot locate Charlie in the dimly lit bar. Then she spots him talking to some women in the shadows on the far side. They are conspicuous by their lack of uniform, displaying legs encased in stockings, and heavily painted faces. They fawn over Charlie, all talking at once, reaching out to touch his stripes, giggling loudly enough for her to hear. Charlie spots her and motions that he'll be a moment. She colours, embarrassed that she could be so naïve. Charlie is a young man, and of course he has needs. When he makes it back to the table, he follows her eyes and reddens too, suddenly embarrassed. 'I haven't . . .' he says.

'Oh no!' says Olivia. 'Don't worry. I don't mind. I mean, what you get up to is your own business . . .'

'I just help when I can . . .'

'Really. No need to explain.'

'This was the last place I came to with Mole and the others . . .'

She holds up her hand. Charlie is saved from further explanation by a couple of friends who come up and thump him on the shoulder. He greets them enthusiastically and introduces Olivia.

They are officers from a battleship that has just returned from operations in the Channel. 'We could have done with your lot at Dieppe,' says the shorter of the men.

'I heard,' says Charlie. 'What a bloody disaster.'

The other man nods. 'Pretty bad for us,' he says. 'Terrible for the Canadians. They took a real hammering.'

'So did the RAF. It was almost out of range for them.'

'That's why we could have done with you.'

'Not up to us to make the decisions.'

'That new Commando unit lost a lot of men.'

The men sigh, staring at the liquid in their glasses as it catches the light.

'Must have been quite some fight,' says Charlie.

The shorter man nods. 'Two Victoria Crosses awarded.'

Olivia senses a profound change in Charlie, something so sad that she almost gasps. But it is only for a moment, and then he raises his glass above his head. 'Let's drink to them all,' he says. 'To those on land and sea and in the air. To His Majesty's armed forces and to all our Allies, wherever they may be. And to the men of the Merchant Navy.'

He nods at Olivia, and she stands too, appreciating the toast to Jack, and the four of them hold their glasses aloft, before the men down their drinks in one and she takes a sip of her own. She looks away. No wonder these men enjoy themselves when they can. Any one of them might be an empty chair next week.

The energy seems to have gone from Charlie after that, and when a group of friends say they're heading back in the same direction, Olivia is relieved that she can go home with them. Charlie offers to escort her, but the offer is half-hearted, and Olivia says, 'You stay. I'll be fine.'

'If you're sure . . .' he says. 'I wouldn't mind another drink.'

As Olivia leaves the bar, she can't help noticing that Charlie is making his way back towards the bawdy girls in the corner. She feels a flash of anger: why is it all right for him to indulge his needs when it is not for her? She watches as he is led to the dance floor by a young dark-haired girl. They pull each other close and swing away into the crowd, another couple clinging to each other in the shadows.

The officers' course at Greenwich is meant to instil some of the history, dignity, and traditions of the Royal Navy into its recruits. Olivia dines in the Painted Hall beneath the swirling paintings and tall columns and gold leaf as the sounds of her fellow Wrens echo around her. She learns her compass points and how to navigate, plot a course, salute. On the wide, twisting Thames, downriver from the shattered docks, they practise things that are second nature to her already – transferring people from ship to shore, delivering mail, going on board, alongside – while manners and respect are drilled into them on land.

Today is a day of multiple celebrations: not only have they passed their exams, and are now commissioned officers, but it is also Gladys's wedding. It is meant to be a day for laughter, a day to push away dark thoughts. Olivia slowly buttons her shirt, gazing at herself in the mirror. It's been a long time since she wore anything other than this uniform. She cannot remember when she last wore a dress. Is it really not since the dance at Loch Ewe? The memory rips a hole in her happiness: Jack is a loss that will always be there, a shadow in her heart. She places her hands on her stomach, revelling in the secret that she holds within. She will have to tell her parents soon, but for now she pushes the thought from her mind.

Gladys is the only member of the wedding party not in a uniform. She has insisted that, for today, she will be the girl she was before the war. She is wearing a blue dress – clothes coupons don't stretch to wedding dresses. It doesn't put anyone off marriage, though. Hundreds of couples are hurriedly tying the knot while on leave, as if getting hitched will keep each of them alive until they next meet.

There are not many guests at the church: Gladys and William's parents, Julia, and Maggie has made it from Southampton. Olivia is pleased to see that Charlie is there too, waving her over into the space next to him on the hard pew. It is the first time she has seen him since they left Spencer and Alice at the hotel dinner a couple of weeks ago.

The marriage service is over in a flash. The vicar has a queue of couples to fit in. Outside, they throw confetti. It flutters to the ground to be trodden into the stony path like Olivia's hopes and dreams. They stop at the church gate, while Gladys's father takes a photograph. Behind the happy couple, the church bells remain silent, as they have throughout the war, only to be rung if there's an invasion.

Charlie puts a solid arm around her shoulder. 'Cheer up,' he says. 'You've got to make the most of the good days.'

He is right: it is easy to let the sadness overwhelm you. She glances at Gladys, looking so radiant, and William, so proud. Maggie is hugging Olivia's other arm tightly, and Julia is dabbing at her eyes with a handkerchief, and somewhere in a tree a collared dove is cooing as if it's just a normal, peaceful day. She knows they are the lucky ones: lucky to be here; lucky to be alive.

Gladys and William have opted for a quiet affair afterwards at Eddie's, before their honeymoon, a night in a hotel down the road; they are both back on duty tomorrow. Faces Olivia recognises swim in and out of the darkness. The parties have grown increasingly frenetic with the influx of American soldiers, who splash more money around as well as the chewing gum, nylons, and Coca-Cola. There are handsome, smiling GIs everywhere, fresh-faced and cocky, so different to the quieter British men, who have been burnt out by years at war.

Maggie is in her element, dancing with anyone who asks, but her eyes are set on one man. She takes Olivia aside, her wide smile leaving a glossy mark on the glass as she sips. 'Would you mind if I . . . You know . . .' she says, nodding her head in Charlie's direction.

It takes Olivia a moment to understand what she means. She stutters for a second before regaining her composure. 'Of course,' she says. 'Why would I mind?'

Maggie shrugs. 'I thought you two had history?'

'Not that kind of history,' says Olivia.

Maggie leans forward and kisses Olivia's cheek. 'I'm so glad,' she says. 'I think he might be The One.'

'I thought you weren't the settling down type?'

Maggie rolls her eyes. 'We all grow up, Olivia,' she says. 'Coming to dance?'

Olivia shakes her head. She watches as Maggie whispers

285

something in Charlie's ear and they swing each other around the floor. She surveys the room – it is hard to believe that these frivolous, frenzied people will be behind their desks or in their cockpits or decoding messages or marching out in only a few hours.

Later, Maggie stands in a group next to Charlie, but talking to a soldier on her other side. Charlie motions to Olivia to join them, but she shakes her head, so he makes his way over to the table.

'You all right?' he asks.

'I think I'm going to leave,' she says, raising her voice above the noise.

'I'll come with you.'

'No need.'

'I want to,' he says. 'Got to be up early.'

She can see he is scanning the room, searching the faces. She thinks of the painted girls she left him with last time. 'Are you looking for someone?' she asks.

'I was, but she's not here.'

'Maybe you should wait for her?'

He shakes his head. 'I wanted to say goodbye,' he says. 'But I need to get back as well. Early start tomorrow.'

Maggie appears at his elbow. 'I'll come too,' she says. 'Don't want to be left here on my own.' Gladys and William have already sloped off, and Julia is settling in for a long night with friends.

They are all staying at the Pimlico flat. It is conveniently near Victoria Station for Charlie in the morning. He may not even bother to sleep. Maggie pours some gin from a bottle in the sitting room. Olivia holds up her hand. 'Not for me, thanks. I think I'll turn in.' She doesn't want to get in the way. She goes to the kitchen, finds a glass for some water. Charlie follows her, his tall frame blocking the light in the doorway.

'Don't suppose I could ask you something?' he says.

She turns. 'Of course.'

'I wondered whether I could put you down as my next of kin?'

She grips the glass, feels a small surge of sadness tinged with pride. She doesn't know what to say. From next door, Maggie calls out: 'Is anyone going to help me drink this?'

'Two seconds,' Charlie calls back over his shoulder. Then he turns to Olivia again. 'I'm sorry,' he says. 'I hope you don't mind me asking. There's no one else . . .'

'What about Aunt Nancy?'

He smiles ruefully. 'Isn't it meant to be the other way round? She's my godmother; she's meant to look after me . . .' He pauses. 'She's certainly meant to outlive me—'

Olivia pulls herself together. 'Of course she will,' she says. 'And of course you can put me down . . .'

'It didn't seem that important to me before but . . .'

'Where are you going tomorrow?' she says, thinking of his case, which is packed and ready by the door.

'It's the Russia run.'

She puts the glass down, feels herself teetering on the brink of darkness.

'It'll be fine,' he says. 'I don't know why I suddenly thought of it. I suppose it seems a bit sad if no one knows that I've gone . . .'

'You shouldn't think like that.'

'That's the way it is . . .'

They are silent for a moment, and then Charlie says, 'You know I'm truly sorry about how I behaved.'

'I know.'

'I just . . .'

'It's all right, really,' she says, laying a hand on his arm.

He puts his hand over hers and they sit quietly for a moment, and then she can't help it. She wants him to know what sort of person she is. Perhaps it will make him feel better. She takes a deep breath. 'Charlie,' she says, 'I'm pregnant.'

She hears the sharp intake of air as he acknowledges the statement. 'What are you going to do?' he asks.

'Keep it.'

'But your family . . .'

'I know. They won't ever accept it. If Jack doesn't come back, I'll have to do it alone.'

'That will be extremely tough.'

'It will.'

'Not just on you. On the child . . . I grew up without my parents. I know how hard it can be.'

'It will have me.'

'That makes it very lucky.'

'Thank you, Charlie.' In that moment she feels an overwhelming sense of gratitude and love for him.

He squeezes her hand. 'I'll do my best to find out what happened to him when I get out there,' he says.

'You've done more than enough already.'

'You're going to need any support you can get.'

'I know.'

'And I'll talk to your parents when I get back.'

'There's no need to do that.'

'I want to. I really admire the way you stick to your guns.'

'We're not so different, after all, you and me?'

'I'm trying to be more open-minded.'

'You're doing a great job of it.'

He shifts and starts to say something, but thinks better of it.

'Oh Charlie. What will happen to us?'

'I don't know about me,' he says, 'but I know you will be fine.'

She gives him a sad smile. Even after all these years of war, it still seems strange to be thinking of death – they should be deciding who to partner in a tennis tournament, or where to sit at a university lecture, or what country they are going to visit next.

'Come on, Charlie,' yells Maggie suddenly from next door, 'or I'll have finished this gin by myself!' They laugh, and then they hear the drone of the bombers and the air-raid sirens start up. The building shakes, and the smell of dust clags in her nostrils as they are plunged into darkness. Charlie moves the blackout curtains so he can peer out into the street. The moon is almost full and it flings pale light across the kitchen, highlighting the contours of his face, the hollows of his cheeks, the furrowed brow. Olivia suddenly wants to reach out and touch him: she can imagine the warmth of his skin, the rasp of his stubble.

Maggie's voice calls again: 'Bring the bloody candles too!'

'I'd better go and give her a hand,' he says. 'Sleep well.'

'You too.' Olivia closes her eyes and says a silent prayer, breathing in the faint smell of him before it disappears.

CHAPTER 20

Jack

It has been five days. They have lost another two men. They buried them near the cliffs, scraping holes into the dark, damp sand with their bare hands. They marked the shallow graves with wooden crosses made from driftwood. Jack can't help but think of the foxes that will surely come; their haunting barks grow closer every day. He has heard other strange noises too, which turned out to be walruses lumbering further round the coast. Neither he nor Grifter nor the Chief has mentioned the polar bear print again. Jack sleeps with one arm over his eyes, trying to block out the light. The landscape never changes. All he sees is the brown, bare beach, and, further away, the rock and snow and water and light, and the smoke from the fire corkscrewing up into the air. He sees it when he has his eyes open and when he has them closed. His body craves night-time and darkness.

At least Carl is better. He can sit up now. But he cannot walk. His legs are a pulpy mess. 'Do you think the Navy will find us?' he asks Jack.

'Any day now,' says Jack, although he is thinking of the same Navy that abandoned them.

A fog descends. It is a relief not to be able to see anything. Jack leans back and closes his eyes, arm slung over his face. The colourless world turns blood-red. The sounds are distorted.

He hears someone squeak in their dreams and is immediately awake and sitting up again because the sound wasn't quite a squeak but more of a whistle.

He peers into the milky mist. Now he wishes he could see that bare beach again. The sound cuts through the fog once more. Jack senses the other men stir around him.

'What was that?' He recognises Grifter's voice.

'Was it a whistle?'

'I heard it too.' The voices fragment in the white of the fog.

Again, a whistle. And suddenly one of their own men is blowing a whistle from a discarded life jacket – and another one, and another. They are all whistling on the beach, and there's a reply whistle from the fog – from the sea, because Jack knows that's the sea out there somewhere.

'Don't move,' says Jack. 'Wait for the fog to clear.' And the men are calling to each other through the fog, but it's like a nightmare you can't wake up from and they just have to sit and wait in the clammy, groping cloud, praying that it's the Navy at last.

The fog starts to clear, like steam from a train. First, Jack can make out shadows. The shadows become his friends, then the cliffs, then the shore. Jack and the Chief move towards the newcomers, their hearts thudding in their throats. The other men hang back. The Chief glances at Jack to see whether to advance. Now Jack can make out the shadow of a ship on the water. Friend or foe? The mist rolls back and the ship comes into focus. He strains to make out the flags. Then relief. It is another American ship from their convoy. It has run aground on a sandbank, having strayed too close to the island.

The Americans are just as surprised to see them. They welcome the lifeboat survivors on board, supporting the weary men against their shoulders or carrying them on stretchers. The crew from the *Aurora* are put together in a mess room. Someone brings hot coffee, but Jack can't drink it because it makes him retch.

His feet tingle and his hands throb as the heat of the ship seeps into them. In the light of the cabin, he takes a proper look at his shipmates. The seven of them are in a filthy state. Their swollen hands and feet are beginning to blister as they thaw. Their faces are black with ingrained dirt. Their hair is matted, and their beards encrusted with food and salt. And they stink: of rotting flesh and filth and sweat. Jack is too tired to care.

The American ship radios a Russian trawler. Jack picks up bits of information. They are not the only men from their convoy to have made it to these islands, called Novaya Zemlya. There are other ships that have been hiding in the Matochkin Strait, a strip of water that separates this half of the island from its other half. They are gathering here, near a lighthouse, from where they will make their final move to Archangel. The thought of being back on the open sea in a ship fills Jack with horror. He could stay and eat seabirds for the rest of his life. But Carl needs help; Jack must get him to safety. His hand goes to Olivia's knife, which has given him strength through all these days. He will see her again. He will.

As he is transferred to the Russian trawler, Jack can see that every ship that has managed to drag itself here is overladen with extra men. They are the lucky ones, the survivors plucked from the sea and from other lifeboats. They cower into the shadows; their haunted eyes barely registering each other. You can't feel lucky when you know that for every one of you there are the countless, frozen unlucky. The men from the *Aurora* huddle together under the Americans' blankets, and stare at their Russian crew. There is a female doctor, the first woman they have seen since the Russian tanker. She is small and neat, but her face is lined, which makes her seem older than her young, sad eyes. The Russians cannot speak English, and the crew of the *Aurora* cannot speak Russian. The doctor hands them salted fish to eat. It is as tasteless as the seabirds. Jack chews it slowly. It is all the Russians have. At least there is plenty of fresh water.

The scrappy new convoy sets off once more across the sea, to finish what they started. Carl communicates in whispers, but at least he can talk. 'I can't feel my legs,' he says.

'It's just the shock,' says Jack. 'They look fine.' It is a lie.

The next few hours are spent in aching terror, each man reliving his last moments on board the *Aurora* with every bump and creak of the trawler. Jack tries to keep spirits up by recounting tales of their training ship, but it only serves to remind them of what they have left behind. The Russians start to shout orders at each other. The mainland is in sight. The ship steams into the White Sea before heading into the mouth of the River Dvina. There, great piles of timber line the banks, long tree trunks stacked high, not sawn planks like those at the Surrey Docks. Enormous logs float past, bowled along by the current. The sparse and scrubby banks are dotted with wooden huts. People who seem no more than scruffy bundles of rags stare at them. And then Archangel rises before them on the coast, looking nothing like it sounds: not heavenly at all.

As they approach the shore, Jack sees the docks are busy with groups of people – men and women – loading and unloading cargo. A man slows to peer at the incoming line of ships, and he is immediately prodded and shouted at by a guard. He stumbles back into line.

'Prisoners,' says the Chief, who has been here before. 'Mostly Russian and Finnish. Perhaps Norwegian.'

The docks are some way from the town. Pine forests stretch into the distance. The men stagger down the gangway. It is hard to tell who is a local, who is a prisoner, and who a survivor. Everyone has the same ragged look, the same weary, gaunt faces. The survivors stand in a confused cluster. Someone waves at them to stay where they are. Another woman appears and instructs them to do something. 'She say to take clothes off,' says the Russian doctor, surprising everyone that she can speak English.

The men shake their heads and back off, but there is nowhere to go. They refuse to take off their clothes. They are not the only ones. The whole quay is packed with men from different ships – Americans and Dutch and British. Those that can still walk stick together in clumps. Those that can't, crawl towards each other, hoping there is safety in numbers. Grifter is trying to talk to the doctor, but she is shaking her head and saying, 'Better here. You must here.' The men look to Jack, but he crouches by Carl, ready to swing at anyone if they come near.

And now Russian guards appear, waving their guns, the bayonets glinting and flashing above their thick overcoats, their faces hidden behind scarves and under their warm hats. The exhausted men shout back at them and the tension swirls, mixing with the stink of sewage that seems to pervade everything. The guards press forward, and the men gather together, shouting back. Jack grips Olivia's knife in his pocket. He will use it if he has to. He keeps one hand on Carl's shoulder.

He hears someone shout: 'Back away. Back away.' He has never been so pleased to hear an English order barked out. Slowly the Russian guards step back into their positions surrounding the men. They rest the stocks of their rifles on the ground. Their shoulders hunch up around their necks as their beady eyes glitter from the darkness, watching all the time.

'Well met, men,' says a small round man with rosy cheeks and little round glasses. 'And welcome to Archangel. I'm Captain Tasker, Royal Army Medical Corps. I'm afraid Archangel is rather basic in the hygiene department. The corporal and lance corporal' – here he nods at the two men accompanying him – 'will take your numbers, rank, and ship names. You need to form two queues. British here, non-British there.'

The men straggle into line, and the medics work their way along, making notes and nodding. When he reaches Carl and

294

Jack, the corporal asks about his burns, whether they have dressed them, whether they smell. He scratches notes on his paper and then whistles at one of the orderlies. They come with a stretcher. 'No,' says Jack. 'I need to stay with him.'

The corporal lays a hand on Jack's arm. 'We'll look after him,' he says.

'You can't take him.' They are beginning to shout at each other above the general commotion. The men on the quay fall silent and watch as Jack feels the anger and panic rise in his throat. An image of Betsy being ushered away from him at the station dances through his mind.

The doctor trots down the line. 'It's all right,' he says, waving the corporal on.

'I can't leave him,' says Jack.

'I know it's hard,' says the doctor. 'But your friend needs to go to a specialist place. We're packed to the gunwales with injured men, and where you're going they've got no idea how to treat something this bad. The Russian hospital is the best chance your friend has. They really know their frostbite and burns.'

Jack swallows. The doctor lays his hand on Jack's shoulder. 'I promise he'll be better off.' Jack sighs. He is too weak to fight. The doctor clicks his fingers at the orderlies, and they gently lift Carl on to the stretcher.

'I'll find you as soon as I can,' says Jack.

Carl squeezes his hand. 'I'm not Betsy,' he says. 'I'll be fine.'

The orderlies climb into the back of a waiting lorry with the stretchers, as it rattles to life and pulls away.

'Right,' says Dr Tasker. 'The rest of you have been deemed walking wounded; fit enough to be debagged and deloused here. I know it's not very orthodox, but it's for your own good, believe me. Facilities are very basic, and we can't risk taking more infection into the recuperation centres.' He nods at the corporal.

'You'll need to remove your clothes now or you'll be spending the night here.' The men look up and down the filthy docks, at the cranes and the sacks and the rubbish and the sewage and the flies. A scrawny man begins to pull off his clothes.

One by one, the rest follow. The prisoners collect their rags, gathering them into a pile to be incinerated. A thickset woman with a ruddy face tries to take Jack's knife away, but he clasps it tightly and yells at her, and she yells back at him, and the doctor appears again. 'Let him keep it,' he says. 'These men have suffered enough.'

She grudgingly releases her grip, and Jack presses the knife to his chest.

A gang of men stands with hoses ready. The Russian guards bark an order at them and the gang begins to work its way along the lines of men.

Jack gasps when the water hits him. The cold makes him forget any humiliation as he stands there like an animal in a farmyard. But even this water cannot get the worst of the grime off his blackened hands and feet. Worse is to come. Now the women start to work their way along the lines. Jack wants to run, but there is nowhere to go: hostile armed guards in front of them; filthy water behind. Dr Tasker and his soldiers gaze into the distance. Somewhere some women are singing a song.

A woman approaches Jack with a razor. She does not meet his eyes. A guard stamps his rifle on the ground. Jack feels the cold metal of the blade against his scalp and the scrape as it is pulled back along his head, gently working around his scar. His hair falls in matted clumps around his feet. He feels the woman's warm hand against his throat as she starts on his beard. The scritch of the razor across his cheek and up his throat. He feels the last scrap of dignity drift from his body. But she hasn't finished yet: 'Up! Up!' she says, and she taps on his arms. The razor scrapes away at the hair in his armpits and then she starts to move around his groin. He grips the open knife in his hand until it digs into his palm and the blood starts to trickle along the blade and drip slowly on to the ground. All his hair is gone. He is as naked and vulnerable as a newborn baby.

Finally, the mosquitoes come, biting and pinching at his flesh. Another woman wraps a sheet around Jack's shoulders, patting him gently on the back. The kindness makes his knees weak, and he almost collapses.

They follow each other in dull shock to a train carriage that transports them like cattle to a hospital, rattling and bouncing against one another. The smell of raw sewage is ever present. When the train stops a short distance away, they are walked to a large building, and then ushered into a tiny room filled with six beds – there is barely space to squeeze between them.

There is something strange about the room. Then Jack realises: it is lit by the soft, warm, yellow glow of electric light. The windows are boarded up. It is the first time Jack has been out of the glare of daylight for weeks.

A slim girl appears. A Russian nurse. She talks to them kindly, but of course no one can understand. Another nurse appears. She points at the beds, indicates that they must get in. Jack peels back the blanket. The sheets are clean at least. The nurse nods, pointing again, encouraging. He sits first, then lies, still clasping the sheet around his shoulders, tucking his legs into his body like an unborn baby, the knife still clutched in his hand. The Russian nurse carefully pulls the blanket back over him and he feels a wave of sleep wash over him, and he closes his eyes, and at last there is true darkness.

When he wakes, someone is massaging his feet. It is the slim Russian nurse. She smiles and nods, says something he doesn't understand. The Chief, in the bed next to him, says, 'Best frostbite treatment I've ever had.'

Grifter, beyond him, gives Jack the thumbs-up.

The sound of propaganda from loudspeakers drifts through the boarded-up windows. The other nurse is busy scrubbing down the room, which, although cramped, is spotless.

Jack is embarrassed. His feet are still grimy and the toes are now pale blue, fatly swollen and covered in red blisters. They remind him of the sausages he used to steal with Stoog. The blisters sting and burn. But the nurse waves him back down as he tries to sit up.

Dr Tasker appears. There is a dark-haired Russian girl at his elbow, who translates between him and the nurse. When he has finished talking to the nurse, he turns to the men. 'You're the lucky ones,' he says. 'You won't be losing any limbs. Goddamned frostbite.'

'Thanks to the Chief, here,' says Grifter.

Dr Tasker nods. 'I've seen the damage done when men try to heat them up too quickly. Sometimes their feet melt without them realising. But yours are treatable. Not too much tissue damage. Good job.'

Jack cannot believe that those swollen waxy things on the ends of his legs will ever look right again.

The doctor touches Jack's head. 'I'm sorry about all that at the dock,' he says. 'It's so bloody filthy here, we have to take extreme measures. This is one of the cleanest places left. It used to be a school. It was requisitioned especially for the British sailors coming off the convoys. We had to fight for it, though. The Russkies barely have any space to treat their own. Poor buggers. And they've given us plenty of nurses, but I'm the only doctor. We're struggling to treat everyone.' He brightens suddenly. 'But not my problem for much longer, thank the Lord. I'm moving on,' he says. 'We're opening a new hospital around the corner at Vaenga. Near the airfield. Much better conditions. All run by our own men. No offence, Anya,' he adds, nodding at the translator. 'It's just so damn overcrowded here.'

Anya smiles. 'We can only do what we can,' she says.

'Where will they have taken my friend?' Jack asks.

'The one with the legs?'

Jack nods.

'To Bolnitsa. It's the only proper hospital. He'll be fine . . . as long as he survived the first night.' Dr Tasker rubs his hands together. 'Best be off, anyway. Got masses of you lot to get through.' He signals at Anya to follow, and they move on to the next room.

When the nurse brings Jack his food, he tries to ask her how to get to Bolnitsa Hospital. She shakes her head at him, proffers the bowl instead. Jack takes it. Inside is a grey soup with something black floating in it. The nurse nods again, mimes eating, pushes the bowl. 'Good,' she says. 'Good.'

Jack takes a sip. It is revolting. Tasteless. Like water with dirt in it. He prods the black thing. 'It's potato,' says the Chief. 'And the white stuff is meat.'

'Not like any meat I've ever tasted,' says Grifter.

'Can't be as bad as seabirds,' says Jack.

'I wouldn't bet on it.'

The nurse returns for their bowls and sees their wrinkled noses and the liquid and gristle still swimming around in the bottom. She is furious. 'This is good,' she says. 'You very lucky. You eat better than any of us.'

Guiltily, they finish every scrap. It is not quite as bad as it looks.

When the other nurse returns to scrub the floor again, Jack says, 'Bolnitsa Hospital?'

'Ah,' she nods and smiles, showing blackened teeth. 'Bolnitsa. Yes.'

'Where?'

She shakes her head, goes back to scrubbing. The sound of the brush sets his teeth on edge. He tries to get out of bed. 'No! No!' the nurse says, pushing him back and shaking her head. She looks worried.

'Yes,' he says, and he pushes her out of the way and heads for the brightness of the corridor. He is just in time to see Dr Tasker leaving with his translator. 'Wait!' he says. But the doctor is already outside, stepping into a truck. 'Please!' Jack shouts. The translator turns, resting her hand on the door-frame. 'Bolnitsa Hospital?'

'You can't miss it,' she says in heavily accented English. 'It is a big building not far down this road. Lots of soldiers wait outside it. Name looks like this.' She writes in a notebook in letters that look like symbols. She tears the paper from the book and hands it to him. 'I warn you, is very . . . basic,' she adds.

'Thank you,' he says.

'Very welcome,' she says and smiles at him, her mouth opening to reveal a natural gap between her front teeth, and another where a tooth is missing. She has a pretty smile, but her eyes are etched with sadness.

'I'm Jack.'

'Anya.'

'Thank you, Anya.'

'Good luck, Jack.'

She turns and trots neatly after Dr Tasker, who raises his hand in a goodbye gesture without turning around.

Back in their room, Jack starts to dress. The men have been given new clothes and boots from British naval supplies. Jack pulls on the thick serge trousers. The material is scratchy and thick, yet somehow soft.

'You look like a proper Navy boy now,' says the Chief. 'What would Mart think?'

Jack pushes his head through the thick woollen jumper and then sits to pull on the leather boots over his sore feet. 'I wish he was here to tell me.' He stands and stamps his sore feet into the boots properly.

'You're crazy,' says Grifter.

'That's good coming from you.'

'You'll never find him.'

'I will.'

'We'll all be transferred on to the next ships to go home.'

But Jack knows Carl is not well enough for that. 'I hope you are,' says Jack. 'But I can't leave Carl.'

The Chief scrabbles about under his bed. 'Take these,' he

says, handing Jack a pair of thick mittens and another pair of socks.

Grifter sighs and shakes his head. 'And mine,' he says, holding them out to Jack. All along the row of beds, Jack is offered cigarettes, spare clothes, soap. He clasps each of their hands briefly. Doesn't dare say anything in case he chokes up. He looks once more around the room. He knows all of their faces as well as his own – even clean-shaven. They have shared something no man should have to.

'See you on the other side,' he says.

The town is filthy beneath its imposing buildings, the odour of decay and the relentless deprivation somehow making it more miserable to Jack than his memories of London in the Blitz. No one takes any notice of Jack wrapped up in his coat. Most of the people keep their eyes averted, avoiding the guards who are always escorting prisoners somewhere. The prisoners wear pitifully thin clothes and old sack cloths on their feet instead of shoes. The locals – old men and women – have dull stares. Only the children seem to be interested, tugging at his coat until policewomen in pointed caps chase them away. The shops are empty. There are piles of fresh sewage on the side of the road, sewers running down to the river. No wonder it smells so bad. Jack brushes a fly from his mouth. Another one lands immediately, its legs tickling along his lips.

The translator is right: the hospital is easy to spot. It rises out of the squalor like something from the distant past, ornate columns leading up to patterned cornicing above wide stone steps. But nearer the ground, the reality is evident: bandaged and exhausted Russian soldiers surround the building: some standing, some leaning, some lying. Their green uniforms are patched and grimy beneath their greatcoats. Their faces are torn and bloodied and dirty. Some will never get up; Jack recognises the waxy stare of death. For a second he thinks back to the lifeboat. But no death is better or worse than any other.

Jack wades through the bodies on the steps. Inside it is

worse. The corridors are lined with the half-dead. They loll on the grimy floors, suffering in grim silence. Men missing limbs, their faces half eaten away, backs of heads missing, or just jibbering wrecks. The smell makes Jack gag; he breathes through his mouth, but that's worse as the stench hits his throat, invades his lungs. He needs fresh air, but he presses on. He must find Carl. Jack glimpses wards packed with beds – there is barely any floor space, but where there is, the men are lying there too. There are two or three men in many of the beds. Those that have sheets are stained with blood, vomit, infection. The stench of urine and gangrene and blood makes his eyes water. Raw sewage seeps under a door. The flies buzz around everything in clouds.

Jack pushes on until he finds a room reserved for foreigners. He spots Carl immediately. His friend is lying on his side, nearest the window – or what's left of the window, since they are all boarded up too, but someone has smashed the bottom board of this one to let in some of the air from outside. Not that you could call it fresh.

Jack touches his friend's shoulder, but Carl doesn't respond. 'Carl?' he says, moving around the bed to squat in front of him. 'Carl, it's me. Jack.' Carl's eyes are shut, his face twitching and grimacing, small beads of sweat on his forehead.

'Hasn't said a word since he got here,' says the man in the bed behind. His voice is ugly, scratching like sandpaper.

'He wasn't this bad when I left him,' says Jack.

'No time to do anything here. Too busy with their own poor bastards coming back from the front.'

Jack looks under the blanket. Carl's legs are white and black. It's hard to tell whether it's the burns or the frostbite or the dirt. The worst thing is the stench: it is the stench of death.

A mumbling and muttering starts up as a nurse and two orderlies thread their way through the ward. The sound builds to a crescendo until the patients are hollering and screeching at each other, and then the noise suddenly stops and a deathly silence descends. The orderlies have stopped in front of Carl's bed. They are old men, creased but burly beneath their stained coats. The nurse is tired eyes haloed by a pristine white head-scarf. She says something to Jack before trying to shoo him away.

'What are you doing?' he asks.

'Moving patient. If not, he die.'

'Moving him where?'

'Operation.'

The man in the next-door bed starts to cackle. 'The guillo-tine! He's for it now . . .' He is laughing hysterically, and so are some of the other men, like creatures from a nightmare, their faces and bodies patched together in macabre ways. The sound of so many men laughing and shrieking is so out of place that Jack feels the anger swell. He would punch the man if all his effort wasn't taken up with trying to hold on to Carl as the orderlies pull him from the bed.

But the orderlies are thickset men, and Jack is still weak. He cannot stop them lifting his friend, and soon he is jogging next to Carl on the stretcher, along the stinking corridor to a room with four operating tables arranged beneath one dim light bulb.

He glimpses a severed limb and a stump in a bucket, and he recognises the metallic smell of fresh blood. On one of the operating tables, a man lies on his back, his stomach gaping, the intestines slithering out on to the table like fish guts. The nurse pushes Jack away. 'No,' she shakes her head and holds him back. 'You stay.'

The orderlies close the door and stand in front of it, their arms crossed, their faces grim, their necks bulging.

So Jack stands there in the corridor while patriotic songs are pumped into the air around his head, and he knows there's no anaesthetic and he hears the grotesque howl of a creature that has been mortally wounded and he feels the bile rise into his mouth, bitter and sweet, and he turns and vomits in the corridor. The orderlies watch motionless, their arms folded, their eyes fixed.

*

Carl is brought out half an hour later. Jack cannot bring himself to look at the bloody stump below his friend's knee. The orderlies carry him back to the bed by the window, but there is someone else lying in it. They turn to the neighbouring bed, which is now empty, but Jack is in front of them, grabbing the man with the raspy voice by the vest and yelling at him. 'Out!' he says. 'Get out.' He knows it is the only place that Carl might get any semblance of fresh air.

The man falls to the floor with a thud. Jack's stomach lurches as he realises the man has no legs at all. He shuffles along the floor on his stumps, back to his bed, somehow clambering up into it, moaning and tutting at Jack. But Jack has seen enough suffering not to care. He helps to lift Carl on to the bed and tuck him in. His friend is delirious, talking about bananas and oranges and the bells of St Clements. The orderlies leave. No one has time to tend the bandages except for Jack. He tears some of the sheet from the end of the bed and uses it to wipe Carl's forehead. He finds drinking water, and begins to nurse his friend again, just as he did at sea, except here there is no fresh air or salt spray stinging his eyes and his mouth, only the smell of death and the feathery wings of the flies that buzz around them, their fat bodies glinting like blue metal in the dim light.

As the long day turns to night, Jack curls up on the floor under Carl's bed, beneath the spiders' webs. He is covered in bites from the bugs that infest the place. He knows he needs to get Carl moved from here if he is ever to recover. But he doesn't know how. He lies beneath the bed, scratching at his itchy skin, the red bites covering every exposed part of him, as Carl tosses and turns and moans nursery rhymes and Morse code. He is not the only one: all the men on the ward mutter and scream in their sleep. Outside the window, washed bandages flutter in the breeze, the stains of blood like wine on a tablecloth.

*

304

The food in the hospital is diabolical – mainly black bread that gives the patients diarrhoea. Jack thinks longingly of the soup he was offered in the recuperation centre. Carl will never recover on such rations. There is no soap to spare, and soon Jack's has run out. The only running water is downstairs as the pressure is too weak and can't push the water up to the next floors. There is no disinfectant, no painkillers, nearly every surgical case becomes septic. There are no bedpans; the men use what they can – bottles, tobacco tins, mugs. In the transfer process, much of the urine ends up either on the sheets or on the floor. Every morning, there is another dead body, another sick patient all too glad of an empty space to crawl into, clutching the crusted sheets between feverish fingers. It is a matter of survival, and Jack is a boy from the streets. He knows how to survive.

Archangel is already growing colder. Summer is almost over. The wind howls along the streets and around the buildings. Two mangy horses drag a transport bus packed with people hunched against the cold. The horses' bony hips and ribs press against their scarred skin. Their eyes and nostrils and mouths are black with flies. The city may look different, but when it comes down to it, one city is much like another, and Jack has no problem identifying the people who can help him. This is a world he knows, scavenging and bartering, where the strong prey on the weak. The children are thin and wiry, their bodies young, but their eyes old. They have seen much suffering. They hang around in gangs, just as Jack once did. He watches them work the streets. Their feet are bare and their clothes ill-fitting: loose strands of cloth frayed at the edges. Their trousers are no more than patched together. Jack cannot imagine how they survive once the snow starts. But for now their pockets bulge with roubles and they are only too happy to trade Jack's cigarettes and clothes for food and soap. He even buys two thick Russian greatcoats, invaluable against the cold. He tries not to think of the men they once belonged to.

It is three days before Carl stops hallucinating. He tries to push himself up on one elbow but he is so weak that he collapses against the pillow. He smiles weakly at Jack. Jack doesn't know what to say. How do you tell your best friend they've lost a leg? Despair is a bottomless chasm. Ashamed, he feels tears well up in his eyes. But Carl reaches out and touches his arm. 'My dad's going to kill me,' he says. 'I'll never make an officer now.'

Jack smiles, swallowing the sob that threatens to bubble out of his chest. 'It's all a load of bull anyway,' he says, and he bends over to hug his friend. Carl is covered in bedsores and bites, but his eyes are bright, and there is even colour in his sunken cheeks. But they both know he needs to get out of here as soon as possible.

Jack risks going further afield, making it to the docks to see if there's any possibility of transport. Thin ice is beginning to form on the river. They will be stuck once it freezes over completely. He wanders among the men on the dock, avoiding the guards, hoping to pick up some familiar English. Someone calls his name. It's the translator, Anya. She is also looking for work at the docks now that Dr Tasker has moved on.

'Did you find your friend?' she asks.

'I did. Now I need to get him to your doctor's hospital at Vaenga,' says Jack. 'Do you think you can help?'

Anya smiles her thin, gappy smile and says, 'I can try. But what about you? Your other friends have gone . . .'

'I'm not worried about me. But Carl needs to get home – or at least somewhere clean – before your winter comes.'

'If you can get your friend here, I might be able to help. I have found work at the naval base at Polyarnoe. It is near Vaenga. They have much need of translators. I leave tomorrow.'

'We'll be here,' says Jack.

They meet at the docks the next day, except this time Jack has Carl on his back. His friend's good leg is missing its toes and he cannot hop. Jack is shocked by how light his friend is, but his laugh is like the old Carl, and his voice is strong. 'You'll never get me there,' he says. 'You could barely carry a plank at the docks.'

'Watch me,' says Jack. His friend clings to his back, and with each step he grows heavier, but Jack remembers how Carl carried Betsy from the river in the rain, and he grits his teeth and makes it without stopping. No one gives them a second look. It is not unusual for people to be carrying heavy loads.

Anya has found a Russian tug that will take them all to the mouth of the inlet. The Russian skipper is wrapped up against the cold wind, only his eyes showing. He nods curtly at the boys as they approach the boat, but Jack is struck by a sudden feeling that he can't do this. He doesn't want to be on the water. His palms grow clammy and there is a fluttering in his chest, but Anya is behind him and the skipper narrows his eyes and the guards on the dock are watching them. He has to do it. He cannot stay here. He takes a deep breath and lifts Carl down into the boat. It is black with coal dust. The sensation of moving water sets Jack's blood racing.

Then Anya takes his arm and they steady themselves and he has Carl to concentrate on. They find a sheltered space in the stern and sit on the grimy deck, their collars turned up against the cold, watching the ships coming and going on the great river around them, all of them glad to be leaving Archangel behind.

The Russians cast off and soon they are clear of the docks and motoring up the river, through the thickening patches of ice, and back into the White Sea. The fresh air blows the mosquitoes away. As they approach the open water, Jack's mouth is dry. Carl lays a hand on his arm. 'A little more space on this boat,' he says. Jack nods and swallows the fear. For Carl, for all of them.

A bitter wind is blowing into the mouth of the inlet from the heart of the Arctic. The tug hugs the bland coastline until they reach another little inlet and motor into a small dock. Anya talks to the Russians and they point and nod and gesticulate. One of the men jumps down into the boat and starts to pull at Carl, but Jack pushes him away. 'It's all right,' he says. 'I've got it.' He hoists Carl up on to his back again and together they clamber out on to dry land. The air smells fresh here, of the sea and faintly of pine needles.

Anya helps them find a British medical officer who takes them to the new hospital. Dr Tasker is there. He doesn't seem surprised to see them. In this country, anything can happen. 'Welcome, welcome!' he says. 'You're my first patient. We're all up and ready for the next influx. Should be here any day now. Poor bastards.'

They are ushered into a shiny, clean ward. The medical officer brings Carl a small mug of fruit juice and a plate of food. He chews it slowly, his eyes closed, a smile on his lips. 'Macaroni cheese,' he says. 'My favourite.'

'That's right, my boy. Close your eyes and think of England,' says the doctor.

Jack feels a great load lifted from his heart. 'He's going to be all right?' It is more a statement than a question.

The doctor smiles. 'The hard work's been done already,' he says. 'We just need to fatten him up and get him on the next ship home.'

'Do you think he'll make the crossing?'

'Absolutely.'

'What happens at the other end?'

'He'll probably end up at the Dreadnought Hospital at Greenwich. Fine place. Run for the likes of you.'

Carl interrupts them: 'Stop talking about me as if I'm not here,' he says. 'I've lost my leg and some toes, not my mind.'

'You wouldn't be alone if you had,' says the doctor. 'Half the men I see have been driven around the bend. Stark raving mad.'

'Well I'm fine,' says Carl. 'But what about you, Jack?'

'I'm all right.'

'Are you really?' Carl tries to hold his gaze, but Jack looks away. 'Can you find him a berth going back, doctor?'

Dr Tasker shakes his head. 'I'm afraid you'll need to be processed back in Archangel. With the other men from your ship.'

'They've gone already,' says Jack.

'You can't stay here. We won't have the room when the next chaps arrive. But they might be able to help at Polyarnoe.'

'I'll work something out.'

Anya clears her throat. 'If you are not staying here, you must come now or the boat will leave without us.'

'Can you help him?' says Carl, addressing Anya.

'I will do what I can.'

'Thank you,' says Carl. 'And thank you for helping get me here.'

She smiles her sad, gappy smile. 'Anything for a friend of the Fatherland.'

Jack feels the anxiety rise in his chest as he realises he is about to leave his friend again. 'Are you sure you'll be all right?' he asks.

'Don't worry about me. I'll be fine.'

'I'm not worried about you,' says Jack, his vision blurring and his voice coming out thick and deep. 'Who's going to keep an eye on me?'

Carl laughs and Jack hugs his oldest friend, feeling the heat of the solid body through his shirt, ignoring the empty space where his leg should be. 'Don't disappear,' says Carl. 'Remember there are people waiting for you. Olivia, Betsy . . .'

But those are names of people from another life, another world. Jack squeezes his friend one last time and hurries after Anya into the unrelenting cold.

When they are out of earshot, Jack says, 'I can't go back to Archangel.'

'We will ask in Polyarnoe.'

'I don't want to ask yet. I don't think I can go back for a while.'

'The crossing?'

He nods because he does not want to give voice to his fear. The hundreds of miles of open sea between Russia and Britain are an abyss he cannot cross until he is feeling stronger. The idea of setting foot on a large ship makes his stomach churn. He needs time.

Anya nods. 'It is possible that I know some people in the hills behind Polyarnoe who might be able to help you,' she says.

CHAPTER 21

Charlie

Charlie is pleased to be back with the squadron, where life follows a set pattern and there is no confusion over romance and pregnant friends. He has a crazy notion that perhaps he and Olivia could raise Jack's child together, and then feels guilty, for he has promised to discover what happened to the man. Perhaps he has survived. Perhaps he hasn't. But whatever the answer, Charlie will be as good as his word and try to find out. It is ironic that if the man is dead, then the child will have a war hero for a father, just as Charlie did. The thought of his father inevitably leads to thoughts of his mother, and what they might have thought of his recent behaviour. Charlie flushes with shame at the memory of Betsy and that night. She may have battered down his defences, but he wasn't entirely innocent: he had wanted her; had wanted to feel what it was like to be with someone who really wanted him. And was it really so wrong when everyone else is at it, when every bar and alley seems full of sexual tension and attraction?

Thankfully he doesn't have much time to dwell on the matter. The Admiralty are ready to start the runs to Russia again after the fiasco of the last one, and Charlie's squadron is going to form part of the first escort carrier to accompany them, defending the merchant ships and their cargo of planes, tanks, food, clothes, and whatever else will keep the Russians going. Charlie pushes all memories from his mind: here, on his ship, he is Lieutenant FitzHerbert, one of a team of courageous pilots tasked with keeping the Bosch at bay. It is all so very straightforward.

They have a new captain, Captain Underhill, another veteran of the First World War, and a leader who knows how important it is to inspire his men. As they set sail, he briefs them: 'We've got our work cut out, men. We are not just fighting the enemy; we are fighting low morale: many of these merchant sailors have already been on convoys to Russia – many have been attacked, many have been shipwrecked. They have lost friends and ships. They have little faith in us after that last bloody hash-up. So let's try and restore some of it. Let's show them that we can still rule the waves together. You're the first Navy pilots they've had to protect them: let's show them what that means.'

Every seaman – merchant and Royal Navy – is aware that the Germans will come at them with whatever they have. Before the ships have even formed up, the repel aircraft station rings in their ears and a Condor rains its bombs from between the clouds. The dark pellets twist and turn in the leaden sky before falling ineffectively into the sea. The carrier ploughs on. The Swordfish pilots are sent up to hunt for U-boats whenever conditions allow. From above, Charlie can marvel at the whole operation. The ships with their Arctic camouflage are scattered across the ocean like the toys that used to lie across his bedroom floor: sloops and corvettes, destroyers and Asdic minesweepers, and, below the waves, the Allied submarines. British, American, Panamanian, Russian – even a French and a Norwegian submarine – surge onwards together.

It is just Charlie and Ned in the plane: there is no room for a gunner now that the cockpit is half taken up by the new radar. Charlie wonders what Mole would have chosen to sing on a day like today: dense, low cloud and pockets of fog. He can't help smiling as he remembers his promise to Alis, and attempts a rendition of 'Cwm Rhondda'. He can almost hear

Mole shouting at him to stop, and he's sure that Ned thinks he's finally lost the plot, but it feels good.

While the Swordfish hunt for U-boats, the Hurricanes intercept the flying boats that buzz around the convoy, trying to stop the German planes returning to report their position. The Luftwaffe shadow them until they are within range of the Norwegian airfields, and then the attacks begin in earnest. The clouds have lifted a little, but the sky darkens with Junkers and Heinkels as the Germans launch a mass torpedo attack. The ack-ack fire and the enemy planes and the Navy retaliations are so loud that the men can't hear the siren to alter course. A merchant ship goes up. And then another: two columns of smoke and dead souls billowing into the air. And still another – until there are six ships missing. Fifteen enemy planes down. Charlie itches to get up there to help, but it is impossible for the Swordfish to take off: the carrier would be a sitting duck as she turned into wind.

They forge on. The flight deck is a continual stream of take-offs and landings. A tanker is torpedoed by a U-boat; Charlie is flying, and goes in for the attack. The U-boat dives, but a destroyer picks it up and the depth charge sinks it, leaving debris slick on the surface. The torpedo bombers return, but again the Navy planes are ready for them. Charlie suffers cramp in his legs from his squashed position in the pilot's seat, but rather that than be like those gunners on the warships, who never move from their turrets – eating, sleeping and dying in them.

Morale is running high. They know they will make it through; the Germans will not stop this convoy, and the Navy will never abandon their merchant men again. The Russian escort arrives to assist. In the mess room, the men laugh and joke. A Hurricane pilot who was shot down by friendly fire has been safely rescued from the sea. 'You needed a bath anyway,' says Ned.

'We could all do with one,' says Charlie, because everything is beginning to smell – of mould and damp. There is no escape:

water drips down the bulkheads on every deck as condensation trickles into their cabins. Even the food is beginning to have a distinctly earthy flavour.

The day before they reach the White Sea they are fogbound. 'We're not even going to be able to see bloody Russia,' says Charlie. As they approach the mainland, the fog clears to reveal seventy Luftwaffe bombers. An American freighter is hit. The Hurricanes are immediately up and then a cheer rings out across the flight deck as more planes appear in the sky.

'It's the RAF!' says Ned.

'What are they doing here?'

'Someone's got to teach those Soviets how to fly our planes.'

Captain Underhill's weary voice addresses them from the bridge. 'Well done, men. The most successful convoy so far. Twenty-eight ships of cargo delivered. No escorts lost.'

But no one cheers: thirteen vessels and countless men never made it.

Charlie and the squadron watch as the convoy is delivered safely to the Russian icebreaker that will take it on through the White Sea to Archangel. Charlie is surprised to hear that the return convoy his carrier will be escorting part of the way back to Britain is carrying a few survivors from the last, doomed convoy. 'Any idea how many?' he asks Captain Underhill.

The captain shakes his head. 'All I know is it's the worst injured. Amputees and the like. The walking wounded have mainly been shoved into compounds, poor bastards. They've gone through all that – injury, shipwreck, survival – to be treated like prisoners-of-war. Shitty Russian food and hygiene. I've no doubt a lot of them won't survive. Ironic after all they've already been through.'

'Are there lists of the men that did make it, do you think?'

'Possibly onshore at our base in Polyarnoe, but I fear it's very chaotic. Did you know someone?'

314

Charlie nods.

'Soon as there's a chance, I'll try and get you there.'

But the carrier is kept busy patrolling the sea as the temperature drops. The fresh water pipes start to freeze. The ice builds up: six inches, eight inches. All day and all night the ship echoes with the sound of men chipping and hacking and whacking where the ice thickens on the flight deck and on the guns, on the island and the rails. If they don't, the ship could easily capsize, pulled over by the sheer weight. Sometimes it looks as though she has been frozen in time: a great castle of ice rising from the water.

Then the sea starts to freeze. Charlie can actually see it thickening as he sits once again waiting for take-off in the chilly cockpit: the heavy snow cools the surface of the water, and an eerie mist starts to rise around the ship. The sea turns grey and cold, congealing to slush, and then into a patchwork quilt of ice across the water. Across the fleet, men shiver on lookout: more than an hour on deck and they freeze to death. If they forget their gloves, they lose their skin as it burns off on the frozen metal rails. Spray turns to ice that lacerates their cheeks. Their ears go numb and black with frostbite.

Charlie starts to worry that he'll never get a chance to find out what happened to Jack. If he was sent to one of the compounds, he could just as easily have died in Russia as well as when his ship went down. Or he could have been terribly injured and repatriated. He could be a war hero or a cripple. Charlie thinks of his shoulder, and shudders. He cannot imagine what he would have done if he'd lost his arm, whether it turned him into a war hero or not. He thinks of his own father, so proud of his part in the previous war, the medals, polished metal beneath bold strips of colour, bright against the navy-blue uniform.

The planes are carrier-bound much of the time, but if it's possible to fly, the Swordfish will take to the stormy skies – they can stay airborne longer than the Hurricanes. But even the Swordfish are suffering. The pitching deck has sent more than one plane toppling into the sea. Another misses the arrester wires and smashes into the barrier, leaking fuel fizzling to life as it catches fire. Charlie almost misses a landing when the carrier suddenly slams away from him as he's about to touch down. But he manages to circle around again, watching as the blue landing lights come closer and then recede as the carrier rises and falls; his fellow sailors specks of black against the great pale piles of snow.

And still the temperature drops. Drips freeze in Charlie's nostrils. Eyebrows and eyelashes are covered in white frost. Water freezes on eyeballs. Inside the ship, the condensation freezes. The men layer up their clothes, winding scarves around and around their faces until only their eyes are visible, but still the cold bites into their bones. Charlie wears his pyjamas under his clothes, only ever removing his boots to sleep. He wonders whether Jack could have been on that return convoy, could have been reunited with Olivia. Whether he knows that he has a child, a future, a dream to cling on to.

It is weeks before an opportunity to go ashore presents itself. 'The Russians have invited us to some celebration for another successfully delivered convoy,' says Captain Underhill. 'Can't say no. I'm taking you with me.'

'Great,' says Charlie. 'Thank you, sir.'

'We'll transfer on to the Russian icebreaker that takes the ships on to Archangel. Then they'll bring us back to Polyarnoe. Should be a bit of an eye-opener.'

The two men are first transferred to a British destroyer. As they come alongside the battered Russian icebreaker, a British man on the Russian ship yells, 'Jump!' and Charlie and the captain leap through the air. The Russian crew reach out with strong, large hands wrapped in thick fur gloves and yank them on to the deck.

The British man introduces himself: 'Jarvis,' he says. 'I'm the translator. Welcome aboard.' He is an animated young man, fresh out of university and a six-month course in Russian. His job is to translate between the icebreaker and the merchant ships that will follow them for the last leg of their trip.

The Russian captain glares at them from the bridge, his lined face bunched deep inside his coat. 'Don't mind him,' says Jarvis. 'He's a big old softie, really.'

'Better go and make myself known,' says Captain Underhill, and Charlie sees the Russian captain's stern face break into a smile as he welcomes the captain in.

Jarvis and his signalman are the only British men on the icebreaker. The ship signals to the merchant ships to line up behind and continue on their way. They enter the White Sea, a carpet of ice that thickens as they draw nearer to the mouth of the River Dvina. High up in the crow's nest a Russian lookout reads the ice as the ship's reinforced bows crunch and smash a pathway. Occasionally the lookout yells down, and Jarvis translates for the signalman, who relays the message via his Aldis lamp to the ship behind. From there, the merchant ships shout through a megaphone to each other: 'Stay in line! Station! Pass it on!' As the ice grows still thicker, ice-breaking tugs come to assist, stopping the ice from immediately freezing again to pinch and buckle their hulls. The straggly line proceeds at a crawl of no more than two knots. Charlie is thankful that submarines cannot operate here under the ice.

'Do you know anything about survivors from convoys getting back home?' Charlie asks Jarvis.

'Not really. You can imagine things are somewhat chaotic when people turn up here. It's difficult enough when we're expecting you.'

'But there have been survivors?' Charlie asks.

'Plenty,' says Jarvis. 'Sometimes the Navy decks are crammed with men whose ships have gone down. They'll risk sitting up on deck all the way if it means they'll get home.'

'What about you?'

The translator shrugs. 'I'm getting fond of the place,' he says.

*

317

The scene at Archangel is like nothing Charlie has seen before: the river is frozen so thick that people, horses, carts, and even lorries criss-cross it. In the half-light Charlie watches as a reindeer pulling a packed sledge overtakes them, scooting along past the icebreaker. Like everyone else, the passengers are wrapped up in thick coats with quilted baggy trousers tucked into felt boots, so that it is hard to differentiate between men and women until Charlie realises that the men wear a fur or astrakhan hat with pull-down earflaps, while the women wear headscarves.

'It'll be time to divert convoys to Murmansk soon,' says Jarvis. 'Unloading these ships is becoming impossible. The tanks and lorries are frozen. Can't even get 'em started.'

'Do they send anything back to Britain in return?' Charlie asks.

'The odd silver fox fur. The rest is just railway sleepers for ballast. They don't really have anything to send. That's why we're here.'

Charlie covers his nose with his hand.

'Horrible, isn't it?' says Jarvis. 'Gets worse when it's frozen like this; can't dump everything into the water and forget about it.'

Charlie takes in the broken crates, rusted vehicles, and potato peelings strewn across the ice. There are even rats scampering about on it. He turns away as a woman crouches down to relieve herself, a yellow stain spreading slowly beneath her. Jarvis chuckles. 'You get used to it,' he says.

At the dock, there is a man fishing in a hole in the ice, among the effluent and rubbish that bobs on the oil slick inside it. A group of men shuffles towards the arriving ships. They are surrounded by armed guards. 'Who are they?' says Charlie.

'Prisoners,' says Jarvis.

'But they haven't got any hats,' says Charlie, blowing on his cold hands.

'Most of them haven't got any shoes.'

'Can't we give them something?'

'Best to ignore them. For their own sakes.'

'Can't we chuck them some bread at least?'

'Definitely not.'

'Where do they come from?'

'We're not sure. They're herded out whenever there's a convoy to unload.'

It is dark when they head back to Polyarnoe. Behind them, the ice closes up around the delivered convoy, sealing it into the city of Archangel. Some of the ships will be stuck there for months. Charlie is relieved that he won't be on one of them. As they motor back through the White Sea, there is nothing to see in the icy blackness around them, until a crown of light bursts from a tear in the sky and the surrounding ice becomes a ghostly carpet of luminous white. The Northern Lights. With a twinge he pictures Scotland, Olivia.

Charlie and Captain Underhill are transferred on shore by more Russians at Polyarnoe. The Russian crew and Jarvis and the signalman come too. Jarvis warns Charlie to accept any checks with as much good grace as he can muster. 'The Russians are a suspicious lot, and we're the only foreigners for miles.' Charlie struggles to comply as his papers are pored over meticulously again and again.

The officers have been invited to dine with the commissar. Charlie asks Captain Underhill if he can go to the naval base first to check the records for the injured survivors who have been sent home. The translator relays the message to the Russian captain, who shakes his head gravely. 'Sorry,' says Jarvis. 'Welcoming celebration first. You mustn't snub the commissar.'

The Russian captain nods. For a moment, Charlie wonders if that is fear in his eyes, but then they are ushered on by their Russian guards, and the captain's face returns to its expressionless stare.

Charlie finds himself in a large heated building with thick

double-glazing. The tables are laid with caviar, fish, smoked salmon, meat, rice, and a seemingly endless supply of vodka. It is a far cry from the rotten fish and scraps of vegetables that he saw at Archangel. The commissar is a genial man who toasts the motherland, and then the British and Russians in their great war against the fascist aggressor. The Russian speeches go on and on, and the British men wouldn't under-stand a word if it weren't for the translators. A friendly British officer on Charlie's table advises him to eat lots of butter to soak up the vodka. 'It really helps,' he says.

'You must come and hear our male-voice choir,' says the commissar, stuffing more food into his mouth. 'They sing every weekend without fail, whether the bombs are falling or not.' The men cheer. Their cheeks are rosy with vodka. They grin at the waitresses and the women who are dotted around among them, but the guards narrow their eyes and the women look away. It is impossible to relax.

Charlie thinks of the prisoners along the coast fishing among the filth. He thinks of the girls in London selling themselves to eat. He has had enough. Feigning tiredness as soon as is polite, he asks to be taken to the British naval base. After much muttering and a lot of assistance from Jarvis, they are both allowed to leave, escorted by a Russian guard. There is another bunch of prisoners clearing the snow from the streets, piling it up along the sides just as Charlie's fellow sailors do on the flight deck. Except these men and women have card-board on their feet instead of thick woollen socks and boots. As Charlie passes, he sees an old man lunge for a crust of mouldy bread that has been thrown out on to a pile of rubbish. The man almost gets away with it, but then a guard notices him chewing, his sunken cheeks working in and out. With a shout, the guard thwacks the old man on the back of the head with the butt of his rifle. The old man crumples to the ground. The other prisoners continue with their work; no one moves to help the lifeless figure. Charlie takes a step towards him, but his escort bars the way, motioning with his rifle for

Charlie to keep on going. The guard's face is impassive and he is unfailingly polite, but the message is simple. 'Remember what I told you,' says Jarvis.

Once they are in the safety of the officers' mess, where it is warm and dry and there are no Russian guards, Charlie turns to Jarvis. 'How can they hit a man for picking up some stale bread?'

'Lucky he wasn't shot.'

'Can't you do anything about it?'

Jarvis shakes his head. 'This is Russia, my friend. Full of suspicion and contradiction.'

'I don't know how you cope. How do you let off steam?'

'Surely you heard the commissar talking about his male-voice choir . . .'

'I'm serious.'

An officer with a dark beard looks up from a paper. 'If you're talking about women, my friend, make sure you steer well clear. Any Soviet woman who fraternises with a foreigner has a tendency to disappear.'

'What do you mean?'

'The Soviets don't like their people socialising with us.'

'Even though we're helping them?'

'Doesn't mean Stalin has to like us. Half the time, he's complaining that our convoys aren't arriving with what they'd promised.'

'They can't exactly help getting blown out of the water.'

'Maybe he thinks we're killing ourselves on purpose.'

'Bloody ungrateful.'

'They're only following orders like the rest of us. Once you cut through the crap, you'll find the Russians themselves are lovely people. Can't fault 'em.'

'What a situation to be in . . .'

Jarvis and the man with the dark beard nod. 'So no women and no parties; what do you do?' says Charlie.

'The usual,' says Jarvis. 'Rowing races and football matches

321

when we have enough men. The Russkies aren't allowed to join us, of course, so we have to wait for you lot . . .'

'That's the only time we ever get any fun.'

'Apart from the Luftwaffe dropping in most days.'

They all laugh. Then there is silence for a bit.

'I hope it's all worth it,' says Charlie eventually.

'It will be,' says Jarvis. 'It has to be.'

The officer with the beard checks through his list of returning survivors, shaking his head. 'No,' he says. 'Oh.' His finger stops. 'Hang on. There's some from the *Aurora* went back in September. Two lots. Look here.'

'Names?' says Charlie.

'Rifter, Gerald; Pedersen, Johan; Mills, Carl.'

'No Sullivan?'

'Nope.'

'Damn.'

'Maybe your man got picked up in the water and taken another way?'

'Is this a record of all the men who made it to Russia?'

'As far as we know. But that doesn't mean it's definitive. People slip through the net. Some are dead. Some don't want to be found . . .'

'Best to seek out one of those chaps off the *Aurora* when you get home,' says Jarvis. 'They'll be the ones most likely to know what happened to your friend.'

'Home? God knows when that will be.'

'That reminds me,' says Jarvis. 'You wouldn't do us a favour? The Russians are asking to see all our mail now. We won't let 'em have it, though.' The translator holds up a handful of letters. He puts his fingers to his lips and then whispers: 'We're sending 'em back hidden inside everyone's clothes.'

'Why are you whispering?'

'Bugs,' he says, pointing at the light.

Charlie opens his coat while the men stuff letters inside the pockets. Half an hour later he is shivering on the quayside

322

while a sentry studies his papers again. Charlie's heart is hammering and he is sure the man will spot the extra padding. But the guard looks him up and down one more time before stepping aside and indicating with a curt tilt of his head that Charlie can go on. He steps into the safety of the launch.

'Come and visit us again,' says Jarvis from the quayside.

'I'll try,' says Charlie. He is sorry that he still has no answers for Olivia, but he is not remotely sorry to be leaving this godforsaken place behind.

CHAPTER 22

Jack

Anya takes Jack to a family whose wooden hut lies in the hills behind Polyarnoe. She follows an invisible track through the myriad paths in the snowy forest until they reach a shabby hut. Only a thin curl of blue smoke rising from the chimney marks its presence in the shadow of the pine trees. Anya knocks on the door and calls out. It is a simple dwelling, with one large room downstairs where the couple sleep and eat and live. Their mattress is partitioned behind a large patterned cloth. Upstairs is a bare attic, used to store food, and too cold to survive in.

An old man and woman are pushing themselves out of their chairs by the fire. They welcome Anya with warm voices, stroking her face and clasping her in a tight embrace. Jack watches with a pang. It has been a long time since anyone showed him such tenderness.

The couple turn to him, and Anya introduces them. 'Dmitri and Elena,' she says. Jack shakes their leathery hands, thick with calluses like his own, though their knuckles are swollen with arthritis. Their skin is patterned with deep lines. Most of their teeth are missing.

'This is a good family. My husband's family,' says Anya. The old lady starts to remove Jack's coat, indicating for him to sit. It is cosy in the hut, thanks to the fire flickering in the corner of the small room.

'I am afraid you can't sleep in here,' says Anya. 'It is too dangerous for them. But there is a room in the woodshed.'

Jack is encouraged to find access to the woodshed through the side of the hovel. The wood is stacked neatly against the wall. There is plenty of straw on the floor, and another cloth that separates his living quarters. There is a low table, and a washbowl. The small window is well fitted, and he cannot feel or hear the wind that sweeps through the forest on the other side. 'They used to have a worker who lived here,' says Anya. 'In better times.'

Jack returns to the hut. Elena is busy stirring a cauldron over the fire. Dmitri pours steaming cups of tea from the samovar, the shiniest and most ornate piece of equipment in the whole shack. They sit and gaze into the flames. Jack feels the tension drain away, his limbs relax. He has a sudden vision of the fire at the bothy, and Olivia's warm hand on his arm. He smiles as he allows himself to picture her. But it is only Elena, offering more tea. He cannot communicate in words, but he smiles and nods his head, which she seems to understand.

'They are the reason I am here,' says Anya. The light from the flames picks out the tears wavering in her eyes.

'I am one of the lucky ones,' she says. 'I escaped from Leningrad. My husband joined up as soon as we knew the Germans were on their way. Thousands of men died – most of them as they were sent in against the advancing Germans. They didn't stand a chance. Food became scarce. We mixed our flour with sawdust. My baby screamed . . . I have never been so hungry. My insides turned in. People died in the streets and we just stepped over them. We had no water, only snow to drink. No power. We were too weak to move the dead bodies. We burnt everything. We put whatever we could find in the stew pots: rats, shoes, belts, cats . . . Only when the rivers froze could supplies come in and some of us get out . . . All those people left behind . . . I cannot imagine what it must be like now. I have heard rumours of people eating people. They couldn't evacuate any more when the river melted. I came by train in the end to Murmansk.' She swallows. 'I am the only one from my mother's family that survived.' The tears swell and drip over her lids and down her cheeks.

'Do you know what happened to your husband?'

'He is on the Eastern Front. I have no news of him.'

'Your baby?'

She wipes her hand across her cheek to catch the tears as they fall. 'My baby did not survive. She starved . . . There was no food . . .' She cannot finish the sentence. She is trembling. 'We became no more than animals.'

Dmitri fills their mugs with a steaming liquid that can hardly be described as soup. Elena strokes Anya's hair, and as the firelight catches the tracks of their tears, Elena starts to sing a ballad. Her voice is as sweet and strong as that of a young woman. Jack cannot understand it, but the meaning is clear. He lets the sound wash over him.

After a while, Anya stands, brushing down her skirt. 'I am sorry,' she says. 'We are not allowed to talk of these things, so when we do, we cannot stop. You must help them in return.' She motions at the couple.

'Of course,' says Jack.

'You can cut wood for them and help them grow food. They have had enough hardship. They are happy to assist you. They know without your convoys, the Fatherland would be lost and more of our families would starve.'

'So why would they get in trouble?'

'This is still Russia,' she says. 'It is a risk for all of us. It is a risk for me too.'

Days turn to weeks. Dmitri and Elena plunder their stores. There is salted fish and some sort of salted meat that is possibly reindeer or yak, and hopefully not dead German as the rumour among the British had it. There are pickled cabbages, and thin, mouldy carrots in sacks. There are still courgettes from the summer, some pickled, others puckered and withered up in the cold attic. There is still a small amount of rice. Jack does what he can to help, swinging the axe in the dusky pink evening light. The nights are getting longer, the world darker. At first, his body ached, but he has built himself back up. He enjoys feeling his muscles tense and tighten and the heat flush through his body so that he can chop wearing only his vest. He lugs the logs for the old couple, and hammers loose slats for them, digs the earth, repairs the roof. Sometimes he imagines Olivia is next to him, carrying a bucket of water or laughing in her easy manner. He is almost ready to return to her. His feet no longer hurt. No one comes to visit except for Anya. Occasionally a Russian soldier skis down from the hills, where Anya says there are British telegraphists listening out for the Germans and Finns. The borders of Norway and Lapland are so close. Most days, enemy planes pass over this uninhabited spot and drone on to Murmansk. In the distance, Jack can hear the boom of guns from the front – and the bombers heading out across other parts of Russia from Norway. Occasionally he spots an RAF plane aiming for the airfield at Vaenga. He prays that Carl has got home.

As the ice cracks and spreads across the White Sea, the temperature plummets further and there is no daylight, only the glow of twilight on snow. The old couple rarely leave the hut, stoking the embers of the fire to keep warm, chewing on bark to stave off the pangs that gripe in their stomachs. Food is very scarce. Dmitri shows Jack how to lay traps for rabbits, but he seldom catches one. When he does, he guts and skins it with Olivia's knife. He remembers her teaching him to slice into the fish in Scotland. He tries to cut a hole in the ice of a lake up in the hills, but it is too thick. He would do anything for her rifle: sometimes he glimpses the deer moving like ghosts through the trees. As the blizzards come, the hunger gets worse, gnawing at his insides, and with it thoughts form like pictures in his mind. He tries to focus on Olivia and the bothy, the boat, the hills, but instead the ghosts of his past begin to inhabit the shadows in the woodshed. The branches tapping on the window at night are Stoog waiting in the alley. The embers of the fire are London burning. He can sense the streets, hear the drone of the bombers, the pavement pounding beneath his feet. He can smell the juicy lumps of meat and the sugary sweet fruit they used to steal. He remembers the tomatoes in the greenhouse with Olivia. Did he ever change? Is he the same boy who abandoned his mother? Who is there to prove he is an apprentice? Who will believe he might make an officer one day? Mart and Burts are gone. Andersson and Russell cannot bear witness. In the darkness of morning, his mother lies broken and alone on the floor.

Elena does the best she can, making watery soups from cabbage leaves and potato peelings, but Jack knows they need more to survive. 'I'll go to Murmansk,' he says to Dmitri.

The old man shakes his head. 'Nothing in Murmansk,' he says.

Elena raises her hands in desperation. 'No Murmansk,' she says.

'I have to try.'

Jack travels to Murmansk with a friend of Dmitri's on a sledge pulled by two reindeer. The driver looks different to the Russians he has met so far: he has a wide, flat face, ruddy cheeks and is dressed in animal skins. He calls and whistles to the reindeer as they pull the sledge across the ice.

But the trip is pointless. The old couple are right. There is nothing in Murmansk. No buildings are left standing. The ground is snow-covered rubble, the mass of brick chimneys all that is left of the wooden houses. The burnt chimneys poke up towards the sky through the dust and snow like a macabre black forest. Through the mist Jack sees people scavenging among the blackened debris, but there are no pickings to be had. Even the buildings that were once cement have crumbled: the cement gone brittle in the freezing cold. All is dead here.

Grim-faced creatures stumble past with their belongings strapped to their backs, their baggy, torn trousers tucked into threadbare boots. Jack walks past an old woman sitting on a suitcase. She weeps silently, the tears freezing to her sagging cheeks.

Jack returns with nothing but a sealskin hat for himself and a small amount of reindeer meat that he exchanges with the sledge driver for the last of his cigarettes. Heavy snow clouds bear down on the tiny hut. The wind has died to a whisper in the pines. A line of Russian soldiers swishes through the wood on skis, their rifles hard and black against their white uniforms. Dmitri and Elena are so pleased with the handful of meat, hugging and nodding at him as though he has brought a feast. But Jack feels the bite of his empty stomach, and he knows that they do too.

His body is mended and strong, but his mind continues to play tricks. Mart leers at him from a corner. Hunger and fear scratch at his soul. The world is frozen; even time has stood still. As he lies in his bed – the only time he is truly warm – he struggles to recall Olivia's blue eyes, the warmth of her hand in his, and her hair brushing his shoulder . . . but then he opens his eyes, and Betsy is crouched at the end of his bed, staring at him, her eyes wide, her body trembling.

'You must know that Dmitri and Elena are starving,' says Anya. 'As are you. They say that if one of them dies, you are to keep their body in the attic, so the other can collect their rations. Then bury them when the weather gets warmer.'

'It won't come to that,' he says, shaking his head at the old couple who are scrunched into their chairs, their sunken eyes closed. They spend much of the time asleep now.

'It might come to worse than that,' says Anya.

They sit in silence until a piece of wood collapses into the fire, sending a shower of sparks up the chimney.

'You are a little like my younger brother, Kolya,' says Anya.

'Dark?' Jack rubs his hand over his hair, which has grown back to hide the scar.

'Not just that,' says Anya. 'He is also a little boy who was made to grow up too fast.'

Jack shifts. 'Where is he now?'

'With the rest of our young men. On the Eastern Front. I hope. Like my husband, I have not heard from him in many months.'

'I have a sister somewhere too.'

'I miss my boys. War is very lonely.'

He nods, and she smiles and reaches out to place her hand on his. The tenderness of her gentle touch makes him want to cry. She moves closer and puts her hand up to his face, leaning in to kiss him. He responds, bathing for a moment in the sensation of intimacy, feeling her heartbeat pulse in her skin, feeling his own begin to race. But then he feels the weight of Olivia's knife in his pocket, and he pushes her gently away. She rests her head on his shoulder and they play with each other's hands, enjoying the closeness, the feel of another human being.

'There is a girl at home?' she says.

He nods.

'She must be very special.'

'She is. She believes in me. Even though she knows some of the bad things I've done.'

'It's not good enough to have someone else believe in you, Jack. You must believe in yourself.'

'I do . . . I did . . .'

'Then why have you not returned home?'

'I can't face getting back on a ship.'

'You are not being honest with yourself.'

'What do you mean?'

'You have been on a ship. With me to Vaenga and to Polyarnoe. There is another truth that you find hard to deal with. Something else that is holding you back.'

He stares at their fingers linked in the glow of the dying fire. 'I was not a good son. My mother died alone. If I'd lived an honest life, then maybe she'd still be around.'

'Or maybe you would both be dead.'

'What if I'm a bad person?'

'I do not believe in such a thing.'

'I can't live up to Olivia's expectations.'

'A girl who loves you does not expect more than you can give. It is you who cannot live up to your expectations. Forgive yourself, Jack.'

'That's easy to say, but you don't know what I'm like, or the things I've done in the past.'

She smiles sadly. 'I have lived in hell. There is nothing that can shock me now.' She stares at him. Her eyes are as deep and fathomless as his own. 'Believe in yourself, Jack. Do not listen to what the others say. You are the only one who knows the truth. Look at the madness of others. We were your enemies. Now we are your friends. The Germans were our friends. Now they are our enemies. The simple truth is that you are a boy and I am a girl and we do what we can to survive.'

Jack shivers in the woodshed. Anya is right. He must return. But he cannot leave Dmitri and Elena to starve. They grow weaker by the day. He cannot bear the thought of dragging either one of them into the attic while the other withers by the fire, alone. His mind switches to automatic. He knows what he must do. It will be easy in the constant dark of polar night. It will be like the old days. He crunches through the snow to Polyarnoe. He watches in the dark, beyond the strange shadows cast by the lights from the buildings. He waits for the Russian sentry to visit the toilet, which is inside a wooden shed on stilts. It is obvious when a visitor is mid-action, as the waste drops down into the river below. Jack watches and waits.

The wind tugs at him, and he shrugs deeper into his coat. Snow is settling on his sealskin hat. As soon as the sentry has disappeared into the hut, he makes his move. He runs as fast as his clothes allow into the nearest building. In the kitchen there is enough food for a week scattered across the counter: salted fish, bread, and some kind of pasta. Jack stuffs as much as he can into his pockets. He can hear the Russians next door fuelled by vodka, singing patriotic songs. He makes for the door, which is wrenched from his hand by the biting wind. He is almost out, when he feels a hand on his shoulder and a voice starts yelling in his ear. It is hard to hear anything above the scream of the wind and his ears are muffled by the hat pulled down over his head. He is yanked back inside. He turns to face a Russian, small eyes glaring at Jack as he shouts in his face, the spit raining in warm flecks on his cheek. Jack raises his hands, and the Russian carries on bellowing, shoving his hands into Jack's pockets and pulling out the food, the bread dissolving into crumbs as he crushes it in his fist.

Two more men and a woman come running from next door, and then the sentry who had been in the hut blows in from outside. Jack struggles to break away, but it is pointless. They have him firmly caught. The woman is holding a rifle. She jabbers at the men. She looks Jack up and down, says something, and the men remove his hat, flipping it backwards on to the floor. Jack blinks in the bright light. They manhandle him further into the room, the woman pointing with her rifle. Jack is so tired. His hands are still in the air and his arms are aching. He tries to lower them, but the Russians shout louder and he tips forward and falls to the floor in a kneeling position with his hands still raised.

They strip him of his scarf, his coat. They pat down his pockets and find Olivia's knife. He tries to grab it back, but they roar even louder and push him away. He wants that knife more than anything. Without it, who is he? Without Mart and Andersson and Russell, who is he?

The Russians are calmer now. Arguing between themselves rather than shouting at him. They can see he has no other weapon. One of the men sends the sentry away. A few minutes later, the sentry returns with a man with a dark beard and harassed eyes. Jack's heart sinks. He recognises the uniform: the man is a British naval officer.

'Who are you?' says the man with the beard.

Jack doesn't answer. Anya is wrong. People will think what they want to think. He looks like a thief. He acts like a thief. He is a thief. 'Are you British?'

Jack just stays there, kneeling on the floor, his arms aching. He is so tired, he wants to close his eyes.

The Russians start to shout again, pushing at him with their hands. They show the officer the knife. He takes it, looks at the initials. 'Fancy knife. Probably stolen.'

'British! British!' say the Russians.

'He doesn't look British,' says the officer. 'Look at his clothes.' He points at the woollen greatcoat and the sealskin hat that are lying on the floor. The Russians poke and point at Jack's trousers. 'British!' they say again.

'Have you got any papers?' The officer is talking slowly and loudly at him, as if he's a child.

Jack stares ahead blankly. The Russians start to yell again. The officer disappears and comes back with another man, also dressed in a naval uniform. The man peers into Jack's eyes, looks him up and down, lifts his jumper up, rubs the trousers between his fingers. 'Look like Royal Navy bell bottoms to me, sir,' he says.

'Rating, you think?'

'Most likely. Look at the tattoo.'

The Russians watch them suspiciously. 'No matter,' says the man with the beard. 'We'd better take him. God knows what this lot would do with him.' They help Jack to his feet. The Russians point at their bread. The British men shrug their shoulders. 'You can still eat it.' The Russian woman cackles at him like a hen scolding a fox. 'Sorry, love, no can do.' The seaman lifts his hand in a farewell gesture. They help Jack back into his coat. The Russians keep the hat. The Navy men usher him out into the snow and the wind, talking to each other behind his back.

'They're sailing at 0400 hours.'

'You'll have to get him out there tonight, then,' says the officer.

'I'll sort it.'

Jack wants to speak, but he can't. He can't make a sound. His palms are damp. His skin feels as if it's on fire. He drags his feet, tries to dig them into the ice as the two men pull him along, leaving tracks like a dead animal. Dmitri will be peering anxiously through the door into the darkness by now. Elena will be stoking the fire.

'Come along, now,' says the seaman. He is a large, strong man. 'Don't be like that.'

Jack struggles again, trying to throw them off. 'You're not doing yourself any favours,' says the officer. Jack gives up. He knows when he is beaten.

They stand on the docks, their breath feathery plumes in the dark, talking to the man in the picket boat. 'It's a strange one. Our men picked him up stealing from the Russians. Hasn't said a word, but then, they often don't, deserters.'

They push him down into the boat. The water stretches in icy blackness in every direction, waiting to swallow him up.

'Don't let him mix with the other men. Mutiny has a habit of spreading.'

'Punishment cells?'

'Certainly.'

The picket boat chugs out across the water. The sway of the deck sets Jack's heart racing. The men drag him on to the ship still struggling. The familiar clank and clang of metal and water fill his ears. They push him in front of them, holding his elbow pressed up into his back. As they descend into the ship, every hair on Jack's body screams to get back outside, but he has been struggling and fighting for weeks on an empty stomach. He is almost all out. He clangs and clanks along the corridor. Past the steaming cauldrons in the galley and the neat beds of the sickbay. Past men in their uniforms, who stop and stare at the struggling man before turning back to getting the ship ready. Past the stores and the purser's office. Everyone is busy. Everything glistens and shines. Everything is shipshape. The ship's Tannoy calls for the men to be at cruising stations. Jack's breath comes short and fast. He feels as if someone is clasping him around the neck. On they march into the bows of the ship, past hammocks slung between every spare inch of pipe. Finally, they stop by a door. The man shoves Jack in the back, and he trips over the metal rung into the room. Behind him, the door shuts with a bang, and everything goes dark.

Jack fumbles in the blackness. It isn't like any other kind of dark he's experienced. It is like the bottom of a coal chute, with the walls pressing in on him. He reaches out with his hands and feels cool metal beneath his palms, with a layer of condensation on what must be the ship's side. The room is just long enough for him to lie down on what feels like a narrow wooden bench. He tries to stand, and trips on a bucket, curses, turns around. From outside he hears the muffled sounds of a ship about to set sail: the men calling to each other, the whirr of the screws, the banging of pipes. He sits down. He was better off in the lifeboat. The thought of his shipmates stabs like a hook in his chest. Faces swim in the darkness: Mart, Andersson, Burts, Dmitri, Stoog, Elena, Carl, Betsy . . . He has let them all down. And what about Olivia? Will she still love him when she discovers he has gone back to his old ways? He's had his chance. He has reverted to type. He curses. His voice sounds tinny and loud and strange as it echoes in the tiny cell. He needs air. He pushes against the cold metal. His chest compresses. His breath comes fast. Someone else is in here with him. He can hear them breathing. He is panting like a dog. He can't get enough air into his lungs. His chest feels as if it is imploding. This is what it must be like to drown. Drowning. He's drowning. In the water again, gasping for breath but can't breathe because the water is filling his lungs and his head is going to explode. But Carl's face swims into view and he has no body and then Burts is frozen stiff and Fred who drank the whisky is smiling and there is Betsy. That's who is sitting in here with him. He reaches out for her in the dark, but his hands find nothing, and then he sees Olivia, shaking her head in despair as she turns away. He digs his nails into his arm, feels the burning sensation as the skin rips. He is breathing easier now. Get a hold of yourself. Outside the great ship starts to grumble and clang to life. They are under way.

CHAPTER 23

Charlie

Mid-December in the Arctic is so dark and cold that even the birds and sea creatures have moved to warmer climes. There is a terrible battle in the Barents Sea, as another convoy from Britain struggles towards Russia. In the darkness, confusion reigns, and neither side is sure of where their own ships are or who is firing at whom. Although all the merchant ships get through, both the British and German navies have casualties in the hundreds and each a destroyer sunk, as well as the loss of a British minesweeper with all hands – a severe blow.

Charlie's world has been drained of colour for so long – in the constant night, the ship and the sky and the sea change only from dark to light grey; there is a grey pallor to everyone's skin. When the opportunity to go ashore at Polyarnoe again presents itself, he jumps at it – even that desolate place is a change of scenery.

Charlie pulls his coat tighter as he is transferred from ship to ship. The wind screeches around him, trying to find its way into every nook and cranny, trying to steal the last of the warmth it can find, even forcing its icy breath down into his lungs. The port is busy – more ships forming up to move out. Charlie watches the shadowy shapes manoeuvre in the darkness. On the ill-lit jetty, a guard checks his papers again, squinting down at the print, his actions slow and heavy, hampered by the cold and the layers of clothing he is wrapped in. Behind him, the snow has been scraped and piled into ever-increasing mounds. Apart from the occasional sentry hunched into a greatcoat, only his hat showing, there is no one to be seen.

Charlie heads for the officers' mess and is pleased to be greeted by Jarvis and his genial grin. The mess is packed – no one wants to be outside in a Russian winter. Somehow the officers have got hold of a billiard table, and the men are crouched around it, ready to catch the balls as they clack out of the pocketless holes.

'Great to see you again,' says Jarvis, pumping Charlie's hand.

'Doesn't look like you'll get home for Christmas after all,' says Charlie, removing his hat and gloves, feeling weightless without his coat.

'Looking increasingly unlikely.'

'Sorry to hear that.'

'Never mind. At least things are picking up a bit here. We've had our fair share of lively recently. Found a deserter stealing from the Russians.'

Charlie shakes his head. 'Some men will do anything to stay out of the war.'

'He's lucky the Russians didn't get to keep him. Who knows what they'd have done with him.'

'Who was he?'

'No idea. No papers or ID, but he was wearing Navy uniform.'

'Maybe he stole it?'

'Unlikely. He seemed to understand English. All he had on him was a knife. Proper fancy one, though. Look at this.'

Charlie looks at the knife in the man's hand. The ridges of the bone have been worn smooth like ivory. The gold brass glints in the cold light of the wardroom. Charlie's eyes widen in astonishment. 'Can I see?' he says.

The man hands the knife to him, its handle warm from his grip. Charlie turns it over and sees the initials: OJB.

'What's happened to the man?' he asks.

'We've put him on the escort with the returning convoy. Should be in the UK by the end of the week. They'll deal with him there.'

'Can I go on board?'

'Too late, sir. It's already sailed.'

Charlie knows he must tell Captain Underhill what he suspects as soon as possible.

The captain is as astonished as he is. 'Why the hell didn't he say who he was?'

'I imagine he's severely traumatised.'

Captain Underhill folds his arms, shakes his head. 'And no wonder,' he says. 'Must've somehow evaded being rounded up and been living out in the woods . . .' He grimaces.

'What can I do, sir?'

The captain stares out into the gloom. 'We can't let them know,' he says. 'They're too far away to signal and we're under radio silence.' His gaze meets Charlie's. 'Look. They're on their way home. I'm sure he'll be fine until they reach the UK. Then this mess can be cleared up.'

It would be insubordinate to argue, but Charlie knows the reality is that no one is safe out here. Not even a Navy destroyer. He returns to his cabin. He lies on his bunk, thinks about the knife, Olivia. He knows he should write to tell her that Jack is alive, and gets out some paper. But then, what if it isn't Jack? What if it's some vagabond, some deserter who stole the knife? That would only upset her. It's not that he doesn't want her to know; he just doesn't want to get her hopes up. But who is he kidding? Deep down, he knows it's Jack. It has to be. He stares at the blank page. He feels a wall build up around his heart like the ice that is forming on the ship, clogging up the winches, clinging to the halliards, the handrails, an inches-thick frost like the icing on a cake.

Everything he turns his hand to is a failure: capturing Olivia's heart; finding Jack. As their futures burn brighter, Charlie's crumbles away to dust.

The ship rises and slams back down, the mountain of spray turning to ice that clatters across the flight deck. In Charlie's cabin, the page remains empty and white as the ice that the men chisel away at, their faces stinging, their hands aching. When it is calm, it is easy to see how quickly a ship can get stuck as the ice thickens into a pack. As the storms return, great chunks of ice fields break apart and then crash together forming new wintry landscapes. The carrier struggles to stay on course. The men struggle to stand, slipping on the icy decks. Lashing straps snap, and men are knocked out by flying debris. More planes slip and slide into each other. Charlie cries out with frustration; his voice is lost on the wind.

They fly in parallel lines back and forth, scanning for the U-boats, watching for the echo on the radar. The sea is always changing. Charlie is always numb. A mist blurs the horizon. The sea is so heavy and the wind is so strong. He cannot rely on his instruments because of the sub-zero temperature and their proximity to the North Pole. One pilot and observer have to be cut out of their cockpit because they are frozen solid where they sit. They had lost the carrier and been circling a rain cloud instead. Who can a pilot trust if he can't trust his plane?

An ominous feeling creeps into Charlie's bones. He tries again to write the letter, struggles to form the words.

And then the news comes that he has been dreading: the returning convoy is in trouble. They too have been hampered by ice and storms, and now they have run into a wolf pack. The carrier sets course to assist. Progress is slow. Although the ice is melting, now great tempests pound the seas. Charlie prays they will get to Jack before the U-boats finish him off. The carrier rolls thirty-five degrees. Mountainous waves up to thirty feet high roll on and on towards the horizon. Gale force winds and squalls of snow and ice scream around them.

340

The carrier rolls forty degrees. The men below deck run from side to side to try to balance a bit, but after a while they are exhausted and they give up, sitting or lying where they are as the vomit rises in their throats. Every roll feels like the last; they will surely go over at any minute. Down in the hangar, the planes smash and bash against each other. Beneath the flight deck, the ready room is kept red so that the pilots' eyes can get used to the dark.

Postie pops his head around the door. 'I'm collecting letters,' he says.

'I'm not finished yet,' says Charlie. He starts to write her name, each letter scratching another graze across his heart.

The call goes up for action stations. Charlie puts down his pen and pulls on his boots. The letter lies on the table, the ink glistening like oil as it dries.

Captain Underhill addresses them in the ready room. 'We're within reach. Two merchants gone already, I'm afraid. And our destroyer has been hit. There's a rescue ship and cruiser assisting. They've picked up some of the men in the water already, but we've no idea how many U-boats there are.'

'How bad's the destroyer?'

'Large hole in her bow.'

'And her crew?'

'Some have made it on to the cruiser. Some in lifeboats.'

'Do you think the U-boats will back off?'

'Not a chance. Hitler's focused all his efforts into U-boats. He's pretty much laid off his surface fleet after we trounced them in the Barents Sea. My guess is those boats are going to do whatever damage they can.'

'Who's going up to spot?'

'At the moment, conditions are too bad.'

'We can't just leave them.' Charlie is thinking of the men struggling in the icy water, of the men in the lifeboats, of the men who have gone before. He is thinking of Jack, somewhere in the holds of the stricken destroyer, once again at the mercy of the Kriegsmarine.

'It's too dangerous.'

'I can do it.'

Captain Underhill shakes his head. 'No.'

'I have to,' says Charlie. He is thinking of Olivia's face, creased with worry, the tears on her cheeks; he is thinking of leave from boarding school when his friends had parents to go home to and he did not; he is thinking that he is still a decent man, even though he has made some mistakes; he is thinking of his father's medals hanging heavy on his chest; he is thinking that he was born for this, now is his chance to shine.

'I won't let you go. You're one of my best pilots.'

'Some of those men have been abandoned by us before.'

'You can't get sentimental in war.'

'If there's no sentiment in war, then what the hell are we fighting for?'

There is silence. Everyone is watching them. Charlie has never been disobedient before.

Captain Underhill sighs. 'If you can find someone to fly with you . . .'

Charlie looks around the room. One by one, the men stand up. Captain Underhill shakes his head and smiles. 'What would the admirals say if they knew what a soppy bunch you are . . .'

'Thank you, sir,' says Charlie.

Ned grabs a rifle as the flight deck crew bring the plane up from the hangar, unfolding her wings, battling against the snow. But these are everyday challenges that all the men are used to now, and the Swordfish are airborne within minutes, lifting skyward one after the other, as the carrier disappears behind them into the thick of a white-out.

They stay low, scanning the waves for the U-boats, Ned watching the radar's screen. Charlie is ready to release a depth charge at any moment. It is the worst weather he has ever flown in. He can barely see the rest of the squadron through the snow, which is turning into heavy, stinging ribbons of

342

sleet, and he can sense the plane is struggling too. It takes all his skill to hold her steady against the driving wind. Then they spot the destroyer listing drunkenly in the waves. Beyond her, the surviving merchant ships flounder, watching helplessly as their protector haemorrhages smoke into the air.

Charlie dips as low as he dares over her so that Ned can get a good look. Around them, the rest of the squadron appear and disappear through the sleet and snow. They circle the destroyer, protecting her from every side, ready to strike when the enemy shows its face.

'Are they all off yet?' Charlie asks.

'No,' says Ned. 'There are still men waiting to get into lifeboats.'

They swing around again, eyes scouring the choppy water for the U-boats that they both know are out there. The sea churns. The wind snatches and screams at them. The plane shudders. Charlie thinks of Mole and the Kid, when he thought he was invincible. When he couldn't imagine losing these people. Then he thinks of Norway. The Blitz. The Channel Dash . . . And now this – the men of the convoys who never make it home. The children without fathers, the wives without husbands. No. He must make this work. This is one thing he will not fail at.

Charlie flies low over the sea again. 'There,' says Ned, and they release a depth charge into the frothing water. The rest of the squadron follow. Charlie can make out the stick figures of the frightened Navy crew who are still trying to cross from the stricken destroyer to safety. They have rigged up a bosun's chair, and it swings perilously across the waves, transferring the injured and the ill through the air. The figures dangle in the blank wetness of spray and sleet, hanging by threads between the two ships, at the mercy of the elements. He wonders if one of them is Jack.

Suddenly Ned yells, 'Two-forty degrees,' as a plane swoops down out of the swirling cloud. The Germans must be desperate to take them out if the Luftwaffe is flying in these conditions. Charlie senses Ned swing the rifle into his shoulder, and hears the shots – a pathetic sound that is ripped away by the wind. The German fires back at them, but Charlie avoids him, dropping the plane lower. He knows they are out-gunned and overrun. The only thing he can do is try to outmanoeuvre his attacker. He swings the plane around and turns on the German. Charlie stays low; he knows the German pilot will struggle to do the same. The German turns his attention to the other merchant ships instead, as another Luftwaffe plane dips down out of the cloud, coming in at a run.

'Bastards,' says Charlie.

But at last the Navy fleet is appearing, elbowing its way through the water, and the gunners start to blast at the German planes, creating a smoke screen to hide the vulnerable merchant ships. Now that they have arrived, Charlie is confident that the squadron can return. He signals goodbye, lagging behind to make sure they leave no stragglers. The pilots raise their fists in farewell and head for the safety of the carrier.

The signalman flashes his message from the cruiser.

'What does he say?'

'Only the captain and his steward to go,' says Ned.

Another Luftwaffe plane is thundering through the air towards them again, firing as he comes. 'Hold on,' says Charlie, and he circles out of the way, turning once again on the German. The German is faltering; only a Swordfish could be stable in such weather. This time, Charlie plunges on him from a height, and at last the German turns and heads back to the coast with Charlie in pursuit. The blizzard is getting worse again. The German has disappeared. Charlie is ready finally to turn for the carrier, but they are in thick impenetrable snow, almost as if they are flying through sludge. The Swordfish is sputtering, struggling against the onslaught.

'We're very near the coast,' says Ned.

'How near?'

'Almost above it.' Charlie hadn't realised they were that close to land. He can feel the wind direction alter. Ned is shouting to him from behind, but he can't make out the words. And all of a sudden there is a bright flash of light beneath them, and the Swordfish makes a choking noise and starts to lose altitude. She won't respond, which has never happened before, and Charlie pulls and thrusts at her, but it makes no difference: she is deaf to his commands. The adrenaline surges through his limbs, every sense on fire.

'Get ready to bail,' he says as loudly as he can over his shoulder. They are being pushed this way and that, and the snow is blinding, and below him is only darkness. He prays it is Russia rather than Norway, and then the plane dies and there is silence apart from the whistling wind and they are falling and he reaches for Ned and he can sense the boy is up too, and they jump, into the stinging snow and the screeching wind and the yawning darkness. He pulls the ripcord. And he is drifting for a moment. Drifting through time and space. More flashes. Guns firing. He glimpses snow-covered ground and hits it with a thump, his legs buckling under him and his face skimming snow. He shouts out: 'Ned? Ned?' but only the wind answers.

He has no idea where he is. Before he can get his bearings, rough hands pull Charlie to his feet and men's voices are shouting in the blackness. He thinks about using his revolver, but there are eight men, and he is still dizzy from the fall. He puts up his hands and one man wrenches the gun from its holster, turning it on Charlie. Within moments Charlie hears more voices and another snow patrol joins them, this time with Ned being pushed along in front. Charlie's ears are ringing, his thoughts scrambling over each other.

'You all right?'

Ned nods, his face pale with shock and his eyes wide with fear. 'Bit of a knock to my leg, but otherwise as well as can be expected, sir.'

'No talking,' says the soldier in charge, in heavy, accented English. The men's faces are hidden beneath tightly-wound scarves. Their hats are covered in snow. For a moment, Charlie wishes they would just shoot him then and there. He is so confused. He doesn't know where he is. Russia, Finland, Norway. He isn't even sure whether these are Germans or Russians, but he soon recognises the language.

'Come,' says the man, indicating with his rifle that they are to walk. 'Come.'

Charlie and Ned stumble in the snow. It is hard to move in their thick flying gear. They march until they come upon an outpost dug into the snow. Charlie's old injury begins to throb. He must have hit it when he landed. The German pushes them down into the shelter and it is a relief to be out of the cold and biting wind, but his thoughts are clouded, running away from him.

'Where is your plane?' says the German, dipping his head and unwinding the scarf from around his face and neck as he follows them inside.

'I don't know,' says Charlie.

'You have destroyed it?' The man has a strikingly angular face: high cheekbones and fair lashes that are almost invisible.

'No.'

'Then where is it?'

'I don't know.'

The German says something to his men, and half of them disappear back out into the snow, presumably to look for the downed plane.

'You won't find anything useful in it,' says Charlie, cursing to himself – there is a charge in the plane to be detonated if this happens, but he had no opportunity to use it.

'Maybe,' says the German.

'What will you do with us?'

'Tea first,' says the German, fiddling with a steaming pot on a rickety table in the corner.

Charlie shakes his head. He won't accept anything from this man.

'I thought all you English like tea?' The German shrugs and

346

sips at the hot liquid. 'I myself cannot see what all the fuss is about. But I will drink anything that might warm me up in this infernal place.'

'Where are you taking us?' Charlie asks.

'Where we take all of you airmen. *Dulag Luft.* Frankfurt.'

Ned looks at Charlie. The German interprets for him: 'A transit camp. For interrogation.'

'We won't say anything.'

'We'll see.'

CHAPTER 24

Olivia

Olivia is with Maggie in London when she receives the telegram stating that Lieutenant Charlie FitzHerbert is missing in action. Both of the Wrens deal with tragedies like this every week, but not always involving their close friends. Maggie is visibly shocked, her pale skin turning almost translucent, her red hair falling dramatically around her drawn face. Olivia may not be so obviously upset, but internally she is devastated. Neither of them can find out any more than that Charlie is missing in the seas off Norway. The prospects are bleak. The girls sit miserably in the gloom of the flat and try to keep each other's spirits up.

Olivia has another worry though. Her pregnancy does not seem to be progressing – her body shows no outward sign that the baby is growing: she has not had to let out the waist of her skirt as she had thought she might by now, nor has she felt the movement of new life. In one way, it is a relief – not to have to explain to anyone – but recently there has been a dull ache there too, sitting heavily in the pit of her stomach. She had put it down to her grief at losing Jack, but now that Charlie is missing, the pain has become more pronounced.

Gladys brings news of Charlie's escapade, so heroically leading the defence of the destroyer from the Luftwaffe. 'That sounds just like Charlie,' says Olivia. They toast his bravery with tea, chinking the cups together with smiles more like frowns, not fooling each other with their false bravado. It is deep winter, and outside the ruined city lies as broken as their hearts in the harsh light.

And then a letter arrives for Olivia from Charlie, written before he disappeared. There is nothing quite as depressing as a letter that has been written by someone who may not be alive any more. The writing runs across the paper, transcribed there by a living, breathing Charlie, perhaps the last words he will ever write. Olivia opens it carefully, pushing the image of Charlie bent over it, pen in hand, handsome face furrowed in concentration, solid, dependable arm moving across the page.

Maggie hovers next to her. 'What does it say?' she asks, as Olivia gasps.

Olivia is shaking her head, astonished. 'I can't believe it,' she says.

'Believe what?' Maggie snatches the paper and starts to read it herself.

'He's alive!'

'Who? Charlie?'

'No. Jack. Jack's alive. And Charlie found him . . .'

'What are you talking about?' Maggie's eyes are as wide as Olivia's, her neat eyebrows arched high.

'He tracked Jack down, and he's alive. It sounds like Jack might have been on the ship that Charlie was protecting.'

'What makes you think that?'

'We know that Charlie went missing protecting the return convoy, and look there' – she points at the paper – 'he says that Jack was safe with the Navy on a return convoy. So he must have been part of the same thing . . .'

Maggie turns from her and walks towards the window, shoulders slumped.

Olivia follows, trying to put a comforting hand on her friend's shoulder, but the Wren shrugs it off. 'Oh Maggie,' says Olivia. 'Please try not to worry. I'm sure Charlie will be fine. He's a survivor too . . .' She is struggling to keep the joy out of her voice.

Maggie glances at her with eyes full of disdain. Her pretty face is red and blotchy. 'You know, if it's true, then it's all your fault,' she says.

'What on earth do you mean?'

'If you can't see, then you're an idiot.' Maggie chews at her lip, then turns her back on Olivia and resumes staring out at the frosty city.

'Maggie . . .' The ache that has been coming on and off for the past week is now pulsing inside her. She rests a hand on her stomach, willing the pain to subside.

'He didn't do it for anyone but you,' says Maggie.

'I don't understand.' Olivia's heart begins to race. She cannot bear that Maggie is so upset. And now there is a sharp stab of pain, and something is not quite right, but she is trying to concentrate on what Maggie is saying, even though she doesn't want to hear the words.

'If Charlie knew that Jack was on that ship, then he went up to protect Jack for you. Not for me. Not for Jack. For you. Because he knew how much Jack means to you. And now he's gone. And it's all your fault.'

Olivia backs away, sitting down heavily in the armchair. She knows it is true. She wants to apologise. Of course it is not what she intended when she asked Charlie to search for Jack. She wants to explain, but the pain is so intense now, and she can feel liquid trickle from between her legs. She won't make it to the lavatory. She bends over double, bracing herself against the floor.

Maggie crouches down, concerned, her face swimming in and out of focus in front of Olivia. 'What's wrong?' she asks, but as the words leave her mouth, it is all too obvious as the dark blood spreads in a purple stain. 'Shit,' she says. 'Why didn't you tell me?' She places Olivia's arm around her shoulder, pulling her up. 'That's right,' she says. 'Lean on me. Let's get you into the bathroom.'

The pain in Olivia's womb has already lessened, but it has been replaced by a different pain, a hollowness that feels as if it might chew her up from the inside.

Maggie starts to run a bath, the steam rises from the gushing water, adding to the fog in Olivia's eyes.

'We need to get you to a doctor,' says Maggie.

'I can't move,' says Olivia. She dares not in case she makes things worse.

'But there might be an infection or something. You need to check it's all . . .' she pauses briefly '. . . to check it's all gone,' she says.

'But it might be all right . . .'

'No, darling. I don't think it's going to be all right,' says Maggie, squeezing her arm and stroking her hair. 'I'm so sorry. So so sorry.'

Deep down, Olivia knows her friend is right. She does not resist as Maggie gently peels away her clothes. She sits there, curled against the sink, wishing she could be left alone for ever.

The doctor's surgery is bright and modern, everything in it sharply in focus. It is a world away from the blurry fog of the hot bathroom. It is a world without Jack's baby in it. The nurse is reassuringly matronly, and the doctor is kind, with a foreign accent and a worn face. 'I don't think the foetus was ever fully formed,' he says. 'It has been dead for some time.'

'Thank God,' says Maggie. 'I'd never have forgiven myself . . .'

But the horror of this – that Olivia has been carrying a dead child around with her without realising – is added to the horror that her baby is gone.

'There should be no infection,' says the doctor. 'I think everything has passed.'

The matter-of-fact way he says it does not lessen the blow. She feels guilty for ever having wondered whether she should get rid of it. And now she has no choice. She feels guilty for having told Charlie about it, who risked his life to protect a dead baby's father. She feels guilty that she did not know that her baby was dead and that she did not mourn its passing until now. She lies on the bed and feels empty. Of emotion. Of life. Of Jack's baby. Of her baby.

'I'm so sorry, darling,' says Maggie. 'I don't know what else to say. Except it would have been so tough . . . You wouldn't have been able to work . . . And your parents . . .?' Her voice tails off. Olivia knows she is trying to help, but she had dealt with all these things in her mind. She would have coped somehow. And now she won't be able to cope.

'It is likely that your friend may have the same problem in the future,' says the doctor.

'What do you mean?' Maggie asks.

'I mean that there's a possibility that she is unable to carry a baby full-term. But at least she knows this now. Next time she conceives, she will need to see her doctor and explain. She will need to keep an eye on things and take it easy.'

If there ever is a next time. Olivia rolls on to her side and pulls the blanket up around her shoulders.

'You should tell your husband. You might find it helps. And he will need to mourn the loss in his own way.'

Maggie looks at him and shakes her head.

'Oh. He did not know?' The doctor is washing his hands, soaping up the fingers and right up the arms.

Maggie grimaces. 'Oh. No husband?' Maggie shakes her head. The doctor dries his hands. 'If it makes you feel better, you are not alone.'

Olivia doesn't answer. She just wants them all to leave her in this room. Leave her with her grief and her empty stomach. Leave her to jump into the black hole.

The doctor bends down. 'I really am sorry,' he says. 'It is refreshing to see someone who is not trying to get rid of it for once. I am just sad it did not work out for you.'

There is suddenly a kerfuffle at the door, and the doctor hurries to attend as a woman is dragged in. She is unconscious

352

and carried by two women who look as if they might be her sisters. The doctor points to a table where they lie her down. Olivia can see the sheen of fever on her pallid skin. The doctor moves purposefully, issuing instructions, his hands working over her body swiftly, the only man in a room full of damaged women.

The nurse urges them to leave. 'I'm sorry,' she says. 'We have little space here, and there are bound to be more tonight.'

'Will she be all right?' Maggie asks, glancing at the lifeless woman as she helps Olivia put her shoes back on.

'I do hope so,' says the nurse. 'Dr Hartmann does the best he can, but these backstreet abortionists . . . They're criminal. Knitting needles, castor oil, gin, soap solution, poison. We've even had girls who have been told to throw themselves down the stairs. Looks like this one's got a ruptured womb. Most of them use unsterilised equipment. It's disgusting. Of course, until it's legalised, we've just got to hope that some of them find their way here.'

Maggie nods. 'Thank you,' she says. 'How much do we owe?'

'Nothing. We didn't do anything. Just make sure your friend rests for as long as possible.'

Rest is not possible. Olivia cannot claim leave; she would have to explain her pregnancy to her CO, and that is something she is not ready to do. No. She will soldier on. She will focus on the happiness that is the imminent return of Jack. She is not the only person who is suffering. She will get up in the morning and paint a smile on her face, just as thousands of people do every day, even though they know they will carry their heartbreak within for ever.

CHAPTER 25

Jack

Jack stands on the cruiser's crowded quarterdeck, half-wishing he had been left behind on the sinking destroyer. The cruiser has made good speed away from the chaos, the planes have long disappeared towards the coast, and the U-boats have been seen off by the Navy. The rescued men are jostling for space, cursing the Germans and talking of home. The sea is less brutal.

A man is elbowing his way through the crowd. 'Sullivan?' he shouts. 'Jack Sullivan?'

The seamen shake their heads and move out of the way until Jack is left facing the man. 'Jack Sullivan?' the man says again.

Jack nods.

'Come with me.'

Jack follows, ready to be isolated again. The sailors stare at him as he goes.

But instead of heading down below deck, the man pushes his way up into the bridge. The captain is busy inspecting charts and talking, but as soon as Jack's escort whispers in his ear, the captain stops what he's doing. He comes towards Jack, his hand outstretched. 'Honoured to have you on board,' he says. 'We've just been told you were part of that July convoy. Must have been hellish. No doubt you have quite some story to tell.' Jack does not reply.

354

Jack's escort says, 'I'm sorry, sir. I think the man is over-whelmed.'

The captain nods, and says, 'Of course. Of course. Anything you need, Sullivan, let the purser here know.'

Although the ship is packed with survivors, Jack is given his own cabin. A steward brings him cocoa and warm food, and he is left alone again. He does not eat. The ship surges and sways beneath him. It takes most of his strength not to let the panic take over. There is a small mirror by the sink. He barely recognises himself any more. He picks up a razor and begins to shave, scraping the grime away. He wonders what it would feel like to score the blade into his flesh. He resists the urge, washing his face and hands endlessly in the warm water instead. When he looks at himself, clean-shaven in the mirror, he is shocked to see his father staring back at him with sad eyes.

After a while, the captain comes to see him again. 'You'll have a proper debrief in London,' he says, 'but I'm going to recommend you for a Lloyds war medal for bravery.' Jack stares at the wall. He thinks about Mart and Burts. The Old Man and Russell. Don't they deserve something too? When the captain has left, Jack washes his hands again, rubbing and rubbing at them until the water grows cold. He cannot bear to look in the mirror in case his father is still there, staring back at him.

They arrive at Loch Ewe without further incident. Jack does not come on deck. He does not want to see the hills and the beaches, or the ships that are waiting to return to Russia. He does not want to see what was the last view of Britain for so many of his friends. The loch is full of ghosts. He stays below deck until they reach Portsmouth, a few days later, and Jack is led blinking into the daylight as the ship docks. The Navy men are lined up along the rails, rows and rows of circular white hats watching another ancient, bombed city roll past.

Jack is taken to the naval hospital. The doctors are amazed by his resilience, shaking their heads and muttering as they

355

tick off their lists. The only signs of his ordeal are slight damage to the toes on his left foot and mild malnutrition. They are happy that he answers their questions with a yes or a no; he is clearly a man of few words. He allows them to poke and prod, regaining his strength during long hours of sleep interspersed by decent food. He is not questioned closely on why he was missing for so long; miraculous stories of survival are still filtering through from Russia. He does not ask them to contact Olivia. He cannot think how he will face her, what he will say, how he can ever explain the last few months. He wants to see her, but he does not want her to see him.

Two weeks later, Jack is due to be discharged. They have given him clean, new clothes, and he is wondering where he will go, which port, which seamen's home, when the ward sister comes to tell him that someone is here to collect him.

And now here is Olivia walking tentatively towards his bed. She looks different somehow. Perhaps it's the uniform.

'Jack!' she says. 'I can't believe it. I'd almost given up hope . . .'

He tries to welcome her, even as he feels his body shrink away. He cannot understand why he is so glad to see her yet his voice is coming out flat and dull. 'Me too,' he says. It is not how he wants it to be at all.

She touches his arm and he flinches involuntarily. 'I'm sorry,' she says. 'You must be exhausted.' Still he says nothing. He wants to, he really does, but he can't think of anything to say. She rattles on: 'You're probably wondering how I knew you were here? Do you remember my friend Charlie? He wrote and told us what had happened. You're a hero,' she adds.

Jack presses his fingers into his eyes. When he takes them away, she is still there, bright, almost glowing, but he feels numb. She tucks her hair behind her ears. 'You're being discharged,' she continues. 'I've come to take you . . .' She stops, biting her lip. 'I'm to take you back to London,' she says. 'If you want?'

He tries to nod his agreement. The move is almost imperceptible.

He hates himself for the lethargy, the inability to communicate his gladness at seeing her, but still he cannot find the energy even to smile.

'Have you got anything else to bring?' Her voice is brisk, forced. He shakes his head. He has been stripped of everything. There is nothing left except for what she sees: a survivor, a thief.

'Come on, then,' she says. 'Let's get you back. I've got a place to stay. Once you're there and you've had a wash and a sleep, you'll feel much better . . .' But he can hear the uncertainty creeping into her voice.

Olivia has been drafted to a shore establishment at Chelsea, so it makes sense to stay at the flat. Maggie is there too, anxiously waiting for the post every day. There has been no further news since the telegram from Charlie's squadron CO.

Jack tries to console her: 'Your friend helped save a lot of lives that day,' he says. 'Not just mine.'

But Maggie turns away, using her red hair as a shield. She seems to have trouble meeting his eyes. She clearly does not want to talk to him, which only makes him feel worse: that someone has risked their life to save someone as wretched as he is.

Olivia fusses over him. There is something sharp and unnatural in the way she laughs sometimes. She is holding something back. Perhaps she has come to her senses. Perhaps she is regretting ever having got involved. He longs to hold her close, but all he can do is push her further away, to avoid the inevitable.

She grabs hold of his hand as he passes. 'I need to speak to you,' she says. Her pale eyes search his face. He dreads what they will find there.

'I've told you. I can't talk about it yet,' he says. He cannot share his thoughts with her, they are too dark, too frightening.

'I know,' she says. 'And I'm not going to make you. You'll do that when you're ready.'

He thinks he will never be ready.

'It's something else,' she says. Her face is clouded, secretive. He wonders what she is about to reveal. He is not sure he is ready for more darkness.

He sits down on the edge of the bed, and she sits next to him, her hand on his arm. He tries not to pull it away, and it stays there, heavy, leaden. He notices something he has not noticed before: the shadows beneath her eyes and the ghost of a sadness behind her smile. He puts it down to her anxiety about him. She clears her throat. 'I've been trying to find your sister,' she says.

A jolt goes through him. He was not expecting that. 'And?'

'I traced her to where your old school was evacuated to in Devon . . .' She withdraws her hand from his arm and twists it nervously in her lap. 'But it seems she ran away, and no one knows where she went.'

Jack sags forward on the bed, putting his head in his hands. 'That'd be right,' he says.

'But it doesn't mean you should give up hope.'

'Hope? Don't talk to me about hope. There is no hope.'

'There's always hope.'

'Don't you see? It means she's dead too.'

'No. Why do you think that?'

'Where else would she have run but home? And you know what happened to that.' He can almost taste the rubble, the dust.

'She could just as easily have gone somewhere else . . .'

'There wasn't anywhere else.'

'A friend?'

'She didn't have any friends. She stuck to me like a shadow.'

'Maybe there was someone after you . . .'

'Stop being so fucking positive.' He cannot help saying it, even though it is exactly what he loves about her. 'Can't you see I've brought this on myself? My mother died alone because of me. Why not my sister too?'

*

358

Jack is sent to talk to members of the naval intelligence staff, who fire questions at him that he finds impossible to answer. He can't sleep. He looks at Olivia and her smooth skin, her perfect smile, but he sees Anya and her gaunt cheeks, her missing tooth. Olivia's attempts at cheerfulness grate on his nerves. Maggie's moroseness is as bad. He thinks about Dmitri and Elena and their empty larder. He thinks about Betsy in the rubble. He thinks about dying. He is already partly dead. He doesn't feel the cold any more. When Olivia says, 'You need to wear a jumper or you'll freeze to death,' he loses his temper. 'You have no idea what it's like to freeze to death,' he shouts.

She is shocked and embarrassed. Tears spring into her eyes. He wants to tell her he's sorry, to take her in his arms and tell her everything will be all right, but he can't. All his strength is taken up fighting the image of Burts, frozen, from his mind; all he can feel in his arms is the weight of the body as they struggled to tip it overboard.

At night he is lost in a snowstorm. He can hear the screams of his friends in the water, and he wakes in sweat-drenched sheets. He scrabbles to reach out to them, but they turn into the broken body of Mrs Knightley in the air raid all those years ago. The less he sleeps, the less he feels. He moves around in the day as if he's still in a dream. His thoughts are fog-bound. 'Rest,' says Olivia. 'It'll do you good.' But the more time he spends lying in bed, the worse it becomes.

Olivia and Maggie are out most days, and some nights too. When Jack is alone, the rooms cave in. Sometimes he blinks and it looks as though seawater is dripping down the walls. Anything he eats tastes dry, sticks in his throat. He needs to do something. To get out. He wanders the streets, but he feels exposed. He sits in the dark flat and feels numb. One morning in the tiny bathroom, he takes a razor blade and presses it into the thin flesh of his inner arm. The pain gives him some-thing to focus on. He scores his flesh again. This time the bright beads of blood join up to make a line. The sensation of pain at least means he is alive. But what is the point of being alive when everyone you know is dead?

He misses that strange other-world of snow and ice where life was on hold, where feelings were frozen. He cannot live up to the expectations that Olivia has of him. He is not the person she thinks he is. He has not left his childhood behind. He is a liar and a thief. He suspects she is beginning to realise that. She has waited for him for so long that even though she is disappointed, she will not say. She is hiding something from him.

'How about some music?' says Olivia, standing to put a record on. As the gramophone grinds to life, the sound of harmony touches something deep down inside the blackness of Jack's heart, and he stumbles to his feet, almost knocking the machine off the table in his haste to stop the notes pouring into him.

He is surprised to feel Olivia's hand grip him firmly. There is a steel in her pale eyes that wasn't there before he left. 'This can't go on,' she says. 'You need to stop being so angry.'

'You don't know what it's like.'

'No, I don't.' He is surprised by her forcefulness. 'Because you won't talk to me. You won't tell me what it's like. But don't you think I've suffered too? Don't you think I felt that emptiness, that fear, that I was just going through the motions . . . I'm sorry you've been through so much. But you're wrong to give up. You have to keep going. Think of your future. Think of us . . .' Standing there in front of him, she is defiant and gutsy, the girl he met in Scotland.

She takes his hand. 'Come with me,' she says.

'Where?'

'You'll see.'

Reluctantly he follows her to the bus stop. They head east, part of a steady stream of buses and cars, pedestrians and cyclists. They ignore the holes where buildings used to be, the barrage balloons that still swim among the clouds above them.

They cross the river, glistening like the rain on the wheel arches of a taxi that slides past.

Eventually, Olivia leads him off the bus and they walk on the dark, damp pavements until they come to a large white building. 'Where are we?' says Jack.

'The Dreadnought Hospital,' says Olivia, glancing up at the imposing facade.

He shakes his head. 'No.' He digs his nails into his left arm.

'You've got to,' she says. 'We should have done this ages ago.'

He shakes his head again.

'I told him you would come.'

'You've seen him?'

'Of course. He's your best friend.'

Jack digs his nails in harder, feeling for the bumps of his scars. He is not ready for this.

'Come on,' she says, opening the door and resting her hand on his shoulder. He shrugs the hand off. 'You need to do this.'

Jack takes a deep breath. He looks across at Olivia, the determined line of her mouth, the expectant raised eyebrow. He wonders when he stopped being the protector and became the protected. 'I'll go. But you stay here.' He needs to do this alone.

The seafarers' hospital is in the grounds of the Naval College at Greenwich, a grand old building surrounded by neatly manicured gardens, where invalids sit on wooden benches beneath stately columns. Jack makes his way inside. A nurse leads him along the hushed, spotless corridor. Their footsteps echo in the silence. The beds in the ward are arranged in neat rows. The windows are open, and clean, white curtains flutter in a gentle breeze. It could not be more different to the Bolnitsa. The nurse ushers him forwards and points. Jack's eyes scan the row of beds, searching for his friend. A man is waving vigorously at him; 'Jack!' he is saying, and Jack can't believe this is Carl. He looks well-fed and sleek, and his hair is cropped short like it used to be. He is as strong and healthy as when they worked the docks together. Except that he can't get out of the bed.

Jack forces himself to walk across the ward. Carl's bed is tucked in, and the soft blanket lies flat beneath the thigh where his leg should be. Here, in the reality of London, in their world, the injury is somehow so much worse.

'At last,' says Carl, grinning and sticking out his broad arm. He grips Jack's hand and pulls Jack towards him, rising up to pat Jack on the back. 'This is Jack, everyone,' he adds, addressing the rest of the men on the ward. 'The man who saved my life.'

The men murmur their greetings, smiling as if they had no cares in the world, but Jack can see that each one of them is damaged. He knows that beneath their smiles lies turmoil and anxiety, the same as his own. For that reason, he barely dares look Carl in the eye. He does not want to see the hurt that must rage there.

Jack bows his head. Carl leans over. 'Can you believe we both survived such a pounding?' Jack pulls his sleeves down to hide his scars. Carl squeezes Jack's shoulder. 'Look at me,' he says. But Jack cannot. 'Come on. It's all right. It's me.'

Jack forces himself to look up. His friend's eyes stare back, not haunted, not scared, not full of the images he expected to see, but bright and concerned – the same eyes that Jack remembers from school. Carl is unchanged. 'I've been waiting a long time to thank you,' he says. 'Where have you been?'

'I don't know. I had a lot to sort out.'

'Too much to come and see your best mate who you snatched from the jaws of death?'

Jack looks away. 'It was you that pulled me out of the water . . .'

'And I'd do the same again tomorrow.'

'But . . . Your leg . . .'

'I'd rather lose my leg than my life.'

'What about all the others? Si and David? The *Pluckston* went down, you know. And Burts and Mart . . .'

'You can't save everyone, Jack. You've got to say your goodbyes and move on.'

Jack swallows. His throat is dry. Carl shifts a bit. 'Look at this ward,' he says. 'What do you see?'

Jack looks up and down the ward properly this time. He sees the recovering men, the lost limbs and the bandages, the burns and the wounds. 'You're not looking at it properly,' says Carl. 'You see a room full of damaged men. But it's not. It's a room full of survivors. And you're one of them.'

'Why did I survive? I don't deserve it.'

'That's the most stupid thing I ever heard you say. Who's to say who deserves it or not? You deserve it just as much as the next man.'

Forgiveness is a soothing balm on Jack's troubled mind. 'When did you become so wise?'

'I've had a lot of time to think.'

'I'd have given up.'

'I've never known you to give up on anything. Make a bad decision sometimes, sure, but give up? That's not the Jack I grew up with.'

'It's hard . . .'

'You think I don't know that? But we'll be fine. We have to be. We owe it to the others. You just need a bit of self-belief.'

'Someone else said that to me . . .'

'So two of us might have a point?'

Jack leans back in his chair and watches his old friend.

Carl smiles at him. 'You've come a long way, Jack. We both have.'

They sit for a moment, listening to the sounds of the other men talking quietly among themselves, playing cards and laughing. Jack feels a peace descend on him. 'I've been horrible to Olivia,' he says.

'You're an idiot, then.'

'She tried to find Betsy.'

'I know. She's visited me most days since her mate wrote

and told her that we made it out of there. She's a gutsy girl, that one.'

Jack nods, thinking of how horrible he's been.

'Why don't you go to Drummond Road?'

'I already have.'

'That was ages ago. Try again. Maybe Betsy's been back knocking on doors too? You never know. There's no harm in giving it another go, and I know Olivia wants to see where you grew up.'

'I'm not sure I want her to.'

'Give the girl a break – she's stuck it out with you so far.'

'God knows why . . .'

'Come on, mate. Keep looking for the silver linings. Bet you thought I could never walk again?'

'Not unless you've met blooming Jesus . . .'

'Watch this.' Carl swings himself upright and reaches down beside the bed. He straps the prosthetic leg to his stump, and, balancing himself against the bedhead, he stands and starts to walk between the row of beds.

Jack doesn't know what to say. He feels a grin break across his face. Carl returns to the bed with a hop and a jump – showing off his new skills. 'Once I get the hang of it,' he says, 'no one'll know it's not real. I'll be able to walk, work – find myself a wife!'

And Jack finds himself laughing with his best friend, in the way they used to laugh down at Cherry Garden Pier.

Olivia is waiting for him outside, chewing her lip anxiously. They catch another bus to Bermondsey. It is not far, and they sit in silence, their ears filled with the sound of traffic after rain, and the shouts from streets busy with people. They pass a group of children pushing a salvage cart packed with old wellies, jagged timber, and a battered pram. Jack watches his old neighbourhood roll by, the smell of wet pavement filling his nostrils, reminding him of days spent on the street. Carl is right. They have come so far. He is no longer a boy of the

364

streets. He is a man of the sea. He puts out a hand and tucks Olivia's hair behind her ears.

She smiles across at him. 'Come on,' he says.

When they have got off the bus, he pulls her close, planting a kiss on her forehead. 'Forgive me,' he says. 'It's been a rough few weeks and I've been an idiot.'

'I could forgive you anything when you're like this,' she says.

They walk along the edge of the park. The anti-aircraft regiments and the tethered barrage balloons still keep watch over the lake he once swam in and the grass he played football on. Even the horse chestnut tree is the same, its naked winter branches proud, regal. He wonders if children still vie for its best conkers in the autumn.

The rubble of his home has been cleared, and they move between the exposed walls where lines of paint mark where the first floor and the staircase used to be. The blackened chimney is vivid against the glowering sky. They reach the backyard and look out across rows of identical yards. Someone has been busy expanding the vegetable plot so that it covers every inch of space, the fine soil tilled and ready for spring seeds. Two girls are playing on the low brick wall on one side. Behind them, lines of washing flap in the breeze. One is sitting, picking her nose, while the other stands, balancing on the wall next to her, pointing her toes. She is wearing a pair of pink satin ballet shoes. 'What you doing here?' she asks.

'I don't know,' says Jack, suddenly self-conscious, feeling like a trespasser in his own home.

Olivia squeezes his hand. 'We're looking for clues,' she says.

'Clues for what?'

'For where someone might be.'

'Who?'

'This man's sister.'

'What's 'er name?'

'Betsy,' says Jack. 'Betsy Sullivan.'

'Never 'eard of 'er.'

365

'The warden might know,' ventures the girl who is sitting. 'My mum says he knows everything.'

'Are they still at the school?' says Jack.

She nods.

'It's worth a try,' says Olivia.

Together they walk back to the pavement, leaving the girls to carry on pointing their toes and swinging their legs against the wall.

Jack's old school is exactly the same as he remembers it – sandbags and stretchers, and, incredibly, there is the ARP warden, the same one who was always on their case, his face more lined and his grey hair thinner. To Jack's relief, there is no flicker of recognition in the old man's eyes. 'Can I help you?' he says. Jack remembers guiltily how they would do anything to avoid this man. He remembers the fight. He remembers the warden helping his mother. He feels ashamed and stares at his feet, his mouth thick with words that won't come.

Olivia takes control. 'We're looking for someone,' she says. 'We thought you might have known her. Betsy Sullivan? From Drummond Road.'

The man thinks for a moment, then starts to shake his head slowly as if trying to clear a fog from his mind. Jack is about to turn on his heel, but then the man says, 'I remember the Sullivans. What a sorry business. Can't remember the kids' names, but I know there was two boys and a little girl. The older boy went to France with the dad. The pair of them never made it back.'

'That's right . . .'

The man continues: 'The daughter was a wild little thing. Just like the other brother. A right pair of scallywags. Always in trouble . . .'

Olivia coughs into her hand and indicates Jack's bowed head. The warden stops and peers more closely. 'You're not . . .?'

366

Jack looks up and nods.

'Well I never,' says the warden. 'I always wondered what happened to you. You needed a fatherly clip around the ear . . .' But he smiles kindly. 'It's a tough neighbourhood. You might not believe it, but I was young once.'

'I heard what happened to my mother . . .' says Jack.

The man's brow creases apologetically. 'There was nothing anyone could have done. Lucky the pair of you were out of it.'

'You mean Betsy wasn't there?'

'Oh no. Definitely not.'

'How can you be sure?'

'I pulled the body out. She was all alone. Besides, I've seen your sister since then.'

'Really?' Jack's voice is high, excited. Olivia is smiling and gripping his shaking hand. 'When? Where?'

'It was a while back. After your mum . . . She was with that no-good lad you used to hang out with. Now that one . . . he's a proper bad egg . . .'

'You mean Stoog?'

'Not sure of his name. Tall, skinny fellow. Bundle of nervous energy waiting to explode . . . Family still live in Snowsfields . . .'

But Jack is barely listening. He is pulling Olivia along the street and shouting 'thank you' over his shoulder.

They walk the couple of miles to the slum area that Stoog grew up in. The houses are practically piled on top of each other, a mixture of brick and wood, tile and muck, wonky chimneys and broken roofs. It's difficult to tell whether this is because of the bombs, or just dilapidation – many were like this before the Luftwaffe came for them. Jack leads Olivia through the narrow, dark alleys to one of the many houses with rags across their broken windows, past boys shovelling bricks and sifting through dust. He raps at the Stoogleys' door. A girl with her hair tied in a scarf answers.

'Agnes?'

'Jack!' Her haggard face lights up for a moment. 'Look at you. So grown up . . .' But her joy turns to worry. 'What do you want?' she whispers.

'Is Stoog here?'

'He hasn't lived here for a good while now.'

'Is he away fighting?'

She shakes her head.

'Who is it?' shouts a woman's voice from inside.

'No one, Mum,' says Agnes over her shoulder. Then she whispers at Jack. 'You'd better go. You don't want to have anything to do with Stoog. He's my own brother, and I can't bear the sight of him . . .'

Jack puts his hand out to stop her closing the door. 'But do you know if he's seen Betsy? Have you seen her? Is she alive?'

Agnes's face pales. A large woman who must once have been even larger shambles out of the darkness of the corridor. Her skin is a washed-out grey and seems to hang in pleats from her body; her features have sunk into the folds of her face. 'Who's this?' she says, the cigarette in her mouth moving up and down with the words.

'It's Jack, Mum. Jack Sullivan. You remember?'

The woman peers at him with gimlet eyes. 'Jack Sullivan? What you doing here? Thought you was dead. So did your poor mother.'

Jack grits his teeth. 'I'm looking for Betsy.'

'It's Stoog you want to ask about that.'

'So where is he?'

'Haven't heard from him for months. Tight little bastard. Don't know what's wrong with you lot, abandoning the women that brought you into this world . . .'

Jack tenses. He feels the old familiar anger simmering in his bones.

Olivia cuts in: 'Is there a forwarding address?'

The older woman starts to tremble, her laughter turning into a phlegmy cough that takes a long time to settle. Agnes

368

looks at her feet. 'Forwarding address?' says the woman, still laughing. 'Stoog ain't the kind to receive letters, ma'am.'

'I just want to find my sister,' says Jack, his voice thick with anger.

The woman stops laughing. She leans towards them, her grey skin papery in the daylight. 'If I were you, Jack Sullivan, I'd crawl back into the hole I'd crawled out of,' she says. 'That girl won't want nothing to do with you, running off and leaving her and your mum without so much as a word. You always were a bad one.'

Olivia squeezes his hand more tightly. He feels the tension in his shoulders. 'Come on,' says Olivia. 'Let's go.' He allows her to pull him back from the door.

'If you do find him,' Mrs Stoogley shouts after them, cackling again with laughter, 'be sure to give me his forwarding address.'

Jack stops in the street, once they have walked a good distance from Stoog's home. He braces his hands against the wall of a building, resting his forehead against its cool brick. Olivia comes up behind him, circling her arms around his waist, pressing her cheek against his back. 'We'll find her,' she says.

'They could be anywhere.'

'We'll keep looking.'

He shakes his head. 'Everything I touch goes wrong.'

'Not me.' She pulls him around so that he is facing her.

He leans his forehead against hers, looks into her pale eyes and sees his own reflection there, and suddenly it hits him, how lucky he is. That despite everything – his past, the *Aurora*, Russia – despite it all, he is here, still living, still breathing, still here on the pavement with the smell of damp brick in his nostrils and the cold air nipping at his skin. More remarkably, in front of him there is this girl, with eyes the colour of the Arctic sea and hair the colour of the midnight sun, and she has waited for him against all odds. And she is here, this strange girl, who shouldn't even be friendly with someone

369

like him, and yet is determined to be with him, standing on the pavement too, with the smell of damp brick in her nostrils and the cold air nipping at her cheeks. And around them the world keeps turning and the traffic keeps moving and the people keep walking by.

Jack takes a step backwards, still holding Olivia, but now at arm's length. The light falls across her face, making the blue of her eyes shine as though lit from inside. It is as if he is seeing her again for the very first time. She smiles a self-conscious smile, a blush sprinkling across the pale cheekbones as she tucks her hair behind her ear. They are both still so young, but he feels as old as the sea.

He drops on to one knee, and Olivia starts laughing and trying to tug him up on to his feet, but he kneels there, feeling the damp from the street soak up into his leg, the warmth of her hand in his, still gazing into her eyes. 'Will you marry me?' he says.

And she is still laughing and trying to pull him to his feet, and blushing, and passers-by are staring, but he doesn't care.

'Will you?'

'If you stand up and stop making a spectacle of yourself . . .'

'I won't get up unless you give me an answer . . .'

'All right!'

'All right, you will?'

'Yes! Of course I will.'

And then he is on his feet and his arms are around her and he can feel their hearts racing in their chests and he buries his face in her hair and lifts her off her feet. And he can do anything. He is invincible.

Later, as they lie talking to each other in the lamplight, he notices a shadow cross her face. 'No regrets?' he says. She shakes her head. He leans up on his elbow, strokes her cheek. 'Is it your family? Are you worried about telling them?'

'No. I don't care what they say . . .'

'Maybe. But they're still your family. It'll be tough . . .'

'They'll come around.'

'There's nothing else you're worried about?'

She pauses for a moment, then smiles across at him. 'Only that you keep yourself safe when you go back to the ships,' she says.

And the shadow is gone.

CHAPTER 26

Olivia

Jack has gone to the Prescot Street pool, with his sea bag hitched up over his shoulder, his brow creased, his face serious, but his dark eyes dancing. Olivia does not try to dissuade him – they all have their parts to play. Her own orders have come through, and she is to be posted to HMS *Helicon*, something that once would have thrilled her. But she is dreading it. Too many memories. Of youth. Of freedom. Of happiness.

There is still no news of Charlie. It is bad enough that he is still missing, but to be part of the cause is a grey cloud that sits heavily in her breast. She misses Jack, fears for his safety out on the seas again. She cannot bear to read the reports any more, does not want to know the name of his ship in case she should see it there in the columns of black and white. She wants it all to stop, so that she can have her happy ending. But there is no end in sight. She is anchorless, drifting. The future is impossible to imagine, but the past invades her mind. Every day she thinks of her baby – their baby. She could not bring herself to tell Jack about it. He has lost too much. But she also wishes she had told him – so that they could mourn their loss together, and because she knows their marriage would be poisoned by keeping such a secret from him. She stumbles along, growing more miserable when she should be thriving.

The night before she is due to leave for Scotland, Olivia

goes to Eddie's Bar with the usual crowd. As always, it is busy and there are plenty of friends and acquaintances to drink and chatter with. But from the moment she arrives, she cannot shake the feeling that she is being watched, that someone is shadowing her. Yet whenever she turns and searches the glowing faces above the sea of navy and khaki, no one catches her eye. She tries to relax into the evening. The lights pick out the flash of polished buttons, regimental badges, stripes of rank, and the occasional splash of colour of women not in uniform. Dancers and drinkers stay close to hear each other above the music, men with hair brushed and slicked into place, women with neat curls held firm with pins. Friends come and go, spots of colour on their cheekbones, their eyes bright with living. Still Olivia feels under scrutiny, the skin on the back of her neck pricking. She loosens her collar and glances about, but there is no one there.

It is not until she is getting ready to go that Olivia feels a feathery touch on her arm. She swings around to see a dark-haired girl hovering at her elbow. Immediately a stab of recognition pulses through her, but she cannot pinpoint exactly where she has seen this girl before.

The girl watches Olivia's friends slip out into the night. Her eyes are dark, made more so by the thick eyeliner painted around them. 'Yes?' says Olivia. 'Can I help?'

The girl squirms a bit, apparently reluctant to speak, but then she says quietly, 'Do you know Charlie?'

And then Olivia realises – of course she recognises this girl – she is the one that she had seen Charlie with on a few occasions. She hesitates, wonders how much the girl knows, does not want to be the one that breaks it to her. 'You mean Charlie FitzHerbert?' she says.

The girl nods. 'I need to talk to him. It's important.'

'You haven't heard?'

'Heard what?'

'I'm really sorry, but Charlie is missing.'

'Is he dead?'

'I hope not . . . We're waiting for news . . . He went down somewhere off Norway . . .'

A look of despair mixed with confusion flickers across the girl's face. 'But when will you find out?' she says.

'I don't know . . . We have to wait . . .'

'But I can't wait . . . There's no time . . .'

'Time for what?'

The girl's eyes shift warily as if she is thinking whether to divulge what's on her mind. Olivia puts out a comforting hand, to encourage her to confide, but the girl shrugs it off, stepping away and unconsciously smoothing her hands over her dress, letting them linger at her waistline. With a searing jolt Olivia recognises the telltale way that her fingers cradle protectively, and at once the loss of her own child tears again at her insides and she has to stop her knees from giving way.

The girl reads her face and laughs, a sharp, bitter sound. 'You see . . .' she says. 'I needed to talk to him . . . but there's no choice now . . .' She moves to leave.

'Wait,' says Olivia. 'Don't go. There's always a choice . . .'

But the girl is not listening. She is slipping away, beginning to push her thin arms into the coat draped over her elbow.

'Stay, please. I might be able to help . . .'

The girl stops, twisting her face back around and hurling her words bitterly at Olivia. 'How? You've got the money to pay?'

'Pay for what?' Olivia grabs hold of her coat, and the girl tries to wrench away and as they grapple with each other, she suddenly stops and gasps. She is staring at Olivia's neck. The blood drains from her face and her eyes grow wider and she manages to yank her coat free, but instead of running, she stretches her hand towards Olivia's throat, and, for a moment, Olivia isn't sure what she is going to do – the girl seems so volatile. But instead of feeling fingers close around her neck, she feels her necklace dig into the back of her neck. The girl is holding the green pendant up to the dim light, twisting it and turning it, searching in its depths for something she recognises.

'Where'd you get this?' she says, her voice a whisper, her hands trembling.

And suddenly the truth hits Olivia: she doesn't recognise this girl because she's seen her with Charlie. She knows her because she has the same dark, wild eyes as Jack, and she says, 'Betsy?'

But the girl has dropped the glass pendant, and she is backing away, tripping against the chairs and bumping into people as she goes.

'Stop!' Olivia calls.

But Betsy doesn't stop, and through the haze of heat from the bodies, Olivia sees tears well up in her painted eyes. Then she turns and runs, barging through the crowds as if the devil is chasing her.

Olivia cannot sleep that night. She fiddles with her necklace in the quiet of the flat until it is as early as she dares to drive to Carl's house. Carl is back with his family and getting used to life on civvy street. He has a job in a sheltered workshop that provides employment for people with disabilities; an increasing necessity with so many injured men returning home. Olivia hammers on the door with her important news. Mr Mills answers, bleary-eyed, but not surprised at being woken. Nights are often broken these days.

Carl comes limping out into the street after a few minutes.

'Take me to Snowsfields,' he says, after she has explained. 'Stoog has got to have the answer.'

'But they wouldn't help last time . . .'

'There's always been bad blood between them and Jack. But Agnes and I used to be close.'

The sky is beginning to lighten by the time they reach the slums. Carl makes Olivia wait in the car. A mist sits over the warren of ramshackle buildings and narrow alleys, and it seems to her that it swallows Carl up. A lone dog trots past, in the same direction as Carl. It sticks close to the shadows, holding its body low as if expecting a blow at any moment.

Then it too is gone and she is left to watch the empty street again, feeling her own yawning emptiness well up inside her.

She is relieved when she finally sees Carl's broad figure emerge, a grim look on his face.

'Got an address,' he says. 'Old Compton Street in Soho.'

'And Betsy's with him?'

He nods curtly. 'Sounds like it.'

'Let's go,' she says, turning the ignition.

'I'm not sure it's the kind of place I should be taking a young lady like yourself . . .'

'You must know me better than that now.'

He slams the car door and glances across at her. 'I thought you might say that . . .'

The rest of the city may be yawning from its slumber, but Soho never sleeps. Olivia feels safe next to Carl. Their pace is slow but purposeful. She turns her collar up against the gaudy music that trickles out of cracks in the buildings, ignoring the whistles of a passing soldier. Carl shoots the man a look, and he backs off, hands raised, as if offended that they could think badly of him. 'Are you sure you want to do this?' says Carl, and Olivia nods. 'One thing, before we go on,' says Carl, stopping to face her, his face serious. 'If she is there, I think you should wait to tell her about you and Jack getting married. She's going to be feeling very alone. Jack's the only family she's got left . . .'

'I'll wait. Maybe it's best coming from Jack?'

'I think that's right. I'm sorry. You know I hate lying as much as the next man . . .'

'It's fine,' says Olivia. 'I understand.' She knows about secrets.

The paint is peeling from the door, which leads to some flats above a shop. None of the bells works. Carl bangs on the wood with his fist. There is no answer. He bangs some more. Eventually they hear the shuffle of footsteps, and a pasty-looking girl with smudged lipstick opens it a crack.

'Shove off,' she says. 'We're closed for business.'

'I'm looking for someone,' says Carl.

'Everyone's looking for someone. Come back later.'

Undeterred, Carl presses on. 'Goes by the name of Stoog.'

The girl hesitates for a moment, as if racking her brain. Then she shakes her head slowly. 'No,' she says. 'No one by that name here.'

'Reginald Stoogley?'

She raises her eyes, as if looking for an answer in the rotting doorframe. Then she shakes her head again. 'No. No one by that name either.'

'Look,' says Carl, 'we know he's here. His family gave us the address.'

'They lied, then,' says the girl.

Olivia can tell Carl is beginning to feel ruffled. He doesn't ask much from people, but he does expect them to be honest. 'I think it's you that's lying,' she says.

Olivia stands square as she feels the girl's eyes look her up and down with disdain. 'I don't know what you think this is,' she says, 'but we don't cater for your sort at all. Try somewhere else.'

Olivia ignores the jibe. 'What about Betsy?' she says. 'Betsy Sullivan?'

The girl starts to close the door, but Carl keeps his hand on it, and the girl is unable to push any further. 'Answer the lady,' he says.

'Don't know no one of that name either. Now fuck off.'

'Maybe you know her as Elizabeth . . .?' says Olivia.

'No. I've told you . . .' Their voices are rising.

'You're not even listening . . .'

A man's voice suddenly calls from inside the building.

'What the hell's going on out there?'

'Some toff and her sidekick sticking their noses in . . .'

'Tell her to sling her hook.'

Carl suddenly straightens up, cocking his head to listen. 'Stoog?' he says. 'Reg Stoogley? Is that you?' He tries to peer beyond the girl into the darkness, but she is blocking his view. 'Stoog? I know it's you . . .' Carl's voice is louder this time, and he easily pushes his way into the hallway. The girl staggers backwards and Carl follows, Olivia behind. The hall smells heavily of perfume and cigarette smoke. There is no natural light because the windows are covered in blackout.

'I know you're there, you bastard,' Carl says again, and Olivia is surprised; she has never heard Carl use bad language before. There is a movement to one side, and Olivia can just make out the thin, tall body of a man in the shadows. He steps towards them as the girl scurries off towards the staircase.

'Well, well. If it isn't the daddy's boy,' says the man, baring his teeth. 'How'd you find me? No, no. Don't tell me. That stupid sister of mine . . .'

Olivia feels Carl tense. 'I'm not here for trouble. I'm looking for Betsy,' he says.

But Stoog is not listening. He is eyeing Olivia. 'You've done well for yourself, haven't you? Pretty little creature. Like the ones in uniform, do you?'

Olivia fights the urge to step away. Now that her eyes have grown accustomed to the dim light, she can see he has small, mean eyes that are darting across her body. She glares back, defiantly, hoping she looks unruffled. Inside, she is quivering.

'Bit hard around the mouth, though,' says Stoog. 'I'm sure I could find you something more suitable . . .'

'Just tell us where she is,' says Carl. 'We know you've seen her, and Jack's looking for her . . .'

'Jack?' says Stoog, and Olivia does not miss the brief look of fear that flashes across his face. Then it is gone, and Stoog is on the offensive again. 'He's alive, is he? Well, you can tell him I haven't seen Betsy since she was sent away. Just about the same time that he did another runner . . .'

Olivia is wondering how they are going to talk him around when she senses another figure move on the stairs. The girl from Eddie's Bar has appeared on the bottom step. Even in the partial light, she is unmistakably Jack's sister. The echo of Stoog's voice dies to a silence as she walks towards them. The building seems to hold its breath.

'Go back upstairs,' says Stoog, his voice quiet and threatening.

But the girl draws closer, walking slowly, as if in a dream.

'I said go upstairs,' says Stoog, spitting the words this time.

But the girl has reached Carl and she is looking up at him with wonder. 'Carl?' she says. Her voice is quiet, as if she doesn't dare say his name out loud in case he is a mirage that will evaporate at any moment.

'Betsy, thank God!' Carl holds out his hand, but she backs away, shaking her mass of dark, tangled hair. 'It's all right,' he says. 'We've come to get you . . .'

'But where have you been?'

'Working on the ships. Like we always said we would . . .' His voice is calm and measured, as if talking to a frightened animal.

'Jack . . .?'

'He's alive. He's desperate to see you.'

'But I came back and he was gone . . . and Stoog said . . . and then Mum . . .' Her whole body is trembling.

'I'll tell you everything. Just come with me,' he says.

'I can't . . . I . . .'

'You can. It's going to be fine . . .' Carl is still holding out his hand.

'But Stoog's looked after me . . .'

Carl snorts as Stoog puts a protective arm on Betsy's shoulder. 'No, Betsy. Stoog's not looked after you. He's taken advantage . . .'

Olivia can see that Betsy is torn, between the man who has offered her shelter for the last few years, and the man who offers her protection now.

Stoog steps closer to her, sensing he's at a disadvantage. 'What about the baby, Betsy?' he says. 'Aren't we going to sort that?'

Betsy's hands go to her stomach.

'Think about Jack,' says Carl. He does not take his eyes from Betsy's face.

'He mustn't find out . . .'

'We'll talk to him together.'

'I can't keep it.'

'I understand.'

Olivia wants to tell her she must keep it. She is thinking of the unconscious girl at Dr Hartmann's surgery. She is about to say something, to intervene, but Carl holds up a hand to silence her. He is still focusing on Betsy. 'It's going to be all right, Bets,' he says.

'Don't you expect to come back if you go,' says Stoog.

Carl talks over him. 'I'm not leaving without you.'

'There'll be no place for you here if you leave.' Stoog is beginning to sound desperate.

'There's a place for you with us,' says Carl.

Betsy looks across at Stoog one last time, but his gimlet eyes give nothing away. She looks back at Carl and his outstretched hand, which is only inches from her, and Olivia can see that she trusts her brother's oldest friend, and she puts out her hand and Carl grabs hold of it and leads her out into the light.

By the time they reach the flat, it is late morning. Olivia is suffering from lack of sleep. Her mind is a jumble of thoughts. She cannot believe they have found Betsy, is overjoyed at the thought of reuniting her and Jack. But now she must grapple with the fact that the girl might be carrying Charlie's baby. She wonders how Jack will react. She wonders how Charlie will react. She wonders what Jack will think of Charlie. She wonders if Charlie will ever know that he has a child. She wonders how it might have been if she still carried Jack's child. She does not know whether to believe what Betsy has told them. She does not know what to say or how to behave.

She settles for making everyone a cup of tea while Carl talks

380

to Betsy. The girl will not even look at her. She is jumpy and agitated, pacing around the flat, picking things up and putting them down. 'I can't have it, Carl,' she is saying. 'I've got to get rid of it. You've got to help me. Before it's too late . . .'

Olivia stirs the tea. She has been doing the calculations. Betsy must be at least thirty weeks gone; even though there is barely anything to show it. 'It's already too late,' she says, placing the hot mugs on the table.

'No,' says Betsy. 'Stoog had someone coming . . .'

Olivia cuts her off. 'Charlie left on September the first. It's now the end of March . . .'

'You have to take me back . . .'

'But the baby will be fully formed. It would be like murder . . . Carl, please tell her. It's too late.'

Carl nods slowly. He has also been working it out. 'She's right, Betsy . . .'

'But Stoog said . . .'

'Forget what Stoog said . . .'

'But how will I look after it . . .'

'There are things we could do . . . Adoption . . .'

'Let's not make any hasty decisions,' says Olivia. 'Let's wait for Charlie . . .'

'You said he's gone.' Betsy glares at her.

'That doesn't mean he's not coming back . . .'

Betsy thinks about this for a moment. 'But where will I have it? Who will help me? What about Jack? What will he say?'

'Don't worry about Jack,' says Carl. 'We'll talk to him. He'll understand.'

'Where will I stay? Can I stay with you?'

Carl shakes his head. 'There's no room. We've already got three families at our house . . .'

'Then there's nowhere else. I've got to go back . . .'

'No!' Carl and Olivia speak at the same time.

And now Carl is looking at Olivia. She starts to shake her head. 'But I'm leaving for Scotland in six hours . . .' She can see the reluctance parading across Betsy's face and she knows that it is matched to the same degree in her own.

'I don't see how either of you has a choice.'

Carl insists that the girls both rest before discussing the matter further. Betsy curls up on Olivia's bed, her dark head lying on the same pillow that Jack's dark head was resting on only a few days ago, the years falling away as she drifts off. Olivia retreats to the sitting room. She dozes in an armchair for a while, but sleep is evasive. There is too much running through her head. Carl watches over them both. He does not trust Betsy not to run. Olivia shifts in the chair, and Carl perches on the arm next to her.

'Do you think she's telling the truth?' says Olivia.

'She's definitely expecting . . .'

'But do you think it's Charlie's?'

'We've got to give her the benefit of the doubt.'

'I can't see how Charlie . . .' But she can. She knows what it is like to lose oneself to longing.

'Bloody Stoog,' says Carl. He lifts his false leg, rearranging it to sit more comfortably. 'Makes you wonder what's the real damage done by war . . .'

'What do you think Jack will do?'

'I think he'll kill Stoog.'

'And Charlie?'

Carl shrugs, defeated.

Olivia tucks her hair behind her ear and fiddles nervously with her earlobe. 'I wish there was some news. I wish we knew if he was alive . . .'

'Will he do the honourable thing if he is?'

'You mean marry her?'

'I don't know . . .'

'He'd certainly do something. He's a decent man . . .'

'Pay for it?'

'Either that . . . Or take it off her hands . . . or . . . I don't know . . .'

'What if he never returns?'

Olivia shifts uncomfortably. 'Actually, he made me his next of kin . . .'

Carl raises his eyebrows. 'So what do you think?' he says.

'I think if it's Charlie's, of course he – or we – should help. But if it's someone else's . . . Stoog's . . . or . . .'

A noise makes her glance towards the corridor, where she sees Betsy framed in the doorway, her black eyes narrowed, unreadable, her thin body tense. 'It isn't Stoog's,' she says. 'It's Charlie's. And if you say he'll pay, I'll come with you to Scotland and have it.'

CHAPTER 27

Charlie

Charlie and Ned are manhandled into a truck. Four guards glare at them, their eyes glittering in the dark. Charlie's head aches. He is disoriented. He has no compass. No revolver. No map. He has nothing. Just the clothes on his back. He can tell from the sun's feeble trajectory that they are heading south, away from Norway, through Denmark and into Germany. With every hour his heart sinks further. He slips in and out of sleep; it feels as though his brain has been rattled and knocked around his skull. He has a scrape down his cheek, and his old shoulder injury throbs. Ned rubs his fingers together nervously. Neither of them speaks.

Eventually they arrive at a camp: a clearing of long wooden huts surrounded by barbed wire fences. Men stand around in the dirt outside, waving at the incoming truck. The stiff figures of sentries keep watch in dotted lines. The truck comes to a halt, and the guards bark at Charlie and Ned. 'Out!' They motion with their rifles.

Charlie lands on the ground, and for a moment he thinks his legs will give way. His body is weak and his mind woozy. He is pushed towards the only brick building, and into a small room. It is empty apart from a bare bed and a small grimy window, which is hanging open. Outside, beyond the drab camp, he can see a hillside laced with glittering streams. His resolve falters.

The guard blocks the doorway. 'Remove your clothes,' he says. Charlie looks at him, unsure. 'Now!' says the guard, waving his rifle. Charlie bends to unlace his boots. The action makes his shoulder burn. His hands tremble. The guard grunts. Charlie unbuckles his belt, steps out of his trousers, fumbles with the buttons on his shirt, peels away the layers, grimaces as the pain shoots through his arm. As he drops his vest on the ground, the guard nods in satisfaction.

He stands there for what feels like an eternity, the cold air sweeping across his skin. But it is not the chill that makes him feel vulnerable; it is the staring eyes of the man standing over him. He tries to remember his training. But he is no longer Lieutenant FitzHerbert. He is Charlie. Naked and exposed.

Suddenly the German spots something and grows agitated. He is pointing at Charlie's wrist. Oh God. The watch. The bloody watch. He was an idiot to keep it on. It had become a sort of talisman. A prize to show off, as well as somehow keeping Olivia close, as if by wearing it, he might retain some hold over her.

'Luftwaffe!' says the man. Charlie tries to regulate his breathing. He takes the air deep into his lungs, lets it out slowly. He does not want this man to sense the fear that is beginning to course through him. The guard barks at him again. 'Luftwaffe!' he says, and pushes Charlie with the butt of his rifle, cold and hard like iron against his naked skin. Charlie's insides are liquid. He has never felt so helpless and exposed.

There is a commotion from outside. The guard moves to the window, peering through it briefly, before trying to close it with his free hand, but he struggles as the catch gets in the way. Through it, in the yard, Charlie can see the other prisoners are still standing in the mud outside their huts. They are all facing the building that Charlie and Ned are in. A sound reaches his ears. It is music – the men are humming a familiar tune, the notes deep and rich, filling the air. Charlie lets the noise sink into him. It is a silly song they used to sing during training. A poor aviator lay dying . . . The tune is the same as something his mother sang . . . Memories of the past flash through his mind: a cricket catch on a sunny day, a picnic with his mother, that first flight with his father, training, friends, flying, parade, the day he got his wings, Mole singing as they fly over the sea. They can take away his clothes, but they cannot take away who he is.

Guards are pouring into the yard and ushering the men, still humming, into their huts. Charlie's guard finally manages to slam the window shut. All is quiet. Charlie locks his eyes on to the cold stare of the German. He unbuckles the watch slowly and holds it out, dangling it in the space between them. The guard indicates that he wants it brought to him, but Charlie smiles and refuses to move. The guard steps forward, snatching the watch, shouting something before retreating with a slam of the door.

Charlie wraps himself in a blanket from the bed. In the ensuing silence, he can hear Ned next door. He taps on the wall. 'Chin up, Ned,' he says. Ned taps back. 'We'll be all right,' says Charlie. 'Just remember your training.'

Charlie waits, sitting on the bed, facing the door. Eventually it opens again and the guard dumps his clothes on the ground, indicating he must dress again. There is no sign of the watch. Charlie takes his time and the guard grows impatient, but Charlie's heartbeat is slow, his hands steady. Eventually he is led to a bare room with a table in the centre of it. A German officer with receding blond hair is sitting at the table. The watch is lying in the middle. 'Where did you get this?' says the officer, narrowing his eyes.

Charlie says nothing. He's damned if he's going to tell this man anything.

'This is a Luftwaffe watch,' says the officer.

Charlie says nothing.

The man slams his fist on the table, the sound making Charlie's heart race again, but still he says nothing.

'You killed a German?' The man slams the table again. 'You will tell me!'

Another man comes in. He is dark, with a squidgy face

386

and kind eyes set behind glasses. The two Germans argue, their voices raised. Charlie's head begins to hurt. The new man has a piece of paper. 'I am from the Red Cross,' he says. He hands Charlie the piece of paper. 'Red Cross,' he says again, pointing at the stamp. 'So we can let your family know where you are.'

Charlie scans the paper. He is not convinced this is an official Red Cross document. 'I have no family,' he says.

'You must fill it in or your mother will not know you are living,' says the man again.

'I have no mother,' says Charlie.

'A wife?'

Charlie shakes his head.

'A sweetheart?'

Charlie shakes his head.

The blond officer interjects. He is calmer now. 'I know how you feel,' he says. 'We are all pilots here.'

'Then you should also know we don't need to tell you anything.' Charlie knows his rights: all pilots are briefed before flying over enemy territory.

'You must fill in,' says the darker man.

'You can have my name, rank, and service number.'

'We need more than this.'

'That is all I am obliged to tell you.'

'We cannot process you unless you tell us more.'

'I'll have to remain unprocessed, then.'

'Where were you flying? What is your ship?'

Charlie shakes his head.

'You will stay here until you tell us more.'

Charlie leans back, crosses his arms. 'Looks like we'll get to know each other well, then.'

The charade goes on for two days before Charlie is freed from solitary confinement. He joins the rest of the prisoners-of-war, all of them airmen, for this is a *Dulag Luft* – a transit camp for air force prisoners – although most of the others are RAF, for the Germans make no distinction between airmen from different armed forces.

Charlie finds a free bunk in the officers' dormitory, beneath a middle-aged man with wildly bushy eyebrows and thinning grey hair who swings himself down to the ground. 'Geordie,' he says, pumping Charlie's hand. 'Welcome to Frankfurt. Where were you shot down?' He puts his fingers to his lips and rolls his eyes from side to side. 'Quietly, though. Microphones in every corner.'

'Norway,' Charlie mouths. The other officers who have come to shake his hand nod their heads, drifting back to their games of cards and their open books.

'Nice to have another Fleet Air Arm chap to liven things up a bit,' says Geordie.

'Do you know what happened to my observer?' Charlie asks.

'Must have been released to another barracks. Divide and rule. You should be able to catch up with him tomorrow.'

Charlie sits on the edge of his bed, head awkwardly forward to stop hitting it on the bunk above.

'It's always a bit disorienting at first,' says Geordie, sitting down next to him.

'Sounds like you've done this before,' says Charlie.

'Almost more times than I can count on these.' Geordie holds out his hands and counts along the fingers. 'I've escaped nine times. Next one'll be number ten, an anniversary of sorts. Got to make that one count.'

'Nine times?' says Charlie.

'Yes. Only problem is, I always get caught and brought back. But one of these days I'll make it. Throw enough shit and someday it will stick, eh?'

Charlie retreats into his bunk, stretching out his legs and putting his arms behind his head. For a brief moment, he feels safe, surrounded by other officers and British men. But then he recalls the barbed wire keeping him from the hills beyond, and he is overwhelmed by exhaustion. He has held out against his captors, but he is trapped. Trapped like the men at Dunkirk.

He tries to fight off sleep, but his eyelids are heavy. He dreams of flying among wispy clouds as the thermals push and bounce at the plane. He hears Mole singing, his deep voice resonating down the Gosport tube. But then he sees the coast of France, marked by a fog of black smoke, the water surrounding it churning with ships – not only the British fleet, but anything that is seaworthy: hospital ships and ferries, sailing dinghies and yachts, tugboats and speedboats, car ferries and trawlers, paddleboats and lifeboats. They are low in the water, so stuffed with extra men that they are struggling to get back across the Channel. Clustered around them like flies are hundreds more men, turning the water white as they struggle to climb to safety. And then there is the beach, black with still more men desperate to escape, and beyond them the chaos on the roads, abandoned trucks and motorcycles, piles of ammunition, guns, provisions, British tanks left empty. Then the marshy ground, the flooded canals and the acres of gleaming tanks and German soldiers waiting to pounce.

Three days later, Charlie is packed into a waiting truck with a group of other men, including Geordie. There is still no sign of Ned. 'I wouldn't worry, old chum,' says Geordie. 'They do at least respect rank here – officers always go to officer-only camps. They probably just think they'll get more from you if you're kept apart.'

They are driven to a train station, where they are packed into a wagon. 'Moving us on quickly this week,' says Geordie.

A young man with a pencil-thin moustache and startlingly blue eyes says, 'The whole place is filling up double quick. We've been stepping up raids, so more of our boys are finding their way here.'

'A last push against the Jerries? Is the end in sight?'

The possibility of an end to war is heartening, but their mood is buoyant for only a short while in the cramped wagons. The Germans watch them constantly. Even the door to the lavatory is wired open; anyone who can face visiting it is

389

scrutinised throughout. One prisoner manages to tear the train map from the carriage wall when no guards are looking. It will be pored over later, giving clues to the men of when to try to escape, where to run. They already know where they're going; Geordie isn't the only one who has been recaptured: 'Sagan, for sure, old boy. *Stalag Luft.*'

The carriages stop often. German soldiers patrol up and down the sides of the stationary wagons, their boots clicking against the ground, their rifles gleaming in the winter sunshine. Troop trains full of German soldiers pass by on the opposite track. The Germans do not seem browbeaten in the least. Quite the opposite. Their uniforms are smart, their boots shiny, their smiles fixed. They are nothing like the dejected, stinking, unshaven prisoners in the wagons. As the temperature rises, so does the smell of unwashed men. They cannot even let fresh air in through the windows: they are all screwed down.

As night falls, Charlie dozes, only struggling briefly when his boots are removed by a soldier. 'In case you run,' says the soldier, cocking his head towards the door, where two more soldiers stand guard. The windows are now shuttered. The wagon is pitch black; the stink of sweat stifling. In the darkness, the men rest against each other, their bodies bumping uncomfortably on the wooden benches as the wagon rattles on.

At some point in the night, the train stops again. The men sleep in fits and starts. They are coupled to another goods train in the early morning. As it pulls on, the guards finally slide the doors open. Most of the prisoners are still asleep, but Charlie inches forward, welcoming the cool breeze. He sticks his hand out, feeling the air touch the skin of his arm and blow into the carriage. It is fresh and cool and he could just as well be on the sleeper to Scotland.

'Enough,' says the guard, and Charlie shuffles back. The guard indicates that he may pass the water and bread around the waking prisoners. They eat slowly, savouring each mouthful; they do not know whether they will be given anything else before they reach their destination.

The lavatory is now blocked. Sewage creeps along the floor towards them. The smell is indescribable. The train stops to let a faster train go past, and one of the prisoners persuades the guards to let them relieve themselves on the side of the track. The men stand or squat in the dull morning light. As the train chugs on again, the guards start to argue among themselves. The man with the startling blue eyes is missing. Geordie laughs. 'Run and run and don't look back!' he yells out into the chilly morning. The guards shout up the train and hammer on the walls of the carriage. It draws to a halt, but the man is long gone. 'Good luck to him,' says Geordie.

At the next transit camp they are kept separate from a mass of other prisoners by lines of twisted barbed wire. Charlie is relieved to be on his side – the other side is filthy: crammed with hundreds of dirty, sick, and injured men. They are standing or lying, or propped up in any space they can find. They have no shelter. The only structure is a high watchtower. Charlie can see the German guards surveying from the top. Beneath it, some of the men have dug holes in the ground in a bid to hide from the wind and rain and sleet. But the holes have turned into sludgy pits, and the men lie there, encrusted in mud and their own faeces. A haze of flies buzzes over everything.

It is the first time that Geordie has not been upbeat. 'I can barely look,' he says. 'Poor buggers.'

'Are they soldiers?' says Charlie.

Geordie nods.

'Why do airmen get treated so much better?'

'It's not because we're airmen. It's because they're Russians.'

Another man adds, 'Others too: Yugoslavs, Serbs, Ukrainians . . .'

'Word is, they're simply chucked into pits when they die. And sometimes before . . .' Geordie cannot talk about this without paling.

As if on cue, three of the pathetic prisoners are dragged

391

away by German guards. They do not even protest, their limp bodies tumble and bump along the ground until they are out of sight. There are three shots. None of their comrades protests. They are too weak to move anyway: their faces gaunt, their eyes sunken, their wrists and hands just skin and bone. Some pull at the last remnants of muddy grass and push it into their swollen mouths.

Charlie glares at a guard who is standing expressionless beside them. 'Can't you give these men some food?' he says.

The guard looks at him in astonishment: 'These are not men. They are subhuman. Socialists and communists. We will not waste food on such undesirables.'

Charlie walks closer to the fence that separates them. An icy drizzle is turning to a stinging sleet. On the other side, a man pushes through the crowd towards him, putting his hand up, as if in greeting. It looks as if he is holding something. The smell of disease fills Charlie's nostrils. The man's teeth are black, decayed stumps. He is trying to say something, but the words are mumbled, his tongue restricted by the pus oozing from his swollen gums.

'I'm sorry,' says Charlie, moving closer. 'I can't understand.' He takes another step, straining to make out the words.

'*Zhena*,' the man is saying. 'Wife. Please.' The guard shouts, and the man stumbles back whence he came.

Charlie can just make out the remnants of a Soviet star sewn on to his shabby uniform. He thinks of the Russians at Polyarnoe, proud and suspicious, wrapped in their warm clothes, checking his papers. He looks back at this creature, covered in filth, emaciated and shivering in the sleet. 'I'm so sorry,' he says. 'I wish I could help.'

The man starts to shout, and suddenly runs back past the guard, throwing himself at the barbed wire, his hand outstretched, a dirty scrap of paper in it. Immediately a shot rings out, that sound Charlie knows so well. The piece of paper floats to the ground, dissolving into a puddle. The body on the wire shudders and then hangs still, the uniform caught on the wire, the thin, bare feet swinging freely in the snow.

The compound for British and Commonwealth prisoners at *Stalag Luft* consists of fifteen long huts surrounded by barbed wire. Charlie has to wear a metal disc with his prisoner number and the name of the camp printed on it. The discs are easy to snap in half, so that if a prisoner dies, the Germans can send the other half back to his family. The officer processing him says, 'You must wear this at all times. If you are found without it – on the inside or the outside – you will be treated as a spy. We do to spies in our country what you do to spies in your country.' He draws his hand across his throat, laughing.

Charlie and Geordie are marched to their barracks and given two blankets. They are greeted by a crowd of men, all searching the new arrivals' faces for friends. They enter their hut and each choose a spare bed in the triple-deck wooden bunks. There is washing strung around the walls and between the chairs and tables. A lanky man with thinning hair greets Geordie. 'Welcome back,' he says. Then he addresses the other prisoners: 'I can vouch for this one,' he says.

'And I can vouch for this one,' says Geordie, pointing at Charlie. The men relax: it is not unusual for German spies to try to infiltrate the camp, so newcomers need to be approved.

The man sticks out his hand. 'Banks,' he says. 'Welcome to Kriegsville.' The hut is warm: there is a coal-burning stove in one corner. Banks rubs his hands together. 'Make the most of it,' he says. 'Coal's running low. We'll be without soon.'

Geordie introduces Charlie to more old friends. 'Barnes and John.' He waves to another man who is deep in a game of chess. 'And there's Spike. He's another Fleet Air Arm pilot.'

Spike holds up a hand in greeting. 'Just can't stay away, can you, Geordie?' he says, without looking up from his game.

Stalag Luft isn't the worst place to be sent – many of the Luftwaffe officers who run the camp are veterans and heroes of the First

World War, and not necessarily indoctrinated into Nazi thinking – but it is still a prisoner-of-war camp. Armed guards patrol the exterior and interior perimeters, between the barbed wire. Their dogs pad along beside them, panting, tongues lolling over sharp teeth. Along the fences are high watchtowers. The guards are allowed to shoot anyone who steps beyond the low warning wire that protects the first perimeter. At night, powerful search-lights send eerie shadows flickering through their huts. The air is punctuated by a cacophony of sharp barks. 'There goes another one,' says Geordie.

None of the men looks up, although Charlie knows that each of them is straining to hear what happens next. He watches John, whose head is always bent in concentration over a table: he is a talented artist who paints cartoons of camp life, soaking food labels to mix missing watercolours, using the end of a burnt stick like charcoal, even making paintbrushes out of his own hair. He is always busy illustrating something: the weekly newsletters they pass around the camp, posters for the plays, his head bent in concentration. But as soon as the hut has been locked for the night, he gets down to the more important business of forgery, painstakingly copying passes and stamps and signatures for documents. The electric bulb that flickers overhead is not enough to draw by, so the men make candles out of margarine, and set them around John while he dabs and scratches, squinting in the dim light.

'Goon up,' says Spike, who has been keeping an ear to the door, and John swiftly covers the documents with a programme for the next concert they are planning. A guard flings the door open and subjects the hut to another random search. The men gaze nonchalantly on, but their hearts are racing and their blood is up. These small risks are worth it, because Charlie soon learns that the overriding feeling of camp life is boredom. They are all bored of the endless inspections and roll calls and searches. Bored of standing around with nothing to do. Bored of the German propaganda. Of playing cricket and football, chess, checkers, and bridge.

The only other moments of excitement during the dull week are when the call comes for Red Cross parcels. These are packed with biscuits, tea, lard, flour, egg powder, condensed milk, cheese, salmon, prunes, jam, cigarettes, and dried fruit and vegetables. Of course, a letter from Olivia would be even better, but there has been no mail for Charlie since he sent news of his whereabouts. In the darker moments, he cannot help wondering whether that means that Jack made it, and now he, Charlie, is forgotten. He pictures their joyful reunion. He hopes that she is happy.

The Germans grow stricter and more agitated as the centre compound expands, filling with American prisoners-of-war. Supplies are low, and, with more men arriving every day, hunger is beginning to grip the camp. Some of the heftier inmates develop a stoop, as if pulled downwards by their shrinking stomachs. As well as softball and basketball, the Americans bring tales from outside. The hopeful news of an Allied victory is tempered by rumours of extermination camps, where prisoners are disappearing; of a mass breakout in another camp on the other side of Poland, where prisoners chose to risk the barbed wire and mines rather than stay in the camp. The men fear they could have to endure the same conditions before long.

Tension begins to rise. The German officers grow short-tempered. The Allies are pushing back. Three prisoners mount a daring escape. They have spent weeks digging a tunnel hidden beneath a vaulting horse. Day after day they have inched their way beneath the camp perimeter undetected, and now they are gone. John's forgeries are found, which leads to more roll calls, more searches.

Charlie is shouted awake. It is a night inspection. The prisoners stagger outside in the cold, shivering while they rub the sleep from their eyes. Inside, the guards search their beds, bundling sheets and blankets on to the floor and tearing the pictures from the walls. Mattresses are left sticking up, and washing strewn in a muddle on the ground. 'This!' says the guard, striding towards Charlie with a tin in his hand.

'It's just a candle.'

'It is *verboten*!'

'For goodness sakes.'

'To the cooler!'

The guard pushes Charlie into the punishment cell. It is a small room with a bed, a table, and a chair. He paces anxiously as far as the room will allow – about three steps lengthways and two widthways. There is a tiny barred window high up in the wall. It barely lets in any light. It is freezing cold.

He loses track of time. Seconds feel like hours. He is only able to stretch his legs properly and see daylight when he visits the toilet block with a guard. He is allowed no book, no cigarettes, nothing. His thoughts fracture. He tries to focus on something – anything. He recites poems he learnt at school. Hymns. He tries to remember Olivia's letters from those early days of the war, forming the words in his mind, then the pictures. He tries to mark the passing of days by scratching a line in the wall for each one. Sometimes Charlie wakes and for a moment he isn't sure where he is. He can feel the movement of the great ocean beneath his ship, but as his eyes adjust to the light, he realises he is still in the cooler. The days fragment into fleeting images: the downward spiral of a Spitfire, smoke spewing from its tail. The thumbs-up of a fellow pilot just before his plane bursts into flames. Thick smoke. The smell of fuel. The scream of a Stuka. The Hurricane's throttle as she banks, banks, banks. London burning. St Paul's Cathedral rising from the ashes. The Polish pilots at the airfield, laughing, hollow-eyed, strewn across the floor, exhausted, patting each other on the back, staring, crying. Sometimes his heart won't stop hammering. At other times, in moments of clear lucidity, in a state somewhere beyond sleep yet still awake, he is taken right back to the beach of his youth, resting his head on his mother's lap, and there is his father, fresh from a swim, rubbing at his hair with a towel, and they are all laughing as the cold drops of water splash on to their hot skin.

Eventually, Charlie is taken to a small interrogation room. A German officer enters. It is not one that Charlie recognises. 'Please. Sit,' he says, pointing at the table. But Charlie shakes his head. 'All right,' says the German. 'Your choice.' He is young, probably around the same age as Charlie. He closes the door carefully behind him, apparently without need for a translator. The action is furtive. Charlie braces himself for the interrogation that must surely follow.

'I am sorry if you are finding this hard. I will try to make it easier for you.' Charlie sees that the man has a lazy eye, as if it can't focus on anything. His English is remarkably good. He pauses to light a cigarette, before handing it over. Charlie is confused, the small kindness is unexpected.

The guard pulls an apple from his pocket and gives this to Charlie as well. It is not just the gift, but the touch of another human being after being so long in solitary confinement that brings a lump to his throat. 'Thank you,' he says, barely able to get the words out.

'It is no problem. Now please, sit. I would like to try to help.'

'Why?' says Charlie, wary of any attempt to break him with false friendliness.

'You were captured with a watch,' says the guard.

Charlie nods, his heart sinking. He waits for the shouting to start again.

'This watch is my watch.' The German lifts his sleeve and displays the watch proudly.

Charlie frowns, confused. He blinks at the German, who nods with encouragement. 'I gave this watch to a friend. I believe she must be your friend too.'

CHAPTER 28

Olivia

Olivia braces herself against the bumps of the train. She is writing to tell Jack that they have found his sister, but she is struggling to tell him about Betsy's pregnancy. She puts it off, deciding it is too important an issue to deal with in a letter. Besides, Charlie should be the first to hear. Deep down she knows it is a secret that has become tangled with the one that already lies in her empty womb.

The train stops and starts, pulling into sidings to let troop trains pass, avoiding bomb damage on the tracks. Betsy's moods change without warning. For the first part of the journey, she is excited and apprehensive, bouncing in her seat like a child while Olivia fills her in on some of Jack's recent life. There is a woman sharing their cramped compartment with her five young children, and they giggle as Betsy echoes Olivia, 'Africa? Russia? A training ship? How tall, did you say?' Happy endings are as rare as bananas these days. But soon she is withdrawn again, and now that the children have no stories to listen to, they also become fractious and tearful while their mother tries to console them with precious sweets.

Betsy reluctantly takes a corned beef sandwich from Olivia. 'If ever there was a reason not to have kids,' she says through her mouthful of food, staring at the agitated baby that is wriggling crossly on its mother's lap.

Olivia glares at her. 'Try and sleep,' she says. 'There's still a way to go.'

For a moment, Betsy looks like a child too, upset by Olivia's harsh tone. 'Did Jack ever talk about me?' she asks.

'Of course. Lots. I even tried to find you in Devon . . .'

'That place . . .' Betsy shudders.

'Do you want to talk about it . . .?'

But she has lost Betsy again; the girl is staring out of the window. Outside, in the corridor, there are soldiers sitting on the floor, their uniforms creased, the leather of their boots wrinkled with use, their rifles propped against the wall. They sit silently, their eyes unfocused, their heads bowed. Cool air rushes in through the open window, replacing the smell of smoke and men with the damp of peat and bracken. Rannoch Moor stretches for miles, patched with brown and green, and blotched with dark boulders. A shallow burn runs along near the railway line, the black pebbles of its bed glistening like obsidian. A herd of red deer hinds lift their heads and stare at the passing train. Their red-brown coats are the colour of the moor. They are so close that Olivia can see their wet noses and their large, surprised eyes. Their ears twitch and they don't take their gaze from the train for a second. And then suddenly they turn and run, flashes of pale rump as they leap and bound away, unaffected by war, impervious to the changing world.

This time they take the train all the way to the small railway station at Achnasheen. From there they get a lift with some young men who are on their way to the new Highland Fieldcraft Training Centre. It has been set up by the War Office: the people in charge are worried about the lack of decent officer material now that so many youngsters are coming up through the ranks. The centre is designed to teach boys to become men, and to increase the pool of officers ready for a final push against the Germans. Betsy switches from scowling teenager to charm itself. She knows how to make the boys grin, encouraging them with smiles and chatter.

The women share the seats in the front of the truck with the driver. The Highlands start to rise around them. Burns cascade down craggy hills into deep crevices; wet rock glimmers in green glens. The land is sparse one moment and covered in dark impenetrable woodland the next. A river appears and disappears on their left as the road twists and curls. Stunted trees teeter on huge boulders. The truck slows to let a ragged sheep cross. It trots nonchalantly in front of them, its wool hanging off in clumps, bracken dangling from its curly horns. Olivia takes in the lonely crofts tucked away in the folds of a hill here and there, feels the peace and space fill her body. Betsy remains unmoved, frowning as they pass the cosy harbour at Gairloch, where small boats bob like seabirds on the rippling water. A cluster of white houses with black roofs lies sprinkled along the shore. They climb a hilly pass, and then suddenly there is the loch opening out before them: the sight still makes Olivia catch her breath. 'Isn't it beautiful?' she says. Betsy shrugs and rests her head against the window.

The truck drops them at the wrought-iron gates to Taigh Mor, and Olivia breathes the familiar tang of peat and salt deep into her lungs. It conjures up a host of memories, not least of the first time she arrived here. She glimpses the stunted rump of a wren as it darts away into the tangled foliage. She hears the blackbirds calling to each other, and, away in the direction of the loch, the seagulls crying. Amid the great swathes of flowers tumbling over each other, Betsy appears thinner, her complexion more grey, her expression more sullen. Olivia reminds herself that the girl won't ever have seen the world in such technicolour – the bold purples and reds of rhododendrons, the creamy pink of magnolia.

They reach the end of the potholed drive, where the house looms above them. The door is, as always, standing open. 'We just walk in?' says Betsy. Olivia nods and encourages her to step inside. But Betsy won't come further than the cavernous hall. 'This place gives me the creeps,' she says.

Olivia goes alone to find her aunt, leaving Betsy to stare at the family portraits through the gloom. For once the grand drawing room is empty of people, and Aunt Nancy is alone. She seems smaller, older. The second lengthy war of her lifetime is taking its toll. She greets Olivia enthusiastically, bustling around her, kissing her cheek and then standing back to admire her niece. 'Where is she, then?' she asks. Olivia tips her head towards the hall. She has had no choice but to confide in Aunt Nancy. Her aunt sighs. 'I knew it would end in tears,' she says in her matter-of-fact way.

'What's that supposed to mean?'

'Would I be wrong in saying you drove him to it?'

'Yes, you would,' says Olivia. But inside she wonders whether her aunt is right. Well, she can make amends now, by looking after Betsy, and the child, keeping them safe.

'I'm sorry. That's unfair. It's just . . .' The pain is evident in her aunt's face.

'I know,' says Olivia, and she reaches out to her aunt, and the two women hug for a moment, each hoping the touch of another human being might fill the desolate space within.

Aunt Nancy releases Olivia. 'I've got to ask,' she says, 'how can we be sure it's his?'

'I've asked myself the same question. But she's Jack's sister. We have to believe her.'

Her aunt paces behind a sofa, leaning her hands on the back of it and looking at Olivia. 'I heard about your engagement,' she says.

Olivia tries to smile, but her family's refusal to accept Jack has hurt her more than she expected.

'You really love him, don't you?'

Olivia nods.

'Give them time,' says her aunt.

'They'll never accept him.'

'They might. The world is changing. Even I can see that now.'

'Tell me why it's so different for Charlie? Why is it all right to do what he's done? Yet I can't love the man I want to?'

Aunt Nancy sighs, shaking her head. She does not have the answers. 'You're too thin,' she says. 'Have you been looking after yourself?'

Olivia cannot hold her aunt's penetrating gaze. 'I'll be fine,' she says.

Aunt Nancy links her arm through Olivia's, steering her back into the hall. 'And what if Charlie doesn't return?' she asks.

'I'll look after them.' Even as the words leave her mouth, she knows that is what she wants to do.

Her aunt nods. If she is surprised, she doesn't show it.

Aunt Nancy introduces herself to Betsy, tries to set the girl at ease, but Betsy is wary. She shuffles from foot to foot, looking as if she might turn and flee at any moment.

Back out on the drive, she says, 'I didn't know whether to curtsey or not.'

Olivia laughs. 'Definitely not,' she says.

'But you said she's a lady.'

'She is, but not the sort you curtsey to.'

'Did Jack come here?'

'Yes. We met up here.'

Betsy scuffs her threadbare shoes into the ground, kicking marks into the peaty soil. 'It don't seem right . . .'

'Why not?'

'You're so . . . different.'

'It doesn't seem to matter.'

'And him meeting the likes of her.'

'I suppose he didn't really. He was here for such a short time . . .'

'Time was, he wouldn't have been able to leave a place like this without his pockets full.'

'We all change,' says Olivia.

'Don't I know it,' says Betsy. There is an edge to her voice.

Olivia leads the way along the track. The sun is beginning to burn the morning's dew off the leaves, turning it to vapour that thickens the air. A cacophony of birdsong echoes through the plants. Tall umbrellas of gunnera tower above them. On their left, the twisted trunks of the ancient rhododendrons line the steep banks, gnarled and impenetrable.

They break out into the sunshine. The bothy remains unchanged on the outside, its knobbly stone facade bright in the sunlight. The lawn that runs down to the beach is still neat and mossy, but the plants in the borders are overgrown, and the campanula has crept up the steps, threatening to break in to the front door.

Inside, Olivia blows the dust from the treasures on the windowsill, replacing them carefully. 'You're in there,' says Olivia, pointing to her old bedroom. 'I'm in here.' She will have to sleep in the sitting room.

She goes to light the stove in the kitchen and returns to find Betsy staring out of the sitting-room window, past the rock pools flashing and blinking in the sun, beyond the orange seaweed that pulses with the lazy rhythm of the water, to the firm lines of the ships that still criss-cross the loch. 'It's even more spectacular when they're not here,' says Olivia.

But Betsy is not looking at the ships. 'It's so . . . bare,' she says. 'Where's the houses? The people? The traffic?' She shudders, then turns to take her bag into the bedroom. As she creaks the door open, there is a horrible screeching noise, and she screams and staggers back into the hall as something swoops at her, a flash of black and white.

Olivia runs to help. Betsy is shaking, her eyes wide with fear. 'Don't worry,' says Olivia briskly. 'It's just a magpie. Must have come down the chimney. I'll open the window.'

'I'm not going back in there,' says Betsy. 'That's bad luck, for sure.'

They can see the magpie now. It is sitting on top of the mirror on the dressing table, its claws clicking against the wood, its eye a polished black marble reflecting the room back at them.

Olivia pushes past Betsy. 'It's fine,' she says, swallowing her own fear. 'Watch.' She opens the catch and waves her hand at the bird. One for sorrow, she is thinking. But whose sorrow? Hers or Betsy's? Charlie's or Jack's? The creature croaks, a raspy, throaty sound, as it spreads its wings and glides away into the fresh air, the light catching the blue sheen on its black wings.

Betsy is still reluctant to enter the room. 'I don't like it here,' she says. 'I want to go back.'

'Well you can't,' says Olivia. 'You've nowhere else to go.'

'It's all wrong. I need to get rid of it.' She is rubbing her hands over her stomach, as if she can erase its contents.

'You know that's impossible.'

'I could throw myself down the stairs.'

'There are no stairs here.'

'I could drink myself stupid.'

Rattled by the bird, and tired from the journey, Olivia finally snaps. 'Just stop it!' she says. 'I don't want to hear any more. Think about someone else for a change. We're only trying to help you. Think of all the people who never have children who have always wanted them. Think about the ones who lose children . . . Think about Charlie . . .'

'It's him that got me into this mess in the first place. If he hadn't gone away, I could have got it sorted earlier. I could have got money . . .'

'That's all it is to you, isn't it?' Olivia lets the rage overwhelm her for a moment. 'You don't care about Charlie. You don't care about the baby . . .'

'You don't know what it's like . . .'

'And you don't know anything about me.'

'I know it always turns out all right for the likes of you. I know that's what money gives you. A happy ending.'

'Even if you had all the money in the world, there would be no happy ending to this . . .'

'But it would never have had a beginning. If I'd come from a family like yours, I'd never have had to work for the likes of Stoog. I wish I never had. I wish it would all go away. I want a happy ending . . .' Betsy is almost hysterical. It is the

404

first time she has let her guard down. Free of make-up and surrounded by unfamiliar things, she is a child again. Olivia sighs. Perhaps it is true, and she will always have the safety blanket of her family, even if she disagrees with them.

She takes a deep breath, gathering her thoughts, the anger and the disappointment and the sadness, pushing them all back into the void. 'Look,' she says. 'If you're worried about support, please don't be. You've got me and Jack. Carl . . .'

But Betsy's defences are already back in place too. 'Me and Jack?' She is mimicking Olivia's voice, and her mouth has twisted into a snarl. 'Don't kid yourself. It'll never work.'

'Why do you say that?'

'You're not one of us.'

The last ounce of energy drains from Olivia's body. 'Just go and rest,' she says. 'I'll make us something to eat.'

Once again, Olivia sets about creating a home, sweeping away the dark, and welcoming in the light. Betsy continues to complain: her bed is uncomfortable, she is bored, there is nothing to do. It is too quiet, too cold. Olivia tries to take courage from the new growth in the world outside – the bulbs that have pushed their way up through the soil and are now in full flower, the birds carrying food for their young, the pale sunlight dappled through new leaves. She smiles as she remembers how much she once hated it here too. She looks at Betsy, this small and vulnerable creature with Jack's eyes, trapped like the magpie on their first night. Olivia resolves to have patience with her, for Jack, for Charlie.

Betsy is fiddling with a loose strand of cotton on the sofa, picking and pulling at it, rolling it between her fingers. There is a call from the front door, and Olivia recognises Ben Munro's voice. He greets her warmly, clasping her small hands in his strong gnarled ones. Olivia introduces Betsy, but the girl shrinks into the background. 'No matter,' says Ben. 'She'll come when she's ready.' He holds out a letter. 'This came for you. Mrs Mather thought you'd want it straight away.'

Olivia looks at the officious rectangle, with its typed address and red stamps. Her hands tremble as she tears it open. She senses Betsy coming closer, her breath warm on Olivia's shoulder. Ben reaches out a comforting hand.

Olivia reads aloud: '"The International Red Cross Committee can confirm that Lieutenant FitzHerbert is a prisoner-of-war. We do not know the address of the camp at which Lieutenant FitzHerbert is located, but he should be able to communicate this direct to you."'

There is a collective sigh, and Ben grins. 'That's good news, isn't it, lassie?'

'Thank God,' says Olivia, suddenly feeling less alone in the world.

'What does it mean?' says Betsy.

'He's alive. A prisoner-of-war, but they don't know in which camp yet. Hopefully we'll get a letter from him soon. Then we can write to him.'

'And tell him about the baby . . .'

'Exactly.' Olivia cannot help wondering whether the relief on Betsy's face is for Charlie or for herself.

Olivia leaves Betsy at the cottage and cycles to the naval base every day. She settles quickly back into her boarding officer duties, inspecting the merchant ships that come into the loch, delivering sailing orders, explaining route alterations, collecting confidential books, as well as checking guns, ammunition and armaments stores. She hears stories of the crossings thick with ice, of more ships disappearing, of U-boats and planes on the attack. Her torch picks out new lines etched by fear and exhaustion across once youthful faces. She clambers back down the swaying rope ladder, dwarfed by the great peeling hulls, pulling her duffle coat tighter and sinking into her white scarf. As she motors out with the mail officer and the ships chuck their fat sacks of mail down into their boat, she hopes one might contain a letter from Jack. But it doesn't, and to her shame, Olivia finds she is relieved, because it is as if her baby and Betsy's baby have become mixed up, and she does not know how to tell him about either now. She convinces herself that she will do it as soon as she has told Charlie. After all, it is his secret, and he should be given the chance to defend himself before the truth is out. Then she is flooded with guilt as she remembers that Charlie knows about her own baby, while Jack does not. The harder she tries to swim, the more she drowns.

There is no time to make new friends. When Olivia is not working, she is at the bothy with Betsy. No one asks about the girl: anyone who sees her – which is not often as she barely leaves the cottage – assumes she is one of Olivia's younger relations. But she could not be more different to them; she is a child, but one who whimpers in her sleep and hoards food under her bed. She can never stick at anything. Her mind leaps from one thing to the next. She paces around the small cottage, moving things, picking at things, balancing a teaspoon on a cup, cracking her knuckles, or she lies despondently on the sofa, staring out across the loch.

'When will we know where he is?' says Betsy, rearranging the cushions, stretching herself out flat, her hands resting on her growing belly.

'Soon, I hope.'

'And you'll tell him to do the right thing?'

'Charlie always does the right thing.'

'You haven't told Jack yet, have you?'

Olivia shakes her head, feels the guilt needle at her again.

'Good,' says Betsy. 'He'll probably kill Charlie. Or me. Definitely Stoog.'

'I'm sure he'll understand.'

'Are you really sure, though?'

And Betsy looks at her with eyes hard as flint, and of course, Olivia isn't sure; she has no idea how Jack will react. All she can do is pray that Charlie writes soon, and that he will have some idea how to sort the whole mess out.

Betsy sighs dramatically and wriggles into another position. 'I can't see what it is you like about this place.'

'If you'd only go out and explore, then you'd discover for yourself.'

Betsy points at her stomach. 'I don't think so.'

Olivia sighs. 'You're having a baby; you're not an invalid.'

'You try lumping this about. Anyway, I don't want people seeing me. I'm ugly and fat.'

'It'll get worse if you don't move around.'

But there is nothing that Olivia can say to persuade Betsy to go out of sight of the bothy, not even a promise of cake with Mrs Mac. In fact, Betsy still regards the locals with suspicion, complaining that she can't understand what they're saying. Olivia wonders if it reminds her of being evacuated – of the Roses, who poked and prodded and checked her for lice. Even when Olivia tries to get her to help on the steps of the bothy, the girl refuses. She wrinkles her nose at the rotting mackerel heads Olivia uses as bait in the creel, and she won't go near a catch – scared of the claws of a large orange crab pinching at thin air, or the small, pink, squat lobsters, fat pincers flailing.

But even though she won't wander, the hours spent lounging on the overgrown lawn in the early summer sunshine set a healthy hue to Betsy's complexion, and her face begins to lose some of its hardness.

At last a letter arrives from Charlie with details of the camp he's in. Olivia is so relieved that she wastes no time in finding a pen and paper. 'Come on,' she says, patting the table. 'A letter will be such a boost for him.'

'I can't,' says Betsy.

'Of course you can.'

'I mean, I can't.' Betsy looks at her hands.

'Oh. I see. How about you tell me what to write, then?'

'Won't you just do it for me?'

'Just try. Once you start . . .'

But Betsy is frustrated, storming from the room. 'Stop telling me what to do,' she says. 'I'm not a kid.' Then she slams the door to her bedroom as though she is.

So Olivia writes to Charlie, once a week, in the correct manner, clearly written on no more than two sides of normal writing paper, as stated by the regulations for letters to prisoners-of-war. She tells him about Betsy and the baby. She tells him that whatever happens, she will make sure the baby is all right. And then she writes about Scotland, because she doesn't know what else to say, and it's almost as if she can make it better – as if she can turn back the clock – by telling him about the arctic terns returning to breed, their rich black caps and blood-red beaks in stark contrast to their elegant streamlined tails, like pale swallows of the sea. She tells him about the dolphin that managed to get into the loch, despite the defences, bursting out of the sea in a shower of glistening water to the delight of the weary sailors. She tells him about the sleek black-and-white razorbills diving for sprats and herring to feed their chicks, so hard to tell apart from the guillemots if it weren't for their stumpy beaks with the white line like trickled paint. And each time she writes, she thinks now is the time to write to Jack too, and tell him. But however hard she tries, she simply cannot: the words will not flow from her mind or her hand as they do to Charlie. And so she does not, and every day her heart grows a little heavier.

Betsy goes into labour a couple of weeks earlier than expected. Olivia sends for Aunt Nancy and a medic, and they deliver it, small and pink and screaming, into a world still at war. He is a boy. Olivia cannot bear to hold him in her arms; she feels it would be betraying her own poor dead baby. She gazes at Betsy, willing her to love the child with all her heart, amazed that Betsy seems so disinterested. Betsy calls him Alfred, after her father. Alfie nuzzles into her child's body, all scrunched and wrinkled. Olivia feels a protective ache surge through her. She wishes Charlie could be here to see. She still has not heard back from him. She wonders whether he has received any of her letters. Perhaps he has been moved on. Or worse.

Alfie is the opposite of his mother, content to gurgle in the drawer they have made up for him, or to lie on a blanket on the lawn, gazing at the slow-moving clouds. But even the best babies can be unsettled, and Olivia persuades Betsy at last that a change of scenery will be good for the child, giving him some distraction, and that Betsy will regain some of her strength and her figure if she uses her muscles a bit more.

They start near the cottage, wandering the shoreline, Alfie swaddled in a blanket and barely visible against Betsy's chest. Around the bothy, the summer flowers are blossoming: blue irises with delicate hearts of gold, fragrant lavender and thyme, white daisies twinkling like stars. It is a riot of scent and colour, and butterflies and bees of all shapes and sizes bumble and float over the top. Olivia hopes Betsy will soften. She shows her the sticky fronds of sea anemones in a rock pool, and the way a petrel skims low over stormy water. Betsy appears untouched, until one afternoon, when she points at three cormorants on a rock. They are standing in the sun, wings outstretched. 'It's like the dirty old men in the park,' she says. 'Showing us their bits and pieces.' She cackles to herself, and Olivia realises it's the first time she has heard Betsy laugh properly, a happy song from a forgotten part of her soul.

She takes Betsy and Alfie to Loch Maree, the magical loch dotted with wooded islands that lies above Loch Ewe. Alfie gurgles on the banks, while dippers hop and dive from the rock around them. On the River Ewe, Olivia shows Betsy how to catch wild brown trout, spotted and supple and tinged a peaty colour, but Betsy is most likely to return the fish, watching them dissolve back into the yellowy-brown depths of their watery home. Sometimes she persuades the girl to paddle in deeper pools, laughing as they balance on the slippery stones. Once, Betsy brings Alfie into the water, and, in contrast to the baby's soft pink skin, Olivia notices that Betsy's is turning brown as hazelnuts and her muscles as hard. In the wider parts of the river, the salmon sometimes leap out of the water, twisting and turning in the air like silvery dancers.

Some of Betsy's wildness has gone. In the early evenings she rests with Alfie on the sofa in the same place that her brother once slept, her face soft like a little girl's, and Olivia thinks that maybe everything is going to be all right after all. But then she remembers that she still has not told Jack, and the lie tightens its icy claw. And still Charlie does not write.

Olivia and Betsy are on a rare visit to Aunt Nancy. While they are playing with Alfie on the intricately patterned carpet, a group of candidates from the Highland Fieldcraft Training Centre are ushered into the drawing room by the company commander. Olivia stays where she is on the floor, but Betsy stands, smoothing her hair and placing herself delicately on the arm of a sofa.

The group has just finished their ten-week course and are heading to the Aultbea Hotel for a congratulatory meal. But first, they have been sent to apologise to Aunt Nancy for using a thunderflash to blow some of her salmon out of the water to eat.

The young men gather in the doorway, looking more like chastised schoolchildren than the officers they are about to become. One of them, a spotty soldier with tousled hair, says, 'We're sorry, Lady McPherson. We didn't realise it would be so effective.'

'That's not really the point, is it?' she says. 'One fish or six: it's theft, and theft is wrong.'

'Yes, Lady McPherson.'

'Thank you for being so understanding,' says the company commander.

Aunt Nancy nods.

'It was the Canadians' fault,' says a voice from the back. 'They showed us how to do it.' Some of the men giggle, and Betsy joins them from the sofa, hiding her smile behind her hand, her eyes shining over the top.

Aunt Nancy is not amused however. 'You can't blame

411

anyone else for your actions,' she says. 'You boys are about to become leaders of men. This is not a laughing matter.'

The soldiers start to talk over each other, but the company commander ushers them out of the room before returning to offer more profuse apologies about how the boys are in such high spirits after finishing the intensive course. Betsy joins the recruits in the hall outside, listening to their tales of exhausting marches and jumping off moving lorries, using cotton grass to dress wounds, abseiling and rock climbing through hailstorms, climbing trees, crawling through the snow, shinning along ropes, passing ammunition across a burn in spate using a tree trunk. Betsy hangs on their every sentence, encouraging them with gasps and murmurs. The young men assume that Alfie belongs to Olivia, even though Olivia can still barely bring herself to touch him. Betsy does nothing to shatter the illusion. Olivia is just glad that the girl seems finally to be enjoying herself.

It is the middle of the night. Pitch black. Alfie won't stop crying. It is very unlike him. Olivia lies on the sofa, listening to the cries, waiting for Betsy to calm him, but the noise grows more insistent. Olivia gets up, wrapping a blanket around her shoulders. She lights a candle and knocks on Betsy's door. There is no answer, apart from Alfie's furious cries. She pushes open the door and pads into the room. The shadows stretch and contort around her until she picks out the drawer with Alfie in it. By now, he is a bawling mass of scrunched-up fury. He has wriggled free from his blanket, and his little pink legs are kicking wildly in the air. Betsy's bed is empty, the rumpled sheets cold. Olivia hesitates for a moment. She has tried so hard to keep her distance from Alfie – not able to trust that she won't be swamped by sadness if she touches him. But she cannot stand and listen to his panicky hiccups any longer. She stoops to gather him into her arms, expecting the cloud of despair to descend, but instead she feels nothing but warmth as she lifts his squirming body.

Alfie tucks himself into her shoulder, and she soothes him, stroking his soft, warm head and moving around, humming a lullaby. He is calm within minutes, his snuffly breathing regular, and his body limp. Olivia checks the wardrobe, suddenly worried that Betsy may have run. But her clothes are still there. She can't have gone far.

Olivia carries Alfie outside, on to the steps. There is no sign of Betsy there either. She stands for a while, relishing the sensation of Alfie's body curled against hers, his tiny legs dangling, his head heavy with sleep. The night sky is peppered with stars, the only sound the rush of water, and, in the distance, the clank of ships at anchor.

When Betsy eventually appears, the sun is beginning to rise in the pale morning sky. The click of the door wakes Olivia from her light sleep. Alfie is still nestled into her shoulder. 'Where have you been?' she asks.

'Nowhere,' says Betsy. Her eyes are sparkling, and a smile plays on her lips.

'Alfie was crying,' says Olivia, acknowledging internally that this must be what Betsy looks like when she's truly happy.

'He looks all right now.'

'Who were you with?'

'What's it to you? You're not my mother.' She is suddenly the Betsy of old: flinty and defiant.

'But you're Alfie's mother. And he needs you.'

'He had you . . .'

'How often have you done this?'

'This is the first time.'

'You need to be careful . . . or you'll end up with another baby.'

Betsy laughs, a hollow sound. 'You think that's what I've been doing? Once a tart, always a tart?'

'That's not what I said.'

'You with your perfect manners and your never doing anything wrong . . .'

'And what about Charlie?'

'You're such a bleeding hypocrite.'

'What's that supposed to mean?'

'It's all Charlie this and Charlie that . . .'

'Charlie's been a good friend to me . . .'

'Well he's with me now,' says Betsy, glaring back at her, black eyes flashing. 'And you're meant to be with my brother.'

'I am with your brother.'

'I bet you haven't told him about Alfie yet.'

'I thought you didn't want me to.'

'That don't make it right. You should have told him. You should have been honest with him from the start.'

'I wanted to tell him face to face . . .'

'Or you're trying to save your Charlie's skin . . .'

'I'll tell him in my next letter,' she says.

'Let's hope for your sakes it's not too late by then,' says Betsy, grabbing Alfie as she retreats to her bedroom, leaving Olivia all alone.

Olivia doesn't mention the events of that night again, but she doesn't tell Jack either. Betsy withdraws once more. She spends her days in and near the cottage, playing with Alfie on the steps or staring into the distance. She won't let Olivia help with the child, and Olivia is relieved in a way, as she hopes it means Betsy is feeling protective of him. Betsy remains aloof, until one autumn morning, when the flocks of wood-cock begin to arrive from Russia and Finland. Olivia has a spare day to go stalking, and she is surprised when Betsy asks to come with her. Olivia accepts the gesture – happy that Betsy is trying to make amends.

They leave Alfie with Aunt Nancy and Clarkson. It is the first time Betsy has been free of the baby during the day. It is also the first time she has been up into the hills. It is a perfect autumn day. They collect Thistle from the farm. Betsy bonds with the pony, stroking his grey neck, whispering in his ear.

'You like ponies?' Olivia asks.

'Reminds me of the rag-and-bone man,' says Betsy. 'He had a stocky pony like this. They used to call on us before the war. Me and Jack would feed it sugar lumps if we had some, or bring a bucket of water on a hot day, while my mum looked for empty jars and rabbit skins and bones if we had any left from Sunday dinner.' She stops for a moment. 'My mum never let us go without,' she says.

'Jack told me a bit about her. She sounds a remarkable person.'

Betsy nods, but her mouth is a thin line again, as if she won't allow more thoughts to spill out.

'Why don't you lead him?' says Olivia, handing her the rope, and Betsy seems pleased with the responsibility.

They climb to the rowan pool and leave Thistle there. Then they climb some more, stopping to take in the high peaks of hills stretching away around them, above troughs filled with liquid silver. Behind them lies the loch, and beyond that the sea. In the distance the Hebrides are wreathed in tendrils of white cloud. A ptarmigan croaks among the heather, easy to spot as the beginning of its winter plumage turns it into a splodge of mottled white and brown.

They rest and eat sandwiches, and then continue, until eventually Olivia spies a suitable stag. She motions to Betsy to drop to the ground and follow, inching slowly forward, head down. Prickly fronds of heather scratch at her chin, up her nostrils. She slides the rifle out and across the ground, jamming it into her shoulder. She uses her bag to rest the barrel on. The rifle is steady. She pulls herself up and forward a little. When she is happy that everything is in place, she slowly lifts her face.

Her heartbeat slows. Time slows. She forgets secrets and pain. The stillness fills her soul. She lines the shot up on the beast's shoulder. She squeezes the trigger. There is a sound like a cable wire snapping as the bullet zips from the rifle and across the lichen-covered rocks, and the stag crumples to the ground.

Olivia stands, reloads the gun. She is ready to give chase if the deer moves. But it doesn't. It is a clear and true shot.

She relaxes. 'He's down.'

Betsy kneels behind her and says nothing.

Up close, the stag is large. A warm yet lifeless body of fur. That's all it takes. One shot to stop a heart beating. To take a life. Betsy and Olivia watch the deep brown stain grow where the blood is soaking away into the ground. Its strong, wild smell fills their nostrils. Betsy bends to stroke the creature's neck, still warm with life. 'I'm glad I didn't get rid of him,' she says.

'Alfie?'

Betsy nods.

'I am too.'

Then Betsy stands and moves away. 'Doesn't mean I want to keep him, though.'

'But you've been so good with him . . .'

'But I don't want to be a mother. I don't want to boil bones in a saucepan and pretend it's soup. I don't want to go without so he can have new clothes . . .'

'You won't have to. Jack and I can help . . .'

'You'd take my baby as well as my brother . . .?'

'That's not what I meant . . .'

'I'm going to go and get the pony.'

Betsy clambers away down the hillside.

Olivia kneels and pulls the stag's head back, manoeuvring the heavy carcass so that it is pointing slightly downhill. She checks its hooves, its legs, its tail for signs of illness. She takes out her knife. She feels for the centre of the chest, warm and muscly. She sticks her knife into the thick hide, pulls it back and forth to make the hole larger. A thick river of blood pulses out, soaking into the bracken and heather. She sticks her hand in, feeling for the white sinewy strand of the oesophagus. She scrapes it clean, then cuts and ties it. With a grunt, she rolls the beast over and uses her fingers to search for the line that marks the centre of its belly. She carefully slices into the skin.

416

She reaches inside with both hands to pull out the rumen, a balloon-like sack of bulging sinews and innards. It is also warm and lumpy, and she works it out of the beast's stomach, being careful not to pierce it.

By the time she has separated the spleen from the belly and tied the oesophagus, Betsy is returning with Thistle. Olivia does not show her relief. Instead, she gently continues to work the entire inside of the hind outside. She moves the guts away from the beast, and then slices the rumen open so that its murky green-yellow contents spread out across the heather.

'There,' she says.

'It's disgusting,' says Betsy.

'It's got to be done,' says Olivia. 'We'd never get it home otherwise.'

Betsy helps Olivia lift the stag on to the back of the pony. When the deer is secure, they start the descent. It has been a long day and they are both exhausted. There is blood spattered across Olivia's clothes, and a streak has dried to a dark rusty colour on her face.

They are traipsing back past the rowan pool when Betsy starts to speak. Her voice is small and tight, and Olivia has to strain to hear. 'Do you think Jack would choose you or me?' she says.

Olivia stops, pulling on Thistle, who tugs his head away from her, annoyed that the food and new bed of straw that are waiting for him are no longer getting closer. 'Don't be silly,' says Olivia. 'He's not going to have to choose between us.' She thinks guiltily of their engagement.

Betsy refuses to meet her eyes. 'He is. You and me, we don't exist in the same world . . .'

'Of course we do. We're here now, together . . .'

Betsy snorts derisively. 'That's not what I mean. Our lives are upside-down. This is what you people call "war spirit". But when the war's over, things'll go back to the way they were. I'll be treated like nothing more than one of those maidservants your kind used to keep.'

'Things have changed . . . Lots of people will carry on looking after themselves when this is over.'

'You mean people like you?'

'I intend to carry on working . . .'

'Then who's going to look after my brother? Have his tea on the table? His clothes clean and pressed?'

'We'll work it out . . .'

'And what of me and Alfie? Would we live there too?'

Thistle nudges Olivia impatiently, yanking at her arm.

'Let's see what happens with Charlie . . .'

'Charlie's not interested. He's never bothered to write. Either he's dead, or he doesn't want to know.'

'We don't know that. Please stop worrying. We'll work something out . . .'

But Betsy is already beginning to move on. Behind her, Olivia notices that the rowan leaves that were orange and gold are now beginning to wither and fall, leaving only the blood-red berries on their naked branches.

Olivia hauls the tin bath in front of the fire in the sitting room. She leaves Betsy in charge of boiling up the water. It always takes for ever, and she is due to deliver some instructions to a waiting convoy. When she returns, the pan has almost boiled dry. She curses. Betsy must have fallen asleep. Olivia shovels more coal into the stove. There is no sign of Betsy in the kitchen. Olivia puts her head around the door to the sitting room, expecting to see Betsy and Alfie asleep on the sofa together. But there is no sign of either of them there, only the dry bath and the embers of the little fire. She runs to the bedroom, calling Betsy's and Alfie's names, but the sound echoes through the empty cottage. The wardrobe is bare. Alfie's drawer is a silent hole. Betsy's bag is gone. She was not trying to make amends. She was saying goodbye.

CHAPTER 29

Charlie

After meeting Hans, the next few days of solitary are not so bad for Charlie. The thin, watery soup is supplemented with chewy meat; once a wrinkled apple appears that tastes of England in the autumn, and there are a couple of cigarettes and some matches. Every week there are coincidences in the camps – men meeting who were at school together – even an American who recognises a German guard as the butcher from his village – but the fact that this is a German who has been to Scotland – and met Olivia . . . It is astonishing. He allows the images of her and of Taigh Mor to flood his mind, replacing the horrors that have lurked there.

Hans insists he interview the prisoner twice a day, on the pretence he is battering him for information. Charlie begins to look forward to their meetings. The German has been well-educated, and the two men have much in common. Sitting in the bland interrogation cell, sharing a cigarette with Hans, Charlie likes to imagine they are old friends having a drink in the pub back home.

Hans likes to talk about his future architect's practice, which he plans to set up to help rebuild the damage of the last years. Charlie jokes that he will run the London office, since there will be strong demand in both countries for construction projects. They both agree that the sooner they leave the camp, the better.

'I suppose we must focus on the good side of being here,' says Hans. 'At least I won't get shot down again by one of your men . . .'

'Nor I by one of yours . . .'

'I was lucky I met Olivia. You were not so lucky that you met Hauptmann Richter.'

Charlie laughs and stubs out his cigarette. 'I suppose we're all doing a job.'

Hans is serious again. 'I cannot do my job any more.'

'Your eye?'

Hans nods, downcast. 'It has not improved in these last two years. This is why I am stuck here in the camp.'

'I'll take you up. After the war.'

'That would be a very good thing.'

They grin at each other, each imagining life after the war. It is all either of them has to look forward to now that their fighting days are over.

'I can't imagine never being able to fly again,' says Charlie.

'Why did you choose to be a pilot?'

'My father. He took me up before I could walk. He was in the Royal Naval Air Service, but carried on flying after the war. He got the bug.'

'He was a hero of your country?'

Charlie nods. 'He flew a Sopwith Camel over the trenches.'

'Ah. The Sopwith Camel. Very effective against us on the Western Front.'

'Bloody nightmare to fly, apparently. They used to say it gave you the choice between a wooden cross, the Red Cross, or the Victoria Cross . . .'

'You should try flying an Arado 66, one of our training planes . . .'

'I love a go in anything.'

'I forgot you British are old-fashioned.'

'What do you mean by that?'

'You will not embrace technology. To think you enjoyed flying that bi-plane . . .'

'The Fairey Swordfish is a dream. The perfect plane . . .'

'The son of a man who flew the Sopwith Camel would say that.'

They are both relaxed, leaning back in their chairs, blowing smoke into the space above their heads.

'You know they flew without parachutes?' says Charlie.

'That would have been the end of both of us.' They both laugh.

'I'm glad you survived,' says Charlie.

'And I you.'

'I couldn't believe it when Olivia told me she had saved a German. I thought it was the most idiotic and dangerous thing I had ever heard . . .'

'I understand. We are told to hate each other. Otherwise how would we be able to murder each other?'

'I don't like to think about how many lives I'm responsible for.' An image of the stricken German battleship frothing in circles flashes in his mind.

Hans shrugs. 'It is war. You have to do what you have to do.'

'Do you have conchies in Germany?'

'Conchies?'

'Conscientious objectors. People who take a stand against fighting?'

'Oh no. This is not allowed in my country. You will disappear. They have turned us against each other. They use children to spy on their parents. My brother is only fifteen, and they are making him fly a bomber in his training for the *Hitlerjugend*. How can they make him do this? A child? What does he know of war?'

'Perhaps he's trying to be like his big brother?'

'We are not allowed to be like anyone but the ideal . . .'

'What made you choose the Luftwaffe?'

'I like to see the world mapped out beneath me. I like to see how we choose to build our homes next to a river or in the shelter of a mountain. Scatterings of humans across the

421

land. I like to imagine how these few houses will grow into a village or a town.'

'I know what you mean. But it's not just that for me . . . It's the feeling it gives me . . .'

'Freedom?'

'That. And – strangely – grounding. It reminds me of my father. Sitting in that cockpit is my earliest memory.'

'My father is the opposite. He is under the sea.'

'U-boats?'

Hans nods. 'And is your father fighting in this war?'

'No. He died when I was six. Car crash. With my mother.'

'I am so sorry. That is very sad. After all that fighting. Not to have a chance to appreciate the peace.'

They are silent for a moment. Then Hans peers at Charlie and says, 'You know, he would have been very proud to see his son now.' And Charlie is embarrassed to feel tears prick at his eyes.

One day, the greatest joy of all: Hans passes Charlie a handful of letters. 'I am sorry,' he says. 'It seems the guards have been keeping them from you for some time. Extra punishment. I will leave you to enjoy them alone.'

Charlie lays the envelopes out on the table, touching them as if they are rare treasures. He removes each letter slowly, dividing them into date order, savouring the sight of Olivia's spidery writing spilling out of the envelopes. He begins to read.

But the letters do not bring joy. Charlie does not take in the depictions of the grey seals singing their mournful song in the early evening near his secret beach. Or how the forget-me-nots have showered the garden with pale blue. Instead he reads of the terrible news of Betsy's pregnancy. He reads it over and over, but the words do not change. He is stunned and horrified and embarrassed. He cannot see how he will ever be able to face anyone again. He remembers that night, of fumbling gratification, so exhilarating at the time, so degrading now.

Self-hatred floods his body. His hands shake. He cannot

422

read the letters again. He shoves them to one side, clutching at them, crumpling them into a messy pile. He feels his heart burn. When Hans returns, his face folds in concern. He bends over Charlie, placing a hand on Charlie's shoulder. 'What is it? What has happened? It is bad news? Has something happened to Olivia?'

Charlie shakes his head. He cannot speak.

'May I?'

Hans touches the letters, but Charlie slaps his hand away. 'No!' Hans reels back. It is the first disagreement they have had. Charlie gathers the letters into his chest, holding them there like something that might explode at any moment. 'Take me back,' he says, without meeting Hans's eyes. 'I need to go back to the cooler. I want to go back.'

That night Charlie's nightmares return. He is all alone, as he was when he was torn from his squadron by Captain Pearce and sent to help the RAF. In the tiny cell, he can smell the aviation fuel dripping from damaged planes. See their dusty, marked frames patched together, littering the runway wherever they had been abandoned by their exhausted pilots. He closes his eyes and sees the RAF pilots, shattered and hopeless after weeks of bombardment and flying without a break. Men who fell asleep where they ate, their shoulders in a half-eaten plate of food, or huddled against the walls of the hangars, or falling unconscious to the runway before their planes had taxied to a stop. Their faces tell of the loss of countless friends; their eyes are bottomless pits, like the one he falls into every time he tries to sleep.

His face twitches, an uncontrollable spasm that happens every few minutes. His eyes flicker open. He is back in the cooler, the walls pressing in on him. He feels disabled. Emasculated. He is a pilot without a squadron. He is a pilot without a plane. He is worse than that. He is a prisoner without a future.

The letters sit in an accusing pile, a testament to his shame

423

and degradation. How can he ever hold his head high and look anyone in the eye again? He does not want the bastard child of a prostitute. He disgusts himself. Now there will be another child like him growing up without a father. The crumple of letters is luminous in the thin light. He shouts until his throat is sore. He punches the wall, and his knuckles bleed. He bashes his shoulder against the bed frame, feels the old injury tear and burn. He throws the letters to the floor, stamps on them, shreds them. He sets fire to the torn pieces of paper, watches his future burn brightly for a second before smouldering to a dribble of smoke.

Hans tries to talk to him, but Charlie will not tell him what has happened. How could he tell this gentle man what he has done? How can he admit that his enemy is a better man than he is? He makes a promise. As soon as he makes it, he feels relief. Whatever happens, he will not return. He will find work in Germany. In France. But he will never go back to England.

'Tell me about the Hurricanes,' says Hans. Charlie knows the German is trying to get him to remember the good things. To find the peace he used to find in the cockpit. But he cannot. However hard he tries. 'This is more like a real plane than those Swordfish? More responsive?' Hans presses him.

Charlie nods. The Hurricanes were more powerful than his beloved Swordfish. With their metal wings, they could dive faster; they could turn better than a Spitfire, particularly at low altitude. He tries to imagine himself back in the single cockpit, to feel the power as the plane lifts into the air. But instead he remembers the Messerschmidts, buzzing angrily, and sees the white trails of tracer fire fizzling through the air like a tangle of ribbons. And he hears the dreaded Stuka dive bombers flinging themselves out of the sky, their stubby legs sticking out beneath them, their sirens screeching. Smoke billows out of somewhere, and, in the flash of yellow flame, he can't tell whether someone is firing or someone is on fire and all the time his finger is on the button firing back. He feels the knock in the tail as he's hit, and he drops her into a corkscrew dive. She plummets down, away from the planes, away from the Polish squadron, and where is Mole? Gone. He is alone. He buries his twitching face in his clammy hands. Even the cockpit is no longer his sanctuary: he will never escape the shame.

In the darkness Charlie thinks about his parents, so full of hope for their only child; he thinks of Olivia, so brave over her pregnancy; he thinks of Jack, so lucky to have Olivia's love and respect – and so much more deserving than he will ever be. He can never go back, but perhaps he can salvage something by trying to be the hero he has so far failed to be. He scratches another line into the wall and blows the burnt remains of Olivia's letters into the dust.

Charlie is returned to his hut. Hans continues to bring news, visiting Charlie whenever he can. The men shutter the windows so that the other guards can't see. Sometimes Hans brings extra provisions – toothpaste, matches. On one occasion, he pulls a dead rabbit from inside his trousers. More importantly, he helps with information about timetables and official documents for the forgers to copy.

The men are busy planning their biggest break-out yet. Banks has come up with the idea to dig not one, but three long tunnels at the same time, the idea being that the Germans might find one, but wouldn't expect there to be three. It is a highly ambitious plan, and will take months to complete. 'We're going to get two hundred of you out,' says Banks. 'Although we'll need more than three times that to help with the construction.' There is no shortage of volunteers: one man's victory would be enough for all of them.

Life at the camp becomes more focused. The prisoners need to be vigilant to spot the spies before the Germans spot them. Charlie keeps lookout. Mattresses, pillows, and sheets disappear to line the tunnels. Forks and spoons are used to dig.

Water carriers and cans remove the sand and soil. Ropes and electric cable are stolen to pull trolleys. The strange-smelling soil is dispersed around the camp, hidden in towels, washing, mugs. Charlie shuffles across the dusty ground, dribbling sand from his bulging trousers. Beds collapse because their wooden planks have been used to prop up the tunnels. The German ferrets search for telltale yellow sand, or lie beneath the huts, eavesdropping on the prisoners: they know the men are up to something, but they cannot discover what.

Hans tells the prisoners to keep a lookout for signs that the Allies are advancing. 'If the Führer is struggling,' he says, 'he will recall as many men as possible to fight. If that happens, stock up on as much food as you can, for you may be moved on too.'

Charlie is happy to talk to Hans when they are among the other men, but he does his best to avoid a one-to-one. He does not want to tell the German what he has learnt. He tries to bury the shame deep by taking the most dangerous tasks for himself, sneaking through the shadows to raid the German food supplies, spying on the guards, eavesdropping beneath their barracks' windows, trying to glean any information about what they plan, what they know.

The months pass. The men dig, hiding more soil in the theatre, the library, across the hockey pitch, anywhere that has not already been filled. John copies and duplicates passes and documents, scratching away through the night. Finally, the time is right. The sky is inky black: there is no moon or stars. The snow lies thick on the ground outside the camp. The only sounds are the patrol dogs panting, pulling on their chains, and hundreds of men's hearts racing. Time scrapes slowly by. A door is frozen stuck. A tunnel collapses. Less than one hundred men manage to barge and scrape their way out before the alert is sounded – a shrill whistle followed by the searchlights snapping on and the guards shouting and stomping through the compound, trying to discover the entrance to the tunnels. Charlie lies in wait for the guards, tripping them over, trying to divert them, until he is dragged by the hair and smashed in the side of the head by a rifle butt. He sprawls on the ground, feels the dirt crunch between his teeth. He prays that some of the men will have got away, beyond the camp to their trains, or anywhere safe.

From where he lies, he can see there are guards in the woods now, lights flickering among the trees, dogs barking. They have found the exits, marked by footsteps in the snow. There are guards in the tunnels. Men who were halfway out scrabble, panting, back into the hut, covered in sand and dust. The guards shout and prod him with their rifles again. Charlie is dragged back to the cooler. He does not care. He scratches another line, another day into the wall with a stone.

In the end, seventy-six men make it out, but seventy-three of those are recaptured. After all that effort, all that digging and shoring up tunnels and pumping in fresh air and removing sand and hiding from the guards and forging and pretending. For three men. But each of them would do it again.

Usually, the escapees are brought back, and the whole charade starts again. But not this time. This time, Hitler wants to make an example, not just of the prisoners, but of the German architect who designed the camp, the security guards, and the duty guards. He sends his feared Gestapo, who come tramping in with their dark shiny boots, their swastika armbands, and their cold eyes. Charlie spits on the ground as they pass, but they do not even look at him. They march on, to where the captured men have been held, to the cooler that Charlie knows so well.

Charlie never sees Geordie again; his tenth attempt is his last, but not in the way he had hoped: he is executed, along with forty-nine others – men from Britain, America, Canada, Poland, South Africa, Lithuania, New Zealand, Australia, and Norway, men who are fathers, brothers, sons and lovers – the Gestapo are not picky. One by one they fall, 'shot while trying to escape'.

*

The men are fashioning black armbands from anything they can find – socks, paper, bedding – to wear in memory of their fallen brothers. A new guard who they do not recognise enters the room. The prisoners turn their backs, refusing to look at him.

'You are to pack your things,' he says. 'Take only whatever you can carry. You' – he prods John in the back with his rifle until he turns to face the German – 'you tell them they must pack. We leave soon.'

'Where are we going?' says John.

'That will be decided by us.'

'When?'

'You will be ready.'

Charlie also turns to look at the guard. 'Where is Hans?' he asks.

'Oberleutnant Schafer is a traitor,' says the guard.

'What's that supposed to mean?'

'Oberleutnant Schafer is to be executed.'

Charlie steps towards the guard, his face drained of colour. 'I don't understand.'

'He is to be killed. For his part in helping you prisoners. The Gestapo do not tolerate such behaviour.'

'You bastards,' says Charlie, and everyone is taken by surprise as he launches himself at the guard. The men turn and try to pull him back, but Charlie is so full of rage that he shakes them off and grabs hold of the German, knocking off his cap and grasping a handful of his hair so that the German begins to shout. But Charlie is shouting too: 'How could you let that happen? He was a decent man. He did nothing wrong but have a bit of compassion. You utter bastard . . .'

Already there are more guards bursting through the door. Charlie lashes out at each of them, shying away from their hands, tearing the makeshift curtains down, ripping the sheets from the bunks, kicking over the table, throwing the food across the floor, swinging the chairs across the room, until four guards have hold of him and haul him kicking and screaming across the courtyard, back to solitary confinement.

CHAPTER 30

Olivia

Loch Ewe is growing less busy; convoys now congregate in the Clyde. The naval base remains, but with a skeleton staff, and soon it will be time for Olivia to be transferred back to London. She is relieved that she is forbidden leave over Christmas. She does not know what to do next. Charlie has still not replied to any of her letters, she has left it too long to tell Jack, and she cannot write to either of them that she has lost Betsy. She is spiralling into a web of deceit, and she dare not imagine what will happen when the truth comes out. She fears for Alfie's safety. She does not believe that Betsy is capable of looking after him alone. She writes to Carl, hoping he will be able to intervene. He writes back telling her not to worry, that he will keep an eye out. But each day she dreads the arrival of the post, in case it contains some new horror.

While her life unravels, the news from the front is at least improving. The Germans are being pushed back; the Allies pressing on them from the west, the Red Army from the east. Parts of France and Lithuania, Greece and Italy are reclaimed. Christmas comes and goes. Winston Churchill recovers from pneumonia more ebullient than ever. The Allies will win the war; it's just a matter of how long it will take, how many more lives will be lost.

It has been a particularly cold and miserable start to the

year, the weather reflecting her inner turmoil. The west coast has been battered by heavy snow and storms. Olivia is woken by the sound of hail against the glass panes that are rattling in the windows. She stares out into the darkness, imagining the great loch frothing beneath the wind, listening to the water running off the roof. She knows the ships will be straining at their anchor cables.

In the distance there is a sudden flash of light. Olivia sits up. Gunfire? Lightning? She fumbles to the window, hands outstretched until she feels the wooden frame, the hail hammering and the wind tugging at it. She presses her face to the cold glass. Outside it is pitch black again, but she knows what that light was. Flares. Something is not right.

She lights a candle. Its lonely flame throws enough light across the room to find her clothes. Not uniform in this weather. She pulls on the thickest, warmest clothes she can find: trousers, woollen jumper, thick socks. In the hall, she wriggles her head into her balaclava, pulls on her boots, searches for the torch.

The wind tears the door from her hand and the candle sputters out. She wrestles the door closed behind her and turns into the vicious cold, angling her head slightly to the side so that her temple takes the brunt of it. A wall of sleet streaks through the torch beam. She runs up to the house, sliding and stumbling in ruts on the way. The twisted trees bear down on her, bending and snapping in the wind.

There is a light on at Taigh Mor. Aunt Nancy is up, her dressing gown tied at the waist. There is a man talking urgently into the telephone in the drawing room, and another staring out of the large French window in the direction of the loch.

'It's an American liberty ship,' says her aunt. 'Hit rocks trying to come into the loch around at Black Bay. The coast-guard's tried to get a line out from the cliffs, but it's too far offshore. The Wrens are on their way from Aultbea . . .'

Olivia is out and running down the drive to the road before she can finish the sentence. She is just in time to flag down one of the trucks that is careering towards her, sending showers of icy water up from its wheels. She scrambles into the passenger seat, the Wrens shuffling up to squeeze her in. The truck is buffeted this way and that by the wind as they race towards the track that leads to Cove, the one she has cycled along more times than she can remember. Past Firemore, and on they bump, peering through the windscreen, barely able to see the track, which is now a slippery quagmire of wet snow. The headlamps highlight horizontal rain, the startled faces of ragged sheep and – once – a herd of deer that has come low to shelter from the bitter cold and snow that still lies deep further inland.

As the track disappears, the truck begins to slip and slide on the sticky surface of slush. They are stuck, and Olivia gets out, squinting against the driving sleet. Three of them struggle to the back of the truck, wedging their shoulders against its cold metal, pushing to free it from the peat, avoiding the spinning wheels that splatter muck behind them.

Eventually the Wrens can go no further. They park and scramble out. Beyond the squealing wind they can hear the crash of sea and spray against the cliffs ahead. Behind them are miles of peat bogs. Olivia's mood is as bleak as the land-scape. She is disoriented, surrounded by impermeable darkness in every direction. She cannot work out which way to go, and then suddenly she spots an extraordinary sight: pinpricks of light spread out among the peat hags and the snow, flickering closer and closer like will-o'-the-wisps. Then Mrs Ross materialises, holding a lamp and a flask of steaming tea. She has a pale, thick blanket around her shoulders, which is covered in a layer of snow. She has crossed three miles of peat bogs and frozen ground. And she is by no means the only one: behind her, more lights float towards them – the crofters are coming to help. Ben and Mrs Munro, the grey-haired MacGregors, the Campbells.

Olivia tries to greet them, but the wind catches the breath in her mouth and forces it back. Mrs Ross nods, and together the women head for Black Bay as dawn begins to break. When

431

they reach the high granite rocks above the beach, it is just light enough for Olivia to make out the awful sight of the stricken ship foundering on the reef. For a moment, the women stand there, their clothes sodden with sleet, their hands and hearts numb. Olivia's own secret beach is only yards around the corner – that place of sanctuary where she used to fish, and where she spent so many happy hours with Jack. Jack. The fear in her heart grows. Any one of the merchantmen out there on that cargo ship could be him. She forces herself to focus, not to let her thoughts run wild.

The waves are too high for the ship to launch its lifeboats, and the men are clinging desperately to her as water surges over them. There is a terrible groan, and the ship cracks in two, and there are men in the water and men scrabbling at the ship and men flung on the rocks and across the bubbling sea, and the Wrens and crofters are immediately scrambling and slipping over the boulders and down to the shingly beach below. The wind rips at Olivia's balaclava and the rocks tear and scrape at her hands and legs, but she is down, where the waves smash against the earth and toss themselves high into the air, falling back down into a seething foam. Wreckage and bodies lie strewn across the shore. Everything is covered in a black film of oil. The coastguard and his men are already here, deep in the surf, pulling bodies from the water. A British escort tug is trying to get a line out to the wreck, but the sea is too choppy, the wind too strong. They cannot get closer or they too will be dashed on the rocks. The last of the desperate figures cling to the ship; the lucky ones are flung inshore, the unlucky dragged away into the churning depths.

All the time, there is a terrible noise like a giant clanging bell, and Olivia realises it is the hull of the broken ship, clanking against the rocks every time another wave tugs at it. Olivia runs to the closest body. He is naked: the clothes ripped from him by the sea; his limbs smashed and pulped by the rocks. She knows it is crazy, but she cannot stifle the terrible fear that it could be Jack. She touches his cold, pale face, clasps the unresponsive hand. For a moment she is glad he is not Jack, but then she remembers he is someone else's lover, someone else's son. He will not wake. She gently lets him go, and stumbles to the next body. Each time she prays, please don't let it be him, please don't let it be him.

Across the beach, fires lit by the crofters are leaping to life. In the weak light, she can see that this sailor's clothes have been shredded and he is covered in black oil so that only the whites of his eyes are showing, but at least he is shivering, which means he's alive. She sticks her finger into his mouth to clear the waxy ball of oil from his throat. Then she drags him towards one of the fires. There are other survivors gathered around its smoky flames. The crofters are gently cleaning the oil from their mouths and ears and eyes too, wiping it away and offering warming sips of tea from their flasks. They wrap the men in the blankets woven by their ancestors, whispering kind words and stroking brows. Their fires offer warmth, and are also beacons for the men still struggling in the water, unsure which way to swim.

Word has spread across the area, and there are more rescuers on the beach now: the latest Fieldcraft Training Centre boys, as well as more naval ratings from Aultbea. They scramble to help the coastguards, scrabbling across the boulders where a survivor is wedged up high, throwing themselves into the sea to grab hands, limbs, rags. The lighthouse keepers help to carry survivors on their backs across the rocks, giving them sips of whisky on the way.

Olivia wades out into the surf. It is so cold that it burns her legs into numbness. She feels the waves pull and pummel at her, trying to knock her over, trying to take her away. She reaches an already exhausted sailor who is attempting to drag one of his shipmates to safety. Her fingers ache with cold. The debris in the water crashes against her, lacerating her legs. They yank the body to shore together, where Ben Munro is waiting with a stretcher. They lie the sailor on it, and she gropes for the end with her frozen fingers. The sailor moans for his mother, the sobs low beneath the shriek of the wind. The snow settles on him as they grapple their way up the cliff. Olivia slips. The sailor cries out. She scrambles up, and they make it a few more inches before Ben slips too. They carry on until they reach the top, then they have to stumble the two miles to the waiting trucks. By the time they reach the ambulances, it is too late. The doctor pronounces the boy dead.

Olivia rests for a moment, crouched against a small rock, her head in her hands. The stretchers of the dead lie in silent rows next to her. She is glad that no one can see she is crying because her face is wet where the sleet has melted as it tries to penetrate her skin. Ben squeezes her shoulder, and then goes to help Mr MacGregor; the aged crofter is struggling towards them with a survivor on his broad back. The living are placed carefully into the ambulances, which race away back down the track to the hospital at Gairloch.

Olivia heads back to the beach. There are no more men clinging to the wreckage of the broken ship above the black water. Now the rescuers are working desperately to recover any bodies before darkness falls again. They will not leave the dead out here in the lonely night. Above them, the crofters scour the cliffs. They find two more men thrown up by the force of the waves. Their bodies are covered in snow, but they are still alive. A bloody trail leads to another man unconscious in the heather. Since the ambulances have gone, the crofters carry them to the hospital, across the paths that they have trodden for centuries. They do not rest until they reach Gairloch.

Olivia feels an arm around her shoulders and the comforting weight of a soft blanket. 'Come on, lassie,' says Mrs Ross, and together they stumble and trip back across the peat hags to her croft. Inside, Olivia sits, stuck in a twilight world somewhere between life and death, while Mrs Ross stokes up the fire and begins to bake bread to take to the hospital.

The next morning, Olivia drives Mrs Ross to Gairloch. There are twelve survivors in the makeshift ward. Sixty-two of their shipmates are dead, some of their bodies lost for ever to the sea. The sailors have nothing: no clothes, no belongings. They are weak and covered in bruises and cuts, but they are alive. They greet the crofters with tears and thanks. They ask Olivia to find paper so they can write and let their mothers and daughters, wives and girlfriends know they have survived, clinging on to life with all the strength they could muster. Olivia thinks of Jack and of Charlie. She scribbles their messages until her fingers are stained with ink and her wrist aches. Mrs Ross delivers her freshly baked bread; others bring eggs and jam, the last of their winter rations – a taste of home for dazed boys so far from theirs.

On the beach, the battered, useless lifeboats lie among the debris thrown up by the storm, and the embers of the crofters' fires still breathe smoke into the air, but at the hospital there is no sign of yesterday's storm. The wind is only a soft ripple on the sea, and the birds wheel and call to each other, swinging through the square patches of leaden sky through the windows. It is after lunch, and Olivia is writing her last letter of the day for a survivor called Skip, when Aunt Nancy appears on the ward, bearing a basket of preserves and winter vegetables.

The nurse rushes over and gives a little curtsey. 'Oh thank you, Lady McPherson.'

'Nothing like healthy food to nourish the body and the soul,' says Aunt Nancy. She drifts past the beds, stopping beside each one to say a few words to its occupant; she is proficient at small talk.

Skip narrows his eyes in a conspiratorial way, and whispers at Olivia: 'A lady, eh? What's that mean? Royalty?'

'No,' Olivia laughs. 'Not exactly.'

'What then?' Skip's hair is beginning to recede, which makes him look older than he is – Olivia reckons about forty. But he is still an attractive man, and there is mischief in his hazel eyes.

'It's hard to explain unless you're British.'

He nudges her. 'Look lively,' he says, as her aunt approaches the bed.

Olivia smiles again. 'Hello, Aunt Nancy,' she says, and Skip's eyes twinkle beneath his raised eyebrows.

'I hope my niece is behaving herself,' says her aunt.

'She sure is,' says Skip. 'I can't believe she'd be anything other than delightful.'

'She's had her moments.' Aunt Nancy does not say it unkindly. 'Any news of Charlie?'

Olivia shakes her head. 'Nothing.'

'And Jack?'

'He's fine. Thank you.'

Her aunt moves on, and Skip says, 'You're a dark horse. First it turns out you're a blue blood, and now there's a Charlie and a Jack? Looks like you got the makings of a heartbreaking tale right there.'

She smiles a tight little smile and glances away. 'It's complicated,' she says.

'Ain't it always?'

'Are you talking from experience?'

'You write what I tell you, and see what you think.'

Skip dictates a letter to his wife. Olivia does not stop his train of thought. He speaks of how he has gambled away their home, the one they built up from nothing and worked so hard to get just right. How the lovely house with the picket fence and the fancy toys and the car and the fine clothes and the jewellery, paintings and ponies could all be taken at any moment. He wants her to know how sorry he is, and how he will do anything he can to sort it out when he returns.

'And even worse,' says Skip as he reaches the end of his story, 'my kids think I'm some kind of hero because I went off to fight the fascists in Europe. The truth is, I ran away. I couldn't face telling them their world was about to come crashing down.'

'And your wife really has no idea?'

He shakes his head. 'Not unless the debt collectors have already turned up.'

'You've got yourself in quite some pickle,' she says.

'And I'll tell you something,' he says. 'Yesterday I almost died. And while I was waiting for the good Lord to carry me away, I realised I didn't want to take my secret to the grave. I was thinking the opposite. How I wished I'd been honest from the start. How I should'a told Rosie straight out. That woman is brighter and braver than ten of me. I love her more than life itself, and if she can forgive me, then we can face anything.'

'What if she doesn't forgive you?'

'The point is, she deserves to make that decision herself.'

Olivia nods.

'Now your turn,' he says. 'Try it on me first. Then go home and write it down.'

Somehow it is easier to talk to a stranger. Olivia tells him about Jack, and about Charlie and Betsy and Alfie. And how she cannot find the words to tell Jack about Alfie, and that his sister has gone. And he probes her gently for more, and she eventually tells him about the miscarriage.

When she has finished, he says, 'You know what you need to do now. Be brave. It sounds as if you can be. Jeez, I know you can be – I saw you last night. If he loves you, he'll understand, and he'll love you all the more for it.'

'Thank you,' she says.

'Anything to help a pretty lady.' He doffs a pretend hat at her and settles back against his pillows. 'Sounds like quite a bloke, this Jack. Ain't done a Russian run myself, but I know plenty who have. Scares the bejesus out of me. He must be made of strong stuff.'

'It's nice to hear you say that. My family don't approve.'

'Don't approve? How?'

'It's complicated . . .' She smiles.

'Back to the old lords and ladies thing, is it?'

She nods.

He laughs. 'Seriously, you should come out to the States. Look me up. We don't stand for that nonsense there.'

'You make it sound easy.'

'It is. You Brits think all the world is here on this tiny island, but it ain't. And when we've kicked this Hitler into touch, you damn well make sure you get out there and find out for yourself.'

Aunt Nancy offers to give her a lift home, but Olivia declines, taking the old path back from Gairloch instead. Before she drops down into Poolewe, she climbs up into the hills behind the bothy, where the snow still lies fresh in the crevices and the temperature drops. She carries on, up beyond the rowan pool, until she is high, where the occasional clump of patchy heather shows through, and great wet rocks lie broken across each other in vast shining slabs. Her hot breath comes out in clouds as it meets the chilly air, but she is warm from the climb. She sits and turns her face up to the dark clouds, feels the cold air cool her hot cheeks as a sprinkling of snowflakes twirls around her. She begins to gather smaller rocks that lie exposed among the ice. She is thinking of their baby, but instead of letting the misery overwhelm her, she relishes the feeling, the imprint of a connection that no one but her will ever feel. She dares to hope that perhaps one day she will experience it again, with another new life. As the sky darkens, she balances the rocks one on top of another until she has built a small cairn. She digs a tiny sprig of dried rosemary out of her pocket. 'Goodbye, my darling,' she says as she tucks it beneath the bottom of the pile. She will never forget, but it feels right that there is a place for her child here among the hills. As she turns to make her way back to the bothy, she catches sight of a large stag standing just below her, head held proudly. She counts sixteen points, a monarch, more regal than any human royal. His neck is thick and solid and there is a scar on his dark flank. He stands still as a statue, watching her, the only movement his soft nostrils dilating and constricting. He does not run even as she passes within yards, just watches as she disappears into the snow that is descending on the glen.

438

CHAPTER 31

Jack

Jack has no trouble in finding decent berths: there is an endless supply of merchant ships that need crew and officers, particularly of Jack's calibre, with his discharge book full of exemplary records. Whenever he is discharged from one ship, he signs on to another, finding comfort in the routine and hierarchy of the vessels, which work in similar fashion, even if the size of their crew or type of cargo differs. The constant change suits him: there is no chance to build meaningful friendships. He travels the world, running the gauntlet of the Atlantic, transporting the arms and ammunition, food and fuel needed to keep Britain going. Although he has not taken the exam, he is now second mate, with responsibilities for navigation and watch-keeping as well as overseeing cargo operations when in dock. As he studies the nautical charts and tide and current, his thoughts settle. He finds he can remember Mart and Burts, Si and David, without being overwhelmed by a black cloud. The scars on his arms begin to heal.

He absorbs Olivia's letters, amazed that she and Carl have found Betsy, and reassured that his sister is safe in Scotland. He longs for the day he will see them both, but still does not take leave, as Olivia assures him it will be easier for them all to meet in London in the new year. And then comes the double bombshell about Betsy's pregnancy – and her own. He

439

is shocked about Betsy, but it is nothing compared to the news that Olivia had carried her own baby – their baby. He cannot believe that she did not share it with him when they were last together in London, but then he remembers the state he was in; he did not make it easy for her. He remains on the ships, trying to work out what he will say when he sees her, building up the courage to face both of the women he has let down.

Then it becomes harder to find a position on a ship: so many are being requisitioned and diverted to the south coast of Britain. The sailors are not stupid; they know that something is afoot. There is a rumour that there is to be a vast assault on the French coast involving thousands of ships. This could be the end of the war – or the end of him. Now is the time to take the leave he has accrued. It is time to face up to his past.

Jack arrives in London on a sunny May afternoon. There are birds singing in the rubble, and the city seems cleaner than when he was last here. He passes some GIs demonstrating the jitterbug on the pavement while onlookers clap and smile. Everywhere he looks, there are uniformed men from every Allied country, many of them walking hand-in-hand with uniformed women. He passes a couple entwined beneath a tree; groups relaxing on the grass. The colour of the advertising hoardings seems brighter; there is expectation in the air.

As Jack reaches the flat, his steps falter. It has been so long – more than a year. How could Olivia still feel the same about him after all she has been through? He stands in the street and removes his hat, twisting it nervously in his hands, but before he raises his hand to knock on the door, Olivia is opening it, smiling at him, gripping him in the circle of her arms.

'I'm so glad to see you,' she says, pulling him inside.

Jack follows her up the stairs. She offers to take his coat, hanging it on the peg in the hall. He is relieved to see that there are no other coats apart from hers. He leans his sea bag up against the wall and follows her into the sitting room. She turns to face him. They are dancing around each other like strangers.

'Well, say something,' she says, her pale eyes searching his anxiously.

The light is streaming through the window, picking out a golden halo above her head. She is something wonderful, something perfect. He is in awe. She tucks her hair behind her ear, and it reminds him of the gangly girl he met all that time ago on the loch. But she is a woman now. A woman who has travelled the length and breadth of the country, giving orders to men like him.

'It's going to be all right,' he says. And as he says it, he is sure it's true, and she nods, and they hold each other again, and he realises that she isn't that different: she still needs him, and his heart swells and he knows he will protect her at all costs.

But there is still the problem of his sister.

Jack yells Stoog's name from the street. Faces appear at neighbouring windows, passers-by cross to the other side of the road. Jack does not care. He keeps yelling until the door opens and he forces his way in, breaking Stoog's nose with the palm of his hand as he does so.

'Where is she?' he says, wheeling around to glare at his old friend.

There was a time when they were evenly matched, but Jack is far stronger now after years of physical work, and Stoog does not even try to defend himself as Jack gathers him up by the shirt. 'Where?' he says. The blood is running from Stoog's nostrils, a dark, glistening trail that flows unchecked from his chin. Jack pushes him away with disgust, and Stoog backs off, holding his nose.

'Betsy?' Jack's voice rings out around the house, sending the dust from the lampshades in the hall, and echoing up the staircase.

Stoog glances to the stairs, and Jack follows his gaze and his heart leaps. There she is. Older, taller, but still the same Betsy, with her tangle of dark hair and her huge eyes.

She is down in the hall in seconds and he cannot believe that she is really here, in front of him. He reaches out and she grasps his hand. 'You know it's not just me any more?' she says.

He nods, noticing for the first time the small child clamped to her hip. Betsy points at Jack. 'Alfie, this is your Uncle Jack,' she says.

The child arches away from him and Betsy tuts and tries to prise his fingers from her waist. She finally unpeels him and places him on the floor, ignoring the pleading hands that grab at her skirt. She turns to Jack, hesitates for a moment, and then they are both hugging and sobbing, and Jack is holding her away from him so he can look at her face again.

'I'm so sorry,' he says as he clutches her to him again. It is all he can say; he is lost for words. Once he thought he was the only surviving member of his family. Now there are three of them.

He crouches down, holds out a hand. 'Hello, Alfie,' he says, but the boy shrugs away again, his eyes large as his mother's. He lets go of Betsy's skirt and falls to the floor. He cannot walk yet. He shuffles backwards. Jack cannot help noticing that his hands are grubby, the nails black with dirt. He stands. 'You're both coming with me,' he says.

Stoog emerges from the shadows, spitting the blood from his mouth. 'She don't want to go anywhere. She's staying with me,' he says. Jack holds up a warning finger, and Stoog stops dead. 'You think you're better than us now, do you?'

'I know I'm better than you,' Jack replies.

'Leave it, you two,' says Betsy.

'Get your things,' says Jack, without taking his eyes off Stoog.

'Don't hurt him, Jack.'

'I'm not going to hurt him. I'm going to kill him.' Jack flexes his hands.

'You won't,' says Betsy. 'You'll leave him alone.'

The child starts to cry, and Betsy lifts him reluctantly on to her hip. A thin dribble of snot hangs from his crusted nose.

'I'm not coming with you,' says Betsy.

'You bloody are,' says Jack.

'I don't want to live with you and Lady Manners.'

'You're not staying here.'

'This is my home.'

Stoog leers at him, cocking his head to one side. 'You should listen to your sister. She's a sensible girl.'

Jack grabs Stoog by the neck and slams him against the wall. 'Shut your fucking mouth.'

'Leave him alone,' says Betsy, her voice high with fear.

Jack squeezes, feels Stoog's windpipe hard and gristly beneath his palm. 'I swear I'll fucking kill him if you don't come with me.'

He senses her move behind him and tightens his grip so that Stoog's breath comes ragged and wheezing.

'Now,' says Jack. Stoog's skin is beginning to change colour, and his eyes are bulging.

'All right. All right.' Betsy opens the door, Alfie clinging to her. When they are safely outside, Jack relaxes his grip, and Stoog gulps great breaths of air, bending double and rubbing his neck, coughing and choking at the ground.

'How could you?' Jack says. 'How could you end up doing this?'

'We all do what we can to survive.' Stoog will not look at him.

It takes all Jack's resolve not to finish him then and there.

Back at the flat, Jack cannot believe that his sister is actually here – in the same room as him – alive and so . . . adult. Almost a woman.

Olivia fetches a cloth to try to clean Alfie's face, but he retreats, shuffling on the floor behind his mother. 'He doesn't remember me,' says Olivia.

'He's been all right. There's a couple of girls who's good with babies,' says Betsy.

'You didn't need to leave.'

'I didn't want to stay.' Her face is hard again.

Throughout that first evening, Jack cannot help occasionally reaching out to touch Betsy's cheeks, her nose, her hair. It is as if he has found a part of himself that he didn't realise was missing. Betsy fills him in with her own story. Jack knows she is leaving parts out, but he is so full of joy to have found her again that he doesn't want to risk it by questioning her, even though something needles at him every time he looks at the child.

When Jack finally goes to bed, he feels such a rush of tenderness for Olivia as he strokes her arm in the dim light. He has the two people he cares about most in the world under the same roof. He can tell she is still awake: her breathing is shallow and her eyes glitter in the dark. 'Thank you for finding her,' he says. 'I can never repay you.'

'You don't need to repay me,' she says. 'Just promise to stay with me for the rest of my life.'

'That's all in hand,' he says, kissing her forehead and tucking her hair gently behind her ears. He falls asleep with one arm draped across her body, for once not haunted by the image of his sister, but safe in the knowledge that she is here, in the next-door room.

Jack is strict with Betsy, laying down rules and not letting her out without him as a chaperone, as if he can force the past from her and replace it with a future. Betsy is different. It is not surprising. Jack does not want to think about how she has survived with Stoog. But after a couple of days, when she appears to have accepted the new tilt to her world, he finally has to ask the question that has been burning in the back of his mind. He waits for a moment when she seems relaxed, playing with Alfie on the floor, tickling the boy until his fat giggles fill the room. Olivia is writing another letter to Charlie at the table by the window.

'Bets,' says Jack. 'How can you be sure that Charlie is Alfie's father?'

Betsy immediately sits up and glares at him. 'You don't trust me?' she says. 'Your own flesh and blood?'

'You're different.'

'Of course I'm bloody different.'

'I wish I'd been there to help.'

'Well you weren't, and now I'm all grown up.'

'Not to me. You'll always be my little sister.'

'I'm no kid any more,' she says, standing and slowly turning around. The light catches the lines on her face, the dips and curves of a woman's body.

'What can I do to make it better?'

'Nothing. It's too late.'

'There must be something.'

Betsy is quiet for a moment. And then she says, 'You can get rid of her.' She points at Olivia, who puts down her pen.

'I can't do that,' says Jack.

'Then you're no family of mine.'

'Betsy, please . . .'

'What is it about her that you so prefer over me?'

'Don't make it have to be a choice . . .'

But Betsy is not listening. Her face has contorted into rage, and she stalks up to Olivia and picks up the paper she has been writing on, then waves it at Jack. 'You'd better watch your back,' she says, throwing the words into the room as if they contain all the anger that has been locked away inside her for so long. 'He's the one she really loves. When he comes back, you'll be for it. Then you'll be all alone. And don't think I'll be there for you . . .'

'Stop it! Just stop it!' Now it is Olivia's turn to be affronted. She stands and grabs the letter back from Betsy. 'How dare you say that? Charlie's a good man and a good friend, but I don't love him . . .'

'Such a good man that he leaves a girl like me in a state like this . . .' She points at Alfie.

445

Jack watches them circle each other warily, the two women he loves: one dark and furious, spitting like a wildcat; the other pale and sad. He knows who he believes, and it is a painful thing. He takes a deep breath and steps forward, sees Betsy angle her head in defiance, the twitch of satisfaction in the corner of her mouth as she glares at Olivia. But it is not to Betsy that he is headed.

Betsy's angry stance deflates with her confidence when she realises that Jack is reaching out for Olivia's hand as the two of them turn to face her. Jack clears his throat. 'You should know that we're getting married,' he says. 'When this is all over. We're getting married, and that's a fact. Now we want you to be part of our family, but the only choice has to be made by you: whether you're with us or against us.'

Betsy stares at Jack: he cannot bear the look in her eyes; there is despair and even hatred there. 'I don't believe it,' she says. 'I won't believe it.'

'It's true,' says Olivia, her voice low and calm.

'Why didn't you tell me?'

'We thought it was better coming from Jack.'

Betsy grows hysterical, pleading with Jack: 'But she didn't tell you about Alfie, did she? If she lied to you once, she'll always lie to you . . .'

'She did it to protect me. Not to spite me.' He is thinking about the other baby, the one that Betsy doesn't know about, and he knows that Olivia is too because she is squeezing his hand hard.

Betsy stamps her feet, and she seems so very young that Jack is reminded of the child he left at the station all those years ago. 'You can't be with her. She's not like us . . .'

'I don't even know what we're like any more . . .'

'I want to go back to Stoog. I know where I am with him.'

'Don't. Stay with us. We'll support you both . . .'

'Why won't you listen to me? I don't want Alfie. I never wanted him. It wasn't meant to go this far.'

Now Olivia raises her voice: 'What do you mean?' she says.

'You think Stoog's all bad. Well he's not. He looked out for me. He kept me for himself. Never made me work like the other girls. We used to blackmail men. I'd go for the married ones. Get them back to the house, and then as soon as they'd dropped their trousers, I'd scream blue murder and tell them how old I was. No need to go all the way. Then I'd threaten to tell their wives or go to the police. They'd pay me extra to keep my mouth shut, and I'd done my bit.'

Olivia shakes her head. 'So why did you pick on Charlie?' she asks. 'He wasn't married . . . And I assume you slept with him . . .'

'Charlie was different. He was the first punter who was actually nice to me. He used to search me out. Talk to me. No one else did that. When he told me his parents was dead and he had no wife, I knew he must have plenty of money to spare. We thought we'd be able to pretend there was a baby and get at least a couple of hundred quid. So him I did have to go to bed with. He didn't want to sleep with me, so I had to work hard at it. Then I actually got pregnant . . .'

'How can you be sure that Stoog isn't the father?'

'Stoog was always careful. He knew what he was doing.' She laughs, but in a bitter way. 'Charlie didn't . . .'

Olivia sighs. 'And you had no feelings for Charlie at all?'

'He was just an easy target . . .'

'No feelings – even though he was kind to you . . .?' Olivia is shaking her head, her eyes wide with disbelief.

Betsy glances down at her hands, picks at her nails. 'When you put it like that it sounds . . .'

'Wrong?'

Jack sighs. 'It was wrong,' he says. 'Can't you see that?'

Betsy looks at her brother, and it seems as if the look is somehow less harsh.

'What happened to us?' says Jack, stepping towards her. 'What happened to you?'

Betsy's bottom lip is trembling. 'You left me,' she says. 'I came home and you'd gone . . .'

'I'm sorry. I don't know what else to say.' He reaches out, but she pushes him away. 'I'll make it up to you somehow . . .'

'You hate me . . .' she says as her breath catches in her throat and she begins to sob. 'I hate myself . . .'

'I could never hate you,' he says. 'You're my sister. Nothing you can do will break that.'

At last she allows him to put his arm around her bony shoulder, as if delivering up responsibility, letting her older brother take charge. 'I'm sorry,' she says. 'It's all so fucked-up. I don't know what I've done . . .'

And now there is something that he has not heard in her voice since he found her: kindness.

'Don't go back to Stoog,' says Jack. 'We're your family now.'

She nods and huddles against him like she used to as a child on Drummond Road.

Suddenly, all leave is cancelled. Jack and Olivia are both called to Portsmouth, into the ten-mile-deep restricted coastal zone that stretches from the Wash in East Anglia all the way to Land's End in Cornwall. Jack stays up talking to Betsy before they leave, convincing her he will return and support her, making her promise she will not run away. He clasps Alfie in his arms, remembering the last goodbye from his own father, the smell of Woodbines, the safety of that broad chest. He persuades Carl to come and stay, to make sure she doesn't slip again. Carl grasps his hand and says, 'We'll be fine. You just make sure you come back safe.'

Mid-summer storms lash the southern coast. The sky is oppressive, heavy clouds pressing down over the darkened world below. Olivia and Jack journey south together along roads jammed with vehicles, a river of military green threading its way beneath trees sagging with rain. Troops and tanks, trucks and medical supplies, aeroplanes and warships, amphibious craft, rations and artillery are amassing on the cliffs and shores, in the harbours and inlets. Jack and Olivia drive in silence. Closer to the coast, the roadsides and fields are dotted with tents and vehicles. There are men sleeping in hedgerows and in gardens. The ports are full. Americans, Canadians, and British men throng the seashores, the docks, the pubs, the houses and – of course – the ships.

Olivia and Jack part in Portsmouth – Jack to find his ship, Olivia to the Wrens' headquarters. They barely dare look at each other because their eyes say it all in a fleeting clash of pale blue and black. Jack does not trust himself to speak. There is a swift embrace. Around them, the streets throng with people behaving in the same way, button-lipped, stifling their emotions, all drowning in the same thought – that something momentous is about to happen that could mean the end for all of them.

For the first time, Jack is on a ship carrying live cargo: soldiers – hundreds of them – pale and anxious, cluster along the guardrails three- and four-deep. Their wet tin hats glisten like the guns and the ambulances that are lashed alongside them on the rain-drenched deck. The water beneath them is a mass of smaller boats, delivering messages and ferrying troops and cargo. Jack strains to see if any of the Wrens at their helms are Olivia, but it is hard to see anything beyond the shoulders of the soldiers crammed like cargo into every space.

The wind picks up, moaning through the waiting guns. The clouds are still thick and low. The ships roll from side to side, pulling and rattling at their anchors. New sealed orders are delivered. Rain trickles down Jack's face as he escorts the Wren boarding officer to the bridge. She has checked their guns, and now she needs to talk to his master. Jack oversees the delivery of the supplies that she has brought: for the final push each soldier is given a box of matches, some anti-seasick pills, a few francs, a map of France, a life jacket, a razor blade, socks, sweets, cigarettes – and, most important of all, sick bags. The day of the attack is put back by twenty-four hours. More sick bags are distributed.

*

The Lancasters head out just before midnight, their thunderous drone reverberating across the sky. The other RAF bombers follow, with their real and dummy parachutists. In the sea below, the ships are so densely packed that Jack could almost jump from one to the next. They groan and heave on the water, waiting, waiting. Jack is on duty when the first ships weigh anchor in the morning darkness. The minesweepers have already gone on ahead, to clear a safe passage. Above them, dawn breaks across the wingtips of hundreds of British and American planes, here to offer support and to drop airborne divisions into enemy territory. The confusion of the last few days slips away, and Jack is in control again.

As daylight tries to pierce the thick cloud, a ghostly morning light turns the water slate grey laced with foaming white. Jack screws up his eyes against the spray, spitting the salt water from his mouth and wiping his hand across his drenched face. There are ships as far as the eye can see – thousands of them – frothing and churning across the Channel. Barrage balloons are attached to some of them, as though a protective herd has broken free from the coast to follow the convoy.

Any spare space is packed with ammunition. Jack knows what that means – he has seen what happens to a ship that ignites when carrying explosive cargo. He looks along the deck to the gathered men. They are bracing themselves against the swell of this foreign world. Their faces are set, their jaws are clenched, their eyes are fixed ahead. He knows they are thinking not of what they are about to face, but of who they are facing it for: mothers, wives, daughters, sisters, friends, home, country. The ship forges on, and some of the men turn their eyes to Jack. He feels a pang as he realises many of them are younger than he is now. They are looking to him for guidance, for a curt nod, a confident smile. As the ship surges and the wind wails, he pulls himself up tall: this is his world.

Jack stands like that even as the first ships hit the first mines; almighty explosions render the air, joined by a barrage from the beach. He walks purposefully among the troops,

450

barking directions, operating machinery, helping the men off the ship, issuing a brief word, a slap on the back. Inside, his stomach churns, but not with seasickness.

Men pour into the first landing craft, struggling ashore. Some have their limbs blown off by the mines in the sand. Jack can't help flinching as a warship opens fire behind him, the sixteen-inch guns pounding into action over their heads. In front of them, the Germans retaliate, firing mortars and guns. The shore is alive with flame and smoke, flashes of orange and billows of white, and the men are caught in the middle. The noise rings in his ears, and the gunpowder burns his nostrils. The tide is coming in faster than the injured can drag themselves up the beach, reaching out for them with deathly grey fingers that turn red with blood.

Still more men are taken to the beaches. They crouch in their boats, trying to avoid the spray of water and bullets, praying that the filthy, flat bottom of this boat won't be the last thing they remember. Strong currents drag the craft sideways. Some run aground on sandbanks. Men abandon ship to wade through deep water. Amphibious tanks sink before they can rumble ashore to help. Boat after boat unloads on the beach, now overrun with men clambering across the fallen bodies of their comrades. Those still breathing are dragged back by the unarmed medics into the landing craft and hoisted on to the empty, waiting ships. Above them the barrage balloons bob to deter the enemy aircraft; they are not always successful. In the distance, the RAF lay a smokescreen to shield the Allies from enemy guns further along the coast.

Jack helps to haul bodies on board, laying them carefully on deck when there is no more space below, ordering the new apprentices to bring them water, to attend to the worst, to calm the whimpering and to cover the dead. He does not let them stop and think for a moment.

They ferry the injured back across the Channel, delivering them to the safety of Portsmouth. The boom of gunfire along the French coast is so loud that it can still be heard from the British harbour. He orders his men to scrub the blood from the decks as they pack more troops, more ammunition, into the holds. The ship creaks and strains, hard ahead to reach the French beaches once more.

The new troops bear the same expression as the last lot: they are ready to do their duty. Jack wonders what happened to the world. They have run out of sick bags, and the soldiers vomit into their helmets. Jack walks among them, offering words of encouragement and comfort, anything he can think of. But nothing he says can prevent the men from trembling as they draw near the thundering warships and the death-strewn beach. Puffs of black smoke turn day into night. Again, they offload the troops, collect the injured, and return them to their home, where a fresh batch waits to take their place. They carry on like that, back and forth, for days.

CHAPTER 32

Charlie

Charlie has lost count of the grooves he has scraped into the wall of the cooler. When the guard comes to release him, the light falling through the open door picks out the scratches, making them look as if a wild creature has tried to claw its way out of the tiny room. The short, fat guard with receding hair – who looks as if he would be more at home behind a banker's desk than in a Luftwaffe uniform – escorts Charlie back to the hut and indicates that he must collect what few possessions he has. John is there, his own things already packed.

'Any idea where we're going?' says Charlie.

John shrugs. 'They say they're splitting the troublemakers up.'

The guards hurry them out across the windblown yard. A truck is idling in the shadow of the main watchtower. Charlie stops, eyeing it suspiciously, reluctant to leave the safety of the place that has become home. 'Where are you taking us?' he says.

'You find out when we get there,' says the guard with the receding hair.

The men all fear they are being moved to one of the camps they have heard rumours about, one of the camps from which no one returns. They refuse to climb up, but the dogs snap

453

and bite at their heels, straining at their collars, and the German rifles form an impenetrable barrier. There is no choice but to clamber in, shuffling up against each other, drawing what crumbs of comfort they can from each other's warmth.

The guard with receding hair and another guard with a flat nose that must once have been broken accompany the prisoners, sitting straight-backed at the rear opening of the truck, rifles between their legs. The great gates are opened, the Germans call out their curt goodbyes, and the truck growls off into the unknown.

They drive through the night, the fear clenching at their stomachs. The guards hush anyone who tries to speak. The prisoners attempt to settle into the journey, avoiding each other's eyes in case the fear is infectious. They doze, each lost in his own thoughts. The fat guard appears to nod off, his head bouncing, jowls wobbling as the vehicle knocks and bumps along the road. Only Charlie and the guard with the broken nose, who is seated next to him, do not sleep.

'Where are you taking us?' Charlie asks.

The guard says nothing, just stares resolutely at his boots.

'You must know you are bound to protect us,' says Charlie. 'You can't just dispose of prisoners-of-war because it suits you.'

The guard sighs. 'We are not disposing of you,' he says. 'You have nothing to fear.'

'Nothing to fear from men who murder their own?'

The man's deep-set eyes flicker briefly across at his fellow guard, but the German is still asleep. 'You refer to Oberleutnant Schafer?' he says, his voice low and quiet.

'And the rest . . .'

'The death of Oberleutnant Schafer was not something I would wish. He was a good man.'

Charlie snorts with contempt.

The German turns his head to gaze at Charlie. Charlie can see there is sadness and resignation there. 'You must know, if you were truly friends with Hans,' he says, 'that we are not all of us the same.' Charlie looks away. The man sighs again and shifts on the uncomfortable bench. 'I am Otto,' he says. 'And I tell you, you have nothing to fear.'

The truck hits another pothole and the other guard is jolted awake. He pulls himself upright, glaring at Charlie, re-strengthening his grip on the rifle between his feet. Otto stares at his boots once more.

The truck eventually rolls in through a new set of gates strung with barbed wire. To the men's relief, it seems to be just another prisoner-of-war camp, with the same low huts and looming watchtowers. The wind still whistles across the bleak yard; the men still have boredom and disappointment stamped on their faces; the dogs still strain at their collars.

Charlie and John slot easily into camp life, Charlie to his raids on supplies, John on the eternal quest for new ways to escape. News that Charlie is a troublemaker has followed him here, and the guards are wary of him, but he does not care. He plots and plans with the others, takes risks that he shouldn't. He has nothing to lose, now that his dignity is gone. He lies on his bunk, staring up at where the mattress above bulges between the missing slats, despising himself for his weakness. He always thought he was a better man than most. It turns out he is worse. How could Jack forgive him for what he has done? How could Olivia? And to have taken advantage of Betsy . . . He is morally reprehensible. The only blessing is that his parents will never know.

The German officers grow increasingly edgy, agitated. One by one they disappear, until only a skeleton staff of older men remains, including the two guards from their previous camp. John – whose German is almost fluent, although he does not let on to their captors – picks up snippets of conversation between the officers, which the British men discuss later in the flickering candlelight of the hut: 'At last the Allies must be advancing. All the fit Germans are being recalled. The Führer needs every man fighting for him.'

Their suspicions are corroborated when news of D-Day filters in via an illegal radio that one of the prisoners has hidden inside his mattress. More good news follows with the liberation of Paris. The Germans are retreating, as well as fighting on two fronts – caught between the Russians and the rest of the Allies. Surely the end is in sight. Charlie and John encourage each prisoner to save whatever they can, mindful of Hans's warning to make provisions in case they are moved on again. The men work hard to prepare rations, building stores of kriegy cake, a mixture of margarine and biscuits, but secretly, none of them believes they will be going anywhere. Surely the Allies will come marching through the gates at any moment to rescue them.

The weeks slip past. Charlie's second Christmas in captivity comes and goes. Europe is in the grip of a particularly harsh winter. Snow blankets the huts, the water is always frozen, and the men struggle to keep warm, burning tables and chairs piece by piece. The coal sheds are almost empty. The sick quarters are full.

And then the order comes.

There is a biting wind, and snow is falling again. The Germans bark at the prisoners, telling them to pack and be ready to move out that night: the Soviets are advancing. The prisoners want to wait, but the guards get angry, shouting at them in broken English. Otto is called to explain; he is often used to translate, as the camp's translators have long since been recalled, and his English is the best. 'Please, Charlie,' he says. 'You must explain to your friends. We have our orders. We are to come with you. There is nothing any of us can do about this.'

Charlie dresses in as many layers as possible: two vests, three pairs of socks, two jerseys, a greatcoat, and a cap. It is clear that he will not be able to carry all the rations he has stored. He abandons the shaving kit for a sleeping bag, and eats as much of the spare food as he can stomach.

Outside the huts, the prisoners are assembling: two hundred and eighty of them heading off into a swirling blizzard. The guards walk alongside, their boots padding silently in the snow. Otto moves among them, strength in his purposeful strides. Men from the sickbay who are too ill to walk are hauled along in wagons by their fellow prisoners. Some of the men have made makeshift sledges to pull their extra supplies, but they soon abandon most of these as they grow heavy with the falling snow, and their arms start to ache.

Charlie knows he must pace himself. He conserves his energy, walking steadily as if he were walking up into the hills at Loch Ewe. On they tramp, a column of prisoners, past empty fields, abandoned vehicles, through silent villages, dragging the ill and frail behind them. The men in the wagons shiver and cannot get warm. Behind them, snowflakes settle in the footprints and in the wheel ruts.

When the men pulling the wagons start to stumble, they swap with those who still have enough energy. When those men also start to trip, the guards indicate they can stop for the night. Two hundred and eighty men cram into an old barn. Half of its roof is missing, the tiles lie broken and crushed on the floor, the rafters are bare like naked ribs against the heavy sky. The German guards huddle in a small group on the sheltered side of the barn. The prisoners-of-war try to do the same, drawing what scant warmth they can from each other's bodies, but they cannot all fit, and the unlucky ones lie beneath the open roof as the snow twirls down on to their tired limbs.

The next morning they march on, through another seemingly deserted village. The occupants hide behind twitching curtains, apart from a small boy who runs out into the street, stones clenched in his mittened hands. He shouts something and launches his missiles, which rain down on the prisoners' bony

457

arms as they pass. Charlie feels the sting, but, compared to the bite of the cold, it is nothing. Most of the German guards ignore the boy; only Otto calls out, crossing the road to place a hand on the boy's skinny shoulder, but the child yells back, pointing at his enemies, indoctrinated to the last. Otto shakes his head sadly as they move on.

The supplies are dwindling. The German guards are hungry. The prisoners mix snow with bully beef. Those that have hoarded rations hide them deep in their pockets. The men in the wagons start to die. The guards encourage the men to offload the cold, rigid bodies, but the prisoners will not abandon their friends to the foxes and rats that leave their telltale signs in the snow and in the chewed flesh of the dead. The prisoners drag the wagons on, trying to ignore the stiffening corpses, hoping they might find somewhere soft enough to dig graves later. They do not. Otto helps to lay the corpses on the side of the road, lifting the bodies gently in his strong arms, removing their RAF dog tags and the photographs from their pockets, trying to keep a note of where they lie. Then they cover the bodies with cut branches until the guards urge them to hurry on.

At the next village, the locals take pity and come out with warm drinks. Charlie could weep as he feels the hot liquid trickle down his sore throat and spread fire through his limbs. Otto thanks the villagers. The prisoners rest for a while. When it is time to move on, Charlie swaps with John to pull a wagon, digging his tired, frozen feet into the icy ground, gritting his teeth as the strap cuts into his bad shoulder. The guards urge them on: glancing backwards, as if they expect the American or Russian tanks to appear at any moment.

At night the men share barns with skinny, ill cattle, sleeping among the rat droppings and filth – and straw if they can find it. John starts to sneeze. Those who develop hypothermia are added to the wagons. The inane chattering of delirious men joins the chattering of teeth.

A fierce wind begins to blow the snow from the roads. The remaining sledges judder and catch at the stones. The prisoners discard them, carrying whatever supplies they can, struggling to pull the last three wagons with dying men onward. Charlie abandons the sleeping bag; he is too weak to carry anything but the last crumbs of saved food. His feet ache and scream with every step, but he dares not remove his boots at night in case someone steals them or his feet succumb to frostbite.

It is not only the prisoners who are out of food; the guards are suffering too. The short guard with the receding hair develops a hacking cough. His footsteps drag in the slush as he weakens; his soft paunch is all but gone. 'He needs food,' says Otto.

'We all need food,' says John.

Charlie offers the man some of his precious kriegy cake. John tries to stop him, laying a bony hand on Charlie's arm. 'Don't waste it on him,' he says.

Charlie brushes him off: 'Look at the man. He's dying.'

'Do you think he would help you if it was the other way around?'

'That doesn't mean I shouldn't.'

'Think about what they did to our boys. And to their own. They're inhuman.'

'And that's what we'd be if we behaved like them.'

Charlie hands Otto the food, and the German feeds it to his sick compatriot, who is unable to feed himself as his hands are trembling too much. The ill man tries to smile, but a tear spills out of his eye instead.

Their depleted column joins another road. There are signs that others have already passed this way. Piles of excrement dot the verges, dark and liquid. The men gag. Dysentery begins to spread through their own group. When the guards refuse to let them stop, the men soil themselves as they march. The stench lingers in Charlie's nostrils until he grows used to it. All that remains of the snow now is a thin sprinkling along the side of the slushy road. Beneath it, Charlie can make out the shapes of more dead bodies.

The prisoners are too weak to pull the wagons any more. They abandon them in the middle of the road. The officers shoot the occupants who cannot continue. Charlie feels a stab of guilt: he is relieved he won't have to drag them any more. They try to bury the dead, but the ground is still too hard, and the guards are urging them on again. This time they pile the bodies together. The dead will keep each other company.

They catch up with a column of refugees tugging their worldly possessions behind them. The people have been refused access to a bridge they need to cross. It is for military use only. Charlie does not know how long they have been here, but many of them have frozen to death in the backs of their horse-drawn wagons, and the bloated corpses of their horses block the road. The prisoners-of-war rummage through the abandoned carts, taking what little food they can find. Charlie tries not to look at the waxy faces of dead children, wrapped for ever in the cold arms of their grandparents.

Soon there is no food left. John catches a feral cat that he spots hiding in a drain outside an abandoned and crumbling farm building. Charlie helps him prise the creature from its hole and then kill it: the cat fights for its life with razor-sharp teeth and claws, hissing and spitting and scratching at their hands. It is surprisingly strong, probably because of a surfeit of rats. Finally, they squeeze the last breath from its body. They dare not meet each other's eyes. Charlie helps to tear it apart, skewering its limbs on sticks and toasting the foul flesh on a fire. They share it among the men, and even with Otto and the other guards – barely a paltry mouthful each, but it is hot and it is meat and somehow that outweighs their disgust. Afterwards, they lie in the sawdust scratching at the lice that crawl through their matted hair and beards. The last kriegy lamp, its wick an old pyjama cord, flickers and splutters out. They are in darkness.

*

In the morning, leaning back against the stone wall of the ruin as it digs into his thin clothes, Charlie hears planes droning overhead. 'It's one of ours,' says John. He's right. Not just one but three. It should be a cheering sight, but as the aircraft fly low above the rabble of men scattered across the ground, for a moment Charlie fears they might be shot at and he falls sideways, covering his head with his arms. But the planes continue, disappearing into the slate-coloured sky behind them.

The guards start to shout and wave their rifles. 'Move!' they say, and once again the men are forced to their feet.

Another road joins theirs, and on it another group of prisoners, traipsing stiffly like men double their ages. The two groups join together. The guards whisper to each other, heads bowed. The prisoners pass on the latest news: 'Big squeeze. Russians on one side. The rest of us on the other. Not long until they meet in the middle.' Hope trickles through the column like the melting snow.

Charlie scratches his arm. Lice have infested his clothes. It is warmer now. He thinks he can risk leaving his coat behind.

John develops a dull red rash beneath his vest. Many of the men have phlegmy coughs that morph into dry retching: there is no food in their stomachs to expel. John clutches at his waist. His joints ache. Typhus spreads fast.

The land is more open here. They reach a field of reeds waving in the watery sunlight. A prisoner with a pair of nail scissors cuts some of the reeds to make a bed for John. Next to him, on another pallet of reeds, lies the German guard with receding hair. Otto tries, but cannot persuade the man to accept food or water. He is too weak to force the guard to take it, so he lies next to him, holding his hand. Charlie is not sure whether he is trying to comfort himself or his friend. He whispers a silent prayer. The weak and frail tend to the sick and dying. The damp air makes Charlie's shoulder throb. He talks about home to the sick men. The rest of the prisoners gather around to listen. He starts to recite from Olivia's early

461

letters, words that are imprinted on his soul. The men smile as they picture the rolling hills and sparkling waters of Scotland behind their drooping eyelids. Only yards away, the hooded crows that often follow them hop awkwardly across the ground, their black and grey feathers dull in the harsh light.

There is a sheen across John's forehead. Charlie touches it with the back of his hand. His friend is burning up. 'You'll be all right,' says Charlie. 'Any day now, they'll rescue us.'

But they do not come in time for John, or for the German. Charlie and Otto haul themselves to their feet and help bury the men together in a shallow grave, the best they can do in the softening ground with their feeble hands. Otto is the strongest man there, but even his empty stomach is concave, and there is no flesh left on his broad frame. Charlie collects stones to mark the final resting place. Even one stone is an effort. It takes minutes rather than seconds. The surviving prisoners copy him, adding to it with their own stones, until it is a cairn like those the Highlanders once built to honour their dead.

Afterwards, Otto and Charlie lean, exhausted, back to back, each feeling the sharp bones of the other protruding through their filthy clothes. Otto's boots have fallen apart, and his feet are wrapped in rags. He has no muscle left, and his skin hangs from his once-stocky frame. They have been reduced to the very core of what they are: two starving human beings pushed to their limits and travelling who knows where.

'Where did you learn your English?' Charlie asks.

'I was a housemaster at a boarding school. I taught rugby and history. I left when they removed our Jewish headmaster who would not allow us to teach the new, rewritten history book. I too did not subscribe to their propaganda.'

'That must have been hard.'

Otto shifts. 'It was not easy,' he says. 'But my anger is gone. And what of you? What is the anger that you carry around? Surely it is not only because of Oberleutnant Schafer?'

Charlie suddenly has the urge to cleanse himself; like confession, he needs absolution. 'There's a baby,' he says.

'There is nothing wrong with a baby . . . A baby is a happy event . . .'

'No. But it's . . .' He struggles to find the words. 'The mother is a child . . . and a whore . . .'

Otto's back remains solid. He does not flinch. 'Do you think you are the only one?' he says.

'Of course not. But I didn't want to be like other men. I thought I was better than that.'

'Better than what? A human?'

'Perhaps.'

'I do not understand.'

'I suppose I wanted to live up to some ideal . . .'

'For who did you need to do this?'

Charlie thinks long and hard. He knows he is near the end. His resolve is battered down. The cold and hunger are eating him up from the inside. Who is he? What is he?

'My father,' he says. 'My parents.'

Otto laughs a bitter laugh. 'We are always trying to impress our fathers,' he says.

'He wanted me to join the Navy.'

'But this is what you did . . .'

'My mother wanted me to marry someone I loved. I thought I'd found her.'

'The whore?'

'No. Someone else.'

'And where is this someone else now?'

'Out of reach.'

'There will be others.'

'Not now. Not after what I've done.'

'We all make mistakes. For every pregnant girl there will be a hundred more. Think of this child – your child – you can be a father to him.'

'How could he ever respect a father who behaved like I did?'

'You would be surprised what children will forgive.'

'No,' says Charlie. 'I know what a father should be like. And it's not me.'

'You set yourself up to fail. There is no such thing as a perfect human being.'

'I just wanted to make my parents proud . . .'

Otto shuffles around and reaches out to hold Charlie by the tops of his arms. 'Listen to me. You know what I see when I look at you? I see a small boy like so many others left on the steps of his boarding school waiting for his parents to come and fetch him. They will never come again. But that does not mean they would not be proud of you. They would celebrate your achievements and forgive your mistakes. I have known many parents, and I know that is what parents do.'

He lifts one of his large hands and touches Charlie's hot face. And instead of Otto's rough fingers, Charlie feels his mother's lips cool against his skin. He feels his father ruffle his hair. He closes his eyes, and the sobs rack his thin body, but he has no tears left to cry.

British planes begin to appear in a continuous stream. The men can stumble only a few yards an hour. Someone marks 'POW' in the ground, and a pilot dips his wings, flying low to salute them. They respond with a feeble cheer. The guards are flustered: a couple of them remove their uniforms and replace them with dead men's clothes. The prisoners are too weak to protest. They barely manage two miles during the whole day. The fields of reeds seem to waver on for ever. The hooded crows hop slowly in their footsteps, occasionally croaking up into the air, but remaining close at all times.

At night explosions and gunfire light up the sky in the distance, flashes of yellow and white tearing a hole in the darkness. Charlie listens to the rustling reeds. Three men make a break for it, squelching away into the swampy ground. The guards that are left are too demoralised to follow.

The next morning, as the prisoners straggle in ragged lines along the muddy road, the water in the puddles starts to jump, and a sound like distant thunder reverberates in Charlie's ears. The men stop. The guards are too weary, too frightened to

464

push them on. They start to talk among themselves, the distress making their voices high and harsh.

The prisoners gaze back down the empty road.

The noise grows louder. The hooded crows scream angrily and wheel away towards the woods in the distance. Some of the guards stumble after them.

'Look!' someone shouts, and British tanks full of Russian soldiers – British tanks like the ones Jack and Charlie delivered to Russia – start to grow on the horizon, larger and larger, an endless column that judders past, bright flags fluttering against the murky green and grey, and the soldiers are shouting down, 'Berlin has fallen! Hitler is dead!' Charlie's knees finally give way beneath him. He collapses with a thud on to the wet ground. Otto stumbles to help him up, reaching down with one of his wide hands to haul him to his feet, but there is no strength left in his once powerful arms, and instead he slumps to the ground too. A tank's deafening rumble fills their ears as it grinds to a halt beside them.

'Look at these poor bastards,' says a loud voice, as one of the men from the tank jumps down. He kneels next to Charlie in the road, calling back to his officer. 'This one's almost dead.' Charlie moves his head to show that he isn't.

'This one's a German.' Charlie hears the thump as the man's boot connects with Otto's ribs, and the German groans. 'Come on, you bastard. Get up.'

Otto struggles to his feet. He is still in his Luftwaffe uniform, though it is ragged and stained with dirt. He cannot stand up straight, but hangs there, bent in the middle. Charlie pulls himself up too. He reaches out to Otto. 'What are you going to do with him?' he asks the man.

'Don't you worry about him.' Another man lands with a thud next to the first, and they start to pull Otto to the side of the road.

'Stop,' says Charlie. 'Can't you see? He's half-dead already.'

'Who cares about that?'

'He's done nothing . . .'

465

The men turn on Charlie and he sees that their eyes are burning with horror and fear. 'If you'd seen what we have, you'd be ready to tear him apart yourself.'

'But you don't understand . . .'

'No. *You* don't understand.' The men are trembling, the pupils in their haunted eyes dilated; they remind Charlie of hunted animals. 'We're taking them to face up to what they've done. They have to see. Locals too. There are so many bodies . . . The smell . . . It's . . .' The men cannot continue.

They indicate to Otto and the other surviving guard that they must get in line. The other guard starts to panic, his voice rising high as he grabs hold of one of the soldiers. He is jabbering and tugging at the man. He cannot explain what he is trying to say as he does not speak any English. The soldier is getting agitated. 'Shut it,' he says.

Otto tries to intervene, to stop his fellow German from panicking, but the man will not be calmed. Otto turns to Charlie. 'He is just thinking that they are going to shoot us,' he says.

'Tell him they won't, as long as he calms down.'

But the German is beyond listening – fear, hunger, shame, and anger flow through his starved mind; there is no room for rationality.

And suddenly everyone is talking at once, and the crisis is reaching fever pitch, and through the cacophony of raised voices Charlie hears the unmistakeable sound of a rifle bolt. The soldier raises his rifle to his shoulder. 'No,' says Charlie, moving to block the barrel.

'Get out of my way,' says the soldier. 'It's all they deserve.'

The German is jibbering, offering prayers and pleading for salvation. Otto is still trying to calm him, and the soldier is yelling and taking aim.

Charlie tries to grab the weapon, and for a moment he grapples with the soldier as he attempts to knock the stock from his shoulder, and Otto is in the sights and Charlie hears the crack of the shot and it makes him think of Scotland and

466

stalking and Olivia and the hills and the loch and a time when he knew what was good and what was bad. His body gives way as the bullet hits his chest and he crumples to the ground. There is mud against his cheek, and he is surprised that the wet earth is so warm. And then a smile spreads slowly across his face, because for the first time he notices that the primroses have pushed their pale yellow heads up through the brown sludge. Spring is finally here.

CHAPTER 33

Olivia

After D-Day, Olivia remains working in Portsmouth, returning to London whenever she can. Jack has rented two rooms in a house in Lewisham. The landlady, Mrs Fields, is a decent woman who doesn't pry. Her husband was killed early in the war, and she is trying to make ends meet. They share the bathroom with one other tenant, but he is rarely there, so it is almost like having their own place. Jack returns more frequently than he has in the past. Betsy has been good to her word and stayed. Every day away from Stoog she grows more settled. She even seems happy to carry out various chores – sorting the laundry and queuing for food while Jack and Olivia enjoy precious hours of leave, tending to Alfie when she needs to, but leaving most of the care to Olivia, who loves to while away the hours with the little boy. Carl is a frequent visitor. Betsy is most relaxed when he is there, but there is always a barrier, a split second between what she thinks and what she says. Stoog is never mentioned.

The war has staggered on, as Hitler tries to swing things back his way. First came the dreadful roar of the Vengeance-1 missile, followed by the silence as its motor cut out, and then the awful, inevitable explosion. People have been once again forced to the rooftops to spot the doodlebugs as they grumble out of the mist towards the city. Londoners are pushed underground and the city is wreathed in the acrid smell of burning and the clouds of dust through which emerge the red and white buses as the blue and yellow flames gutter on the pavement where lampposts once stood.

The V-2 missiles follow, deadlier and more powerful than their predecessors. The Woolworths at New Cross – a shop that they have often taken Alfie to – is obliterated in a single strike, along with almost two hundred shoppers and people queuing for trams outside, with more than another hundred seriously injured. Survivors crunch through ankle-deep glass and rubble, while the white-suited medics and nurses move their temporary shelters to this latest tragedy in the city.

The attacks are relentless and indiscriminate, but Olivia is not afraid any more. It is simply part of life.

There is still no communication from Charlie. Olivia hunts for information through every channel she can, but news coming out of Germany is scarce. It is as though he has simply disappeared. He has already missed Alfie enjoying his first ice cream, and now dim-out, when lights are allowed to be left on unless there is an air raid; the boy thinks that the nights are festooned with lights shining especially for him. But Olivia cannot sleep. Disturbed by the unfamiliar brightness in the dark, she prays for news.

The year stumbles on; the three of them stumble on, held together by Alfie. He is something they can focus and agree on, with his innocent smile and his eyes wide with wonder, always trying to reach for what he wants, however hard it is, learning to stand alone, to walk, balancing on both feet, determination etched into his face. Alfie, who reminds Olivia of Charlie every day that she sees him.

There is a small garden in the communal square outside the house. Its railings have been removed, supposedly to be melted down to make weapons. Olivia and Betsy sit on the grass while Alfie gazes open-mouthed at the barrage balloons floating in the sky. He wants to join the young boys searching for shrapnel in front of coils of barbed wire, just as his mother and uncle once did, but he is too small and unsteady to keep up with them. Betsy distracts him with an orange she has procured. It is the first he has ever tasted, and they laugh as he bites into the juicy flesh, screwing up his nose and sticking out his tongue, and then his hand, asking for more. Suddenly there is a streak of silver through the March sky. Though far away, the explosion is so loud that Olivia huddles Alfie up into her arms and they run inside. Together they stand at the window, Alfie perched heavily on her hip. He presses his nose to the glass and watches through the criss-crosses of tape as the ambulances pass by at full speed, bells clanging, stretchers piled in the back.

'I just wish it would stop now,' says Olivia. 'I'm fed up with it. I want to get on with my life.'

Betsy bites her nails, distracted. Her eyes are fixed some-where a long way away. 'It's not much of a life,' she says, and Olivia is not sure whether she is talking about her past, present, or future.

They find out later that the rocket fell through Smithfield Market and on to the railway below, killing another hundred people, many of them women and children who were hoping to buy from a large consignment of rabbits, just as Jack and Betsy might have done only five years earlier.

And then, two weeks later, the rockets stop and the sound of the doodlebugs is replaced by the music of a song thrush in the garden outside the house. And a week after that, they receive the official news that Lieutenant-Commander Charlie FitzHerbert is dead.

Olivia is at Greenwich, chatting to fellow Wrens. Officially it is VE Day, a public holiday, but many have congregated here to listen to Churchill's official announcement of the surrender signed in France the day before. There is relief that these harsh years are over, but some of them are also wondering what an end of war means to women who are mechanics and radio operators, torpedo Wrens, mail officers, night vision instructors, and couriers. Olivia has received a letter from Charlie's bank manager stating that he has left all his money to her as his next of kin. It was almost too much to take in, but she has already made enquiries about setting it up in trust for his son. And now there is a messenger pressing a handwritten letter into her hand from a recently repatriated POW. Olivia examines the writing, prays that it might be Charlie, miraculously plucked from the confusion in Europe. But of course, it is not. She opens it slowly, dreading what she will find inside.

The letter is from a German officer, Otto Weber. He writes briefly of Charlie's story, and includes his address, saying that he has marked the coordinates of Charlie's grave so that she will be able to find it when peace allows. He tells her how he hopes one day to be able to explain to Charlie's child how his father died, a true, selfless hero, a father to be proud of. Inside the envelope is a handful of soil and the pale, dried petals of a primrose. Olivia holds the letter to her lips, hoping that she might find a last scent of Charlie there, but she can smell only the earth and the ink. Charlie has gone.

Olivia leaves the building for the last time then, making her way home through streets hard to negotiate. The pavements are teeming with people, but they are also cracked and marked with craters, remnants of war. The crowds are growing, men and women, old and young, gathering together in tentative celebration, for VE Day is not just a celebration, it is also a memorial to the men who won't be coming back.

The shop windows are full of bright rosettes and buttonholes. People are climbing ladders, hanging bunting and flags and streamers above the battle-scarred buildings. The city is no longer grey, but fluttering red, white, and blue, and lit by the smiles of thousands of people who can finally contemplate a future.

Jack is waiting with their cases. Olivia changes out of her uniform and folds it on to the bed, where she intends to leave it. She takes hold of Alfie's hand, and the three of them make

471

their way to the train station. Once again they are travelling up to Scotland, this time to the church at Poolewe, where Aunt Nancy has arranged a small service in memory of her godson.

Her aunt meets them at the station and drives them along the now-familiar single-track road. Olivia sits in the back with Alfie, with the windows open, pointing out where the buzzards soar and the cattle cool their hooves in the burns, watching the breeze lift his hair as he giggles in delight. She hopes the landscape will imprint itself in that same part of his mind as his father.

They pass Gairloch, and rise up towards Loch Ewe. The sky is deep blue, the hills are rich green flecked with pale rock, and there at last is the loch, sparkling and glimmering, empty of all but fishing trawlers, oozing out towards the sea. Alfie points and bounces up and down. It is his first glimpse of the wide ocean, of the far-reaching horizon, and the hint of infinite possibilities.

They stop next to the tiny stone church, where the river tumbles and froths towards the sea. A faint scent of wild thyme lingers in the air. As they enter the churchyard, Olivia is astonished to see that so many people have congregated here that they cannot fit into the little church. They are standing in clumps among the gravestones, quietly talking among themselves. There are all the locals, of course – Mrs Mac, whose face crumples as soon as she sees Olivia, before encompassing her in her thick arms and kissing her hair. There is Mac, eyes bright and body wiry as a bird, smiling up at her from beneath his cap. 'This is Callum, and these are Hamish and Mary and wee Gus. Not so wee any more,' he says. He does not mention Angus. The children are dressed in their Sunday best and they smile at her with ruddy cheeks, and she wonders which of them don't have a father any more, and she smiles a greeting at their mothers. Then Greer shakes her hand, and she notices he shakes Jack's hand too. And then there are Mrs Campbell and the Rosses, Mrs Ross dabbing

472

at her eyes. And the MacGregors, and beyond them more men, young and old, who she does not recognise, returned from the war. Everyone murmurs a greeting, and she allows their support to wash over her.

They move onwards, into the cool, dark church. As Olivia's eyes grow accustomed to the light, she sees that even in here, there are people standing at the back and along the sides, because every pew is packed. The air is heavy with the scent of flowers from the garden at Taigh Mor.

As they move down the aisle, she sees Carl rise and nod at them, and she recognises the pretty girl sitting next to him and Betsy as Agnes Stoogley. And around them are other men representing the Merchant Navy – crew and officers that Jack has worked with, proudly wearing their Merchant Navy badges on their jackets. There is Julia, lifting her hand in a brief wave, and Maggie, her face painted, her lips red as the rowan berries, a new man on her arm. Next to her is Gladys, holding her pregnant belly protectively, William's arm around her shoulder. They are almost at the front. Olivia recognises Ned, the young observer who was captured at the same time as Charlie. He has fattened up now. In the pew next to him and behind him are numerous men of the Fleet Air Arm and the Navy, a sea of naval uniform, gold braid, and polished buttons.

And there, on one side at the front, are her parents – her father older and more drawn than she remembers, her mother apologetic, eyes searching for hers – and her older sisters, Amelia and Grace, all of them virtual strangers to Olivia after so much time apart. And finally, on the other side, there is Aunt Nancy again, with space next to her for Olivia and for Alfie and Jack, her eyes filled with a sadness for the man she thought of as her child. Olivia kisses the older woman on both cheeks and threads their arms together as they sit down. She understands only too well that bleak chasm in Aunt Nancy's soul. On her other side, she grips Alfie's hand more tightly as he settles between her and Jack, his little feet swinging, a solemn look on his round face. Jack glances across at her over Alfie's blond head and smiles his reassurance before taking hold of the boy's other hand as the vicar clears his throat and starts to speak.

Afterwards, a Royal Navy bugler sounds the last post in the graveyard, while Alfie roams down to the river with wee Gus. The boys play among the thorny clumps of gorse, throwing stones into the river. No one cares that their best clothes are getting dirty.

Aunt Nancy grips Olivia's hand. 'Are you going to come back to the house for food and drink?'

'Of course,' says Olivia, squeezing back.

She walks over to her parents. Her mother is wringing her hands, her father is resplendent in his captain's uniform. 'Father, this is Jack.'

He nods and sticks out a hand. 'Pleased to meet you.'

'Are you coming home?' says her mother.

And Olivia thinks about the years that have passed. The ships and the Wrens, the bombs and the wrecks, the drinks and the parties, the weddings and the funerals, the loch and the ships, the loch before the ships, the touch of a man's hand.

She leans against Jack's shoulder. 'We're going to make our own home,' she says.

Before she joins the reception at Taigh Mor, Olivia goes for a walk on her own – not to the bothy, but up into the hills behind. She leaves her shoes, relishing the feel of heather and rock beneath her feet. She passes the rowan pool where she spent so much time with Jack. She dips her toes into the icy water, sees their pale shape distorting against the stones. Then she continues to climb, past the rock that she scrambled out on to when Mac's sheep got stuck. Past the outcrop where she first saw Hans. She climbs until she reaches the warm, flat rocks and the cairn she built to her baby. Now she stops and turns to survey the world beneath her. The sky is empty of planes. The loch is empty of ships. The world is as it should be. It is such a gloriously clear day that she can see everything. She can see the bothy, white against the Scots pines, the rickety boat that she fished in with Jack, the crescent of sand where she swam with Charlie. She crouches down, reaching out to touch the stiff roots of heather, breathing the smell of the earth deep into her heart; the mixture of peat and bog myrtle, crushed beneath her feet as she climbed. She spreads her fingers across the rocks, feels the heat of the sun in their ancient roughness. Then, from her pocket she pulls the dried primrose from Otto, and she places it carefully beneath the cairn.

She stays there for a while, where she feels as close to her lost baby and her lost friend as she is to the living. As she turns to walk down the hill, she sees the same red deer stag with the scarred flank and the majestic antlers. They stare at each other for a moment, before it bounds away inland, towards the great expanse of undulating hills that make up the Highlands. Before her, the sun is a path of gold, illuminating the sea that she is about to cross with Jack. Above her, an eagle soars on the thermals; the whole world curves beneath it, and the sky is endless.

Historical Note

This book began with family stories, but grew into a fascination with not only the Arctic convoys but also the journey to adulthood in a time of crisis. My grandmother and her sisters, aged between nine and eighteen, were on holiday with their Aunt Nancy in Scotland when Neville Chamberlain declared that the United Kingdom was at war with Germany. Their father, a captain in the Royal Navy, sent word that they were to stay where they were rather than coming home, in case of a Nazi invasion. Aunt Nancy returned to London, and the five girls were left alone – something that many other young girls might have found frightening, but not the FitzRoy sisters.

I always took the story of my great-grandfather surprising them in their Scottish idyll when he arrived for tea in his minesweeper sloop (and later entertained his bored daughters with a tour of the guns) with a pinch of salt, thinking that it was a myth shrouded in the fog of time. But of course, when I eventually looked into it, the truth was far more astounding. For ironically, that safe haven became Port A, a secret naval base for Royal Navy and then Merchant Navy ships to refuel and assemble in. Sometimes the loch was so full of ships that locals said you could have walked from one side to the other across them.

Winston Churchill was not wrong when he described the Arctic convoys as 'the worst journey in the world'. They suffered comparatively more losses than any other Allied convoy, the majority of those merchant ships. In fact, the

Merchant Navy lost proportionally more men than any of our armed forces during the Second World War. The youngest of these were children – a boy rating would typically be fourteen or fifteen years old, and inevitably some were even younger. The older of my aunts were teenagers then too, and I started to imagine what it might be like to have your formative years defined by war.

While the characters in this novel – and their ships and squadrons – are entirely fictitious, the historical events are as accurate as possible, with the odd alteration that I will try to list below.

The first Arctic convoy, Operation Dervish, left from Liverpool in August 1941, but none of its ships stopped at Loch Ewe on the way home. Although nineteen of the seventy-eight Arctic convoys left from the loch, the infamous PQ17 – described by Winston Churchill as 'one of the most melancholy naval episodes in the whole of the war' – did not, but I have taken the liberty of allowing Jack's ship to refuel there on its way to assemble in Iceland.

The false alarm that sounded across London on 3 September 1939 came minutes after Neville Chamberlain's radio broadcast. Here, I have imagined it a few hours later.

The German submarine U-39, which fired torpedoes at HMS *Ark Royal* on 14 September 1939, did so as the carrier launched her Blackburn Skuas in response to a distress call from the merchant ship SS *Fanad Head*. I have delayed the U-boat's attack so that Charlie's Fairey Swordfish can display one of the things it was best at – spotting U-boats – on his return. It is true that Swordfish went to assist the *Fanad Head*, and also true that U-39 was the first U-boat of the Second World War to be sunk, giving up the first German prisoners-of-war the same day.

There was no aircraft carrier at Scapa Flow the night that HMS *Royal Oak* was sunk – although aircraft carriers did anchor there. The Commander-in-Chief of the Home Fleet, Charles Forbes, had ordered many of the ships to disperse, as there were rumours of an attack, so the anchorage was relatively empty.

There is no record of an aircraft carrier coming into Loch Ewe in the summer of 1940, but *Ark Royal* was deployed from Scapa Flow, so she was in the area.

Charlie's aircraft carrier is an amalgamation of carriers, and its various captains are not meant to represent any real people. There was no Squadron 858 of the FAA, and none that saw such service as Charlie's, although Squadron 825 drew pretty close, having operated in the Norwegian campaign, the sinking of the *Bismarck*, the Channel Dash, and on Arctic convoys.

The Norwegian campaign in spring 1940 saw the first airborne torpedo attack of the Second World War, launched by Fairey Swordfish from HMS *Furious*, and those ancient bi-planes saw a lot of action at this time, on reconnaissance, attack and anti-submarine patrols, but there are no reports of a mistaken attack. Lieutenant Commander Bob Selley RNR (Retired) told me how he was once sent up to spot in appalling Arctic weather. When his engine cut out, Bob had to jettison his flares and depth charges (unarmed) to save weight, lighting up the convoy as he did so – because the weather was so bad he had been unable to pull away from the carrier. His captain gave him a dressing-down for giving away their position, but Bob was simply relieved to have landed safely (the wind had got the propeller going again before landing).

In May 1941, Fairey Swordfish did indeed make a crucial contribution to the sinking of the German battleship *Bismarck* after a torpedo damaged the ship's steering gear. Remarkably, no planes and no crew were injured, unlike Charlie.

There is no bothy down by the loch in the grounds of Inverewe house, where Taigh Mor is based, and nor did the owners of Inverewe have anything to do with intelligence, as far as I know. However, Pool House, just up the road in Poolewe, was requisitioned by the armed forces and used by the RN as a headquarters of Russian Arctic and North Atlantic convoys from Loch Ewe. It was also here that Lord Rowallan

– CO of the Highland Fieldcraft Training Centre – was based. My grandmother's older sisters stayed in the cottage that can still be seen today by the gates to the National Trust's Inverewe Gardens. The two youngest girls stayed in little more than a gardener's shed with two beds in it, behind that gate lodge.

The SOE did recruit ex-FANYs of the First World War for roles in intelligence, including communications, and there were training centres up in Scotland, although none at Loch Ewe. The SOE Norwegian Naval Independent Unit operated the Shetland Bus from Orkney and Shetland, running agents in and out of Norway and ferrying supplies, usually on boats crewed by local men with sound knowledge of the waters.

Winston Churchill visited HMS *Ark Royal* and other ships of the Home Fleet when they refuelled at Loch Ewe in mid-September. This was before the sinking of the HMS *Royal Oak*, but I have made it afterwards.

There are no recorded sightings of German aircraft over Loch Ewe until 1941 – here I have them earlier. The Germans clearly knew about the base, as they mined HMS *Nelson* in December 1939 at the mouth of the loch, so it is not inconceivable that they would have sent reconnaissance planes. An empty lifeboat was found in 1941. In 1944 a Junkers 88 crashed on the Scoraig peninsula. Three of the crew died at sea, but the *Unteroffizier* survived and made his way to the only house for miles. The story goes that none of the women at home spoke German, and the officer spoke no English, so they communicated in Latin. As far as I know, none of my aunts ever found an airman hiding in the stables.

I can find no records of Germans escaping from Great Britain in the Second World War, although two prisoners-of-war did manage to steal a training aircraft in November 1941, and only failed to escape as they ran out of fuel. I like to think that Hans would have checked the fuel gauge before he took off. There are reports of Nazi spies and sympathisers.

Jack's training ship is based on the *Vindicatrix*, a wooden training ship for boys joining the Merchant Navy, which was moored on the Sharpness canal, although none of the teachers or characters are based on real people. The *Vindi*'s figurehead is on display at Gloucester Waterways Museum. The Sailors' Home in Liverpool was demolished in the 1970s, although the Pearly Gates were preserved, and can be seen at Liverpool One, a memorial to all the merchant sailors who passed through the home's doors.

I have kept the place names 'Polyarnoe' and 'Archangel', which would have been used at the time; they are now called Polyarny and Arkhangelsk.

There were many Wren training establishments in Scotland, but Olivia's is fictional. Olivia requests to become a boarding officer in the summer of 1942, but this option would only have been available to her from 1943.

Survivors of PQ17 did use sheets to disguise their ship in the icepack, and some survived in lifeboats for days, some refused to be rescued, fearing they would only be attacked again, some made it to Novaya Zemlya, some even cooked seabirds, and the American ship SS *Winston-Salem* ran aground on the island. It took two weeks before anyone knew what had happened to many of the men, despite searches by aircraft and ships. Stalin thought the Western Allies were lying about how many supplies they had really sent because he could not believe so much could have been lost.

The American merchant ship *Greylock* was attacked and sunk on the homebound convoy RA52 at the end of January 1943. The entire crew was rescued, but none of its RN destroyer escorts was holed at the time, and nor did any aircraft carrier launch a Swordfish to assist picking up crew from a Royal Navy destroyer or a merchant ship.

The Dreadnought Seamen's Hospital was established at Greenwich in 1870. It seems to have remained there until 1986, but I can find no records of injured merchant sailors using it during the Second World War – this could be because nearly all pre-1948 records were destroyed when the hospital was bombed. It still exists to provide care for seafarers, but now as the Dreadnought Unit at St Thomas's Hospital.

The real Trojan Horse escape at *Stalag Luft* III was in October 1943; I have mentioned it earlier. The Great Escape was in March 1944, while the *William H Welch* wreck was February 1944.

I would like to add that while the characters Olivia and Nancy bear the same names as my great-aunt and great-great-aunt, who were at Loch Ewe in 1939, they are in no way meant to be anything like them and are entirely fictitious characters – as are all the persons in this book. I just wanted to pay homage to my ancestors.

Loch Ewe is still used as a refuelling place by NATO ships, as well as for maintenance of warships. Wreckage from the SS *William H Welch* can still be seen at Black Bay, as can the old gun placements and pillboxes dotted around the loch. At the end of the track beyond Cove, there is a memorial stone commemorating those who sailed from Loch Ewe and never returned. The Russian Arctic Convoy Museum Project hopes to build a multi-site museum around the area as a lasting legacy to all who took part in the campaign, which would be wonderful.

Acknowledgements

There are very many people who I would like to thank –
veterans, researchers, historians, librarians, museums, families,
authors, and websites – who helped me in my research, but
their names would fill another book. However, I would like
to say a special thank you to the following:

The Russian Arctic Convoy Museum Project – and George
Milne in particular – for their help, and for trying to provide
a converging point for anything to do with Arctic convoys.
They are guardians of some incredible artefacts and stories.

Lieutenant Commander Chris Götke, Mr Neil 'Fraz' Fraser
and Katrina Campbell at the Royal Navy Historic Flight, RNAS
Yeovilton, who let me admire the Royal Navy's Fairey
Swordfish – one of only three in the world that are currently
flying – and who answered technical questions.

Commander James Ekins for further technical expertise and
incisive suggestions, and who brought the Navy to life with
his boatswain's call and rum barrel.

Susan Watt, editor and publisher, who somehow saw and
understood what I was trying to do, and who worked tirelessly
to get me there (a job not dissimilar to holystoning an endless
expanse of deck).

My agent, Heather Holden-Brown, for her no-nonsense
advice and support over the years.

My grandmother Amelia and great-aunt Barbara, and their
sisters, Olivia, Mary and Kathy, for their indomitable spirit, ability
to tell stories and love of the countryside, particularly Scotland.

483

My husband and three children, who have followed me around many museums and chilly naval trails without complaining once.

Most particularly 'my' veterans: Bob Selley, Fleet Air Arm pilot, whose humorous chats and anchovies on crackers I miss enormously; David Chance, Royal Navy translator, whose experiences of life in Russia imbued me with a sense of love for that country and its people; and my neighbour Jock Fison, who kept meticulous records, and is the only veteran I know who sneaked a camcorder on to his ship hidden under his coat. All three of them have crossed the bar, but their wonderful writings, drawings and recordings will live on.

And finally, to all the men and women who fought for our freedom on land, at sea and in the air – and especially the Merchant Navy, without whom the outcome would have been very different.

We, Who Live Now

Who can blame us,
We, who live now,
For taking all we can, with both hands,
For living to the utmost of our capacity,
For being thoughtless of others,
When the future is for us a thing uncontemplated,
A shadow in a fog,
A quicksand,
A mirage.
We have nothing to build our lives on,
We who live now,
Knowing that the cliff crumbles under our feet
And that the sea beneath is fathomless.
Do not blame us,
Who snatch what we can,
Our lives are different to our past lives,
And more frightening,
For even if the cliff holds
There is still a very long way to go.

Olivia FitzRoy, 1943